W9-BUF-267

# COME THE
# MORNING

# SHANNON DRAKE

# COME THE
# MORNING

Kensington Books
http://www.kensingtonbooks.com

KENSINGTON BOOKS are published by

Kensington Publishing Corp.
850 Third Avenue
New York, NY 10022

Kensington and the K logo Reg. U.S. Pat. & TM Off.

Library of Congress Card Catalog Number: 98-066230
ISBN 1-57566-383-X

First Printing: April, 1999
10  9  8  7  6  5  4  3  2  1

Printed in the United States of America

# Prologue

## Scotland, The Borderlands
## The Year of Our Lord 1127

He was dead, he thought. He had died from the great battle-ax of his opponent, and had entered into a new world.

It was strangely familiar. It smelled of the sweet grasses of the sweeping plains, and of the fresh, clear lochs that lay like teardrops scattered across the borderlands. If it was heaven, and it must be—for surely hell could not smell so sweet—then heaven was filled with flowers and thistles and the rich smell of the earth. And, he discovered, managing to open his eyes at last, heaven was blessed with a sky brightened by a strange gibbous moon that cast an eerie glow of bloodred light down upon the earth.

Then pain set in; he wasn't dead. He lived. Yet his skull pounded as if it had been rent in two. He nearly groaned aloud, yet some instinct kept him silent. He gritted his teeth and inched up on his elbows and looked about the field.

So many men . . . limbs pale in the moonlight except in those places where they were bathed in blood, and there he saw darkness and shadow. The sweetness on the night air was not just that of long green grasses and of flowers; it was the sticky-sweet scent of spilled blood, blood soaking the landscape.

The land was covered with the sad, grotesque carnage of battle. As it had been before, he realized dimly. As it would be again.

The pain roared to a greater life within him. It threatened to steal his consciousness again. He became aware of the feel of night-wet grass against his flesh. Each small wound burned, each greater injury seemed alive with all the fires of hell.

Dead, so many dead, and he was so nearly dead himself. He

had been left with the slain, he realized, by friend and foe alike, for not far from where he lay was a small cottage made of earth and stone. Light radiated from a fire that burned inside it; those who had survived the carnage had gone there to dress their wounds and make their plans.

Please God, his father would be there, he thought. His kin.

Yet even as the hope flashed through his mind, so did fear and a certainty of knowledge. Dead or alive, his father would never have left him. He realized his hand lay upon cold flesh, and he looked to his left. His heart shuddered within his chest; tremors seared into him, hot, scaling his spine, cold, ripping into his limbs. Tears welled in his eyes.

For his father, William the Great, lay at his side, blue eyes opened and unseeing upon the sky above them, chest cleaved by an enemy's sword.

"Da!"

He whispered the word in a husky cry of agony, reaching for his father's head, his fingers traveling lovingly through the deep auburn curls that graced it. "You cannot leave me, Da! You cannot leave me. Nay, ye canna leave me . . ."

He could dress for battle, wield a sword. And he was tall and strong, a promising youth, the men had all said. But seeing his father dead, he knew that he was just a lad, and he knew that whatever the jokes and the laughter had been, and even the pride, he was a boy still, with far to go to equal not only his father's great prowess and strength, but his wisdom, mercy, and judgment as well.

But age didn't matter, nor could his anguish change what was. Love could not bring back the dead, nor change the outcome on this battlefield. He'd have to be a warrior now, he knew. The tears within his eyes fell unashamedly down his cheeks. Great William was gone, with all that he had taught, and all that he had given. And there . . . with the moon coming from behind a cloud, he could see *more* of the field of slaughter. Just feet away, he saw his father's brother, proud, handsome, laughing Ayryn, as close in death to William as he had been in life. Now he was stretched across the sweet rich grass as well, arms splayed as if he reached out to embrace heaven itself.

"Ah, Uncle! You cannot leave me, too!" he whispered again. "You cannot leave me alone."

A scream rose within him, fierce and terrible. It threatened to tear from his lips. Again, instinct rose to serve him. He mustn't make a sound. He fought down his cry of pain, a sound that would have ripped across the grasses, a howl of loss, a moan of primal fury, rage, and agony. Instinct served him well; he did not betray himself. He heard footsteps, and he swallowed down the threatened sound along with the bitter bile of anguish that filled his mouth from what he saw of this day's most terrible work.

Footsteps . . .

Furtive in the night. Footsteps moving quietly through the grass. He saw the forms of those who were coming. They began to circle the crude cottage where the Scottish survivors had gathered after the savagery of the battle.

He held his breath. Studied the men who came. Their enemies.

He lay still as they passed by him.

Da! He wanted to cry out again, warn the men and his father that an enemy walked with silence and menace among them.

But his father was dead; his uncle, too.

I am alone, he thought again, the wretched, dreadful truth. Alone in the world, of all his people. Those who loved him would never speak his name again.

He waited.

And he watched.

And when the last of them disappeared around the cottage intent upon a silent assault, he began to rise. He staggered, nearly passing out from the pain that swept through his head as he came slowly to his feet. He paused, letting the pain subside, gathering his strength and awareness. Then, he, too, began to move furtively through the grass.

Michael, Lowland chieftain of the MacInnish family, listened to the talk that went around the fire. He'd been born himself at Dunkeld, the most ancient home of Gaelic and Celtic being. A younger son, he'd come here to this fine sweeping borderland when he'd taken his wife, the last of the MacNees, the traditional owners of this fair stretch of earth. But the MacNees were no more, for since olden days, conquerors had come here. The Romans had at last been stopped by the fierce Highlanders and rugged terrain beyond; the Vikings continued to raid inland even now upon occasion. And always, the English—or those purporting to be English, such as the new Norman aristocracy—came here. The lands were rich, good. Men held tenaciously to them; men became a part of them. Perhaps they came to seize land, but instead they became one with it, they became Scots.

Aye, now they were Scots. Often considered barbarians, they had never been conquered by Rome; the first time a Roman commander, Agricola, had severely beaten the Caledonians then in Scotland, he had been called back to Rome. Soon, all Britain had been deserted by the Romans. Different Celtic and Teutonic tribes had come in, the Picts, the Scots, the Britons, and even Anglo-Saxons. The kingdom of Scotland remained a land inhabited by different peoples, and they still had their differences, but since the day of the great Kenneth MacAlpin, king of the Scots of Dalriada, they had begun to become a united country.

Now, there might have been something resembling peace in the region. King David I reigned over Scotland; a king whose sister had married Henry I of England, whose wily father, Malcolm III, had battled William the Conqueror, and if he hadn't exactly won those battles, he had still maintained a separate and largely whole Scotland. David had come to his kingship having watched and learned from his father and brothers before him; he had grown up in England and prospered at English hands, while he had also watched his family struggle with the results of the Norman conquest. He wasn't a young man, but a king in his prime, a mature, wise, and wary man. He never forgot that any king held a precarious position, and that the world was a dangerous place. Some resented his upbringing in the Norman court, but by blood, he could draw many ancient loyalties. His mother had been the sister of Edgar, Atheling, Saxon royalty before the coming of the Conqueror. He'd learned the power of fighting, and the power of alliances. Yet the Scots, like Michael, supported and upheld their king despite this, and their hatred and distrust of all things Norman. Despite many of his Norman ways and Norman leanings, David had proven himself, as a leader, and as a Scotsman, determined on his own identity, and that of his country. He was a warrior, ready to go to battle. Though relations sometimes remained diplomatically stable with their southern neighbor, along the border there was often war. David meant not only to keep the lands traditionally Scottish; he longed to push the borders and keep the English from his heartlands. In order to do so, he had granted Scottish lands to some of the important Norman families with whom he had become familiar. With the tact of a good fledgling king, he had taken care to give lands where the chieftains of old had died out, where disputes among heirs might arise. By taking care, he had allowed for the very ancient races of his homeland to accept—if grudgingly—still another arrival of a different people. David had put down an insurrection in 1124 when he became king, and God knew, Scotland being the warlike, rugged land it was, he would put down insurrections again. Feudal laws, many not yet a century old, vied with the ancient ways, and it took power, force, and cunning to rule the Scottish people. David, thus far, was proving himself a most able man. Still, two main threats remained to challenge his power: here, along the border, and from the Vikings, who were ever on the lookout for opportunities to gain an advantage. David had studied history. Of all the factors that might have gone into the Saxon king Harold having lost England to the Normans, he believed that the Viking invasions to the north at the time of the Norman invasion to the south were the main cause. The Vikings hadn't beaten Harold, but they had weakened him.

Yet no king's power seemed able to stop the savage skirmishing here on traditional borderlands and tonight, though Michael had managed with very little time to gather together numerous chieftains and their men, he had been assaulted hard by Lord Renfrew, a nobleman of Norman descent unsatisfied with the lot of land he had drawn in Yorkshire. Joined by mercenaries from a Danish army, he had marched northward, sending farm inhabitants fleeing ahead of him. He had plundered the churches and abbeys he'd found along his way, and ravaged many a poor young woman, so had come the news this morning. And Michael had called upon his people, his clan and his clan associates, and they had gathered to defend the land.

Now, many of their number, many of their finest, lay dead or dying. And around this fire, the survivors argued their position.

Thayer Cairn, a huge burly man with the strength of an ox, stood to cast more kindling upon their small fire, seeking the warmth on his hands. Firelight rose around him, casting his face in an eerie shade of red.

Red, like the blood that stained the hills.

Michael felt an uncanny chill seize hold of him as he watched Thayer; his vision blurred. The small cottage seemed misted in red. "Where is the king with his troops when we need him and his help?" Thayer demanded. "The call has gone out; we are set upon and with no relief in sight!"

Michael stared at the fire. "We can't go condemning the king for whatever speed or lack thereof keeps him from us. We must depend on ourselves here and now."

"Aye, Michael is right!" Fergus Mann said, from the left of Michael. He'd seen his brother and oldest son fall; his second and third son remained at his side. The wiry old graybeard warrior still had his wits about him in his intent to salvage their situation now. "The king matters not; what we do in these next few minutes is most important. I say that we must gather our wounded and disappear across the hills to the crags and cliffs by the lochs. Our only hope is to regroup. If they pursue, for the time being now, we must escape to our brethren in the hills."

Michael heard a thumping sound and frowned. He glanced at Thayer. "Who's on guard?"

"McBridie guards the doorway."

Michael made a silent motion that Thayer should try the door— and see to the welfare of McBridie. The warriors in the cottage tensed, but even as Thayer cast open the poor wooden door, a cry went out. A yellow-haired Nordic warrior charged where the door had been—and great Thayer was pinned through the shoulder with the man's razor-honed pike. He let out a cry like a bull, yet even then, more of the enemy flowed in behind the Norseman; they burst through the thatch-covered windows. In seconds, the twenty-odd Scotsmen who had taken refuge in the cottage were dead or injured.

Michael alone held his sword when a tall man, clad in chain mail and leather, strode through the doorway. Lord Renfrew. He ran his fingers through his short-cropped russet hair, smiled, and reached for the youngest of old Fergus Mann's sons, catching the lad by the hair in an instant and placing his small sword to the boy's throat, flush against the vein. He held the boy and stared at Michael, the chieftain.

"Ah, now! 'Tis Michael, himself. Laird of these lands," Renfrew's dark eyes narrowed even as his thin lips curled into a cruel smile, and he mocked the pattern of the Gaelic speech. "Throw down your sword, Michael. Do so. The lad will live."

"It's a trick, Michael!" the lad, Patrick, called out.

"What terms?" Michael demanded.

"Terms?" He nodded to his men around him. "Bind the men's hands, now, and be quick and thorough. You've got to take great care, you know. They're the result of years of tribal invasions.

They've even got enough of your good Viking blood in them, eh, Ragwald, to fight like wild creatures." He glanced at the Norseman who had either killed Thayer or left him grievously wounded; then he stared down at Thayer. Thayer could not say; he was slumped to the ground. Renfrew looked back to Michael. "Your sword, Michael. Now. Or I kill the lad."

"He'll kill me anyway!" Patrick stated gravely, swallowing down his fear to make the statement.

Perhaps the lad was right, Michael knew, but in their current situation, it seemed to make no sense to hasten Patrick's death. Michael cast down his sword.

Renfrew smiled with a nod, acknowledging his pleasure. "Bind him," Renfrew commanded, indicating Michael.

The Norseman at Renfrew's side did as commanded. Michael didn't fight as the man tied his hands behind his back. He looked at Renfrew.

"What now?" the Viking asked Renfrew, having finished binding Michael as commanded.

"Bind them all," Renfrew said, "for they will submit to me. They will be my prisoners."

One by one, the men were bound, and when the task was completed, it was Michael who asked once again the question that Renfrew's Viking had already put forward.

"What now?"

Renfrew smiled. "Now? What now, indeed? You are worthless, the lot of you, as hostages. Could I keep you, working you men as slaves? I assure you, many a once-proud Saxon lad still serves his master in England. Ah, it's a fine thought, such proud, noble warriors enslaved to me! But, alas! I'd be ever wary of my back. There's little choice in it, I think. Now, I let my men amuse themselves. Now, I hang you poor savage bastards, one by one. Take him first!" he commanded, indicating Thayer. "He's half-dead already, but such deadweight should make a good fall, eh? We can test the rope for the others."

The attackers filed out of the cottage, kicking and shoving the bound Scotsmen, laughing as they struggled to manage Thayer's great bulk. The last of them departed through the cottage door; it was the Norseman who had so swiftly skewered Thayer. He paused before leaving. "You'll pardon us, good Scotsmen, eh? We'll not leave you hanging long."

Laughing with pleasure at his own deadly humor, he exited the cottage.

"You should have kept your sword, Michael," Patrick said glumly. "You'd have brought down at least one of the great, ugly bastards."

They could hear deep, guttural laughter in the night as the enemy struggled still with Thayer's body. Then suddenly, they were startled by a thumping sound within the confines of the cottage. A large dark shadow fell behind Patrick, who had been pushed closest to the rear thatched window. Patrick gasped, then held his tongue.

"By all that's holy—" Michael began, but Patrick threw up his hands, freed from the leather ties that had bound them. The shadow rose. It was Great William's lad; Michael had seen him fall in battle, seen him crumple atop his father. He'd been sure the boy, Waryk, was dead. But he lived. Streaked with mud and blood, he was a length of darkness. All that was light of him was the blue fire in his red-rimmed eyes as he stared around himself at the men left to their turn at death in the cottage. Not fourteen yet, he stood well above many a full-grown man with the breadth of shoulder that would eventually fill out with power. This had been his first test of arms, but Michael had seen him work with his father often enough in the open fields, learning his swordplay.

"Sweet Jesu," Michael breathed.

The lad started toward him. "Your father, your brother," Waryk said quietly to Patrick, indicating the bound hands of the others in the room. "I'll free Michael."

Yet even as he approached Michael, the Viking warrior appeared in the doorway once again. "What's this, eh? A nit left alive among the dead lice! A young one for the hanging, this now!" he declared.

Waryk reached down for Michael's discarded sword. The blond giant laughed. "A cub would fight with wolves, eh? Have it your way. May not be so merciful a death as the quick snap of a rope, for I'll slice you from stem to stern, my fine boy!" he claimed.

The muscled warrior laughed and used his great strength to swing his battle-ax. Waryk watched him for no more than seconds, then let out a cry. The cry filled the night, like something unearthly, borne on the wind. He charged the man straightforward, and before the man's ax could fall, the "nit" had pierced him through the gullet with his sword. Lord Renfrew's Nordic mercenary fell to his knees, shock lighting his eyes 'til death glazed them over.

All in the room stared. Patrick paused in his attempts to slice his father's bonds. Michael forgot that nooses still awaited them all.

"What goes in there?" came a cry from outside.

"Quick!" Michael ordered.

Once again, Patrick and Waryk set forth to free the men. They worked in swift silence. When another of the enemy came to the door, Waryk spun around again and, this time, met a swordsman. The clash of steel alerted those outside that there was trouble in the cottage, where the last of those they had conquered should have been making peace with their Maker.

Now it was the Scots who had the advantage, for as each attacker crossed the cottage threshold, he was set upon. Soon the blood ran thick beneath the firelight, and men tripped upon the bodies of others as they fought. Renfrew's men began to back away, stumbling in their haste now to be free from those so intent upon vengeance. They were followed by the Scots.

Out in the moonlight, Michael was so fiercely engaged in battle that he was unaware at first of the sound of horses' hooves pounding against the earth as a troop of men approached them. He hammered the head of a combatant with his battle-ax, then swung quickly to see who was riding down upon them as at last he heard the thunder of hoofbeats.

The king. The king had come. His warriors pitched themselves into the battle with the enemy.

*Their enemy.* Now outnumbered. Dead and dying on the field of those they had slain before.

Yet David was commanding mercy; the survivors were casting down their weapons. The sound of a single fight was all that remained, steel clanging against steel in the night.

Michael saw that it was the lad, Waryk, son of the man they had called Great William, known as William de Graham. The boy had Norman and Viking blood of his own in his veins; his father had traveled northward with the king from borderlands farther to the east, lands invaded time and again by the Vikings, and ruled by them for a time as well. 'From the gray home', or so the name—according to both the Norman and the old English. But the name might have been borrowed from the lad's mother as well. Legend had it that the most ancient of the Scottish people, the lad's mother among them, had introduced the name Graeme into the borderlands. The boy's maternal border kin might have come from a family with an old and illustrious Scottish history. A Graeme had been a general with the armies of an ancient king from the very early years of Christianity, King Fergus, and this Graeme who had served him had led the king's army when it had breached the Roman wall set against the "barbarians"—the old races of Scotland. Graeme's Dyke still existed at the remnants of the old wall. God knew. Names came from anywhere. Some men were just Thomas, Michael, Fergus, or so on, and some took on their father's names, which became their family names. His own great-grandfather had been Innish, and now, he was of the family, clan MacInnish, just as a Norseman might be Eric, Olaf's son—though with the Norse, he was more likely to become Eric Blood-Mace or the like. Even the king's family name, Canmore, had come from his father, and the old Gaelic Caenn Mor, meaning big head.

It had become a noble name.

Whatever the ancestry in the boy's name, it didn't much matter. Today, the lad was showing his worth as a man.

His worth, and his pain. Anguish that created raw courage and defied fear and even death.

Men fallen all around him, the boy fought still. He had taken on Lord Renfrew himself, and no matter how the skilled, hardened, and experienced Renfrew attacked, battered, and countered, the lad was there.

Waryk had found his father's sword; he fought with it. When Renfrew dared breathe, the boy charged him. Renfrew was skilled. He charged, and charged again, his onslaughts merciless, but the Graham neither lost his balance nor his sword. What advantage Renfrew had in power, the lad countered with speed and subtlety. Still, it appeared that the boy, battered, black-and-blue, and crusted with blood, must eventually give. Renfrew attacked with a practiced, relentless aggression, his great muscles swinging his sword again and again with grim determination. He would not cease until he had killed.

Yet right when Renfrew lifted his sword above his head to slice down with the coup de grâce, Waryk de Graham used Renfrew's bid for momentum against him. He swung his sword upward with a startling, eerie force, impaling Lord Renfrew just below the ribs.

Renfrew clutched the sword, dying. He stared at the lad, still arrogant, stunned, and in disbelief.

Yet there was no denying death. When the man fell at the foot of the lad, the boy didn't move. He didn't reclaim the sword. He stood there shaking.

Michael hadn't realized that the king, still mounted, sat his steed just to his own back. The king nudged his horse forward. "My God, who has bred this lion pup?"

"Your own man, sire," Michael said wearily. "Great William who lies yonder."

"Ah!" David said with understanding.

"I shall see to the boy," Michael promised. "William was married to the last of an ancient family. The lad's mother was my own distant cousin, Menfreya, who is now long deceased. The lad has no more real kin, so his friends must be his family."

"Nay, good man. Be his friend, and his family, but I shall see to him, I will be his guardian now, and I warrant that one day he will be a great warrior—and then he will be my champion."

David, already a mature man, virile, a king of whom the united Scots claimed themselves proud, walked his great steed to the center of the carnage, where the boy still stared down at the dead man, shaking.

"Young Gra—ham!" the king called. He was well versed in all three languages that might have been spoken among his peoples, the old "Scottish" or Gaelic, the "Teutonic" or English, and the Norman French brought over by William the Conqueror and the fruitfully reproductive knights who had accompanied him. Now, he spoke the Scottish tongue, placing a heavy Gaelic accent and burr upon the syllables. The lad did not at first respond. "Graham!" the king repeated.

The boy looked at him at last, as if realizing it was his name now being called. David—tall, lean, handsome in his saddle— looked down upon the lad, who had promise of an even greater height and physical power. He assessed the lad carefully. David was no fool. He'd had years to study the art of kingship; he'd seen the power of the Norman kings. He'd seen their weaknesses, and he knew their strengths, and strength, he had determined, lay with people.

Though he learned much among the Norman-English, he was the king of Scotland, and he was loyal to the Scots. This was his kingdom. He weighed all men, friends and enemies, carefully.

He was a good judge of character, quick to find both the frailties and virtues within a man. Now, he weighed the lad.

"You are the Graham," David said gently.

The boy's shoulders jerked in a spasm. He moved at last, turning to look at the place upon the battlefield where his kin lay dead.

"I am," he said. He fixed his piercing blue eyes upon the king. He had just slain a giant. His lower lip trembled, his eyes glistened with tears. His family lay dead. "I am, sire. I, alone."

"Your father was a fine man. A great man. I cherished him, as a warrior, and a friend."

"Aye, sire."

David looked around at the men who had survived both battle and treachery. In silence now, they watched the scene unfolding. David dismounted from his horse. He drew his own sword. Nothing so gained the loyalty and love of people as pageantry, and recognition of heroic deeds well-done.

"Kneel, boy!" he commanded.

At first, the boy did not seem to understand. Perhaps he thought David meant to slay him.

"Kneel!" the king commanded.

The lad Waryk fell to one knee. The king set his sword upon his shoulders. "I, David, by the Grace of God king of this united Scotland, do knight thee here and now for incredible valor upon the field of battle." His sword still set upon the lad's shoulders, he looked around at the fighting men of the field and his own escort of armed men and nobility. "Waryk, son of William, you are now Sir Waryk Graham, in honor of your father's kin, and your mother's. All here have witnessed your courage, and these events. They will know that from this day forward, Waryk, son of the great William de Graham, that though I can give you no such title now with lands to support it, you shall be known as Laird Lion, you will be my champion, and I will look out for your interests in the years to come for this night's work. When the time is right, lad, there will be much to be gained, perhaps through advantageous marriage. Sir Waryk de Graham, Laird Lion! Your father's honor lives on in you."

The lad stared up at the king. Bloodied, bruised, covered in earth and sweat and mud, he grasped the king's hand. His eyes were bright with tears he would not shed. The king had given him the greatest gift he could offer in honoring his father, and the mother he could scarcely remember. "Sire," the lad said, his voice tremulous, "I will serve you until death."

"That, Laird Lion, I will expect from you," David said wryly. "Rise, my boy."

So commanded, the lad came to his feet once again.

"You are the Graham, my boy."

"I, alone, sire," he said, his tone now weary, the weight of the night's work heavy upon him.

"Tonight, aye," the king said kindly. "But you will create your own kin, my boy. Trust me," he murmured.

And his thoughts were already on the future. For he was a king. And his newly made knight of the realm had just become another pawn.

The game of his life had just begun. There were any number of moves possible for this lad.

# PART I

## The Viking's Daughter

# CHAPTER 1

H is method of warfare had changed somewhat in ten years. Not completely. Waryk, Laird Lion, still preferred his sword to any other weapon; it had been his father's blade, William's claymore, and he wielded it still.

Today he sat atop a great warhorse and stared down the hill, watching the assault on the king's small fortress of Localsh. Fifty mounted men-at-arms were in his command to quash the rebellion, reputed to be far greater than what he discovered here. The garrison at the fortress, however, was no more than twenty men, plus the artisans, masons, clergy, and freemen who lived within and about the walls of the fortress. Stonework, so recently begun, was being torn down. The defenders had prepared for a siege rather than striking out at the attackers; the garrison in the castle was small, enough men to defend, not enough to attack. But now, the defenders were beginning to lack food, water, arrows for ammunition, oil to pour upon those attempting to scale the walls. The rebels could be seen preparing their weapons of assault; catapults to storm the castle with rocks and flaming debris, rams to break down the gates, ladders with which to send men over the walls.

Watching the rebels from a distance, Waryk frowned. This was not what he had expected. With neighboring England now in something of chaos with Henry I dead and his daughter, Mathilda, fighting his nephew, Stephen, for the crown, many of the Norman barons were stretching their wings and reaching out for whatever power they could seize. While even the Scottish king's personal troops were known for their wild appearance—Waryk commanded a comparatively small cavalry—and foot soldiers whose raw courage most frequently created their victories, these fighting men were sad, lacking even leather armor, breastplates or protection. Some carried the poorest shields. They appeared to be no more than disgruntled serfs, with little strategy, or knowledge of warfare. Their dress was poor, more Norman than Scottish, not unusual here in the Lowlands. Granted, the death of King Henry I of England had thrown a great deal of confusion into England and the borderlands and Anglo-Scottish relations, but this still seemed strange. A knight prepared for war with the full treasury of a king—even a Scottish king, as some would say—he himself was well mounted and armored, a coat of light, finely meshed mail over his wool undergarment and under his surcoat of deep rich blue. A single metal plate protected his chest, and his helmet was metal as well, though many of his men preferred the protection of leather to that of steel. His eyes as deep and disturbing a blue as the color on his surcoat, stared out from a helmet with a sturdy nose plate. His own blazon, that of a flying falcon, was embroidered on his surcoat and on the rich trappings worn by his horse.

He was close to where he had fought so many years ago, he thought. He had come far from there, only to return. Once, he had been a boy, ragged and undisciplined, no shield, no armor, fighting for . . .

His life.

*Why* were the men below fighting? He thought of the way they had struggled then, so poorly armed, and yet, they fought for their homes.

These men were assaulting a fortress.

"Waryk?" Angus, his aide in all things, spoke his name, reminding him that he and his armed troops were staring down at the battle scene. He became aware of the restive movements of the horses behind him.

"They are like a peasant army," Waryk said.

"They are hurtling burning oil, as we speak," Angus pointed out dryly.

"Aye, but why . . ." Waryk murmured. He couldn't ponder the question—as Angus had said, the attackers, no matter how sad, were attempting to kill the defenders of the king's fortress. Waryk lifted a hand, indicating they should charge from their vantage point atop the high cliff, and take the enemy swiftly. God knew, he didn't want to lose his own men, though it disturbed him to believe he was embarking upon a slaughter of his countrymen.

He turned in his saddle. "For God's sake, keep alive what men you can! If not for mercy's sake, for that of knowledge, my fellows! Angus, Thomas, ride with me against the siege machine. Theobald, Garth, and you three MacTavishes, take the men with the ram. The rest of you, storm the fellows at the gates, seize the ladders. Now, we ride for God, for king, and for country!"

He lowered his hand, and kneed Mercury, and they began a thunderous charge down the cliffs, and to the aid of the beleaguered fortress.

There were, perhaps, a hundred rebels, outnumbering Waryk's forces, but in no way were they capable of outfighting them. He hadn't wanted a slaughter. Killing men for different loyalties was always difficult, many a fine man died that way. He had learned that there were good men among the king's Normans, among the Scots, among the secluded tribes, and even among the Vikings. These rebels looked like Celtic barbarians of old; some were painted like the ancient Picts.

They fought like berserkers.

And in his slashing and slaying, Waryk was greatly disturbed to find that the enemy seldom sought mercy. Continually assaulted by more than one man, he was forced to kill, rather than threaten and keep a man alive. As he fought, he found it more puzzling still that he heard snatches of different languages as the men shouted back and forth to one another, seeking to make a retreat. Norman French, Gaelic, old Saxon English, Norse, all were being spoken. And men fought to the death, the enemy calling threats to one another, or they fled.

Even the Lowlands in Scotland offered tremendous opportunities for retreat and shelter, heavy forests, rolling, sweeping hills, making lightning-quick assaults and equally fast retreats not a matter of cowardice, but of strategy. Some of the rebels continued to fight as berserkers, but more and more began to flee. Hunted down toward the rich forests, they turned and fought again. Freed from fierce attack at last, Waryk turned to see Angus facing a single man. When Angus would have brought his great battle-ax down upon his opponent, Waryk rode hard upon him.

"Angus! We need him alive!"

Angus held his ax at Waryk's command, and Waryk was certain Angus's burly combatant understood every word that had been said, but the man looked toward the forest, his eyes grew huge as if he were expecting an evil spirit to spring out upon him. He then took a reckless lunge toward Angus, forcing Angus to raise his battle-ax in self-defense.

The man's bare head was struck; he fell dead. He'd meant to die, Waryk realized, rather than answer any questions.

"I'm sorry, Waryk, but he came straight at me, expecting me to cleave him!" Angus said, amazed.

"Aye," Waryk said, staring down at the dead man. He shook his head. "What man fights so hard, with so little, and is afraid to live?"

"Damn me, Waryk, if I know."

"We'll go to the fortress, see if we've any man so much as half-alive."

The fortress at Localsh was small, a tower built upon an old Celtic formation, rude wooden walls to surround a courtyard for marketing by the neighboring freemen and the tenants and serfs of lesser chiefs and lairds. Sir Gabriel Darrow, keeper of the tower, was greatly relieved by the lifting of the siege and the coming of Waryk's troops, but he, too, seemed to find the attack disturbing. A gruff old soldier, survivor of many a battle, he told Waryk that the initial attack had come out of nowhere, madmen in paint streaming out of the forest, slaughtering all the men they found in the fields, and demanding that he open the gates and surrender Localsh, or all would be put to death when the fortress fell.

"I've seldom seen such brutality, and for so little reason," Sir Gabriel told them.

"There's reason aplenty," Angus commented, "what with the English king dead and his nephew a thieving bastard."

Waryk arched a brow to Angus, who supported their own king's position. David had respected Henry and supported his daughter's claim to the throne. However, Waryk knew his king well, and, though he didn't say so aloud, he was aware that David was a powerful opportunist who would seize this advantage to push Scottish borders if he could.

"A Norman lord comes," Sir Gabriel continued, "and he wants more land, more servants, more to do him homage. The Vikings attack and plunder, rape, and kill, but with the intent to enrich themselves. These men came to destroy, to slaughter men, to lay waste the land. Why, I do not know."

Even as Sir Gabriel spoke, Thomas and Garth dragged in a fallen rebel. He bled profusely from wounds to his temple and chest, and he was barely conscious, but Waryk knelt by his side on the stone floor before the hearth in the small tower room.

"For whom do you fight, man? Is this an attack against the king of Scots on behalf of Mathilda of England, or her cousin, Stephen?"

The man's eyes opened on Waryk. He offered him a half smile. "Have you a son, my great, mighty, lord?"

"Nay, man, not as yet."

"Then you do na know."

"You're dying, man. If you've a son and you give me the answers that I need, I will see to your boy, raise him to fight like his father, under my protection. I ask you again, for whom do you fight?"

The fellow coughed, spitting up a trail of blood. "Ye wouldna reach my boy, great laird. You bleed yourself. All men bleed."

Waryk hadn't realized he'd been nicked in the fighting. He bled, but hadn't felt the injury. "Aye, I bleed, I wear many scars. But I don't fall, and if I were to fall, others more powerful would come behind me. Give me your boy. I can grant him the king's protection."

The man shook his head painfully. "You would never reach him in time, before . . ." he said. He gritted his teeth tightly against the pain assailing him.

"I swear to you, I will do whatever is necessary—" Waryk began.

But the man shuddered and died. No man, no laird, no king, had power over death.

"What is it that a man fears more than death itself?" Sir Gabriel demanded.

"The death of all he loves," Waryk said quietly. He rose, and looked at his men. "No other survivors?" he asked.

"They fled, or died, Waryk," Thomas told him.

"Have the men set to work strengthening the defenses," Waryk said. "We'll leave an additional fifteen men and supply the fortress before we leave, Sir Gabriel. Added strength until we know what this disturbance is all about."

"Maybe we'll never know," Sir Gabriel said.

"I think that we will. Aye, I think that we will," Waryk told him. "Eventually. All men fight because they want something. I believe these battles are like the tips of the icebergs off the northern waters—we've not begun to see what lies beneath."

\* \* \*

Two days later, with much work accomplished to shore up the walls and defenses of Localsh, Waryk and his men, minus those he would leave behind, departed.

Before turning back toward Stirling, he and his men rode the border, a powerful presence in the name of the king of Scots. As well as seeing to the welfare, strength, and loyalty of Scottish lords, they stopped at a small English castle, where they were entertained by Lord Peter of Tyne, an English baron who had managed to keep his border region peaceful despite the many disturbances in the region. His castle was strong; he had at least sixty of his own men trained for battle and joust. In the midst of the trouble between Stephen and Mathilda, he maintained a strong neutrality, and, due to his proximity to Scottish land, kept a close allegiance with King David of Scotland.

Peter was Waryk's own age, the son of a noble who had grown up at the court of Henry I with David of Scotland. Listening to Waryk's account of what had occurred, he seemed at a loss as well. "There is a tremendous schism in England," he said. "One day, a man is killed for supporting Stephen; the next, five men are tortured for their loyalty to old Henry's daughter. Strange things are happening."

"Aye, but Scotland has enough of her own troubles without being embroiled with those of the English!"

"Hard to say, when so many Normans, and Anglo-Normans, call themselves Scotsmen. And when we all keep our eyes on David, knowing he will seize what he can to the south!"

"Aye, but if these men were involved in this fight between royal English cousins descended from the Conqueror, why go against the king of Scotland?"

"Someone is stirring up trouble, but who, I do not know. I will, of course, keep my eyes and ears open."

"Ah. You will be on the lookout for a Scottish king?" Waryk asked skeptically, grinning. Peter was a cunning fellow, often blunt, never reckless.

"Aye, well, the Scottish king sits on his throne, at the moment. While the English . . . my loyalty lies where it is most expedient."

Waryk laughed, they drank together, the night wore on. As the fire in the hearth slowly died, he saw a woman in the shadows of the hallway, waiting. Eleanora. Peter had long been a friend, and if they were ever to become enemies, it would be in the open.

Here, he had relaxed, weary from the perplexing battle, and he had lain half-sprawled in his chair. Now, his muscles tightened. He gave her a slow smile, finished the ale in his cup. "Peter, I'll say good night, and accept your hospitality."

"Indeed, you must be exhausted," Peter said.

"Aye, that I am."

"My sister has waited long enough?" Peter queried, a brow arched in good humor.

"Apparently."

"Aye, brother!" Eleanora cried. "Enough of this talk of battle and men who crawl from the forests like mindless monsters to die."

Waryk walked over to Eleanora. The widow of a wealthy English laird, she was now an independent woman, but she loved him, and had been his mistress now many years, though the times he saw her were far too infrequent. She took his hand, and with a subtle smile, led him through dim corridors. Soon, they were within her rich apartments in her brother's house. The light was very low, scented candles burned. Her clothes were quickly strewn. She was a voluptuous woman, the fullness of her breasts was emphasized by the flickering light and shadow of the candles. In the privacy of her room, she was passionate, experienced. He caught her to him, hungry for the taste of her, a kiss, the feel of her breasts in his hands. She responded with a sweet urgency, glad of his touch, wanting more, wanting it quickly. Upon her knees, she unbuckled his scabbard. She took him in her hand. Battle was soon forgotten.

He had meant to stay longer at the welcoming bastion of Tyne, but while he was there, a messenger arrived from David, urging him onward to Stirling with moderate haste. Something had happened; Waryk knew the king, and he knew he was being summoned for a reason. He bid brother and sister good-bye and started swiftly toward Stirling, where the king, who frequently moved about the country, was in residence.

They rode late one night when they came across an armed guard bearing the king's colors. They were challenged in the name of King David, and Waryk quickly called out his own identity, then found that he faced an old friend, Sir Harry Wakefield, an older man, but one of the king's closest advisors. Dismounting, he greeted Sir Harry, curious to know what he was about. "Is there some new action? Has fighting broken out anew?" he asked him.

"Nay, Laird Lion! Why, 'tis nothing but escort service I am about. The death of an old laird sends his child to the king, and so I am entrusted with her safety. We have heard about the fighting. Across the country, my friend, you are known for your great victories."

Waryk inclined his head, though he was tempted to deny the praise. What had he done but slaughter madmen who had seemed to have no purpose?

"There's another copse, just yonder," Sir Harry told him. "You and your men may rest, Laird Lion, for no one will pass this road without my challenge!"

"My thanks, Sir Harry. Angus, what say we do as he suggests and make camp here. Have Thomas tell the men."

The cry went out down the ranks. Angus knew that Waryk trusted in no one man alone, and that if Waryk had told him to take his rest, then Waryk meant to stand the first hours of guard duty himself. Sir Harry, pleased to be of service, saluted Waryk. "Truly, we heard you made quick business of those raiders at Localsh," he said.

"Aye, Sir Harry, but I fear they'll rise again."

"The king has new enemies?"

"A king always has enemies, old and new." Waryk dismounted, giving his horse to one of the pages who rode with him as the lad came to tether the destrier for the night. A rustle in the trees alerted Waryk and he spun, his sword unsheathed, as a second mounted man rode onto the trail. "Sir Harry—" the man called, a thunderous note in his voice to mask his concern.

"It's all right, Matthew," Sir Harry said. " 'Tis Laird Waryk, the king's champion, returning from battle."

"Aye, sir, Laird Waryk," the man said, sounding somewhat relieved. "We've strength against an enemy tonight!"

"Have you had trouble?" Waryk asked.

"Nay," said Matthew. "But there are always troubles then, are there not? Especially in this, an old laird dies, he leaves a daughter ..."

"Aye, well, we will be here tonight, and tomorrow, we'll wait for you to break camp, and follow behind. If anyone is following, we will know. If that serves you well, Sir Harry?" Waryk didn't want to imply that Sir Harry might really need his assistance in the simple task of escorting an orphaned heiress to the king.

"Laird Lion, it sits well enough with me!" Sir Harry said. "The lady's own men are with us; when we see Stirling, they will double back, and when they have passed you by, you will know we are safely on our way down to the fortress."

"Aye, then."

"Matthew, ride the trail south, and I will move to the north," Sir Harry said, and Matthew turned on his warhorse to do as commanded. Sir Harry lifted a hand in salute to Waryk. "I will leave you to your rest, m'laird."

Matthew turned his mount to cover a distance of the northern road. As the light from Sir Harry's torch faded, Waryk saw the glow of the campfires where the lady and her escort rested. They were some distance away through a thicket of foliage and trees, yet Waryk found himself drawn curiously to a sudden flow of movement in the night. He strode to the side of the trail, and, setting a hand upon a large oak, looked through to the group of men, shadowy figures all, drawn around the fire.

The campfire burned brightly in the center of a large clearing, flames licking upward in the night, blue and gold, mauve and crimson. From his distance, Waryk could see that a girl spun before it. He was too far away to make out her features, but close enough to feel there was a pretty sense of magic in the scene. Perhaps it was the late hour of the night, the slight blanketing of fog rising around her like an ethereal mist. Her dress was long, silver-white, touched strangely by the fire glow to embrace a rainbow of netherworld shades. Her hair was the color of the blaze, yellow-gold, highlighted with just a touch of fire. Like a sprite, she glided around the fire, dancing with the seductive allure of an ancient Celtic princess, capturing the breathless attention of everyone present. And then she spoke. Her voice was magic, crystal clear, and he realized she was telling the tale of St. Columba.

"What sin he committed, no man is sure, but he crossed the Irish Sea, and came to our sacred Iona, his strength created by God's own hand. And there he built a great monastery, and the people began to come to him. There had been men before, come with tales of Christ and the Church, but none was Columba. He was an artist, preserving our Celtic beauty, a scholar, and his monks toiled hard and long, creating pages of beautiful script. But most of all, he was a warrior knight, and he proved to the people the power of his will, and his God, for he came upon Loch Ness, and there he was defied by a great dragon. A sorry, wretched creature, it had plagued the people, stolen the children, consumed, as homage, many a fair maiden. Columba would have no more. He challenged the dragon to come for him. The creature rose from the deepest, blackest depths of the loch and, shedding the crystal water it shook from its great head, breathed fire upon Columba, yet he raised his great shield, and the fire returned to singe the dragon, and thus, the dragon was blinded. And Columba drew his great broadsword, and slew the dragon, and the people, who had grown hungry, feasted upon their enemy." She raised her arms, stretched to the heavens on her toes, then bent low, her hair sweeping around her in golden rain as she bowed deeply, laughing even as she did so. As she rose again, lifting her hands, Waryk thought she was indeed enchanting, and she had great pride, a spirit of independence—and a definite wild streak. He was glad Sir Harry was her escort, and that he had been left to battle madmen.

Her tale was completed, and applause rang through the forest. Then the sound of a lute could be heard, and the gentle tone of a harp came as well, and there was laughter, light voices, dancing in the trees.

Then suddenly, the music hit a discordant note, and the sweet sounds of it faded into the night. "The king's Normans are here," he heard someone say. The words were spoken quietly, but somehow they carried through the night. Then a strange whispering began, and then there was silence.

He remained against the oak, teeth gritted. Aye, David had brought many Normans with him. He fought with Normans, and he fought against Normans. Still, somehow, the words were disturbing. He'd received many advantages in the king's court; he fought with good armor, steel protecting him over the wool of his tartan. Many of the men escorting the young heiress had been clad in the typical leine croich, long pleated wool garments loose enough to allow a man to fight, yet supposedly offering some protection in the folds of material. But his own mail and plate were worn over his tartan, a pattern created for his father by the finest of the wool workers of his mother's family, the Strathearns. As much as any man, more than most men, he was a Scot. Often, he knew, priests, clerics, and poets wrote of their being barbarians. Many in the Christian world claimed that though Rome had not conquered the Scots, they should have; much had been gained across Europe from the Romans—roads, aqueducts, laws, literature, more. Waryk thought that it was true; no one could match the Celts for the beauty of their jewelry and the works done by Irish and Scottish monks in the last centuries were some of the finest ever. But they needed to learn from their enemies, he thought. If they were going to fight the Normans, they needed to be as well armed as border friends and foes.

The armor he wore beneath his surcoat might be Norman, but he was a Scot. His father had paid for their place in this homeland with his blood. He had shed his own upon it often enough.

He moved away from the oak. He was tired, and he was going to get some sleep. God alone knew what the king was planning next.

And his sleep was haunted by a dancer. She moved through his dreams with steps as light as quicksilver, her cloak of golden blond hair—just touched by a crimson flame—swirled with her, ever hiding her features.

He reached for her, wanting to see her face.

But she swirled, and in a field of mist, she was gone.

# CHAPTER 2

They emerged from the trail through the thick-forested crest, and there she lay. Stirling.

Seated upon her gray mare, Mellyora looked down upon the town where the king was in residence at his fortress. It was an ancient place. Even the Romans, in their quest to seize Britain, had come this far, but long before that, the old tribes had made it home. As dusk came now, as twilight touched the valleys, crags, and waterways, it was a beautiful picture. The fortress walls rose proudly, the colors of fall highlighted the sweeping dips and mounds of the landscape around them. The reflection of the setting sun upon the water gave it the appearance of sparkling with dozens of gemstones, brilliant stars that glittered and beckoned. One far field was dotted with sheep, now being herded in by a pair of lads and their dogs. Before the walls, near the water, the fishwives cried out their husbands' catches; the clang of an armorer at work could be heard on the wind.

Mellyora loved Stirling—the hills, the forests, the greens and mauves, the beauty of the crags. She loved all of her homeland; this was far different from Blue Isle, where the waves could beat against the rocky shore and the cliffs with a wild, white vengeance. Here, all was calm, peaceful, and serene.

Yet, from her vantage point she could even see downriver, far downriver, to a field of tents and makeshift housing: a Viking camp. She bit lightly into her lower lip, feeling a strange level of excitement. *Her uncle was near. If there was trouble, her uncle was near . . .*

"My lady, we must ride."

She nodded. It was Sir Harry who had spoken. The king's man, not her own. Sir Harry had come for her. She hadn't thought to come to the king, not yet. She had still been in mourning. It had been inconceivable that Adin should die, and she had not been able to think, to feel, to do anything other than miss him. But when the king's men arrived to escort her to David, she'd realized her situation. The king had sent an escort; she hadn't insisted on bringing her own. A few men from her home had ridden this far with her, along with one of her women, Jillian, but though Jillian would ride on with her, her own retinue of men-at-arms would leave her now. They would return to guard Blue Isle, while she went on to the king. She was the lady of the isle. She wanted the king to know that she trusted him, as he should trust her. Not only was she protected by the escort he had sent, but the king's conquering cavalry was riding this way as well.

There was little to do but trust the king.

She would vow her allegiance to David as her father's heir, and then she would speak to him, honestly, pleadingly, as she would have spoken to Adin. It was the best strategy.

"My lady, we'll leave you now."

She turned to Ewan, grave, serious, concerned for her, gray eyes upon her as he waited for her to insist that he remain. He had been somber since he had heard that the king's men-at-arms had ridden behind them last night.

But no matter his look or his concern, she did not ask him to stay. She had to do this alone.

"I'll be home soon, and I shall miss you all," she said. She smiled at Ewan, then spoke to the others from Blue Isle, "Darrin, Peter, Gareth, thank you for the escort; protect Blue Isle as you protect me. I leave my home in your keeping, and thank you for your company this far. I know, of course, that I am well guarded by the king's soldiers."

"Perhaps we should continue with you," Ewan said, his eyes still upon hers.

"Ah, now lad, the fortress lies ahead of us, and I'd die for your lady, as would any king's man," Sir Harry Wakefield, the king's chosen messenger, told Ewan, not unkindly. Sir Harry considered himself a far stronger escort; he was a king's man, knighted, trained at arms, a warrior who had survived many battles. Ewan was a clansman, a warrior from a wild countryside still considered barbaric by many of the more southern inhabitants, people highly influenced by the Norman population in England that seeped ever more into Scotland.

"I will be fine," she said. She loved Ewan. From her childhood, he'd been her best friend. With his dark blond hair and gray eyes, he was handsome, serious, and dependable. He was worried about her, they were all worried about her, her people, her advisors, everyone. She had been summoned before the king. All lairds and ladies must pay homage to the king, she had assured them all. The king was her godfather. He loved her, she had always been able to charm him. She believed in her power to maintain her position. And Sir Harry was an old friend as well. He was the leader of the five armed men sent by King David to protect her on her ride through the countryside to Stirling. The gates of the city were within view, she knew she was perfectly safe.

"Sir Harry, if you'll excuse us just a moment, I'd have a moment with Ewan, who will safeguard my home in my absence," she said.

"Aye, my lady, of course."

She moved her mount back into a copse in the forest, and Ewan followed there. Her mare nuzzled his gelding. She reached out and touched Ewan's face. "Don't fear for me."

He shook his head. "I'm not afraid."

"You look so sad."

He smiled, an awkward, lopsided smile. He wasn't going to argue with her.

"Ewan, I am strong. I can take care of myself."

"Mellyora, David is the king. We've all told you that, we've all warned you—"

"And I will do the king homage."

"He'll think you haven't the strength—"

"But I do."

"Mellyora, take care in your arguments. Take care what defiance you make, don't put yourself into danger. You don't seem to understand that if you're attacked ... well, you can be in danger."

"How so?"

He suddenly drew his sword, aiming it at her throat. But she saw the motion coming, and she carried her own sword in a slender leather scabbard at her hips. Her steel touched his even as he tried to prove his point.

"You were saying, Ewan?" she murmured softly.

He shook his head, eyes lowered as he rued the fact he hadn't moved faster.

"I'll be all right. Have faith in me."

"Aye, that I do. I'll pray for you, my lady."

She smiled, sorry that he seemed so insulted that she had easily rebuffed the attack that was to prove her weak. She inched her horse toward his, discreetly looked about to assure herself they were alone, and leaned forward to plant a gentle kiss against his lips.

"My lady MacAdin!" she heard Sir Harry calling. "We must ride on; it is getting dark!"

She sat her mount primly again, but could not help smiling mischievously at Ewan once again. "I'll be all right. I swear it. I love you. I vow my heart to you, always."

He lowered his head, inching his horse forward once again. He took her hand, and kissed it tenderly. His gray eyes touched hers with devotion. "Whatever happens, my lady, I will love you. I swear it." He looked at her as if he were saying good-bye. She could not bear it.

Heedless of Sir Harry's anxious calls, she leaned over again and impulsively kissed Ewan one last time. "Soon. I'll be home soon, my love."

They rode from the cover of the trees and parted ways. As they slowly loped down the crest toward the fortress she remembered the words: "The king is anxious to see you today, my lady. He insisted, today. He has much to tell you."

*And I have much to tell him*, Mellyora thought.

It didn't occur to her that she might not have the opportunity to tell him exactly what she was thinking, what she wanted, and what she intended to do.


"Mellyora, I have carefully chosen this marriage for you," the king said firmly. He could sense her resistance, it seemed to bound off her like the hot, angry rays of the sun on a summer's day.

Time and the passage of years had changed King David little. If anything, he was stronger, more assured, and more aware that being a king often meant maneuvering men. Alliance could be far more advantageous than the strength of hundreds of fighting men. Being a man who had lived through much and gained a certain wisdom regarding people, he never judged a man, a friend or an enemy, by his birth. Certain Englishmen, overly imbued with their own sense of power, attacked his southern borders, but his wife was a Northumbrian heiress, and he had many supporters among her people. Henry I of England had been partially responsible for raising David, he had taught him, he had given him many of his lands, and his wife. But Henry had died two years ago, and the English monarchy was in chaos with Henry's nephew, Stephen, fighting with Henry's daughter, Mathilda, for the throne of England. This made the English nobles more powerful as each faction vied for their help in the dispute. Border lords were a danger, they always would be. Naturally, they considered him a danger, and naturally, he was pressing against the line of the kingdom.

Then again, there were still the Vikings.

He had never disliked a man simply for being a Viking. God knew, even the royal house of Normandy evolved from Viking contributions. The sea pirates had raided far and wide, into France, England, Ireland, as far away as Russia and the Mediterranean, and certainly into Scotland. The great invasions which had first cast such horror into these isles were now several centuries in the past, but wars with the predators were not so far away that a Viking menace could be taken lightly. In the early years of the last century, his own royal ancestors had been forced to pay homage to the Dane Cnut, who had been recognized king of much of England. And it had just been in the year 1098 when the Norwegian king Magnus III, known as Magnus Barefoot, had savaged his way through Orkney and the Hebrides, held his position, and made a formal treaty with David's brother. Aye, Vikings were a greater danger than border lords. He didn't intend to lose any of his land to the Vikings. They were a threat.

They always would be.

He had sent for Mellyora so quickly after her father's death mainly because Vikings were so dangerous. He had accepted her homage, then told her his plans for her future—immediate plans—because Vikings were so dangerous.

And the lass before him was far too Viking for her own good, no matter her maternal ancestry and her dead father's loyalty to Scotland, and to him. Adin had been proven. This was a girl facing him, one with dangerous desires and dangerous kin. But she was also an heiress with an outstanding inheritance. A stubborn heiress, dangerous herself. Even if she thought herself loyal to him, she could be manipulated. She was his own godchild; he had stood by her father, recently converted to Christianity, at her birth, and he had watched her grow. Now, she was his ward. He had mulled her future for a very long time, firmer plans revolving in his mind as Adin had continued to mourn his wife at her death, refuse to marry again, and thus, fail to sire a male inheritor. He was greatly pleased with his decision; he was a king who granted time for an audience with his poorest subjects on an almost daily basis, and he was quick to reward those who served him.

Not only was this girl one of the most wealthy heiresses in his realm, she was young, stunning, healthy, and vibrant. Many men had asked the king for her, most discreetly, while her fierce father lived. He had firmly turned down all pleas and entreaties. There were few men who deserved such a prize, and such power. A power which required a love of Scotland, loyalty to the royal Scottish house of Canmore, and a sense of the new growing nationalism. Perhaps the kings of Scotland had been forced to pay a certain homage to the kings of England; the lines of a separate country had been drawn, and through both warfare and diplomacy, God willing, they would only strengthen.

And by God, his errant young ward would understand, and do his will. Without question. He was a good king, and he knew it. Honored for the introduction of new laws, creating new commerce, minting coins, and more. He was a strong and intelligent king, a warrior and a statesman. He could be both merciful and merciless. And watching her now, as she stood before him, silent, chin set stubbornly, he knew that it would not be easy to be merciless.

But by God, she had too many Viking kin. And Vikings were dangerous. They always would be.

They had stared at one another now for a very long time, he thought. Too long a time.

"Your marriage will take place, and, my lady, you do understand my position?" David said, his tone courteous—and unyielding.

She still did not respond.

She stood like a stone statue, as if she were a carved creation of mythical beauty crafted by the talented hands of an artist to grace the king's great hall at Stirling. She evenly returned the king's stare, betraying no true feelings with either the slightest movement or expression. The perfect marble smoothness of her face remained cool and impassive; the endless deep blue of her eyes remained fixed upon the king.

*She intends to fight me,* David thought. *But perhaps not here, not now. How?*

She hadn't disputed him yet, but then again, neither had she agreed with a single word he had said since he had turned down her bid to remain in power herself in those lands which had been held by her father until his recent, lamentable death. He had summoned her to Stirling to give her the good news about her upcoming marriage. Amazingly, she had come to pay homage as her father's heir, expecting that he would allow her to remain lady of the isle in her own right. He had known she'd wanted to speak; he hadn't given her a chance. He'd immediately told her his plans for her.

And she didn't like them.

His fingers curled around the arms of the handsomely carved chair. He hadn't seen her in quite some time, Mellyora, granddaughter of a Norse king. What could she think? She knew herself that Vikings were dangerous. They had proven it time and again over the years. David himself had made treaties with the Vikings, he respected the Vikings, and many northern islands were ruled by Viking jarls. Adin, her father, however, had been unique. Different, powerful, he had seen fit to become a part of Scotland. Not many of his kind were quite so willing to settle into the political structure of a unified Scotland under one king, and kin of Adin's still ruled many of the isles off the coast of Scotland. His brother, Daro, Laird of Skul Island, was camped just outside Stirling now, here to negotiate with the king. Mellyora still had powerful family from her father's homeland to help her if she saw fit to go to them. Still, the king was strong himself in his own domains, and he would have his way.

Mellyora was also a descendant of one of the most ancient Gaelic families in all of Scotland. Through her mother's kin, she should have been his most loyal subject. David was aware that although he had spent many of his formative years in a Norman court, it was acknowledged by his subjects that his mother had been Saxon royalty. And from his father's side, he could trace his heritage back to the great Kenneth MacAlpin, and some believed that the line of Scottish kings went back even farther, with their royal line descending back first to ancient Egypt, then on to Spain, Ireland, and from there, on to Scotland. As king, in holding his country together, he had learned that bloodlines could be important, and that sometimes, one had to be very, very careful in mixing blood.

Not that much care had gone into the mingling when Mellyora had been born, so legend went. Adin had simply come, seen, and conquered, and whether his bride had been willing or not at the beginning was anyone's guess. No matter, the blood mixed in Mellyora's veins had created a young woman with the best of both parents—truly an asset to any king. She was perfectly formed, with a slim, supple body, beautifully curved. The bone structure in her face was exceptionally fine. She moved with the grace of an angel, and her striking blue eyes gave her both power and a sense of the mythical or mysterious, as if she might have been bred from old Adin's Nordic gods. Her hair was purely golden, nothing pale about her blond at all—it was touched with a hint of red fire, and it was thick and rich and lustrous and fell down her back now freed from any plaiting or restraint. He was certain that she had worn her hair down, flowing freely, just as she had come to him dressed in a blue-linen shift—not a piece of jewelry or adornment upon her—because she had calculated that such plain apparel would signify more than mere loyalty to him. She had come before him as she might have come before her own father, a true daughter who most naturally swore love and devotion, and therefore deserved to be completely trusted in return.

Simply clad, she appeared all the more noble. She was tall for a woman, a regal gift from her father, for he had towered over men. She was incredibly still, shoulders set, back straight. Despite her height, she was delicately built, as her mother had been, with fine, chiseled features, high-set cheekbones. Her face was in perfect proportion with her large blue eyes. Honeyed brows handsomely arched above them; she had a small, well-formed nose, and full, generous lips. Perhaps those lips were just a bit grim now—her one telltale reaction to his dictates.

Ah, yes.

And there . . . along the elegant line of her throat, a pulse ticked furiously. She was angry with him. Livid.

David smiled. At least she knew her place, and did her very best not to betray her anger.

His smile faded. Either that, or she plotted against him. She was part Viking. Too much Viking. And *Vikings were dangerous.*

He determined her marriage would take place as soon as was humanly possible.

"My dear?" David prompted.

"I understand your position, sire," she said.

Ah, yes. She *understood* his position.

She didn't agree with it a bit.

Well, he understood her position as well. What she hadn't completely comprehended as yet was that *he* was *king*. And, therefore, it was his position that must not just be understood, but *obeyed*.

"You do then accept my plans for your future?" David asked.

"You know that I have always been your most loyal servant. As was my father."

She paused. The king watched as she struggled with her emotions.

Great Adin was not long deceased. He had been a bear of a man, tall as a god, gifted with a thick mane of red-blond hair, rich beard, and flashing, icicle eyes. Men had admired him, women had loved him. Yet, even after the death of his Gaelic lady, he had remained loyal to her memory. However the marriage had begun, he had loved her. After her death, his constant companion had been his daughter. He had ridden with her, read with her, practiced at arms with her, sailed the sea with her.

Perhaps he had even taught her about going a-Viking. Raiding, plundering, seizing land that was not hers.

Strangely, David had never questioned Adin's loyalty once the Viking had come to him for term. But in the midst of what appeared to be incredibly robust health, Adin had died. Drinking with friends, jarls, and chieftains, he had suddenly constricted, turned white as snow, and fallen.

All through the night, the king had heard, this daughter of his had sat by his side, clutching his great hand.

She had continued to do so, even after his death. As he was shrouded for burial in the chapel where he had been baptized into Christianity himself, she had sat by his side.

And even then, the king had heard, she had kept vigil, refusing to leave the chapel, to eat, to sleep, to cease her prayers, until Adin had been dead three days, and only then had friends and the strange Gaelic priest, Phagin, convinced her that she must leave him at last.

Watching the king then, she cleared her throat. "I do repeat, sire, my father was your most loyal servant. I learned all that I know from him. I would always be your most loyal subject as well, ever more especially—with greater determination, care, concern and *responsibility*—were I granted faith and freedom to see to my own affairs. A husband of my own choosing, when I choose to take one, would be—by God, I do solemnly swear—a most loyal subject to you, sire, and to no other man."

"Well spoken, my lady—and with all the passion and fervor of youth. But you are a young, very beautiful woman, Mellyora. More temptation than you can imagine to those who would covet both your person and your lands."

"I have in my household the most able men—"

"Who serve you. None who can claim to be lord."

"None who rule me," she snapped back, losing—if just briefly—her iron hold upon her temper.

David lowered his head, smiling. He looked back to her gravely. "My dear, I am well aware of the power and strength of your will. However, it is the strength of your sword arm that worries me."

"I manage quite well," she said evenly. "I have been taught by masters. Those incredibly skilled in the arts of survival."

*And invasion!* David thought, suddenly wary. There were more pressing matters than this of trying to convince a headstrong young heiress that she was not a power to stand alone—especially when he didn't dare be anything but suspicious of her closest male kin. Admittedly, other Vikings had often interbred and made Scotland their home, as had Adin. But though Adin's brother had sometimes fought with the king's troops, he was a younger man, and the company he kept was not entirely trustworthy. Adin had married a Scottish heiress. Daro's loyalties still remained in question. Not that any of that mattered in this; David had made up his mind about Blue Isle, Adin's fortress.

"Lady Mellyora, you will bear in mind that I am your king. Your overlord, and your godfather. Your well-being was entrusted to me by both your father and your mother. And it is your welfare that I have in mind. Though I do applaud that strength and will of which we speak, I must still repeat—"

"Strength and will and wit, my liege," she corrected him. "When a stronghold is besieged, it is not saved by one sword arm alone, but rather by the talents of the main defender—directing others to action. Of that, I am highly capable."

"Mellyora," David said, losing patience completely, "I have spoken. You will trust in my ability to see what is best for you—and Scotland."

"Since I am a woman too weak and witless to judge for myself, sire?"

David stood and approached her, amazed by her blunt sarcasm and the force of her resistance. When he stood directly before her, she still met his gaze steadily. Then her lashes swept her cheeks and he could see that she was trembling, though with fear that she might have pushed him too far at last, or with simple fury that she had not gotten her way, he did not know.

"I have chosen a man for you—"

"You have chosen a man to whom to give my property. I am but an appendage to it." Her eyes flashed to his. He had known her since she was a child, and she was taking grave advantage of that relationship now. A fact which tempted him to treat her as he might a very young child of his own—and take her right over his knee.

She was too old for such treatment—and so was his knee. But he grew tired of this argument. He would win, because he was king—he commanded great armies, and since he did, he could surely get one small woman to the altar. Yet it was irritating that he could not feel that he was truly winning the battle with his words and logic alone.

"You may retire, Mellyora," he told her curtly.

"But, sire—"

"You may retire!"

"Retire, indeed," she said. "As you wish. I give you all homage, King David, as is rightful. But now, though the hour is late, I will take my leave and return home—"

"Nay, lady, you will not."

Her elegant, honey-shaded brow arched. "Am I a prisoner then, sire?"

"You are my guest."

"Your guest."

"Indeed, my lady."

"And if I wished to leave—until the wedding, of course?"

"Pray, my lady, do not wish to do so. You would find it most difficult."

"Ah. Because my sword arm is not so strong."

"Good evening, my lady," he said firmly. But she refused to go down without a further fight.

"I feel, sire, that you do not truly appreciate the strength that may lie within one's mind, and that neither gender nor muscle power has a thing to do with that strength."

"I have heard you, Mellyora."

"You have the power, my lord king. But if wits were to allow me to leave, then I would be free. Wouldn't that be true, my lord?"

He leaned toward her then, wagging a stern finger beneath her nose. "My lady, you should take care. You'll find yourself not only confined to Stirling, but to your chambers," he warned.

"Perhaps."

"Oh?"

Again, her lashes lowered. "Sire—"

"By God, Mellyora, leave me be!" David thundered, and at that, at last, she braced herself with clenched teeth, pausing. It was on the tip of his tongue to inform her that he hadn't summoned her to Stirling just to hear about his decision regarding her future, but to meet her prospective bridegroom as well. A messenger had recently assured him that his fighting men were nearly home, that they had tarried only to follow after the escort given to Mellyora.

The Lion had led the men engaged in the fighting.

But then, as yet, King David hadn't informed Laird Lion of his coming nuptials, either. It hadn't been until Adin had so suddenly died that the king had firmly decided that Mellyora was the right reward for the lad who had grown to become his most respected warrior knight. Other rich properties had become available over the years, but they'd been encumbered with aging heiresses who could not give the man the family he had lost. Young women were always available, but those as richly landed as this Viking's daughter were few and far between. The question of Waryk's future had remained a concern until now since David had never imagined Adin's death at such a time as this—the Norseman had seemed like a god himself, a Wodin to live forever. He'd been young when he'd taken his Gaelic bride, still little more than a boy himself when he'd produced his daughter. David had not thought that the lass and the riches of the property would have been his for the granting so soon.

The king's head pounded. Laird Lion would ride in triumphant;

a warrior loyal to the king, a sword arm strong in valor and ability, and his king would present him with a bride who was not only unwilling, but brashly determined to make quite certain everyone should know it.

"Mellyora," he said angrily, "you will honor me, cease this fight, and leave me be."

"Well, sire, then, as you wish, I shall obediently leave you be," she said quietly, but her blue eyes still carried dangerous light, and despite the soft way she spoke, her voice was edged with anger.

"Shall you?" He crossed his arms over his chest.

"I'm disturbing you, so I will take my powerless wits and leave you. Your prisoner—no, your guest—since I couldn't possibly escape your great strength or that of this fortress."

"Lady, you test my patience."

"Do I? Your pardon, it is not my wish to cause you trouble, merely to allow you to see that the mind is an incredibly powerful tool. Especially when it seems I am challenged to prove its force and potential."

"M'lady," the king said, inclining his head politely, "do let your mind work as it will. One of my men awaits just beyond the door to escort you back to your chambers."

"You know, sire," she said, "before God, not even a king can force a maid to marry."

The very quiet of her tone made the words an irritating rebuke. She was maintaining her temper, he was losing his. He wouldn't have it. He was the king, and she was a pawn—his pawn, to be moved where and when he deemed it important.

"Before God, my dear, you may be surprised. Two can play a game of power and wit. Don't underestimate what I can and can't do. And as to force, perhaps I will leave that matter to your future husband!"

She smiled at him suddenly, sweetly. Even his determined, angry, and aging heart felt a warming trend—if not a melting. She was lovely, volatile, one minute so furious, and the next, gazing at him in a manner which could be almost tender and caring. She was his godchild.

"Sire, I am thus challenged. Of course, we both know that I can't possibly manage to escape your fortress here at Stirling, but if I did . . . would I then be free to choose my own future?"

"You will not escape."

"Of course not, but if I did . . . ?"

"You will not escape. My mind is set."

"If you are so certain, then surely we have a bargain?"

"My lady—"

"If I escape, then I am free," she said, as if that settled that matter. Her smile remained radiant, and she stepped forward suddenly—just as she had as a child. She touched his shoulders, came to her toes, and kissed his cheek.

"I make you no such promise!" he said sternly.

"But if I escape, I am free," she said. "I learned well from you and my father. Possession gives a man great power to hold a property. Freedom gives a woman great power to negotiate. I'm also, sire, adept with a sword, a knife, and especially, my mind. I'm stronger than you see, sire, and I pray that you understand," she said with determined dignity. Then she turned at last to leave.

Shoulders squared. Head very high. She didn't run from the room, but walked, as graceful as a goddess floating upon clouds. She walked with confidence. Slowly.

She was giving him a chance to summon her back. To talk more, argue, come to some different conclusion regarding her future.

Despite her sudden smile, and even the old affection of her kiss, she remained a stubborn, determined, and seething young goddess.

"I should wed you to a pruned old wife-beater, lass!" he swore after her, following her suddenly with long, angry strides. Oh, yes, he granted her a will of pure steel; she would argue with God himself on Judgment Day, so it seemed.

Just outside the great hall, he found that Sir Harry Wakefield—an old friend, a knight who had served him long before he had become king—waited as he had expected, as escort for the Lady Mellyora.

"Sir Harry!" the king said.

"Sire?"

"The lady and I have engaged in something of a game of combat—of wills, so it seems. You will see that she is returned safely to her chambers, and that she does not depart her chambers again until she is summoned before me once again."

"Indeed, sire."

Mellyora merely smiled. Yet even as she smiled, she cast the king a sharp, challenging assessment, then slipped her arm within

Sir Harry's. "As if I could best the king at any combat!" she said, and laughed as if the possibility of such a thing was entirely absurd. "It will be good, Sir Harry, to know that you're guarding me."

They departed down the hall. David watched them, telling himself that he had a trained knight decked in partial mail watching one lone woman.

He decided to double the guard on her door, and to let it be known that the Lady Mellyora was not—under any circumstance—to leave the stronghold at Stirling without his express permission.

If she so much as tried . . .

Well, she'd be brought back.

In chains, he thought grimly.

*Easy, my fine sir, easy . . .*

*After their first passion had been spent, Eleanora had seen his wound. A scratch, he'd told her. A wound, still, she'd told him. Vulnerable to infection.*

*Easy, mine is a gentle touch . . .*

*With such sweet words, Eleanora worked her balm into the slash he'd received against his upper arm. And when she was done, she'd crawled atop him, naked, sleek, glistening in the light of the fire, entirely comfortable with him, with herself. They'd been together so many times through the last years, she knew how and where to stroke, she made love like a tigress, she had a throaty laugh, a way about her . . . battle might be fierce, the world a wearying place. They'd had so little time before he'd been summoned back to the king. He'd been puzzled, angry, and disturbed about the fighting, not a good companion. Yet he often came to her angry or weary, and she never minded, in a matter of days, hours, minutes, whatever time he had, she would offer her own brand of distraction. She asked nothing in return . . .*

"Waryk?"

Interrupted from the depths of his thoughts, Waryk glanced at Angus, riding next to him. "We've almost reached the king."

"Aye."

Waryk turned slightly, looking back at the armed men who rode behind him. They had fared well in the fighting; they were mounted men, trained in the use of a multitude of weapons. The past action remained puzzling, and one that Waryk found more disturbing since he grew more certain it had been instigated from elsewhere. Granted, the northern English nobles were exceptionally dangerous at this time, with Henry's daughter and nephew struggling for his throne, but, as Sir Gabriel had said, a Norman lord would usually strike with greater strength and purpose, and make a claim on property, riches, and titles. He wasn't sure what the enemy had been rebelling against, or what the rebels had hoped to achieve. Despite their camp of the previous night, his men were more tired from marching than fighting.

Angus was right, he had let his mind wander, and they were nearly at the gates of Stirling. Torches blazed along the walls, and the fortress seemed alive in the night. Above him, the sky appeared far more fascinating than the lights of the city. The night was clear, and stars dotted the heavens like jewels cast against an endless black sea.

He reined in, slowing his horse. "Angus, my friend, I think I'll leave you here."

Angus frowned, arching a brow. "Waryk, you are the leader of this company. Stirling lies ahead. The king summoned you. He will be anxious to see you, he'll want to hear what you have to say. You were eager to reach the king, remember? We've ridden hard to come here quickly, you've sent messengers ahead telling him that you will see him tonight—"

"Aye, that's true. But the night is long, and we've ridden faster than I thought we could. There's time. And I'm not sure as yet what I have to say to the king," Waryk told Angus. "Tell our liege that I will ride in shortly and report to him immediately upon my arrival."

Angus still wasn't pleased. "Waryk, there's a Viking camp downriver—"

"Aye."

"You plan to ride alone—"

"I do. The Vikings downriver have come here to negotiate with the king, they are not a group of maddened berserkers out to kill off the Scottish, man by man. I'm not going downriver. I plan to stay here, along the embankment."

"For what?" Angus demanded, puzzled.

"Time alone, Angus, a precious thing."

"You can be alone in your chambers at Stirling—"

"It's not the same as having the stars over your head. You needn't worry about me. We are back to civilization. The gates lie just ahead. No one more dangerous than a fisherman roams here. I'll take good care. Bring the men in. Report to the king. Tell him I'll be with him very soon."

"Waryk, you're no longer wearing any armor, not a plate, not a coat of mail—"

"I have my knife," Waryk said quietly. He looked back to Geoffrey of Perth, the lad serving as his gall-oglach, or armor-bearer. The boy was careful with all his belongings, polishing and tending his claymore, shields, mail, and plates constantly. Waryk had shed his fighting attire last night, and now, he realized, in his simple tartan and wool cloak, he looked more like some of the wildmen he had fought.

"Waryk—"

"Angus!" he groaned. "You are a good man, a good protector. Now be a good friend, and give me some peace."

Waryk lifted a hand to the trail of mounted men following behind him. He turned his horse and rode downriver, into the night.

Angus, watching him go, shook his head. No one man was an army.

And Angus had enough Viking in his own blood to be worried about the situation. Civilization! Angus snorted to himself. God alone knew what danger a man could come about in the dark of the night, even with a field of stars above.

# CHAPTER 3

"All men are tyrants!" Mellyora declared, closing the door to her chambers at Stirling. She had just given Sir Harry her sweetest and most flirtatious smile and sincere thanks for his safeguarding of her.

Jillian MacGregor did no more than arch her brow at the words. She was far more Mellyora's friend than her maid since she had all but raised her. She now continued to work on her tapestry, her demeanor calm, her fingers not missing a beat in their steady rhythm.

"I thought you were quite fond of the king, dear," Jillian said. "And you were so confident in seeing him."

For a moment, Mellyora wished fervently that she could be more like Jillian. Nothing seemed to disturb her. Jillian had been her mother's best friend and maid as well, so she had lived through some turbulent times and apparently weathered them well. Such peace with the world must be pleasant. Despite her perhaps forty years or so of life, Jillian's heart-shaped face remained serene, unlined, and lovely. Her hair had gone to a gentle silver, which complemented her soft ivory coloring and light slate eyes.

Yet when Jillian turned those light gray eyes to hers at last, Mellyora saw the glitter of amusement within them. Jillian had known the outcome of Mellyora's meeting with the king. She— along with all of Mellyora's advisors—had warned her it would be so. Even Ewan had said so. When she arrived in Stirling, the king would not let her remain lady in her own right of the isle, and he would have plans for an immediate wedding.

"My feelings for the man do not change the fact that he is a tyrant. And you apparently know exactly what happened when I went in to see him."

"Aye, the servants in the castle are all talking about it. Everyone thinks the union will be perfect. And you must remember, David believes he has a right to make such arrangements. He is a king."

"That may be, but must the word be synonymous with tyrant?"

"Mellyora, if you think about this rationally, I know that you'll agree David is a king with a kingdom he governs wisely. He has earned the love and loyalty of his people. He seeks to avoid any more bloodshed than he must endure to keep his kingdom together. Remember, there were tremendous battles when he took the throne in 1124. He fought again just a few years ago when insurrection among the clans began again. He must have the strongholds and castles of Scotland peopled with men he trusts. Especially with the current problems among the English royalty."

Mellyora listened to Jillian's words, knowing there was truth to them, but resentful nonetheless. "Indeed, the English problems. Trust me, the king will use the English problems to his advantage. He says he must stand strong against the border lords when we know he will push the borders. The king trusts only certain men, does not trust *women* at all," she said.

"Mellyora—"

Mellyora moved swiftly across the room, sinking to the floor in front of Jillian's chair. "Why can't he understand that I will be loyal?"

Jillian shifted her work on her lap, then sighed, stared at Mellyora, and answered flatly and truthfully. "Because you are a Viking's daughter."

"My father was loyal."

"Your father, my lady," Jillian said more gently, "is dead. And being king is not easy, and ruling such a rugged land of wild, proud chieftains and nobles from ancient tribes as well as those from more recent invasions and immigrations is a dangerous task, at best."

"Aye, my father is dead, and we are a wild land. But my father did not fret to leave his beloved homeland to me."

"He acquired his beloved homeland through your mother."

Mellyora sat back, irritated. "Are you going to argue with me as well? The land came through my mother, all the more reason it should be mine. Argue that!"

"Me? Argue with you? To what point? You heed nothing that I say, though I do continue to do my best to instruct you in what is fact—and must be seen, construed, and accepted as simple fact.

The land came to your mother by tradition, you'll remember it was your father who held it in a powerful grasp!"

Mellyora rose, pacing the chamber as restlessly as a great cat. If she escaped, she was free. Whether David liked it or not. Because if she escaped, she could appeal to her father's kin for help until she could reach some compromise with the king. He hadn't even given her a chance to tell him that she wanted to marry Ewan. Even David should have been pleased with her choice of a husband.

Ewan was a Scotsman, born and bred, even if his mother's family did have a bit of Viking blood as well. It didn't matter. Ewan MacKinny was chieftain of his father's family, and the MacKinnys had held their lands from Mellyora's mother's family back unto the ancient times. The MacKinnys had provided countless fighting men for the kings of Scotland for hundreds of years. Many had been knighted, many had shed their blood for what was now unified Scotland. They were a proud and noble people, and the king should welcome a MacKinny as laird of her lands.

The king simply didn't know it. Because he'd never given Mellyora a chance to explain. He'd accepted her homage, and told her that he was arranging for her marriage to one of his finest warriors, his own man, Laird Lion.

"Because he's a tyrant," she said aloud, still furious, and looked at Jillian. "He believes that he can order me to do anything if it's his will and that I don't matter in a decision regarding *me* at all. I'll not allow it."

"Mellyora!" Jillian murmured, distressed at last. "You've lived on Blue Isle too long, refusing to realize that it is a small part of a greater world. Come now, be reasonable. David is the king. You do not allow or disallow with the king!"

Mellyora shook her head, her eyes wistful. "It wasn't always like this, you know. The *Normans* are the ones who began so many of these wretched rules by which we live. My mother died so long ago, I admit, I don't remember her well, but I do remember her telling me about the old days. When Scotland was very wild, and there were many kings, different people, old gods, old ways . . . and women owned land just as men. She told me about wiccan beliefs—"

"You're talking about pagan beliefs!" Jillian warned her, making the sign of the cross over her breast.

Mellyora smiled. "In the wiccan religion—the pagan ways— the earth was the mother, and women were respected and loved.

And if we were living before the wretched Norman influence changed everything, I might well hold the land in my own right—"

"Might and might not. Don't you understand, your rebellion is just what he fears? You don't see it, but the Viking threat is very real. It is within living memory that the Vikings seized Scottish holdings. Your father proved himself a Scotsman, he became one of David's best friends. I'm certain that the king loves you—"

"But he doesn't respect my rights in any way, Jillian, and I've never given him cause to doubt me. I came here longing to give him nothing but my love and loyalty, and where did that get me?"

"I'm telling you again, whether you blame the Normans, the decade, or Divine Power, you have no more rights than a child. And the Vikings are too close, and David feels they rule enough of land that should belong to Scotland, and he doesn't intend to lose any more to them."

"It's all so infuriating! I'm the rightful heiress, through my mother, and my father. I hate the Normans, and I hate the influence they've brought!"

"The Norman influence came before you were born. I loved your mother, but she shouldn't have told you stories about a woman's right being any different. Like it or not, the king holds the right to give you—and your land—to whom he chooses in marriage."

"Well, then, I must somehow change things myself. If I can avoid the king, I will find a way to be free."

"Avoid him? Avoid?"

"All right . . . escape him."

"What?" Jillian rose, watching as Mellyora moved quickly about the room.

"If I escape him," Mellyora called over her shoulder, for she had found a window crevice within which to crawl, "I am free."

"The king said this?"

"I have just left the king," Mellyora hedged. "It is what will be."

"You're so certain?"

Mellyora withdrew from her window nook to come back into the room again. "If I escape him, I can see to it that he and I actually negotiate, and bargain, and then, he must keep his part of a bargain. My uncle Daro, jarl of Skul Island, is here in Stirling.

Called to a meeting with the king. I'll appeal to his men, and he'll see to it that I cleanly escape until our good King David is forced to see reason."

"Mellyora, kings are seldom forced to see reason—"

Mellyora shook her head firmly. "I disagree. Kings are often forced to see reason—most often, it is upon a battlefield when they discover that their many men cannot beat another king's men! Look at our country, how so many very different sections are now ruled by one king of Scotland. This is partially through the will of the people who interbred and shared the space, and it is also partly because one king became more powerful than the others. He should listen to me—I could be a threat to him. God knows, enough of the outer isles are ruled by Vikings."

"Mellyora, I know that you are well aware of the history of our country. Most of these people you speak about have been here for hundreds of years, but the Vikings often remain separate, and as you say, they rule many of the islands. King David is wary of your Viking relations as it is, Mellyora. Yes, you are a danger. Become too great a danger, and he will crush you before he lets you threaten him," Jillian warned carefully. "Please, you simply must take a good long look at your situation and realize that the king has no choice but to step in and decide your fate."

Mellyora paused, watching Jillian. She was sorry to see her so distressed, yet at a loss as to why she couldn't make her understand her position.

She bit into her lower lip, dismayed by the sudden, almost overwhelming desire to burst into tears that seized her. She could not believe that her father had died. She had loved him dearly, the world was so empty without him. She'd never known anyone quite like him. Adin had possessed the strength of ten men; he had been born a Viking. Yet his greatest power had always been his intelligence, his greatest strength, his gentleness. He had talked to her endlessly about her mother, keeping her alive through the years for Mellyora. He had attracted warriors, priests, artists, and poets to their home, he had made their great hall one of the most hospitable residences in all of the country. He had taught her to ride, to defend herself with a sword, even how to wield a heavy crossbow. Through his eyes, she had seen their world, as it had been. He had taught her that all men and women were worthy of interest and respect, no matter what their beliefs or the land or circumstances of their birth. From him, she had learned that friends were priceless, and that power and riches were gifts and responsibilities, and that she must always take care of those who called her lady, rather than seek for them to take care of her. He had loved her, taught her strength, kindness, independence, just as her mother, who had been uniquely wonderful as well, had taught her to have spirit, to believe in herself. She had given her a taste of a different magic, telling her the ancient Gaelic tales, and showing her the beauty of Celtic crafts. She'd been blessed with a lilting laugh, and flashing eyes, and a smile that was as warm and brilliant as the sun. She'd been proud and assured, a perfect wife for her warrior husband, and she'd taught Mellyora always to speak her mind, and to fight for her rights.

But now, they were both gone. And even as she learned to live with the pain of her father's death, she was discovering that her position was far more perilous than she had ever imagined. She wasn't just alone, bereft of those she had loved most in the world. She was in danger of losing her independence and becoming nothing more than someone's *acquisition*. She had been a cherished daughter, treated with kindness and respect. After Adin's death, Ewan had been there, keeping everyone from intruding on her grief. But now she was alone, and about to be cast to a wretched stranger who would simply seize everything that was rightfully hers. And what was she to do? Forget the man who had been her friend, her support, and her comfort forever? Her heart was not so fickle, her love not so lightly given.

"Mellyora, you're frightening me, I beg of you, you must take some time with this matter. Be calm."

Mellyora walked to Jillian, taking Jillian's small hands into her own. "I can't possibly be calm. I tried to be calm, I tried to talk to David, to be logical, intelligent, and reasonable. He refused to listen to me. I've heard of this Laird Lion before. I'm to be wed to a *Norman*."

Jillian shook her head. "That's not what I've heard!"

"An old, slimy, hoary, battle-scarred Norman who served the king while he was in England. Jillian! You saw the king's men when we camped—they were all Normans!"

"I saw the king's men at a distance, and decent armor does not make a man a Norman. Mellyora, I don't believe that this man the king intends for you is a Norman. I have ears as well. I've listened in the servants' quarters, and I tell you, that servants' gossip is by far the best. They call this knight Laird Lion. He is no Norman, but a lad found single-handedly taking on a raiding party of Normans when the king came upon him. He is a warrior covered in glory, so I have heard."

"A lion, indeed!" Mellyora muttered. "Certainly, compare the man to a lion. Like all Normans, he most probably likes to hear himself roar. There is simply no justice in this world, yet maybe the name is apt. Even with the animals, it's the lioness who hunts for food, while the lion sits about and sleeps in the sun. There you have it—exactly. This male beast would lie in the sun upon my land and reap the rewards of my family."

"You've not even met him."

"I've no desire to meet him. I'm very afraid that once I've met him, I'll find my fate is sealed," Mellyora said, gazing past Jillian's shoulder to the window again. Then she met Jillian's eyes firmly. "You're also forgetting the fact that I have vowed my hand, my life, my love, elsewhere."

Jillian stared back at her. "And that, my dear, was foolish. You hadn't the right to vow anything anywhere to anyone."

"I had my father's blessings on my choice!" Mellyora insisted somewhat desperately. Adin hadn't actually granted her permission to marry Ewan MacKinny, but he had been aware of their friendship, and that it had been very close. She'd known Ewan ever since she could remember. They were just three years apart in age and since she had been very young, he had been trusted as her guardian about her father's lands. His father had been what they called "The" MacKinny, a chieftain in his own right, the head of the largest family who held their lands from Adin. When Ewan's father's had died, Ewan had taken on the cloak of being The MacKinny. Ewan was a quiet, gentle man, as he had been a quiet, gentle boy, listening to her rages, angering her only when he pointed out that she might not be quite fair in her assessment of one situation or another. She couldn't forget the way he had looked at her when they'd parted.

*As if they'd been saying good-bye.*

They had swum together in the lochs, ridden fields, cliffs, and hills, studied Latin, French, English, Gaelic, and even Norse together, played at science and mathematics, and read endlessly, translations of the Greek tragedies, Italian romances, so much more. They could laugh together, argue together, roll in the grass together, sit in long silences. Ewan held no surprises for her; he listened when she spoke. Life with him would be all that she wanted.

She could not accept the thought that she would not only have to bear the agony of losing her father, but endure seeing a strange Norman lackey of the king take his place. She really wasn't a fool; she understood the way the world worked, just as she understood King David. But while she had breath to fight, she could not allow the king's lackey to take her father's place—or her own. She couldn't simply lie back and allow her life to be taken without fighting the best battle she could wage.

Mellyora looked to the window in her room at the fortress. It was very small; this was a defensive fortress, built strongly from stone.

Yet the river ran by it; if she could just get to the river, she could reach her cousin Daro's men.

"I cannot argue this any longer!" she announced with sudden determination.

Forgetting Jillian, Mellyora hurried from her own larger chamber into the smaller one behind it where Jillian slept. The window here was cut a bit larger—and let out onto a wooden platform of battlements.

She could easily step outside the window. And there was scaffolding set up where they continued to work on the battlements. In the darkness, she could swing down the wooden scaffolding without being seen, and, if she enwrapped herself in one of Jillian's plain brown woolen capes, she could simply walk out the gates.

What then?

At the river's edge, she'd have no choice but to steal a boat. Not steal. She smiled suddenly. King David had been the first Scottish monarch to mint his own coinage. She'd leave the boat's owner a handsome coin bearing the king's own image.

"Mellyora?" Jillian called to her.

Mellyora hesitated. "Go back to your tapestry, Jillian. I am sorry to have upset you. I need some time alone," she said.

She softly closed the doors between the two rooms.

Quietly, she dug into Jillian's travel trunk and found the cloak she required. She slipped it around herself, drawing the hood low. It was a deep brown color, and would blend well with the night.

Mellyora crawled onto the window seat and squeezed her

length through the narrow window. She leapt softly down to the wooden battlement beyond the window and hurried along it.

She paused, seeing the distance between the place where she paused and the scaffolding just beyond. She inhaled, wondering if she was willing to risk her own life for her freedom.

Freedom was a gift worth many risks. She'd heard it said, many times, by many men.

It would be a long fall if she made a leap—and didn't catch the crossbeam of the scaffolding.

Ruling was wisdom, her father had taught her. Decide if it can be done. And if it can be done . . .

Then do it with courage.

She stepped back.

Ran . . . and leapt.

She caught the crossbeam, swung down upon it, caught a lower beam, and then another, and another.

She jumped the last few feet to the ground.

The common courtyard at Stirling was not crowded, neither was it empty. By night, fishermen returned from their journeys along the river; wives rushed home from the last of their bartering; wool, dye, and food merchants closed up their stations for the night. Mellyora blended with them. Nearing the gates, she hurried to walk close behind a peddler leaving the city walls. To someone watching, it would appear she was a woman walking with a brisk pace to keep up with her husband.

Outside the walls, the peddler started down the southward trail, to the village. She parted ways with him, nearly running now as she hurried toward the river.

At the docks there was a great deal of activity, despite the hour. She veered away from the docks, heading downriver. Daro's men would be encamped in the fields southward, so she would want to move downriver.

She hurried along the damp embankment until she saw an unattended boat. A small rowboat, pulled up tight on the embankment. She looked carefully around, but no one was about, so she hurried over to the small boat. Both oars were in place. She remembered that she wasn't going to become a thief—not when she didn't have to become one. She slipped her hand into the pocket sewn into her shift and curled her fingers around a small silver coin. She would toss it onto the shore where the boat had been once she had gotten it moving.

She started to push the boat from the mud when, suddenly, something seemed to rise from the embankment.

She froze.

Not something. Someone. A man. Darkly cloaked as she was herself. He seemed to rise forever, huge and towering in the darkness.

A gasp caught in her throat as a man's voice deeply shouted out, "Thief!"

Could she get the boat out and away before he reached her? Never.

He came closer; he was already almost upon her. His strides were long, fluid, and swift, and he gained on her position so quickly she hadn't a prayer of getting away on the river.

She watched him coming, trying to remain calm, to think, to calculate—quickly!—and yet the sure menace of his graceful speed sent panic searing through her. She could manage a sword in her own defense, but she had fled without a sword.

So much for thinking.

She had a small knife at her calf, but he was probably well armed . . .

She couldn't get away swiftly enough in the boat. She could only hope to escape on foot. She turned to run.

Yet even as she did so, she was caught. She gasped as she was enwrapped in large, steel-like arms. Her feet were swept off the ground as she tried to escape, and she was brought crashing downward to the soft river embankment.

She landed hard, inhaling desperately for air.

She tried to rise, and could not. He was there, ready to pounce on top of her. She slipped her hand down to her calf, reaching for her knife. Her fingers grasped it and she wriggled desperately, turning to her back. She managed to bring her arm up, and aim for a place between the man's ribs.

Before her blow could fall, her wrist was captured. Long, ruthless fingers sent a searing pain into her wrist. Against her will, she dropped the knife.

She couldn't breathe, for the towering stranger with the steel muscles had straddled her form.

"Now!" he thundered, his voice husky and deep. "Now, thief! Where do you think you'd be going with that boat? Answer, and answer quickly, or I'll slit your throat!"

# CHAPTER 4

She had to fight the waves of fear cascading over her, despite the fact that the wretch was atop her in the pale, wavering moonlight. She could not think clearly if she allowed fear to rule her.

She saw him now far more clearly than she wanted—his form, not his face, for annoyingly, his face was hidden by the shadow of his hood. He was heavily, tautly muscled beneath his encompassing cloak.

The garment gave her pause, and sent her mind spinning once again. The cloak was wool fashioned in a complex Scottish style, with the strands so tightly knit together to render the garment nearly completely waterproof. Each strand was colored with vegetable dyes to create a pattern that would signify a certain part of the country or a people. Talented weavers were creating the *tartans* more and more often these days, remembering the exact shades and number of dyed strands by marking them upon a stick, so that the coloring could be repeated again and again. The style of clothing belonged to Scotland, and not to the Normans who had been invited to settle lands at the king's request. If the garment was any indication of the man, he wasn't a Norman usurper.

Did it matter what his nationality if he slit her throat and her life bled away, here in the mud? Slit her throat, with what? Was he armed? Aye, she thought, he would have a knife sheathed at his calf, just as she had carried. A sword? He wasn't wearing a scabbard now, or was he? Where had he come from? There was a small hut of stone and mud on the riverbank, and a horse grazed nearby. Was it his boat, or had he come by way of the huge warhorse with the battle accouterments, looming in the shadows?

Would he kill her? What was he doing here, alone, on the

embankment? She started to shake; then she was furious with herself. Death was one thing. Dying without a fight was completely another.

"Get off me!" she commanded.

The ox! He ignored her. And she would, she assured herself, prevail.

The man was, she determined, the servant of some greater lord. A fine example of good Scottish breeding; his height was commanding; his body form and muscle structure were formidable. He would serve nicely as a knight—he could surely be trained to possess an incredibly powerful sword arm. Indeed, he was certainly strong enough—all but breaking her into bits now as he straddled atop her.

"Are you daft or deaf? Get off!" she repeated, with confident authority.

Still, he didn't move. She felt him staring down at her curiously, his face still masked by his hood.

"So a lass would steal a boat," he said simply.

She could see his torso and legs. Beneath his cloak he wore simple woolen hose, a linen shirt and another overshirt or tunic of like design as his cloak. His clothing was not of poor quality, but it was muddied as if he had worked or traveled long and hard in it. Perhaps he could be made to travel just a bit longer, and a bit harder.

"I'm not *stealing* anything, good fellow," she said, wincing inwardly as she heard a slight waver in her voice. "I warn you, get off me now!"

To her relief, he listened at last. He stood, catching her hand, dragging her to her feet before him. He remained very close, and though she was tall for a woman, he was much taller, and his nearness made her more uneasy. She was alone on a riverbank with a strange man who might well be dangerous, and who may not realize he challenged a ward of the king—and had already had the audacity to wrestle her to the mud.

She had no choice but to hold her ground firmly; one of the first lessons she had learned in life from her warrior father was that you must never let a potential enemy know that you're afraid.

"You must pay attention now. I'm not a thief!" She turned her hand over, producing the silver coin she'd intended to leave as payment. "But I've need of transportation south, and am quite willing to pay with this good money. It seems you've been traveling long yourself, but perhaps your master would not know if you traveled a bit longer. If you'll take me, you will have the money and your boat, and I can pay even more for your services."

"Can you now?"

He reached out, and it took all her courage to remain dead still as he pushed her hood fully back, studying her face in the moonlight.

She thrust his hand away, but her hood had already fallen, and he could clearly see her face while she could still see almost nothing of his.

She felt a great resentment rising within her. He hadn't been thrown to the mud. His cloak remained in good condition—the hood pulled low over his forehead.

"Don't touch me," she warned him.

"I didn't touch you. Merely your garment."

"Don't do so again. I warn you, men could well die for less."

"Really?" He was casually intrigued, and it seemed that he had all the time in the world.

She did not.

Her patience began to wane. "You must take heed with your every liberty. I do give you fair warning that I am a lady of this land, and if you serve me well, you will prosper, and if you cause me harm, you will die."

He lifted a hand suddenly, indicating the boat. Relieved that he at last seemed to understand her position and situation—and his possible gain from it—she quickly collected her fallen knife from the ground and scampered in. She then crawled to the aft of the small vessel, leaving him the center-seat plank so that he could row the boat with the oars in the locks there.

He pushed the boat from the shore and stepped into it as it shot from the bank. With balance and ease he came forward into the center of the small vessel, took a position in the center seat, and picked up the oars. One swift surge with the oars on his part and they were all but flying across the water.

She would move far more quickly with him rowing than she could have possibly prayed to move on her own power.

But though she wanted to feel relief, she remained disturbed. She felt him watching her beneath the shadow of his hood. They were out upon the water when he spoke to her again, his voice rich, deep, husky—and menacing.

"A lady, eh?"

"Row, and mind your business," she said.

"A lady, alone, in the night. When there might well be cut-throats and thieves about, rapists, plunderers, ravagers—simple opportunists?"

Was he threatening her? *Yes, fool, most apparently!* she warned herself.

"As you know, I carry a dagger on me, a gift from a Viking friend. It is sharper than any sword you can imagine, and the Viking taught me to use it quite well."

"Aye, so I saw."

"You took me by surprise; it will not happen again. If you've any intent to harm me, you should truly rethink your designs," she informed him. She was careful to keep her voice firm and level despite the fear rising within her.

He didn't respond to her warning, but continued to ponder her situation. "A lady at night, alone on the river, demanding services—and threatening those she commands to serve her. There can be but one explanation to such a situation, so it appears to me. Tell me, my lady, just whom do you seek so desperately to escape?" he demanded.

"I should give you an answer to such a question—so you can demand a ransom?" Mellyora inquired. "I've nothing to tell you. Row. I'll pay you in silver coins, in gold."

"So you've told me. But I have you now, at my mercy, one might say."

Mellyora stared at him, determined not to show a flicker of fear. "I swear," she said quietly, "alive and in one piece, I can make you far richer than you could make yourself by causing harm to me. Touch me, harm me in any way, and if I do not cut your heart out here and now, you will, I promise, die a tortured death. You will writhe in pure agony—pierced, bludgeoned, bloodied, and burned—before your body is hacked to pieces and fed to the crows."

"You are both imperious and bloodthirsty," he replied.

"You wretched bastard! How dare you sit there and criticize me—"

"You're quite certain of your power. Which makes me think that you are running from none other than the king himself." He leaned forward. "Why?"

Mellyora gritted down hard on her teeth, trying to control both her temper and the trembling that had seized her. Aye, she carried a knife in a sheath at her ankle. And aye, she'd been schooled well in the use of weapons.

But training and fact were two different situations, as she was now discovering. When he'd pinned her on the riverbank, she hadn't had a prayer of reaching her knife. And if he truly threatened her now, what would happen? Could she draw her knife out and injure him severely enough to keep him from slaying her in return?

Part of winning in battle was knowing when to fight, when to feint, when, even, to negotiate.

"What is this to you?" she asked, not wanting to risk a physical battle. "I can pay you very well—there's no need to ask for any ransom. You'll receive money, and there's the end of it. What more do you need to know?"

Beneath the encompassing wool of his cloak, she thought that his great shoulders shrugged. "Whimsy, I suppose. I'm curious, quite intrigued. And I do well enough, you see. I am not in great need of your money."

She sighed. "Then let this be inspiration for helping me quietly now to reach my destination. I could, truthfully, have you arrested and possibly hanged or otherwise executed for accosting me as you did on the riverbank."

"How strange. It seems to me you want nothing to do with the law of the land."

She exhaled with a great deal of exasperation. He was demanding a story. She'd give him the truth. "Fine, if you want a story, entertainment, then you shall have it. I am Scottish. Well, perhaps my father wasn't exactly a native, but my mother's people have been here so long that they are part and parcel of the land. I am, as you've suggested, a ward of the king. My father died recently and unexpectedly and King David has determined that he must give me and my land to a horrid, wretched, despicable, pockmarked, miserable Norman-bastard of a friend and supporter. I have determined that I will not be so given."

"Ah . . ." he murmured. Had she received sympathy from him at last? "I see."

"So you do understand, and you'll help me, and I'll make you richer than you are, even if money isn't a tremendous concern to you."

"I'm still confused."

"Why?"

"Just where is it that you're trying to go?"

"Downriver."

"Why?"

"I've kin there."

"There's nothing but a Viking encampment downriver."

"Yes, I know."

"You're kin to Daro the Viking?"

"He's my uncle."

"Are you also kin to Bjorn Hallsteader?" he asked sharply.

"No," she said, surprised at his tone, but nonetheless pleased that, for once, he didn't know what he was talking about at all. "Hallsteaders hail from Denmark; my father was the son of a Norwegian jarl."

"Danes, Swedes, and Norse have been known to fight together."

"Aye, and Vikings have fought for the king."

"Still, you intend to pit the Vikings against the king?"

"No! And how dare you assume that my Viking kin would take arms against the king? I simply intend to remove myself so that I may be in a better position to explain my feelings and situation to the king."

"If you intend to cause bloodshed and insurrection, you had best be able to explain yourself."

"I do not intend bloodshed, or insurrection! My father was a Viking who loved Scotland, and the concept of a united Scotland, more than you can imagine. And good God, but you are presumptuous! What is any of this to you?"

"Oh . . . nothing," he murmured. His attention was suddenly directed to the right oar. He seemed to be struggling with it, twisting it around in the oarlock.

"What are you doing?" Mellyora demanded. "Don't play with it so, you must be careful—you're ripping the oar out of the lock—"

Even as she spoke, the oar slipped from the lock, and into the water.

"Och!" he gasped. "M'lady, would you look at that!"

"What have you done?" she asked with incredulous dismay. Was the man dangerous—or simply an impossible clod?

"The oar," he said sadly.

"Yes! The oar—"

"It fell right through the hole."

"Of course, you fool! You wrenched the oar free from the oarlock! That is what happens if you take an oar from the lock and don't hold it—"

"Dear Lord!" he exclaimed suddenly.

"What?"

"There went the other one."

"My God, but you can't be such a fool. How can you sit there tormenting me with a million questions while you haven't the sense to hold on to the oars—"

"My dear lady, I'm so sorry, but you mustn't worry," he said cheerfully, and suddenly he was standing.

"Now what are you doing?" she asked incredulously, staring up at him.

"I said not to worry—"

"Don't worry!" she repeated, staring at him in disbelief. "Please, God, I don't mean to be cruel, but you're a clumsy oaf and you've created pure disaster for me—"

"I'll swim back to the shore and acquire more oars."

"That takes time!"

"Rest assured, lady, I'll be back for you—and your gold of course. Don't be distressed. I promise—I vow to you—that I will take you exactly where you should be once I return."

"How could you have done this to me? I am desperate, and time is so important. How could you? You should be horse-whipped, beaten—"

"Tortured? Burned at the stake, perhaps? Broken on a wheel?"

"Perhaps no less!" Mellyora said in rising dismay. In all her life, she'd never treated a servant with anything but kindness. All men were unique, she had been taught. In the eyes of God, the simplest man deserved the greatest sympathy.

But God had never seen fit to inflict her with such a wretched fool before. He had done so now. Now, when she was in the gravest peril. And this man wasn't just a wretched, clumsy, oaf, he was an insolent one as well, taunting her as he made a mockery of her getaway.

"Broken on a wheel, but left alive to burn at the stake!" she muttered angrily.

"M'lady, I will come back," he said. She realized that he was about to dive into the water when he doffed his cloak and cast it upon the seat where he had been sitting.

She saw his face at last.

His eyes were searing and powerful. She found herself staring at him, as he looked back at her.

In a moment of surprised silence, she studied him. His hair was rich and thick, shoulder-length, dark auburn. His features were handsomely, strongly formed. His jaw was quite square, his cheekbones were high and broad, giving him a rugged and commanding appearance. His eyes, which had so caught her attention, were deep blue in color, almost cobalt, large and set beneath well-defined, arching brows.

He was young, she realized, yet somehow hardened for his years. He was exceptionally striking, powerfully masculine. There was something imposing and indomitable about his appearance that unnerved her. His eyes touched upon hers with a raw, chilling determination.

"Wait—" she began on a whispered breath.

"Nay, lady, wait for me. You'll just drift for a bit—downriver, the way you wanted to go. Lie still and take care, and I will be back."

"No, wait—" she cried.

But he had dived into the river, leaving her in the boat. Oarless, and stuck on the water.

Barely moving at all.

Damn him!

Once he had entered the water, she shivered, then shook off the unease he had caused her and concentrated again on the seriousness of her predicament. He hadn't understood the complexities of her problem at all. She couldn't just drift. She had to reach the Viking encampment quickly—before the king discovered she was gone, and sent men after her.

Far away, he broke the surface of the water.

"Wait—!" she tried crying again.

But he dived into the depths of the river once again, and when he broke the surface this time, he came up far from the boat, swimming hard with long clean strokes. He couldn't possibly hear her.

And the distance they had come! Far from either riverbank.

Farther still from where she longed to be.

She swore. "What kind of an idiot loses both oars?"

The river was muddy, dark, and deep here. The oars were gone, beyond all hope. Unless they were to surface and float . . .

She looked about, searching the surface of the water. No. Fate was not smiling her way. The oars were not reappearing.

She sat in the boat, watching the moon in the night sky. She wasn't moving at all, the current should be taking her at least at some decent pace!

Mellyora clenched her hands into fists in her lap. Oh, God, if only her father had lived! Or if only the king had taken heed of her words. She raged against the fact that no one seemed willing to listen to wisdom and logic—not when it came from a woman.

She had really thought David might at least have given her pleas some thought. He was a good king, a strong man who had made great strides in making Scotland a unified and more powerful country. She didn't want to betray him, argue with him, or hurt him in any way.

She simply had no choice. This was her life. Kings liked to play with lives of others by the hundreds. It was part of what they did, of what they were.

Yet independence was part of what she was, and what she yearned to have. She told herself again that she didn't want to defy the king; she simply wanted to be in a better position to compromise with him.

It seemed that she sat forever, weighing her problems. She realized that she was afraid, that she didn't know what David would do if he believed that she had really betrayed him.

Once she was free, she could prove her loyalty.

Where was the fool who had lost the oars and gone to shore for more? Was he in the act of betraying her? He'd been gone so long now.

Did she dare sit here any longer?

No. Staying here, vulnerable, in the center of the river wouldn't do at all.

She stood, calculating the distance to the shore, then dropped her cloak and cast off her shoes and hose. The night was cool, the water would be cold. No matter, she had to risk it. She stripped down to the linen shift beneath her blue gown, hesitated a moment longer, then gritted her teeth tightly. She was a good swimmer, a strong swimmer. She could manage the distance, and the cold.

Determined, she dived into the water.

The cold engulfed her.

\* \* \*

Waryk touched bottom, and walked through the last few feet of water to the embankment. There, he sank to the ground for a moment, lying back to breathe deeply, shake his head—and laugh. So he looked like some rich man's servant, did he? Well, he was somewhat battle-stained and road-weary. Still, just who was she?

An heiress. The proud, blond beauty who had danced before the fire and told her tale about St. Columba. He realized that he had never asked Sir Harry just who the heiress was. And now, David was about to give her to a brutal old Norman knight, or so she believed. She might be right. Who was the king wedding her to? He did reward those who served him, and many who served him were of Norman descent.

The night was incredibly calm. The lady, whoever she might be, could sit and fume on the water for hours.

He might have been a bit more understanding, he chided himself, sobering. Having spent time, if brief, with Eleanora after the skirmishing, he should have had a greater sympathy for a lass with an aversion to an arranged marriage—especially to a man she would consider an invading monster.

But arranged marriages were the way of the world for young noblewomen, and she should have learned that fact from a very young age. Not to mention the small matter of his own loyalty. He was the king's man—and in her present course of action, she was the king's enemy.

The Norse were her kind, so perhaps she didn't realize that the Vikings were dangerous no matter how many alliances and treaties were made. They were a proud, fierce people, and fond of ruling in their own way. The king ruled a united Scotland, but David was aware that he was never really safe on his throne, that they lived in violent times. Maintaining his united Scotland was always a battle.

Still . . .

He felt a moment's pity for the girl out in the boat. She was young, he thought, and he had known from the moment he seized her that she was of noble birth—and in a dangerous position. She had been lovely, despite her temper and determination. Exceptional, in truth, regally tall, young, and beautiful, tender, ripe—magic. He had thought so, listening to her tale, watching her dance. She was a prize, certainly, and David was a king to recognize any asset he might control—and he was in debt to many of the Norman knights who had ridden with him and helped put down the small insurrections against him when he had first ridden north to take the crown of Scotland. Waryk could well imagine the girl's aversion to becoming the wife of an old decrepit Norman—a man perhaps two or three times her age whom she would still consider a foreigner.

Ah, but if the king discovered her treachery, she would be sorrier still. And no matter what Waryk's sympathy for her, there was little that could be done if David had made up his mind. When the king discovered her escape, he would be furious.

He was glad once again that he had been the one sent to fight the madmen and that Sir Harry had been given the task of watching the heiress. Still . . .

He would retrieve her from the boat himself, Waryk decided, in due time, without saying a word to the king. He could try to make her understand that kings often had no choice in their course of action. He could try—yes. He doubted that he would be successful.

He looked up at the sky. She might have played havoc with his dreams, and he knew that she and her party had considered him part of the king's Norman contingent last night, but still, tonight, the lady on the lake had caused him a great deal of amusement. Thanks to Eleanora, he was certain. Remembering her ways always soothed his temper. She was an Englishwoman, loyal to England, but that loyalty was such a part of her exquisite making that he had to forgive it. She spoke her mind, but paid heed to his every thought and opinion. She was aware and discreet; passionate and adventurous. She was both his friend and his mistress, a companion to entertain him, a vixen to stir his senses. Marriage to Eleanora, however, had never actually occurred to him until recently, not because she'd been widowed but because she was an Englishwoman—and because he'd known that his fortune and future would most probably be made through marriage to a landed heiress. However, he wasn't poor, nor was Eleanora. He had lands of his own, left through his mother, a Strathearn heiress. Eleanora had a fair amount of wealth in jewels and coin from the incomes granted her after her husband's death.

Marriage just might make sense. The king had grown up among the English, surely meant to stretch his borders with the English civil unrest, and Waryk had begun to muse that David might see a match between Eleanora and Waryk as advantageous.

Eleanora had not spoken so bluntly, but Waryk knew that marriage would please her. She'd served Henry of England as she had been ordered, and now she was free to marry where she wished. He'd almost mentioned the possibility to her when they had last lain together, yet he'd refrained, disturbed about the battle he had just fought and aware that he would need to do some convincing with David of Scotland. Still, the more he thought about it, the more convinced he became that David would surely realize that she would make him the perfect wife.

Waryk looked to the water and spoke softly aloud. "Ah, yes, lass on the lake, whoever you may be. Thanks to Eleanora, I will return you to the safety of the king's court as quietly as I am able. I will see that your difficulties grow no more serious than they already are!"

What she planned was damned close to treason, no matter how she tried to word her intentions. He wondered if she was aware of just how serious her actions were, that she could lose her head for conspiring against the king.

He stood and whistled softly, and his ebony warhorse, Mercury, came trotting toward him along the shoreline, startling the poor old fisherman who was wandering along the embankment. Waryk realized that the old fellow was looking for his boat. It was pure happenstance that Waryk had paused by the boat on the riverbank that the lady had chosen for her night journey. He had always loved the water. Lying on the embankment, studying the stars, the sky, and feeling cool breezes—untainted by the scent of blood—always seemed to soothe his soul. This area of the river just outside Stirling had always been his favorite place. Quiet, with none to disturb him except the occasional fisherman.

The fellow here now was grizzled beyond belief, and sadly confused. " 'Tis here I left her, of that I am sure," he muttered to himself. He looked at Waryk. "Now, I am not daft, m'laird. I do converse with meself now and agin', but that merely for some form of company since the fish do not talk much. Great sir, have ya nae seen a boat about, perhaps rowing itself out on the river?"

"Indeed, I'm afraid I have seen such a vessel," Waryk said. He produced a silver piece—with King David's image upon it— and presented it to the fisherman. "Take this for your boat, my good fellow. And come tomorrow, I'll see that your boat is back."

The old man's eyes widened and glazed. "Great God, but I

care not if ye make kindling of that rat trap fer a silver piece such as this!"

"Go spend it then," Waryk said, leaping atop Mercury's back. "Ah, but wait. If you would be so good. Do me a service as well, and I'll see you receive another coin. Your boat is there—you can just see it downriver. Keep your eyes trained on the water, and see to it that the boat does not somehow reappear here on the shore. There's a lady upon it, and I will be back for her."

"Aye, sir! As ye wish it!" the fellow cried delightedly. "I'll keep my eyes hard upon the water, that I will!"

"Have you a name, man?"

"Aye, sir, I am Milford. Who may y'be, me fine, great young laird?"

"I am Waryk—"

"Laird Lion!" the man cried with pleased approval.

Waryk arched a brow. "I'd not imagined I might be so readily known."

Milford laughed happily, the sound of his voice a wheezing cackle.

"Laird Lion—ye be known far and wide. Every Scotsman loves a warrior who bests his enemies—if he not be one of the enemies himself. 'Tis glad I am to make your acquaintance, good sir! Believe it or not, in me younger days I rode with a man named William who served the king. I admired your sire, young Graham. And ye've my loyalty yerself this night."

Waryk nodded with a wry smile in response to Milford's accolade to his father's memory.

"Thank you. My father was a great man, and glad I am of your loyalty, Milford. I will return as soon as I'm able."

Waryk nudged Mercury and rode the short distance to the fortress, the heart of Stirling. He was hailed by the guard at the gate, identified himself, and entered the courtyard. There, he turned Mercury over to a young groom and hurried to reach his own chambers at the fortress.

The hour had grown very late, or very early. He hadn't planned on spending so much time with the lady on the lake. Alan of Ayr, manservant to the king, caught him when he had barely entered the long hallway that led to the knights' quarters.

"Laird Lion, the king would see you now."

"I know that I must see him, Alan. But if you'll note, I'm dripping wet. Give me leave, and I'll wash and change before coming to see the king. I had not meant to keep him waiting awake through the night."

"Laird Waryk, the king did not stay awake—he has risen again since it is almost dawn. The king would see you now."

Waryk shrugged. "Aye, then. I will come."

His shoes squished upon the floor as he walked the distance to the great hall. David was there, pacing. It looked as if this might be a long discussion, Waryk thought with dismay. He'd meant to leave the unwilling heiress for some time to consider the error of her ways, but he had not meant to desert her entirely. It might take some time before he could go back for her, and under those circumstances, he'd have to mention the lady to the king after giving him a report of the battle in which he'd rather too easily managed to keep hold of the king's domains.

Daylight was coming, and too quickly, Waryk thought.

She might be in greater danger, for the river would fill, and the Vikings she longed to reach might be ever closer, moving about by day . . .

He would have to reach her quickly. He would keep her escape secret if he could, but if he could not . . .

She would have to meet the king's wrath. There was no other way.

Or else she might well make good her bid for freedom, and they'd both be in danger of charges of treason.

Of being hanged, or beheaded.

Or even drawn and quartered.

Vikings could be very dangerous, he had never deceived himself on that issue. Vikings, in all sizes, and all shapes. Even a Viking's beautiful daughter.

Perhaps, he thought, a strange foreboding sending a tremor of heat along his spine, especially a Viking's beautiful and wayward daughter . . .

# CHAPTER 5

"Sire," he said, entering the king's great hall, bowing briefly upon a single knee before rising. "I can report—"

"Nay, you don't need to report a word of your deeds, for many great words have preceded your arrival."

"I'm sure that Angus exaggerated my deeds."

"Messengers reached me before Angus came to give a report. You're dripping, by the way, Laird Lion."

"I stopped by the river."

"Aye, you've had a fondness for water all your life."

"And the stars. Your pardon, perhaps I should have come straight here, but—"

"The leisure time was yours, well deserved. But tell me, did you fall in the water?"

"I went for a swim."

"How curious, it was a rather chill night. Were you chasing water nymphs or the like?"

Waryk grinned. "I'm afraid I ventured too near the water and, thereby, wound up wet."

"Umm," the king murmured, aware there was more to the story, but not persisting at the moment. "Whatever your recent adventures, you have returned home triumphant. You gave chase to the rascals, left men in attendance to build new fortifications, and have done us all proud. Perhaps most important is the fact that you have ably and loyally supported me, and no shift in the political wind has ever steered you from that course."

Waryk lifted a hand in gracious acknowledgment of the king's words. "Well, you see, sire, I learned my loyalty as a boy," he said lightly, but then added on a serious note, "This new action has disturbed me, David. It was much like that which we fought westward a few months before, and farther to the north and east on the border a few months before that. It's as if there is some unseen, unknown enemy creating dissension where there should be none."

"Angus told me that you battled a group of ruffians, none of them ably trained."

"Aye, that's what's so strange. We fought freemen with little language or education, and perhaps serfs from some of the new Norman domains. Men pushed to battle, more afraid to live than to die. To a man, they escaped into the woods, or died. We've tried to take men alive, but they fight us as if we are demons, and I can't make sense of anything they ramble as yet. It has been the same again and again."

"There has always been minor insurrection. And now, with Henry dead, men are easily swayed to fight for his daughter Mathilda against his nephew Stephen, or to fight for Stephen against Mathilda, and to cause trouble simply for whatever power might be seized in the midst of it."

"Men must fight for some belief. Warriors would declare for Mathilda, or for Stephen. As far as Scotland goes, my lord, there are few Lowland Scots who do not recognize you as their king and overlord. I believe there is an enemy we have yet to unearth, someone more powerful than those poor fools we are forced to slay, and I am puzzled and angry that such an enemy doesn't show his face."

"Vikings?" the king inquired dourly.

"Vikings are men who believe that their gods honor them for fighting with boldness and courage. I've yet to meet a Viking who chose to hide in battle."

"In the end, Waryk, it's our strength that keeps us victorious, whatever enemy we fight. Don't dwell on questions when you haven't the resources for the answers."

"But we can't ignore—"

"I ignore nothing, Waryk, you know that. I'll be all the more wary. And that is the heart of the matter, Waryk, leading to the arrangements we'll now discuss."

"As you wish, but—"

"There's recently been a death that leaves a vast property open for the taking, Laird Lyon. I am pleased, at last, to have found the right holding for you. I knew, when I found you battling against all odds as a boy, that you would be a great champion for me. You have never disappointed me, Laird Lion. I will honor you, and you will serve me well to become overlord of that property."

Curious, intrigued, and wary, Waryk realized that he had been gone several weeks and was out of touch with events that had been occurring in the king's realm. He didn't know what great holding had become available, but though the king had promised him rich rewards for a long time, he had never allowed himself to dwell on what the rewards might be, or why it took the king so long to find them. There had been times when he'd wondered if his "great rewards" had been words and nothing more, but not even that had mattered. Since the night his father and other kin had died, he'd followed the king.

*Eleanora . . .* he thought.

A vast property, the king had said. Now, after the king had told him what property, he could bring up the subject of marriage to his English lady. He felt a strange trembling inside. Time had come. Here, tonight, was his reward. Land. Home. And soon, his family. What he had wanted, what he had craved. "Sire, I am naturally curious, and of course grateful, especially since I have found a woman I would call my wife—"

"Wife?" David interrupted, arching a brow.

"Aye, David, a good match, I think. I've given the matter a great deal of thought, and I think that I've found a proper lady, a wife whom you'll approve—"

"Nay, Waryk, I fear not," the king said impatiently. "The lands come with an heiress."

"What?" Waryk said, startled. Uneasy, and as yet, not sure why.

The king shook his head with impatience. "An heiress brings the land and the reward, Waryk. A great warrior has died. The laird is dead, but he left a daughter. With her marriage to you, she remains the lady there, and I keep the peace with those who will honor her house. The property I am talking about is coastal property along a fine inlet, an island and mainland, and they create a gateway to the Hebrides, and you know the old chieftains, and their sense of loyalty. Her mother was from one of the most ancient Scottish houses. The land, I promise you, is rich. Waryk, I believe you've learned that little in life comes without a price, but a price, I think, that will be painless. You've yet to see this heiress. And imagine this, a stone castle nearly as old as the land, where the foundation was built by the Romans out of a natural rock formation, where the first Normans built upon the old foundations, and created a solid fortress against marauders from land and sea. The surf may be tempestuous, but trade between the isles, England, Ireland, more, is constant. Goods arrive on a daily basis, crops grow in abundance, and sheep and cattle thrive. Many a man would kill for these riches, and many men have died to protect the land. Its position is advantageous, and it's imperative that the laird in power be a Scotsman, loyal to the crown of Scotsmen, and to no other. Vikings rule an area far too near."

David had spoken lightly at first, then grown serious and Waryk answered in kind. "I'm grateful, of course. But—"

"Waryk, if ever you have served me, serve me now. There is nothing to protest. I told you, men would kill for what I am offering you, and I'm afraid that many will die if it is not seized and held with an iron fist. Great care must be taken that Lady Mellyora's lands be kept securely within my grasp, for though the great fortress lies upon an isle, the property stretches onto the mainland as I said, and there are trails there that lead directly to the Highlands. The lands are a connection with the chieftains, and with the sea, and they command vast, strategic stretches, should any of our Nordic neighbors see fit to raid again. You'll see it soon enough. The fields are rich, the artisans there are some of the most gifted in the country, the armorers are surely the finest in all the isles."

"Again, I'm honored, but—"

The king came before him again, interrupting sharply, "You've not dishonored this woman you would have made your wife?"

"It's not a matter of honor or dishonor. The lady has been my mistress for some time. I'd not, I'll admit, thought of marriage until recently."

"Mistress!" the king exclaimed, frowning. "Then what of her birth? What man—what father, brother, uncle—would allow this without challenging you—"

"David, she's a widow with the English king's permission to choose her second husband—"

"English!" David said, irritated.

"Sire, you married an Englishwoman. The woman I would wed is the Lady Eleanora."

"Ahh . . ." David murmured softly, shrewd eyes on Waryk. Then he shrugged. "Indeed, she's a beautiful woman."

Waryk lowered his head. On the one hand, he felt a strange excitement, a sense of beginning. The king had never lied to him. If he said that the property was vast and rich, then it was so. He'd known poverty, and he'd lived off the land. He'd lived at the king's court as well, and yet, though he'd slept in many a soft bed after many a rich meal, he'd not had a sense of a home. Not since his kin had all perished. He was hungry not for riches, but for a place to call home. Yet he had meant to marry Eleanora. He'd known whores as well as ladies, courtesans, and dairymaids. She had captured his mind, and his desires. It would be a good match. He didn't know if he was arguing with the king, or himself. "Sire, I've served you in many things—"

"Aye! So continue to serve me when I am trying to reward you with a great treasure. My dear lad, are you turning down a chance at tremendous wealth and power?" David demanded indignantly.

David had been born to be king. He had watched the English kings, he had watched his parents, and then his brothers, rule before him. He was capable of laughter, amusement, mercy—and fury, determination, and now, a quiet but very regal outrage.

"Nay, never. I am grateful. But—"

"I'm sorry about your liaison with Eleanora; I'm fond of that saucy English lass myself. But I know that you're no fool, and you've known that I've been waiting for many years now for the right situation to give you the titles and position you deserve as my champion. You are a warrior, lad, who has learned the ways of harlots and whores along the line of battle, and you're a knight who has too often lured the romantic notions of impressionable young women. I will see to it that Eleanora isn't too sorely disappointed with your marriage. By God, my man! You have known since you came to serve me upon your father's death that yours was a political destiny—that I would make it a great destiny, that you would not die a common man. You know your duty is to me—and to Scotland."

Waryk stood still, feeling the cold of the river water that dripped from him. It was one thing to argue with the king. It was another to have his loyalty to Scotland questioned.

David was right; *he should have known this, expected this. Nothing came without a price.*

Yet still, the concept of being handed a woman because she came with a rich property was not a pleasant one. The feelings of warmth and laughter—and admittedly, lust—that had so intrigued him when he had been with Eleanora could be forgotten for Scotland. But despite his loyalty to the king, there was one thing he had desired above all else since the horrible day when his father and so many others had perished.

He wanted children. A family.

And if his rich property came with a gnarled, bent old witch of a woman, he would be denied the one thing that he had fought for all these years.

"I would simply like to hear a bit more about this land—and the heiress. David, you cannot doubt my loyalty to you or my country," Waryk said. He wanted to ask more specific questions, but he was interrupted as the doors to the great hall burst open and a woman rushed in, frantically seeking the king's attention.

"Sire!"

The woman was slim with an abundance of flying silver hair. She rushed to the king. "Sire!" she repeated. Trembling, she bowed deeply before David, about to continue. Then she noted Waryk in the room. She was too distressed to note that Waryk was dripping river water on the floor, but she was evidently dismayed that she found the king in conference with one of his knights. She spoke awkwardly then, staring uneasily at Waryk, and stuttering out her explanation. "Sire, I—I . . . My apologies, I did not wish to interrupt, I—"

"You may speak, Jillian. What has happened?"

"But, sire—"

"Come now, speak up, Jillian!" David said impatiently.

Jillian tore her eyes from Waryk and looked at the king at last. "She's gone."

"What?"

"Mellyora, sire. She's gone."

"Gone?" the king exploded.

The silver-haired woman cringed and nodded again, glancing uneasily back at Waryk. She moistened her lips to speak, forcing herself to look back at the king again. "She's—gone."

"She can't be."

"But she is."

"How? I had two men on guard at the door—"

"She left by the window, sire, I believe."

"But there was a great drop to the courtyard below—"

"Scaffolding, sire. If she left through the window, she might have jumped from the parapets to the scaffolding. She is fleet, graceful, and quick. And . . ."

"And what?" the king said, his voice something like a growl.

"Desperate," Jillian told him.

"My God!" The king roared with an explosion of anger. He slammed a fist down upon the long table in the center of the great hall with such a vengeance the wood groaned. "Damn her, but . . . my God!" he repeated. "The traitorous wench. I didn't believe that she would really defy me, blatantly disobey my will. I will find her. I will stop whatever treason she plots! She will regret her stubborn determination to defy me. She will pay the price for treason, and I will be entirely justified in whatever way I choose to mete punishment upon her—"

"Your pardon, sire, please, but you'll have apoplexy!" Waryk warned. But he was suddenly feeling a chill himself, an awareness. He should have known, though he still didn't want to admit . . .

"She will be found, and certainly, but if you'll excuse me, just who in God's name is this 'she' who is gone?" he asked carefully.

The king had been distracted, but he stared at Waryk. His eyes were still blazing with a fire of fury and disbelief. But he paused in his tirade, his brow arching slowly as seconds passed. Then he spoke, more calmly than at first.

"The 'she,' Laird Lion, is Mellyora. Mellyora MacAdin. She has managed her escape. Sweet Jesu, but I underestimated her! I never thought the wench would risk her own life to defy me!"

The king had yet to really answer him, but did he need the truth spelled out. Aye!

"Who, sire, is Mellyora MacAdin? What is her treachery? Is she your prisoner? Is she guilty of some misdeed?"

"She had been my guest. The child of an old and noble friend. Nay, she isn't guilty of a crime—I correct myself! She wasn't guilty of any crime. But now, she is very close to committing treason. Indeed, if I weren't such a merciful man, I would call her a traitor this minute!"

Still, the king hadn't spoken what Waryk already knew, and Waryk insisted he do so. "Why is she so anxious to escape? Is she an errant wife, a—"

"Oh, errant. You might think so, since she defies my command. To marry you. She's your heiress, Laird Lion."

"Mine?"

"Aye!"

And he knew, of course, with certainty. What a fool he had been not to realize the situation instantly. The lady on the river was his intended wife. He might have reasoned it then; he might even have realized it when he spoke with Sir Harry, and realized that he had been summoned back just when the heiress had been coming to the king . . .

He was the man from whom she was running. He was the wretched, horrid, despicable "Norman" she had been told she was to wed. And rather than do so, she was running to her Viking kin.

He swallowed hard, fighting to keep a hold on his temper.

She had tried to use him not just to escape the king—but to escape her marriage—*to him*—as well. He remembered all the things she had said. By God, but she was arrogant.

She didn't know him; he didn't know her, he rationalized with himself. But logic didn't help the sudden searing of his temper. The hint of emotion and understanding he had felt for her plight dissipated like fog beneath a burning sun. *She* was the woman the king intended for him.

Wonderful. He had wanted a wife and a family. He had taken a loving, passionate woman as his mistress, and just when he had realized that she would be a loving, passionate wife as well, he was being told he was to receive a headstrong lass. A girl who was stubborn, reckless, determined, far too young to begin to understand the shaping of a nation. She was careless, foolhardy, irritating . . .

He paused in his thought, remembering his encounter.

Young.

Yes. If nothing else, she was young. Gentle, definitely not. Loving? Never. Warm? As ice. Passionate? Only in her determination to be free from him.

But then again, his greatest fear in being given an heiress had been that she would be a wizened old woman, incapable of giving him the sons he craved.

She wasn't exactly an old witch.

She was in possession of all her teeth, something he must acknowledge, since it seemed life was all a bargaining game. Good skin, good bone structure, fine lines. She was sound. Aye, definitely healthy. Strong, capable, fleet and graceful—as her woman had said.

But she was much more, and he had seen that already. She

was not just young and healthy. She was *formed*. In body—and mind. She was cold as ice in her will to fight, hard as nails in her determination. She was beautiful as well. What was the word he had thought in connection with her earlier?

*Ripe!* he reminded herself. What she didn't see in her reckless desire to be free was that she was young and vulnerable, and risking herself in a way she might possibly not understand. Or else, she understood her peril completely, and just didn't care. What could be worse to her than being given to a man she had determined to be one of David's Norman knights? She was hotheaded and wild, and certain that her will alone was enough to change her destiny.

Enough to defy a king.

*Yet, even before he had seen her features, he had heard her voice, seen her before the fire, and she had haunted his dreams . . .*

His temper continued to surge despite the fact that he was a stranger to her. He was dismayed to realize that he felt a greater sense of fury against Mellyora MacAdin than he did loss for Eleanora. His pride, he thought ruefully, took precedence over his heart. Minutes ago, he had felt a measure of sympathy for the lady on the river. But he'd envisioned a different future then for himself. His life had been changed here, in this room, in less than a quarter of an hour. This was the way of the world. He couldn't have Eleanora, and Mellyora MacAdin could not have her freedom. The lady on the river now deserved no sympathy. She was no longer an amusing young woman in a sad situation, but an obstinate, disobedient, and disloyal subject of the king.

Which made him remember that she was still sitting out on the river, where she plotted and planned to join with her Viking kin.

"I shall find the lady," he told David.

"What?" the king asked, distracted. He shook his head. "You've been on a battle campaign, and just come to court. I'll send other knights to find her, I'll send out an army, I'll—"

"Trust me, sire. I'm not tired. I shall find the lady," Waryk swore. He didn't explain to the king that he had more at stake than other men, nor that he knew exactly where to find his errant heiress. The king, he knew, had made his decision. He would brook no arguments. The lady was Waryk's. So he would find her. She would remain cold as ice, he was certain. He couldn't force her to accept him, to want him, or to care for him in any way, and he wouldn't insult either of them with such an effort. But he could force obedience, to the king, and to himself, and he would do so.

He inclined his head to the woman Jillian, bowed to the king, and started from the great hall, his shoes still squishing.

Indeed, he would find her.

Outside the king's hall, he paused, plotting. There were a few things he needed to do, some orders he needed to give, before retrieving his reluctant soon-to-be bride.

Because once he found the lady, he intended to keep her.

"Angus!" he called, bursting in on the man who kept quarters adjacent to his own.

It was early; Angus hadn't slept long, but at Waryk's summons, he was instantly up, reaching reflexively for his scabbard and sword.

"There's no need to seize arms—yet," Waryk said dryly. "I've been to see the king—"

"Aye, then, you've heard," Angus said, studying Waryk.

"Aye, I've heard," Waryk said. Apparently, everyone else at Stirling had known his fate while he had idled his time under the stars and in the river.

"Ah, well," Angus said. "Lady Eleanora will understand. I know of the inheritance. It's a place beyond imagination, the wildest beauty known to man. You love the sea, Waryk, there's no place finer. And the lass, well, you'll be pleased, she's young. I saw her once, as a babe, and she was the prettiest little creature ever. She was the heiress we camped near last night, Sir Harry's charge. If I'd but known, I'd have insisted on seeing her. Aye, now, I know, women change, but it's said she's grown into one of the most beautiful women in our country and beyond. I'm sure you'll be pleased when you've met—"

"Angus, we have met, so it seems—"

"Where, when?" Angus asked, puzzled; then he suddenly noted, "Waryk, you're wet. Soaked."

"Aye, that I am. We met quite by accident. I didn't know the lady, nor does she yet know me."

Angus lifted a brow slowly. "And she is why you're soaking wet."

"Aye."

"Well, dry off, change man!"

"Not yet. I'm off to find my lady again, you see. And she has a penchant for water as well. I'm learning these things about her, you see."

"Oh? Shall I come with you to find her?"

"No. I'll find her myself."

"And tell her just who you are, I imagine!"

"No. Not yet, Angus. But once I've brought her here . . . well, once I've done so, we'll want to keep her. I'm not sure when I'll return with her. When I do, inform the king. And alert Sir Harry, and Tristan, I think. I'll count on you to keep close guard on these halls."

"You think she'll try to escape you?"

Waryk smiled grimly. "I know she'll try to escape me. But she won't. No matter what she thinks. I am curious to discover, though, just how far she is willing to go."

# CHAPTER 6

By the time she came to the embankment in the night, Mellyora was freezing and exhausted. She had lost direction in the darkness, and it had seemed to take forever to reach the opposite embankment.

There, she had found a fisherman's lean-to, a hut of stone and mud like the one on the opposite bank, and it had seemed compellingly welcoming, a break against the chill wind of the night. Even with the Viking camp so close, she had paused there just to rest for a few minutes. Shivering, weak, and weary, she had longed to start out quickly again. But the swim had exhausted her more than she had thought possible, and she realized she had slept very little in weeks now, hardly doing so since Adin had died. In the small hut she'd closed her eyes, she'd dozed, and when she opened her eyes again, there was light, and there were fishermen on the water, and she could see the little boat she had borrowed the night before. It was just a few feet from shore, as if it waited for her. It had drifted close to the embankment. Amazingly, in the light of day, she could see the oars. They had surfaced, and they floated close to the drifting boat. The day was nearly as chill as the night, and her clothing and cloak were in the boat. It wasn't far at all. She could reach it with just a few minutes' swim, and take it the rest of the way downriver to the Viking camp. If she were found walking along the embankment, she might be in for some grave difficulties. She decided she needed the boat.

Without a fool young oaf to lose the oars for her again! She wondered vaguely what had happened to her boatman of the night gone by. He hadn't returned for her. Or had he? He wouldn't have seen her in the hut. He would have to think that she had either found her uncle or perished in the darkness. His fault. With luck, he'd feel guilty for being such an idiot and for assaulting her in the first place.

The river was deep and wide and very cold. Mellyora's teeth chattered, her bones ached, she could barely force herself into the water, and then to keep moving. But she knew the harder she swam, the greater force she would exert, the more warmth she would generate within herself. She really had no choice, not anymore. Perhaps it had been foolish to plow back into the water— it seemed more so every second—but she had done it, and therefore, she had to keep going. Everything she had done since her audience with the king might be conceived as foolish, she admitted to herself. If she didn't freeze to death or drown now, she might have broken her neck earlier. But she didn't have many weapons with which to fight, and it was one thing for kings to believe they had the right to command the future, but since that future was hers, she had to wage war with the king in whatever way she could. She wouldn't allow any of it to be foolish. Achieving her goals would be vindication. She would keep herself from freezing, and she would reach the boat, secure the oars, and find her uncle. She was a good swimmer, a strong swimmer, and she would make it.

Finally, raising her head to draw a breath, she saw the boat. Relief filled her. In the not so far distance, she could even see the Viking camp, men up and about now, women working at their cooking fires.

Before long, she'd reach her destination. Which she needed to do. The king would have men out any minute, searching for her. Maybe it would take until midday, when Jillian realized she didn't sleep, and alerted the king that she was gone.

Yet just when she thought another hard kick would bring her to the boat, she felt a startling new force against her. She gasped, gulping in water as she was suddenly jerked back. She wasn't alone in the water. Someone had seized her and was pulling her back, trying to drown her.

A hand was upon her waist. She twisted, kicking and clawing with fear and desperation, her nails digging into flesh. She was released; she started to sink. She kicked hard and shot to the surface, desperate for breath.

She had barely breathed in before hands closed around her again. Being held in the water instantly panicked her; she was certain an enemy was trying to drown her. This time, she tried to bite. Her teeth met flesh. The arm in her mouth slammed against her with such a power that she released her grip, stunned, and certain she was about to die. The arm around her was like a cordon of steel. But she wasn't being drowned, she was being dragged out of the water. In deep dismay she realized that she had swum so hard only to be dragged back to the embankment once again.

She kicked and wriggled, trying to twist around so that she could assess her enemy. She could barely move, scarcely breathe. In seconds she found herself slung down upon the embankment. She was so cold, it was hard to fight. Her assailant was about to come over her; she caught the rich mud in her hands and cast it upward, into his face. She struck him, twisted, and started crawling to freedom.

But he was suddenly before her, bare feet staunchly embedded in the mud. She turned again, and he was upon her, arms wrapped around her waist as they rolled on the embankment. She flailed furiously with her fists, fighting the man, desperately wishing herself back at the fortress at Stirling. For the moment, she cursed herself for her foolishness in thinking she'd had a real chance at escaping the king and finding the freedom she had been willing to risk so much to find. Who was this madman who had risen from the river like a sea monster? What had she done, had there been any other means of reasoning with the king? Was she about to be raped and murdered? Her knife remained at her calf, and she reached for it, drawing it from the leather sheath. She didn't want to die, she was terrified, but she couldn't just lie there like a frightened lamb and allow herself to be slaughtered without a fight. She tried to raise her weapon high, to bring it down with a worthwhile effort . . .

"So you're a traitor, thief—and would-be murderess!" she heard as long fingers curled around her wrist with such strength that she cried out at the pain, forced to release the weapon. She was slammed down upon her back, and her assailant was over her. Her knife was in the mud, and her wrists were pinned above her head while his face hovered grimly just above her own.

She inhaled sharply, seeing the monster who had assailed her.

"You!" she charged. It was the wretch who had lost the oars and left her in the river.

Apparently, he didn't feel guilty for his first assault. He was attacking her once again.

"Aye, lady, I said I'd be back."

"You loathsome, despicable creature! First, you desert me in the river, and then you assault me and attempt to drown me! How dare you! I tell you, you are in sorry shape, you wretched fellow, there is no question now, you will be treated severely, you will pay—"

"I don't think so," he told her.

She fell silent, staring up at him. His eyes were more chilling than the night. Deep blue Arctic frost. His features were fierce, tense, frightening.

He was back. After the night. He should have been gone, he should have rued that he had seen her in the first place, and he should have stayed far away when word went out that the Lady Mellyora had escaped Stirling Castle.

Had he decided to demand a ransom for her after all? Did he intend to kill her? No, what value would there be in her murder? Yet, he looked angry enough to throttle her then and there, and she thought it was far more than the chill in the air that was causing her to shiver.

She tried to be calm, and perfectly still. Not fighting him, she hoped to muster her strength if the moment came when she might slip free from him. "You know," she said with solemn warning, "you are making a grave mistake. You don't understand who I am—"

"No, I understand exactly who you are."

"All right, I may be at odds with the king, but if he knew that you had nearly drowned me, that you—"

"I wasn't trying to drown you," he said, and assured her, "You would be dead now had that been my intent."

"Then—"

"I was trying to help you out of the water."

"Were you? You're lying, you bastard, you were rough and cruel and brutal—"

"I'm not lying, you little witch! You were rough and cruel and brutal. You started scratching and biting and fighting and left me little choice but to drag you out—perhaps a little less than gently."

She narrowed her eyes, wondering at his words when he was obviously furious enough to do her great damage. He was shaking, she realized, as if he was expending considerable effort to keep from doing her bodily harm. A renewed sense of unease swept through her.

"Why did you attack me in the water?"

"I didn't think you were going to make the boat."

"I'm an excellent swimmer."

"Indeed. That's why you got nowhere last night."

"I was cold, and tired."

"And weak," he said.

"I was doing just fine on my own."

"But now you're with me."

"You still don't understand, do you? Terrible retribution will come your way. You'll be—"

"Disemboweled, hanged, drawn and quartered?"

She stared at him. How dare he be so mocking when such a fate might well await him?

"Yes!" she lashed out. "In fact, if you don't let me up immediately, when I see the king, I'll see to it that you receive exactly what you suggest—you'll be disemboweled, hanged, drawn and quartered—and then your pieces will all be burned and the ashes cast to the wind!"

He rose and looked down at her. "My lady, I don't think so."

He reached out a hand to her. She stared at him in absolute amazement. Refusing to accept his offer of assistance to rise, she inched her way to her knees. Watching him distrustfully, she then scrambled to her feet on her own.

His eyes raked over her in the daylight. She felt her face flood hot and red with color. She was now sorry for the fact that she'd cast off all but her linen shift, for she knew that the thin, wet material clung to her flesh, exposing much more than it concealed. In fact, the mud that clung to her in various places was probably far more concealing than the remnants of her rich clothing. The way he studied her was strange and unnerving; she felt as if she were a prize cow on the block, and that any minute he would ask to look at her teeth. There was no warmth in his gaze, just appraisal and assessment. She felt again the power of his size, and she was tempted to inch away from him, then run again for all that she was worth. But he would catch her, and she'd be thrown back into the mud again. There had to be another way to escape him.

"Let's go, shall we?" he said.

"Let's go?"

"That's right."

"Where?"

"Why, to the king, of course. So that you can have me disemboweled, hanged, and drawn and quartered, in that order, then burned and my ashes cast to the wind."

He was taunting her, of course. He was an outlaw, she was suddenly certain. Or, perhaps he was a disgruntled chieftain. One way or the other, he intended to abduct her, take her to some hiding place, and use her as a hostage in his own negotiations with the king.

"Come on!" he said impatiently. He started toward her and she backed away, very wary.

"You really haven't begun to imagine what lies at stake here. I can help you, or hurt you. If you're in trouble, I can help you. Daro will reward you richly if you deliver me safely to him. He can give you money, he can take you far away on one of his ships. He—"

"He can also disembowel, hang, and draw and quarter me, right?" he inquired.

She shook her head. "No. You must believe me, the Vikings are no more vicious than any other men in our world. They will do as I ask, and in truth, I detest violence—"

"Indeed, m'lady, you most certainly could have fooled me!"

"Sometimes threats are necessary when—"

"Dealing with lesser men?" he inquired.

She shook her head. "Damn you, I said nothing like that at all—"

"Ah, but you implied."

"I did not."

"Lady, your vessel awaits."

He pointed to the boat. It had now drifted to where it was just a few feet from the shore, not twenty feet away from them.

She shook her head. "I'm not moving until you tell me the truth regarding your destination."

"Fine. I told you, I'm taking you to the king."

She didn't believe it for a minute. "What king?" she inquired suspiciously.

He crossed his muscled arms over his chest. "There is only one, m'lady," he said with such deep passion that she was suddenly very afraid. He meant it. He wasn't taunting her. He meant to take her back to David.

"No . . ." she gasped. "Oh, my God, you do mean to take me back to the king, to betray me to him! You are taking me back to David for whatever reward you think that you can get from him. You left me, deserted me on this river, just to find out how much I might be worth to him. You are the worst kind of mercenary outlaw, how can you be so cruel and callous and traitorous—"

"You are the traitor, m'lady," he reminded her.

"Never! You don't understand, you won't understand—you *refuse* to understand! I'm not betraying the king, I'm only seeking ways to negotiate—"

"To defy the king, to refuse the rightful lord to whom he intends to give you—"

"Me—and my property!" she said sharply.

"There's always property involved when the lady intended is as noble as yourself."

He accented the word *noble* and she knew that he was mocking her and that he didn't find her noble in the least, which irritated her further. "Property is all that the king sees."

He arched a brow. "Oh, I believe he sees more than just the land involved. Perhaps he sees Viking invasions as well."

"You know, you are a reckless fool. You should take care. I am a Viking's daughter."

"Perhaps that's the very point the king sees most clearly." He let out an impatient oath. "Come, m'lady. You were behaving like a foolish child from the beginning if you thought that the king would not be involved with your future. It's all a game of power and land, isn't it? Surely, you're aware of that. And we're all of us pawns within that game. Now, shall we go?"

She shook her head, backing away from him again. "You're not listening to me. If you understood, you'd help me. You're a Scotsman. You should be outraged for me! The king intends to reward one of his Norman, lackey henchmen—"

"You consider this man nothing more than lackey, one of the king's henchmen?" he demanded.

"Aye, a terrible one at that!"

"And a Norman?"

"Can we dare forget the Conquest? That we were spared, and England taken?"

He shrugged. "Curious. I've heard the man is Scottish."

"You've heard lies," Mellyora corrected him, praying that he was beginning to understand her position. "His father was in the king's command before he came here from England. I don't care what he chooses to call himself, the truth is that he's a Norman, an invader, a wretched, horrible old Norman knight—"

"A wretched, horrible old man?"

"Yes!" she cried. "Do you understand?"

He lifted his arms in a shrug. "Indeed. Poor girl. It's such a pity, such a wretched, wretched situation . . ."

"So you'll help me?" she cried hopefully.

"Ah, lady . . ." he murmured.

"Aye!" she said, stepping closer. She stared up into his eyes, very bright against his muddied features. She barely breathed, praying.

He smiled.

"You will help me!" she whispered.

He caught her hands, held them between his own. "Not if the sun fell from the sky this very minute!" he told her flatly.

She gritted her teeth and counted, fighting for control. No good. She drew her hands from his in a fury, aware that he had baited her, that he was laughing at her. She tried to tell herself that she had to be very careful, she was risking her future—not to mention her life and limbs—with every word and action.

But it was just no good.

She slapped him with all her strength and did so with such speed that he didn't manage to stop her. However, the moment her handprint embedded on his cheek, she was sorry for her action. His eyes became as sharp as knives, as hard and cold as winter ice.

She turned to flee.

He reached for her, and his fingers caught her linen shift, ripping the material. Heedless of the fact that she was losing the garment, she kept running. Aware that he was behind her, she veered toward the water again, praying that she could plunge into the depths and swim far enough beneath the water to elude him . . .

The cold stung her. Despite the chill she'd felt on the embankment, the water was still colder. She plunged deep, but to no avail. Like a demon from the depths, he seemed to be there before her. She found herself dragged out of the water and slammed down on the embankment again. This time he stared down at her with such a fury that she began to tremble. Her shift was in tatters, she was all but naked. She closed her eyes, not wanting to meet his, desperately afraid of what move he might make next.

"D—don't . . . d—don't . . ."

"Don't what?" he demanded.

"Don't . . . er . . ."

"Ah! Assault you? Steal your virtue? Tell me, have you any virtue?"

Her eyes flew open. She met his crystal gaze. "You are an arrogant fool. You can bring me back to the king, and he can give you whatever reward it is you so crave, but if you touch me—"

"Ah, yes, here you are in all your perfect, naked, noble beauty! How tempted I must be!"

His mocking, dispassionate tone startled her to silence, but trying to keep her eyes locked with his, she didn't feel assured.

"Let me up!"

"Let you up? When I'm so tempted? Could I bear to let you up, you and all your perfect noble beauty?"

"Why are you torturing me like this?" she cried, wondering if she were more afraid, or humiliated. Both made her more desperate, and more reckless. "You don't dare harm me in any way, and we both know it. You—"

"Umm, well, that depends. As you say, there are different Vikings. Norse, Danish, Swedish. And they all enjoy a good *negotiation*. Perhaps your relatives would like you back chaste and in one piece; then again, it's amazing what men will trade in a negotiation. There are still Scottish rebels who might pay a pretty price for you, and not care too much whether you come tarnished or not."

"My relatives will kill you if you . . ."

"If I?" he inquired politely.

She felt her cheeks flooding with bloodred color. She felt the pressure of his body against hers, and the cold of the air against her bare flesh. He stared at her, and she didn't know what he saw. She longed to crawl beneath a blanket, to close her eyes, pretend she had never left the warmth of the castle that night. She started shaking, badly. The day was cool, the river cold. She told herself it had nothing to do with fear. She knew she was lying. She had to think carefully before speaking.

But she gasped, shivering with a greater violence as he touched her cheek, stroking her face with his knuckles. He spoke to her, his voice so deep and husky it seemed to slip beneath her skin, and touch her oddly. "Oh, so noble! Noble face, noble breasts, noble . . . well, everything must be noble, eh, my lady? Such a great, beautiful, noble bounty!"

Fear escalated, her temper soared, and she panicked, lashing out at him. This time, he was ready, and she didn't land the first blow against him. He caught her wrists, and pinning them down, he stared at her again in taut anger, no longer mocking her. "I suggest you stop."

"I suggest you go to hell!" she spat back, yet his eyes then touched her in such a way that she kept talking, quickly, else give away the depths of her fear.

"I'm freezing!" she cried. "I'll die on you, and I won't be worth anything."

"You're not going to die. Well," he mused, "unless I lose control completely and strangle you."

She forced herself to glare at him. "Whatever you're going to do, do it—or let me up!" she challenged him.

"Do you know, m'lady, you've bargained, you've ordered, you've used all manner of words. Except one."

"And what is that?"

"Please. Ah, but then, perhaps you're not accustomed to using it."

"I'm very familiar with the word."

"Then?"

"However, I'm not accustomed to using it with a bastard mercenary who's attacking me!"

His eyes narrowed. "Try it. What have you got to lose?"

"Let me up. Please."

He smiled.

"Let me up, *please!* What are you doing now? You said that you'd let me up—"

"I said that you should try it. But you did call me a bastard mercenary."

She gritted her teeth, then thought that she should really get a grip on her temper. No matter what he said. She needed to pretend to acquiesce to whatever foolish thing he said, if it would get her up.

"I'm freezing. Pl—"

"Naturally, you're freezing. You're soaked, and you're naked."

"Pl—"

"And you've been swimming in a wretchedly cold river."

"I know why I'm freezing—"

"I'm not warming you in the least?" he inquired.

She shook her head. "You're chilling me," she said softly. "I've never been so cold in all my life."

"Tell me, are you really afraid yet?" he asked.

She frowned. Of course she was afraid! She would never, never let him know it.

"Cowards such as yourself do not scare me," she said.

"What a pity. I was about to let you up!"

"Oh!" she cried in sheer frustration. "Please, I'm afraid, I'm very afraid—please let me up."

He leaned closer to her. "You're not afraid, and you should be. You think that your birth and the king's distant hand can protect you. Well, it can't. You're with me, and I won't let you up, and you don't know what I'm going to do. You are a ward of the king. Basically, m'lady, he owns you. You, and your person, and you have risked both, and, therefore, you're guilty of treason."

"No! I've done nothing but—"

"Arrive in the midst of a situation where you are naked and freezing on a riverbank with a stranger ten times more powerful than you are."

She fell silent, staring at him. If he was really so dedicated to the king, he wouldn't touch her. And she could prove that strength lay in many areas within the human mind.

She closed her eyes for a long moment, then looked up at him with a tremulous shudder. "Please! You've made me very afraid, and I'm so cold . . . aye, I was wrong. If you've come to take me back to David, do so, *please*. I will beg his pardon, I . . . I'm so cold."

Again, she closed her eyes, shivering violently. She hadn't lied in some respects, she was certain that her lips were blue, and she was very afraid, pinned, unable to escape.

"Why don't I believe you?" he murmured, and her eyes flew open and met his.

"I don't know," she grated. "I'm telling you the truth."

He shook his head. "You are a liar. A wretched, petty liar, but we'll change that."

Despite his words, he came to his feet. She started to scramble away, fully aware he meant to help her up.

She lifted a hand to him, pleading, "No, don't . . . don't touch me. I'm getting up, I'm coming along."

She stood, awkward, and so cold that her teeth were chattering as she hugged her arms around herself, feeling more vulnerable than she ever had in her life. He had stripped down for his swim, but he still wore a knit wool shirt, and that he pulled over his head. When she shied away from him then, he let out an impatient oath, jerking her close so that he could slip the wet shirt on her. It was better than nothing. She didn't move then, but stood before him with her head down, now shaking violently.

"Come."

He caught her hand and started walking along the embankment to the boat. She stumbled after him, not meaning to protest at that moment, but so cold that she could barely move. Once again he swore, pausing to sweep her up into his arms. She clung to him to keep from falling, uneasily aware of his physical power. His naked arms, chest, and upper abdomen were defined with muscle. With dismay she thought that he was no one's servant hoping to become a knight; he was already a warrior, a knight, one of the king's men who had trained with the very heavy weapons and armor of war.

He stepped into the boat, set her down, and shoved off from the embankment. He pointed to her cloak and tunic, left behind when she had first decided to leave the little vessel—a lifetime ago, so it seemed.

"Get dressed."

She reached for her things, starting to slip the tunic on top of his shirt.

"M'lady, I'll take my shirt back, if you don't mind."

"But I do mind—"

"Why should you? I've already seen all that you have to offer."

"I wouldn't want to commit more treason."

He smiled at that. "But I do want my shirt."

She stared at him, feeling a ridiculous surge of anger inside her once again. He liked to bait her. Fine. He was the king's man. And her "noble bounty" was something he mocked.

"As you wish," she told him, and she pulled off his shirt.

She tossed the garment toward him. He caught it; they stared at one another. The cool breeze caught her naked flesh, but she took her time, pretending she had lost her tunic again with the pile of clothing in the boat, and searching through her clothing. When she found her tunic, she pretended to have difficulty with the garment before slipping it over her head. As she did so, she started, frightened, afraid she had taken her taunt too far, for he was right next to her, nearly touching her, reaching for her cloak.

He practically threw it on top of her head.

Then he sat again, staring at her. She returned the glare.

He reached for his shirt. As he did so, the oar started to slip from the boat.

"The oar!" she cried.

He fumbled for it. Too late. It was gone.

He swore.

"Oh, my God, not again! You really are a fool—"

"One more word and I will strangle you!" he promised. "You needn't worry this time!"

He tossed his shirt down and slipped over the rim of the boat, back into the water. He was going for the oar, she saw.

Then she realized that the second oar was still in the lock. She hastily changed her position, trying to maneuver the small vessel with the one oar. It wouldn't move at first, but then she jerked the oar from the lock. She spun herself in a circle, but then she managed to slip the oar in and out of the water, changing sides, and set the little boat out on a straight line across the water.

She dipped the oar to the left, and couldn't lift it. She struggled with it, then gasped. He had reached the boat. He tossed the lost oar aboard. Desperate, she tried to strike him with the oar she was using. He ducked. He rose on the other side of the boat, and she spun around in time to catch him on the shoulder. Then she realized that she had begun a brutal fight, and that if she didn't win . . .

She struck out hard, and wild, very afraid. Then she saw she was beating the water. He was gone.

She sat back, shaking. Tears stung her eyes, horror filled her. She forced herself to breathe deeply, and she tried to tell herself that she hadn't just murdered a man, and if she had, it had been in self-defense, she didn't know just what he had intended for her.

Still, she felt a wave of wretched misery engulfing her. *Whom* had she killed? He'd been young, a king's man. A knight. A man loyal to the king. Perhaps he'd encountered dozens of the king's enemies, and returned triumphant, and she had murdered him in cold blood upon the river in the midst of a beautiful fall day . . .

She looked up at the sun, figuring it was well past midday. Early afternoon, now? Her stomach growled suddenly, and she was horrified that she had murdered a man, and felt hunger at the same time. She had to stop sitting there, stunned and appalled by what she had done. She had to move. She had to reach the Viking camp. In just another few hours, it would be dark again.

Shaking, she tried to pull herself together.

Then she screamed again, for *he* was back. He wasn't dead, and she was indeed in grave danger. With a sudden impetus, he came shooting out of the river like a water demon, hiking himself over the edge of the boat with swift force. She thought he meant to kill her when he wrenched away from her the oar she had wielded. She cast her arms over her head and ducked, awaiting his deadly blow.

She began a swift, silent prayer, the Hail Mary, waiting, waiting . . .

The words of the prayer faded from her thoughts as nothing happened. She lifted her head at last.

He wasn't looking at her. He was seated in the middle of the boat, adjusting both oars again. She dared to breathe. She should have kept her quiet. But she was shaking, and she couldn't quite manage to do so.

"You're alive."

"No thanks to you."

"I didn't mean—"

"To kill me? Aye, I think you did."

"But you haven't—"

"Killed you? No, my lady, I have not."

"I see," she said. "You wouldn't want to return me to King David dead or bruised."

She could see him gritting his teeth together as he shook his head in wonderment. "Well, m'lady MacAdin, you're right. I don't want you dead, maimed, or bruised. You do know something about fighting, and I grant you this, you're very brave, or incredibly stupid."

"I almost killed you," she reminded him.

"Nay, lady, you did not."

"You were gone a very long time—"

"I watched, my lady."

"Just as you disappeared last night—"

"Again, I watched, my lady."

"All that time?"

"Nay, not all that time. But much of it. You barely made it last night. You were too tired for the swim. And too cold to go on."

"You watched me . . ."

"Aye, that I did. Shivering in that little hut, taking to the water again—"

"Why, you bastard—"

"Careful, I might think that you're not fond of me, lady."

"I pray you'll die on the spot!"

"My lady, with your ways, you are far more likely to die."

She fell silent for a moment, then told him softly, "I just want to be free."

He stared at her in return. "Don't we all?" he queried after a moment. He rowed with his words, rowed hard. They were soon back to the shore where they had first begun their journey in the little boat the previous night.

Taking no chances, he lifted her from the vessel as they beached. He set her upon the shore, and watching her, whistled. She was startled as the huge horse she had seen grazing the night before slowly trotted down to them from the trees by the roadside above the embankment. She assessed the animal. It was a warhorse. Huge, well tended, a scar here and there. An animal in its prime, but one which had seen action. Wide-set eyes, broad shoulders, sturdy haunches. Powerful limbs. It could carry the weight of a man in armor and still race into the fray with good speed.

The horse nuzzled the man, and she found herself studying her far too familiar stranger with greater unease. Who was he? "Ah, Mercury, you are a good fellow!" he told the animal.

"Would Mercury happen to have a bit of bread in his saddlebags?" she asked, surprised herself that she managed to do so.

He probably wouldn't share food with her if he carried any with him. She had tried to kill him.

But he shrugged. "Maybe," he told her, and he flipped up the leather flap on a saddlebag. Inside, wrapped in a small linen square, was not just bread, but cheese and a portion of dried meat. He offered her all the food, and she was surprised. He watched her balance the lot of it, then indicated a dry spot beneath a sapling oak. She walked to the oak and sat, biting into the bread with hunger and feeling, despite her wretched position, a sense of fulfillment and pleasure as the food began to take away the hunger pangs that had assailed her.

She stared out on the water, eating. In a few minutes, she was filled, but she pretended her hunger still, taking tiny bites of food as she watched him. He didn't sit by her, but waited, eyes broodingly upon the river.

"You came back, and just watched me all night?" she inquired.

"If you wanted to sleep in a small mud hovel rather than the warmth of the king's hospitality, I felt it wasn't proper to disturb you."

"Ah, well, you've disturbed me now."

He shrugged. "The morning was nearly gone when you made your move, my lady. Wearily, so it seemed, at that. I didn't want to bring you back drowned."

"How kind."

"Darkness is falling again."

"The mud hut is actually quite comfortable."

"What a liar. You are accustomed to warmth and comfort— and the men in your life tripping over themselves to see to your comfort."

"You don't believe in such courtesy."

"I don't believe in anyone walking over me." He hunched down beside her, and she was startled again by both the classic handsomeness of his features and the hardness within them. He seemed a rock. She felt a slight chill, seeing the way muscle rippled with his every breath, and remembering how she had tried to kill him. She needed to be thankful for her sex, she thought; he surely would have killed a man in return, no quarter given. Yet, did it matter? He was young, powerful, and striking, a warrior from a noble house. She had underestimated him last night. He meant to turn her in to the king. She still meant to escape.

Fall . . . nearly winter. The light did not stay long. Here, beneath the sapling oak, a breeze stirring, the coming twilight was suddenly beautiful. The air played upon the water, and it rippled. A fresh, cool scent seemed to stroke her cheeks. She was warm in her cloak, filled with his food. She felt renewed. Her strength was revived, along with her faith in herself. If only someone would come along. Help. What story could she come up with to tell an unwary passerby? There were fishermen out on the water. They'd be coming in soon, with darkness so quickly looming before them . . .

"Don't even think about it, my lady."

"About what?"

"Seeking help from me through a fisherman. I'd have to kill him, and his death would be upon your hands."

She flushed, wishing he could not so easily read her mind. She stood then, dusting bread crumbs from her hands. He stood at her side, pointing toward his horse.

"M'lady, shall we."

She hesitated. When she had feared immediate rape or death, the prospect of returning to Stirling had been a good one. Now, she knew she was facing nothing but the king's fury. Just how angry would he be? How far would he go with her to prove his power?

"Now, my lady!" he said, his tone taking on a harsh quality.

She swallowed, shaking her head, wondering if he'd realize now that her obstinance was more fear than defiance. "I . . . can't. I'm not going anywhere with you," she murmured. "If we could just—"

"No, we couldn't just," he said quietly.

She stared at him, assessing him once again. She held very still. She was dressed, but still damp, and the breeze sweeping by her was cool, but good. She felt strong again. They were near the castle, too near the castle. Her chances were slipping away. She had to reason with him, or outwit him. Reasoning might be hard now, since she *had* tried to split his head open with the oar, and she had drawn her knife on him, twice. She'd not retrieved it the last time. She shivered as she stood there, realizing his height allowed him to tower over her. He was, she thought again, a man to make her very nervous. In the prime of life, still young, but a man fully formed, a warrior trained. Powerful, striking, yet so chillingly so, for his sculpted features were set in lines so harsh and impassive that she felt tremors begin sweeping through her, touching her with a strange sense of both panic and warmth.

She moistened her lips. "We've had a chance to talk, to know one another." *Too well,* she thought. He'd touched her, grappled with her. She knew the feel of him, the scent of him, his warmth. "Look, I'm not going with you!" she said again, taking another step from him. "Understand me. You think you're in control now. But things can change. The Viking camp is just across the river. If I screamed, they might hear me. Think about just how close we are to my kin! A fisherman, aye, you could easily slay a poor fisherman! But what of a berserker? Now, please. Pay attention, hear me, heed me. I'm not going anywhere with you!"

He didn't even take a step toward her. He smiled, shaking his head with both fury and exasperation. "Oh, lady, you're so wrong. Indeed, you will be going with me, anywhere I say, everywhere I say. When I say."

"We'll see what the king has to say about that!" she snapped.

"Make up your mind! Are you threatening me with the Vikings or the king?" he demanded.

He was angry—yet amused at the same time again, she thought. Shaking his head, he turned away from her to pull the small boat they had used higher up on the embankment, as if he meant to make sure it was there at a later time. As he did so, she saw her opportunity.

His horse was huge, but she was an excellent rider—once again, because she was a Viking's daughter. Perhaps she wouldn't be able to make an unassisted leap upon his back were it bare, but the horse was saddled. She was agile, and had been riding forever.

The stirrups were high but she managed to set a foot in the left one and vaulted herself easily up onto the warhorse. Her heart seemed to fly. She nudged the animal with her heels. "Go, boy, please, for the love of God, go, save me!"

The great horse leapt forward, pawing the air, hitting the ground.

They began to race. She felt the cool air. Felt the earth, flying beneath them.

She felt a taste of triumph, and freedom.

Then she heard a whistle.

The horse came to a sudden stop, pawing the air. She managed to keep her seat, but then the animal swung around and began racing again. Back toward the very place from where they had come. The horse galloped with lightning speed. She saw the man ahead of them, and she sucked in her breath, certain that he was about to be run down.

But once again, the warhorse came to a stop. A dead stop. This time, she couldn't control her own momentum, and she vaulted cleanly over the horse's head.

Luckily, she landed on soft, clear ground. Still, it felt as if she had broken every bone in her body. As if her head had cracked open.

She knew she had to leap up, to run on her own. She tried to do so, but the world was spinning. Looking up at the sky and the stars now spinning above her, she realized that twilight was turning to night. Stars were appearing.

"My God, but you are one stupid, stubborn woman!"

"No!" she cried out desperately.

But it was too late. His hands were moving over her, checking for broken bones or injury. He touched her in the most intimate ways, but didn't seem to think she had a right to demur or take offense. He made a snorting sound of disgust, then lifted her up despite her groan of protest. She was cast over his shoulder like a hunter's kill as he mounted his horse.

Maybe that was close to what she was.

He had hunted her.

And now they rode through the night. He with his trophy, returning to the king . . .

# CHAPTER 7

She must have actually dozed, because she opened her eyes, disoriented for a moment. Then she realized that she still lay over his shoulder, her head against his back as they loped closer and closer to the fortress at Stirling. She felt beaten, weary, cold through to her bones.

She was almost glad when she heard him crying out to the guards at Stirling. She heard the change of the horse's hoofbeats, the clopping against stone, as they came to the courtyard of the fortress.

He dismounted with her. She tried to rise, praying that she could revive, scream for some assistance from this zealously loyal madman, and demand to be put down, but she didn't need to scream; he was already setting her on her feet. As he did so, she wavered. She knew she was going to fall flat onto the dirt and stone, but he caught her, sweeping her up into his arms.

"Is she injured, m'laird?" she heard a groom inquire. "Shall I send for the king—"

"Nay, lad, she's weary, cold, and worn, not hurt. I'll take care of her, and see the king."

*Not hurt!* she thought indignantly, yet even as she tried to struggle against him then, she went still. She stared up at him with concern, suddenly realizing what the stableboy had called him.

*M'laird.*

She'd realized belatedly that he had to be a fighting man, a knight, or a rich patron's man-at-arms. No man was built so without hours practicing with the heavy accouterments of war.

But he wasn't just a knight, he was a laird.

She fixed her eyes on his as he walked into one of the residence entrances of the fortress, and not through the main doors which would have led to the great hall—and the king. "M'laird? Well, *sir*, where are you taking me now?"

"To a place where you can rest until I've had a chance to see the king."

She continued to stare at him, furious, powerless. "I shall kill you for this one day, I swear it."

"M'lady, it seems I shall have a harder time preserving your life than my own, though I am aware of your intent to end my existence," he said impatiently, his strides long as they moved down a hallway. She looked around herself uneasily. This section of the fortress held residences for the king's court, and his most trusted advisors and champions.

She struggled up against him. "I demand that you take me immediately to the king."

"You may make demands from here until hell freezes over, m'lady."

"Damn you, where are you taking me?"

"Not to a dungeon, m'lady," he told her, amused. "Though that might not be such a bad idea."

He stopped in the corridor, using a foot to push open a heavy wooden door.

"Where—"

She broke off. He opened the door to a large room with handsome tapestries hung on the walls for warmth, a huge fireplace against one wall with rich furs strewn before it.

"Whose room is this?" she asked.

"Mine," he told her, and entered with her. Once inside, he strode to the bed set in an arched inner chamber against the wall.

She leapt up; he pushed her firmly back. "You'll wait here."

She shook her head desperately, so tired, but now more dismayed than ever regarding this strange man who'd come after her so relentlessly. He obviously had great influence with the king, and she had so little time left for any argument or fight. She'd been gone more than a day now, she thought, and the king would indeed be furious. "Please! Please!" she begged him, rising again and placing a hand gently upon his arm. "Don't do this! Don't leave me here trapped. Help me. I swear that I do honor and love the king, but he is wrong in this. He intends to give me to that despicable—"

"Wretched, decaying, old Norman, Waryk de Graham."

"Aye! You know! Oh, God, you must understand, there is another way. If you'll just help me—"

"But I won't. Excuse me; I'll be back, m'lady."

He walked away from her toward the door, and she shook her head again, following.

"Wait!"

"What?" he demanded, stopping and turned back with exasperation.

"Help me get out of here. Please. Help me escape that awful man. I swear, I can pay you with riches you can't begin to imagine. Viking gold."

She swallowed nervously as he reached her once again, standing before her, handsome face cast at a devilish angle as he looked down upon her.

She clenched her fists at her sides. "Aye," she told him.

"Hmmm . . ."

"Lots of it!"

His smile deepened. "Tempting. But then, so much has been tempting tonight. But what if I weren't interested in gold?"

Her heart seemed to skip a beat. "What do you mean?" she asked him quickly. She was afraid that she knew exactly what he meant. How strange, when he'd mocked her so. Yet, she had tried to tempt—and irritate and disarm—him. Had she been more successful than she had imagined? He was obviously a virile man, yet . . .

She assumed as well that women were easy for him. He was built like steel and rock, and he was young, and his features were handsome, his smile even sensual. Was he mocking her again?

He smiled slowly, watching her, as if reading her mind. "I have a fair amount of gold," he said, stretching out an arm to indicate the richness of the room. "Plunder, you know. Battle gain."

"All men want to be richer," she said, moistening her lips.

"Well, riches mean different things to different people, don't they?"

"Not to the king," she murmured bitterly.

He shrugged. "What can you offer besides gold?"

"Jewels, Celtic art, you wouldn't believe how fine some of the ancient pieces of jewelry we have are . . . and we have ancient manuscripts, excellent armor, horses—"

"But they aren't really yours to give, are they?" he queried.

"Indeed, they are. They are riches that have belonged to my mother's family—"

"At the moment, it's irrelevant to whom these things really belong. They're not what I had in mind."

She met his eyes, feeling a strange sensation as if both fire and ice were filling her veins. She suddenly wanted to run from him with a greater urgency than that with which she had fled the fortress, and yet she was backed to an alcove, so there was nowhere to go. She decided on boldness.

"You mocked my 'noble beauty' before, m'laird. What would you want with it now?"

"I've been on a long battle campaign," he said with a shrug. "You might be a pleasant diversion."

"You certainly had plenty of opportunity for . . ."

"Rape?"

"Aye."

"Yes, I had dozens of opportunities. But rape the king's ward?" he taunted softly with mock horror.

"Seducing her would be better? You said that risking my person was treason. Wouldn't such a bargain make you guilty of treason against your beloved king as well?"

"I'm not the one desperate to barter here, m'lady. My motives are my own. You are the one attempting to negotiate, so my sins need not concern you. You're the one who needs to ask herself the soul-searching questions. How far are you willing to go to escape this marriage?"

"To hell and beyond," she murmured softly, eyes lowered.

"Ah, really?"

"What are your terms?"

"You, here and now."

"Never. What a foolish negotiation. You could betray me."

"Then?"

"I'll meet you anywhere—once you've let me free to reach the Vikings."

"How would I know that you'd meet me as agreed?"

"You'd have to accept my word."

"What if you were captured again by the king's men? You'd still owe me a tremendous debt. I'd be out the reward of having brought you back here."

"But I thought you weren't interested in gold and riches."

"We were making a different bargain."

"I'd keep the bargain. No matter what, if you let me free now, I swear I'll find a way to pay my debt."

"Are you lying?" he inquired. She shivered fiercely, forcing herself not to wrench away as he lifted her chin to study her eyes.

"No," she told him. She swallowed hard. Of course she was lying. But if she escaped and found Daro, and this knight came after her again, he would die. She would warn him that that was the way things were. And that would keep her from paying any debt.

"Where and when do you intend to pay this debt?" he asked her.

She hesitated, knowing that she had to take great care. He seemed serious, he might really let her go. He'd mocked her, and laughed at her, but now he seemed to want her, and she had to use whatever weapons were available, be those weapons wiles, lies, and deceit. Yet she had to take care that her every lie had a grain of truth, else this enemy might too easily see through her.

"There's a forest northwest of the fortress, no more than an hour's ride, where a high crag just begins to shoot up from a valley. It's the king's land, do you know it?" she inquired.

"Aye."

"There's an old hermit's cottage deep in one of the copses; the king uses it when he's hunting, so it's kept in good repair."

He arched a brow slowly, studying her in a way that unnerved her once again. "I am familiar, I do know the cottage," he said. "Go on."

"If you let me go now," she whispered, "I'll meet you there on the night of the next full moon."

"The night of the next full moon?"

"Aye."

"That's two weeks from now."

"Aye."

"You'll be there?"

"I swear it."

"Take care, m'lady. If you swear to me, make a vow, I'll not let you break it. You would imperil your immortal soul, and your life, and we wouldn't want that to happen. Not when you court death so frequently with such determination."

"I said I'll be there," she told him.

He watched her, nodding. "You will be," he said softly. "And still, I give you one last chance to think this through. Is this a bargain you really wish to make?"

She inhaled and exhaled nervously. "Aye!"

He suddenly turned away from her. He strode across the room and stared into the flames that burned in the fireplace. "I'm not going to help you escape, you know," he told her harshly. The anger that deepened his voice was all the more unnerving. "I'll allow you to leave the room. You'll have to escape the fortress again."

"I didn't expect your help," she said anxiously, moistening her lips. She looked longingly to the door.

"You could be brought back to the fortress within minutes," he warned her.

"I know! Leave that to me, I know how to escape the fortress," she told him.

"So it seems," he said dryly. He spun around, staring at her again. "But if you're caught, and you're wed to this Norman lout, how will you carry out your vow to me?"

"If I'm caught again, I'll agree to whatever the king demands. And I'll no longer be a prisoner."

"But what about your intended husband?"

"There are always ways to . . ."

"Deceive an old man?" he suggested. "Especially a wretched, decrepit, Norman lackey."

"You're being horrible, despicable," she told him.

"No," he said seriously, "I'm in the process of making a bargain. I want to be sure you'll keep your part of it. I'm not being wretched, just thorough."

"I don't owe anyone anything. I'm being manipulated against my will, so what I do to or against a Norman who remains little more than an invader can be of little consequence to me. I've made no vows to anyone, no promises. The king makes promises for me. I will keep my part of the bargain I have made with you!"

She felt as if she were being wound more tightly with each passing second. She kept seeing the door. A thick door, yet once opened, it was a gateway to freedom. Freedom. Anything that she could say or do to escape seemed right at the moment.

"So that is it?" he said.

"What do you mean?"

"Your final word?"

"Aye, that's it!" she snapped.

He lifted a hand, indicating the door. "Go."

She kept her eyes on him all the while that she slipped past him, anxious to reach the door. She was certain that he planned some trick, that he would stride forward and accost her as she reached the exit. But he didn't make a move. He watched her impassively, yet she noted the pulse beating furiously against his throat. He stood so very still, allowing her to leave. She was almost quit of him. What did it matter?

*What matters,* she thought, *is the way that he stares at me. As if I were a witch or a demon, some godforsaken creature, horrible in the extreme.*

She opened the door, and still he watched her. He was going to pounce upon her, like a tiger, a prowling wolf, and when he did, he would rip her to shreds. He would wait, and watch—he had watched her before, letting her suffer through the night!—like a cunning predator, and at the last possible moment, he would make his move.

But he didn't. She opened the door, and exited the room. She leaned against the door for a split second, expecting it to explode open behind her. But it didn't. She took a deep breath and tore down the hallway.

Her footsteps were almost silent as she sped for the doorway. She had no idea of the hour, but it was fully night, and the darkness and shadows would hide her once she reached the courtyard. She couldn't take any more chances. She had to slip into the stables, find her horse, and think of something to say to the night guard. On horseback, if she cleared the gate, she could reach the bridge, cross over, and ride hard. Stop for no one, nothing.

She spun around a corner, seeking the entrance where they had come into the residence hall of the castle. Yet when she had nearly reached the door, she skidded to a dead halt, for a man had stepped into the doorway.

A guard. A big man, large enough for the bulwark of his frame to fill the entire space of the doorway.

She backed away. Perhaps he hadn't seen her.

"Lady Mellyora!"

She gasped, stepping backwards again. It was Sir Harry Wakefield. The very man she had eluded earlier.

"Come, m'lady, the game is up."

"Sir Harry, if you'll just step aside . . ."

"Now, ye know, m'lady, that I cannot."

She turned to run down the hall in the opposite direction. She rounded a corner, unfamiliar with the corridors, but certain that there had to be other exits from the residence halls.

There, ahead of her, lay an archway. She ran toward it, dismay filling her along with an awareness that she was beginning to run in circles like a cornered rat.

She turned left toward an archway. And there, at the opening which should have allowed her access to the courtyard, stood another of the king's men. This man she did not know, though he seemed vaguely familiar. He was huge, bald, and his right cheek was deeply scarred. He looked like the sorry end of many a long battle, and seeing him, she was suddenly forced to realize the enormity of what she was doing, that she was fighting a king. She had defied David, and he had discovered her missing, and he had sent out the most hardened, vicious, and mercenary of his troops to find her. She had been so desperate that she had allowed her captor to play her for a fool. He would have known that the entire fortress would be alerted to be on the lookout for her. He had probably helped plan for it to be so.

She turned quickly, hoping she had done so before the bald man could see her. Racing wildly down the next corridor, she saw a tapestried alcove to her left. Slipping behind the tapestry, she leaned against the wall, gasping for breath, breathing deeply as she debated her next move. Should she try running up a flight of steps, perhaps finding an escape by way of the parapets once again? Should she hide a while, wait? How could she possibly escape now when the king had warned every guard to be on the lookout for a wayward young woman?

She suddenly became aware that there was breathing other than her own going on in the alcove. She caught her breath, and held it. Someone else was in here. Someone silent. Someone trying to hide as well, or someone waiting to pounce on her?

She fought a rising sense of fear and reminded herself that these alcoves were the place of many a secret tryst, and she assured herself that she was cornered with someone equally determined to keep his or her presence quiet.

She braced herself, hearing footsteps in the hall. "Have you seen her?" one man called to another.

"Aye, the Lady Mellyora came this way, but where she ran from here I do not know," came the reply.

"Warn Tristan she'll try the south entrance next," came another voice.

The voices and the footsteps faded. Mellyora remained frozen, waiting. Then she heard a soft whisper. "Mellyora MacAdin?"

It was a woman's voice.

A woman could betray her as easily as a man. She held silent.

"Mellyora!" The voice was a whisper, hesitant, afraid. "Mellyora! It is Anne Hallsteader."

Mellyora exhaled on a long breath. "Anne! What are you doing in this alcove?" Anne was the daughter of the youngest son of a Danish jarl and a MacInnish heiress. Her father had been slain soon after her birth, and she had lived with her mother's family since she'd been a child. Her home was north in the Hebrides, but close enough to Mellyora's island fortress that they had seen each other often enough over the years. "What are you doing here?" she repeated.

"You tell me first. Why are they looking for you? What have you done? Why are you hiding here?"

"I haven't done anything," Mellyora replied quietly. She was growing accustomed to the darkness in the tapestried alcove. She could make out Anne's shape, just feet away from her. By day, the tapestries were drawn back and richly carved chairs allowed residents and guests to sit and talk in small groups in relative privacy. By night, Mellyora had heard, much more went on, though she often wondered how, since this evening was proving that the alcoves could be crowded.

"I swear, I didn't do anything. I'm just avoiding the guards— obviously," Mellyora said. "My father died, you know. I am the king's ward."

"Aye, I've heard. They say he will wed you to one of his men."

"Aye, and I'm seeking to . . . leave."

"You're in dire trouble," Anne said with sympathy.

"Anne, what are you doing here?"

Anne was silent a long time.

"Anne!"

"I'm—meeting someone."

"Who?"

Again, Anne was silent.

"Anne, sweet Jesus, I'm in the trouble of my life! Whatever you have to say cannot be worse."

"Daro," Anne said.

"What?" Mellyora was so startled that she nearly shouted the question.

"Sh!" Anne rushed forward, clamping her hand over Mellyora's mouth. Mellyora wiggled her head, indicating she wasn't about to shout again, and set Anne from her.

"Daro! My uncle Daro?" Mellyora demanded. Perhaps she shouldn't have been so surprised. Daro was her father's younger brother, blond, bold, brave, and handsome. After the death of a friend, he'd taken over a rocky stronghold in the Irish Sea called Skul Isle. He was somewhat wild by nature, he was most often David's ally, and while Mellyora's father had lived, there had been peace between them. But Daro and the king were arguing or mediating about some point now, which is why her uncle's troops were camped down the river. She had thought that Daro was with his men.

"Please, Mellyora, be quiet! With David so strong now, my family wants nothing to do with Daro; they say that he will bring heartache and trouble to us all!"

"Dear God, I would never betray either of you—the man is my kin!" Mellyora assured her friend. If she weren't in so much trouble herself as it were, she might be amused. Anne had always seemed so steady and serene, the least likely candidate for an illicit affair with such a man as her uncle.

She heard footsteps again and inhaled sharply, staring at Anne. Sooner or later, the guards would draw open the tapestries and drag them both out. She hesitated, then clutched Anne's hands. "Tell Daro I need him. Tell him I'm a prisoner about to be wed to one of the king's lackeys. I need his help, but he mustn't be reckless, I don't want lives lost, I . . . I . . . I don't seek a battle, only escape!"

"Mellyora, what—"

"Get back!" Mellyora told her firmly. "And don't fail me, please, don't fail me!"

She gave Anne a little thrust, pushing her far back into the darkness. Then, hearing that a guard was coming near, she slipped from behind the tapestry.

"There she is! Ah, lady, but we were about to flush you out!" Sir Harry stated, striding angrily toward her.

"I can make my own way, Sir Harry," she said. She turned away from him only to realize that the hulking bald man was making his way toward her. "I can make my own way!" she repeated.

She didn't like the look of the man she didn't know. Unnerved, she tried to run past him. He reached out and caught her.

"Sir Harry!" she cried, trying to free herself from the huge stranger. "Sir Harry, tell this brute that I can make my own way—"

"Sir Harry has gone on, m'lady," the bald man told her. His voice was deep and husky with a deep Highland burr.

"Let me go," she said. "I don't know you, I'll see the king with Sir Harry—"

The man spun her around. "Sir Harry is gone on about his business," the man told her. "I will escort you—"

"I can make my own way to the king."

"I think not."

"I'm not running anymore. I know that you've managed to hunt me down. I will go straight to the king, you may follow me if—"

"M'lady, it is the middle of the night. The king is not to be bothered with your tantrums now."

"My tantrums? Fine! Well, you may follow me to my own chambers then, and I will await his summons."

"No."

His fingers were clamped around her arm. She stared at her arm, and into his eyes. There was something fierce and merciless there.

"Come with me. Now."

"You just said that the king—"

"The king is not to be bothered, ye'll come with me now to the laird."

"Nay, I'll not accompany you!" she declared, wrenching hard to free herself from the vise of his grip. She clawed at his arm, wriggled and struggled, all to no avail. He started down the corridor, and she had no choice but to follow, she was nearly lifted off of her feet. All the way she fought, clawing, pounding, kicking, trying to bite. He barely noticed. She was no more annoyance than a gnat. She'd struggled so desperately that she hadn't even realized where they had come until they were there.

He opened a door in the hallway, and thrust her in.

She had come back to the point where she had begun, she realized with a sharp gasp of dismay.

The man who had become the nightmare of her life stood before the fire, his back to her. He'd donned a clean shirt under his wool, and his still-damp dark hair had been brushed back.

"She's here, m'laird," the bald man said.

"Fine, Angus, thank you," he said casually. He didn't even turn around.

The door slammed as Angus departed.

Mellyora stared incredulously at the back of the man standing before the fire. Her fury rose along with the sick sensation that filled her as she knew she had lost.

"You cheat! You liar, you bastard!" she accused him, shaking, her voice tremulous with the depths of her anger. "You let me go just because you knew you had men in these corridors who would drag me back. You let me escape just to humiliate me—"

"I let you escape to see the futility of what you're trying to do," he interrupted with weary impatience. "You've taken a knife to me twice, you attempted to beat me to death with an oar, and still, here you are. I'm tired of your games, and that's the end of it."

There was no sense in her action, but she couldn't control herself. Her very world seemed lost and all because of this wretched king's man. She flew across the room, slamming her fists against his back with a thunderous vengeance as she stuttered out her fury, not able to find words to describe just how despicable she found him. "You vile oaf, you bloody bastard, you're a lying, conniving, sneaking, wretched excuse of a man and I'll never forgive you—"

He spun around, and she backed a foot away from him. His eyes were narrowed as he told her, "Whether you do or do not forgive me for your own acts of foolishness and treachery mean nothing to me."

"Nothing!" she cried. "It is all nothing to you!" In a frenzy she flew against him again, her fists now thudding against the wall of his chest, which seemed to mean nothing to him either. "I don't know who you think you are," she warned him passionately, "but I will not forgive or forget ever, and I will hurt you, I swear it, for all that you have done to me!"

With a sudden, lightning-quick movement, he'd had enough. He captured her wrists tightly. She struggled, still in a frenzy of anger, but he shook her and she was forced to go still, staring up into his eyes. For a moment she was afraid that he would strike her down in return, his eyes promised such violence, but he did not retaliate. "I don't give a damn if you forgive me, forget anything, or spend your life seeking revenge, but you'd best be warned. I gave you a chance, you made a promise. And when you make a promise to me, you will keep your word!" He assured her with controlled anger.

Promise, what promise? Oh, God, yes, to meet him at the king's cottage in the forest!

"Never! Never!" she assured him, outraged. "You lie, you cheat, you tease—"

"Tease? M'lady, you put the goods right on the table! You're treacherous and disloyal, but the cards are played, and you're in my power. Like it or not. I even tried to warn you not to bargain, that the odds were against you. I told you how things would be, I gave you every chance—"

"I haven't had a fair chance all evening!"

"That's what happens when you set out to betray the king."

"You're not the king!"

"But you are in my power, and that's the way it is," he told her, thrusting her from him.

"What can any of this mean to you?" she cried in exasperation, warning herself that she must keep her distance from him. "The king sleeps, he cannot be bothered with me, so what can any of this matter—"

"It matters. And the king may be sleeping, but he is still waiting to see me. Regarding you. So, if you'll excuse me . . ."

He moved past her toward the door. She stared after him, tears stinging her eyes. She wanted to race after him and pummel him again, but she clenched her fists at her sides, afraid she had already dangerously tested his temper; and she didn't want him touching her in return. "Damn you!" she cried out with passionate loathing. "Damn you a thousand times over!"

He ignored her, and despite all her instinctive warnings and simple logic, she ran after him, clenched fists raised. She landed no blows, for he caught her wrists again, and held them tightly, generous lips tightly clenched into a grim line as he stared down at her.

She looked up at him searchingly. "Why are you doing this to me? Who are you?"

He paused, arching a brow to her, a deep frown burrowed into his brow. Then he suddenly smiled, released her wrists, and bowed to her deeply in a complete mockery of the courteous gesture. "Of course, how forgetful of me, we've not *formally* met. Strange, isn't it? I mean, we are beginning to know one another, aren't we? But as to your question, well, I am he, my lady. That awful man to whom you are to be given, my lady. That wretched, decaying, decrepit, old Norman, Waryk de Graham. However, my father was not a Norman, though there might have been some Norman blood—even Viking—in his veins. My mother was from one of the oldest families in the Lowlands. So you see, I'm not a wretched decaying old Norman at all, but a wretched decaying not-terribly-old Scotsman. Now, if you'll excuse me . . . ? I really must see the king. He has been deeply concerned regarding your whereabouts."

Oh, God. She'd never even suspected . . .

She was so stunned and dismayed that for once that evening she couldn't move or speak.

He turned and opened the door to exit the room, and still she couldn't move. She stood staring after him, shocked and shivering, her mouth formed into an O.

Then she found life. "Wait!" she breathed.

No. It couldn't be. It couldn't. After all that had passed between them. She should have known. She should have sensed, but it couldn't be, how horrible, please God, he was lying, it was a jest, a cruel jest . . .

"Wait!" she cried again, flying after him this time.

"What?" he asked sharply, pausing and turning back.

She stopped just inches before him, heart pounding, her breath coming in gasps. "You're not—you can't be. Please, don't do this to me. Tell me . . . the truth. You're taunting me again in revenge—"

He stepped back to her, capturing her chin before she could move away, his hold so strong she couldn't possibly wrench free from him. "There may be many things I would do for revenge, m'lady. But this is not one of them. I am Waryk, Laird de Graham, known as the lion, or Laird Lion. And you are about to be my wife. You're not fond of the situation—so you've advised me, and I must admit, I believe you, you've made your feelings incredibly clear. But I must tell you, you were certainly not my choice either, lady. And now that we've met, I can assure you that I find *you* to be headstrong, wayward, immature—and amazingly *foolish!* But the die is cast, and you will be my wife, and if you want war, I've spent my life in battle. Few men are better fighters. Do you understand?"

She wrenched her jaw free from the bite of his fingers at last, frightened and dismayed to the depths of her soul. "I'll see you in hell!" she whispered.

He smiled. "So you shall. If that's as you would have it, I can promise you that our marriage will be hell."

He turned again to leave her. She was still shaking. She shouldn't have spoken as she had. Perhaps there was still hope of ending it all if he wanted the marriage no more than she did.

"Laird Lion, wait—"

The door slammed in her face.

"Wait!" she pleaded again.

The only answer she received was the sound of a heavy bolt sliding into place with a thud.

"Please!" she whispered, leaning her head and hands against the door. But her plea had come far too late.

He was gone.

And she was damned.

# CHAPTER 8

Daro Thorsson was a proud man, a brilliant strategist, and a warrior brave enough to lead any advance. He was also, he thought sometimes, the last of a dying breed. For hundreds of years, his father's people had been the scourge of the seas. They had raided the British Isles, Finland, Russia, the Mediterranean, and gone down the Seine to threaten Paris itself. They'd made strongholds everywhere, and few places where they had roamed and raided were now left without Viking names, customs, manners, dress, and crafts. But the world was changing.

England, not so long ago, had been split into kingdoms; Alfred had risen to unite Wessex against the sea invaders, but even after he had first forced his nobles to fight against a common enemy, Vikings had ruled. The Danes had become kings in the north until mixed blood, as much as treaty or might, had stepped in to unite the country under Edward the Confessor. Scotland, too, had been a wild, divided place, with the heirs of one great man battling another for precedence. Northern outposts had islands that had been ripe for the taking. The invaders sometimes came in, plundered, raped, robbed, and committed mayhem, and then left. Sometimes they stayed, and in time, the people there forgot they had been the invaders, and the place was then left stronger for the presence of the new warriors breeding with the older stock. Many of the islands dotting the coast of Scotland, especially the north, were still ruled by Viking kings or jarls, and at the highest and lowest levels, intermarriages were frequent. It seemed strange to him sometimes that most men were so quick to call the Vikings barbaric since he'd yet to see much civil behavior between the English and Scots when they battled, and since all of the British Isles were peopled by different tribes—Angles, Picts, Gauls,

Scotia, Jutes, and more—and all the different tribes had waged war to make the land their home. No matter. The raids of long ago were ending, and it was becoming a more set if not a more civilized world. And the legends about the glory of going a-Viking were often stories that entertained and hid the fact that men went a-Viking because there was so little left for them at home. There was too little land for the food to sustain them, too few fish when winter set in, too few resources. Not that that mattered. The world was, he believed, a better place because of the Vikings, and he did have his little spit of land in the Irish Sea—nothing so grand as Adin's great isle, but a place to call home, a place to rule, a place to bring a bride—Skul Isle.

It was well into the wee hours of the night when he moved carefully along the hallway at Stirling. Despite his tall, muscled structure, he moved silently and with ease—life, though changing, had not been without its pitfalls and battles, and he could fight like a berserker or stalk an enemy with a tread as quiet as the flight of a falcon. He'd left Norway at the age of ten with his older brother Adin, and he'd learned from Adin, and learned well. Sometimes, there was as much power in silence and stealth as there was in any force of arms. Not that he was afraid of being accosted; he had a right to be in the hall that night. He and his men were camped just north of the city because he was here to negotiate with David. More land for more service to the king. His presence here would not be questioned; he was an invited guest this evening.

But he had waited until this time—just hours after the last of the merchants and tradespeople had closed down their shops and carts in the courtyard, and just a few brief hours before the farmers would come in with their produce and the fishwives would begin hawking their husbands' catches—because it was perhaps the only time when he might arrange a tryst within the confines of the fortress itself.

He strode the corridor with swift, silent confidence, but still, when he reached the alcove, he entered it carefully, searching the corridor for any other sign of life before slipping inside the break in the hanging tapestries. Once there, he barely mouthed her name.

"Anne?"

"Daro!" She breathed a reply and slipped instantly into his arms. He knew they were alone and he allowed himself the pleasure of simply feeling her warmth, of touching his lips to hers and reveling in the passion that instantly stirred to life. The emotion he felt still awed and amazed him. He'd known many women, some decent, some not. He'd learned the tricks of the whores of a dozen different countries. Sex was cheap enough in the cost of life, and to make their way in the world, prostitutes were easy as well. He'd never known that he could feel this simple thrill of warmth, that holding a woman could mean more than the final act, that he could, in fact, lie awake, thinking of a woman's scent, the flash of her eyes, the sound of her laughter, the very way she looked at him.

Of course, his love was not without lust. He mused that the architect of the fortress here must have had an illicit love for some damsel inside, for the alcoves were so perfect for such meetings as this, if only for this brief time of privacy long after the witching hour. There was seclusion, there was excitement, for there was danger here as well.

It felt that his blood pumped hot; she came to him so quickly, so eagerly. There were no words between them at first, other than the whispers of one another's names. The taste of her lips, the fire of their kisses led them to a swift and desperate fumbling with their clothing. He hiked her up: she wrapped herself around him. The very lack of time for tender play between them increased the rise of his urgency and her desire. That which was forbidden was often more exhilarating, and she delighted him with a sheer, bold, wanton hunger that matched his own. In seconds he had her back against the far wall, and her long legs were tight around his hips. She bit into his shoulder to keep from crying out as he thrust into her, and she locked herself to him with a trembling but steel-like strength as he spent himself in a swift thunder. The dig of her teeth sharpened against his shoulder as he drove into her hard, spilling his hot seed into her and precipitating the sudden shudder that swept her as she climaxed as well. She went limp against him, and the night, the darkness and the shadows, enveloped them for precious seconds as they both reveled in the wonder of each other. He was more aware of the passage of time than she, quicker to passion, and quicker to step back. He set her down, straightening her clothing and his own, yet before he had fully adjusted his breeches, she was back into his arms, her whisper now plaintive and agitated. "Oh, God, Daro, I don't know what we shall do, I won't be able to bear it, I won't, there has to be a way out—"

"Bear what?" he interrupted sharply, wondering what had happened since they had last stolen moments outside the great hall after one of the king's recent banquets. They had talked about marriage then, and the best way to bring the matter before her uncle, her guardian, and her family. She had been convinced at the time that they would meet with little opposition. Her grandfather might have been a jarl, but her father was dead, and she had been raised by her mother's brother and her stepfather. She wasn't a landed heiress, but her mother had set aside the small hoard of Viking gold and Celtic relics left her by her father, an adequate dowry when the time came for her to wed.

Her arms around him, she looked into his eyes. "Daro, they've decided that I'm to be given to the church!"

"Wait. They—who? How did this come about? There was no talk of you entering a convent before. What has happened?" Daro demanded angrily. He had wanted to go straight to the king with his request for her hand, but she had felt the need to speak with her kin first, certain they would never allow her to marry a Viking if she didn't make them understand that he wasn't ever going to sea again, and that he was as settled as any man who had come to Scotland to make the country his home.

"I never had a chance to say anything to anyone. Uncle Padraic came to my room here and told me that he intended to make arrangements for me to enter the convent of Sisters of Mercy, and that my dowry, given to the Church, would help atone for the vicious raids gone into the acquiring of it. Padraic is hateful toward the Vikings, any Vikings, he doesn't care if they're Danish, Norse, or Swedish. He thinks my father's blood has made me wild, and that the older I grow without the help of daily prayer and devotion, the greater danger into which I pitch my immortal soul. I'm also a danger to the good name of my mother's family—Padraic's family. I never had a chance to say a word to anyone. If I could have only spoken with Michael . . . but he is on the king's business. He would understand, he says that a man's belief and his loyalties make him trustworthy, not his place of birth. Padraic claimed that he has spoken to the king, and the king has apparently agreed with him that Viking blood is dangerous. David is afraid of Viking strength as well."

"I won't let them rule us. We'll run away," Daro said.

She inhaled sharply, she shook her head in misery. "Daro, we can't; the king's forces would come after you, you haven't the strength on your own to defeat his power."

"We can run far away. To the island, all the way to Norway, if need be."

"Oh, Daro!" She touched his face, and shook her head again. "I love you. I won't let you do that. This land means so much to you, I know that. You don't want to go to battle against the king—"

"I shouldn't need to do battle with anyone! My brother was Adin, respected, admired—and trusted."

Anne gasped again. "Oh, my God, Daro, I forgot . . . oh, dear God, I'm so sorry—"

"What?"

"Mellyora is here, in trouble. She said that she was to be wed to a Norman laird—though I had heard it was Waryk, Laird Lion, the king meant for her to wed. Perhaps it is he, and she thinks that he is Norman because of all the things said about the way the king found him as a child. She is probably not aware that he was more Scotsman than Norman. Or perhaps I am wrong, and it is another man the king planned on her marrying, I'm not at all sure. But she tried to escape the fortress," Anne said. "And she was discovered—in fact, she gave herself up to the king's men before they could have a chance to find me behind the tapestry. She said that I had to tell you that she needed you."

Daro lowered his head, closing his eyes for a moment. Damn them all. Damn the king, and damn Anne's self-righteous family. The Highlanders were little short of barbarians—even the most "civil" of the Scots and English practiced the most savage punishments and executions. And they would damn him for being a Viking. Anne's Scottish uncle intended to dictate her life, while he hadn't even been told about the plans made for his niece's future, while the king used her as he might any pawn. It was true that Mellyora probably did not know Laird Lion—she hadn't accompanied Adin often when he came to court, preferring to entertain guests at Blue Isle. If the king meant to reward his great champion, then Mellyora and the isle would be choice compensations.

Daro bore no grudge against Waryk. He had ridden with the man, and fought beside him at times. But if Daro and his kind, the Vikings, were to be held as pariahs, he'd be damned if he'd have no say in the disposition of his own niece, Adin's only child. Especially when so many of the loyal and trusted men in Scotland did have Viking blood themselves.

"Where did they take Mellyora?" he asked Anne.

She gazed into his eyes, obviously anxious. "She said that she didn't want lives lost, that she wanted help, but that you must be careful. She doesn't want your life, or your future, risked, Daro."

"Do you know where she was taken?"

She shook her head. "No, I heard Sir Harry's voice, and then the voice of another man. They were saying that she wasn't to be taken to the king, but to the laird—"

"Waryk's chambers. They took her there," Daro said.

"She'll be heavily guarded—" Anne said.

"There will be a bolt on her door, and one man left to see that an alarm is raised if she attempts to escape," Daro said. "She could not possibly escape, not without help."

"Daro," Anne said softly, "if you help her, you'll become the king's enemy. We'll have no hope—"

"As it stands, we have no hope. If I am holding my niece, and the king has plans for her, then there will have to be room for discussion."

"You intend to use her, the same as the king," Anne said unhappily.

"Not the same as the king. She's my brother's child. She's asked my help because she knows I will defend her."

"But if you defend her, we are lost," Anne said.

He gritted his teeth hard. "I don't know what Mellyora seeks to do. I won't know until I've seen her. I have no other move at this time than to help her escape, and give her my protection, of course. But to do so, I must get her out of here along with"—he paused, staring down at Anne tenderly—"with you," he finished softly.

Anne inhaled on a reckless breath. "All right!" she breathed. Then, quickly, "Nay, nay, it's not all right! The king will seek to kill you."

"We've no choice. Let's move, carefully, Anne. We'll see who guards her door." Daro pulled the tapestries apart and looked out into the corridor. "Meet me here," he told her swiftly, "tomorrow night. Keep your eyes and ears open throughout the day, I will do the same." He kissed her, and started to leave. He returned, kissing her once again with passion and promise. "Tomorrow night," he told her. "Trust in me."

The king drank wine from a chalice, staring at the flames in the hearth of his great bedroom. In warm, sweeping robes, he still appeared very much the warrior king, strong despite the elegance of his apparel.

"Eric Bloodaxe," he said broodingly, looking over at Waryk. "King of Northumbria less than two centuries ago. Cnut, who ruled much of England. Magnus, who seized much of Scotland." He stared at Waryk. "Adin was a most unusual man. Who could have foretold his death? And who in God's name would have thought that his daughter could escape with the skills of an acrobat?"

"She is returned," Waryk said smoothly.

"The banns are cried; the wedding takes place in two weeks."

"Do you wish to see her?"

"No. Where is she?"

"My chambers."

"And she was not plotting treason?"

Waryk was surprised to realize that he didn't want the king's wrath against Mellyora rising to any greater extent. "She simply wanted her freedom, that is all."

"Daro is here to negotiate Viking service, so he has said," the king mused.

"I've fought with Daro in your service. He is a brave man, and a clever strategist. He is very much Adin's brother," Waryk said carefully.

"He's a Viking. And I fear that he will be displeased if he discovers his niece's intent to remain free. Surely, she was seeking his help. You mean to tell me that Mellyora was not hoping to plot insurrection along with her uncle?"

"I don't think she would ever want to take up arms against you, no, sire." Was that the truth? She was willing to go far to escape her fate.

The king made a snorting sound and swallowed more wine. "I'm tired, and weary of her. But I warn you, what I've heard is that there's a young man from the coast land by the isle. And he has Viking in his blood."

"David, I've been told that I have Viking in my blood."

"I don't hate men for being Vikings," the king said. "I merely mistrust them. Well, my fair lass from the Blue Isle is back. You are apparently feeling more kindly toward her than I at this time."

"What shall I do with her? I think that my quarters are more secure, a safer place for her—"

"Do with her what you will," the king said. He shook his head. "I am disturbed by these attacks against the borders now, as you warned me I should be. I'm anxious to find out if Daro is as loyal as his brother. Attacks divide a kingdom. The border skirmishes keep me from watching the Nordic rulers to our north. Mellyora MacAdin had best take care . . ." He lifted his hands. "See to her; do what you will. If she causes much more trouble, she will simply be displaced."

"Pardon?"

"She can remain my guest forever," David said evenly. "In a dungeon, in a convent, wed to a Saracen with a dozen wives, I care not. I will not be defied, not even by my own godchild. If she commits treason, she will lose her head. I'm just, I'm merciful—but traitors die, and that is the law."

"I don't believe she means treason. The Vikings have been among us for centuries now, as enemies and friends. Your ancestors used the Vikings for their own aims, David. Malcolm II gave his daughter in marriage to Sigurd, the Norse earl of Orkney, and strengthened his influence in the north by so doing. Malcolm II extended many borders, if I may remind you, Scotland to the Tweed-Solway line, Lothian, the alliance of Strathclyde. It was through his daughter's marriage, however, that his might, that of the *Scottish* king, was felt across the land."

"I am aware of history and strategy, Laird Lion. And I am seeking strength through marriage. When alliances and peaceful means do not suffice, there is nothing left but bloodshed."

Strangely chilled, Waryk left the king soon after. He had scarcely left the king's chambers when he heard footsteps coming quickly behind him. He turned.

It was Jillian, Mellyora's woman.

She was anxious, drawn. "Laird Waryk . . ." she began, then paused. "Is she well?"

"She is tough as steel, as you know."

"Aye, but . . ."

He arched a brow.

"May I go to her?"

"Soon enough."

"Please don't judge her too harshly. She never thought her father could die, that there could be a different life . . . she doesn't so much despise you, but she has been in love, you see—"

"Aye." He studied Jillian for a long moment. "How far has this love gone?"

"Why, they've been friends since childhood, close, you see . . ."

"How close?"

Jillian looked at him, then grasped his meaning, and seemed horrified by all that she was giving away. "Oh, I don't believe that . . ."

"Aye?" he said sternly.

"I don't believe . . . I . . . don't know," she whispered.

"Thank you for your honesty."

"Please . . ."

"Aye?"

"Please don't hurt her."

"I don't intend to hurt her."

"You'll not . . ."

"If she loved this young man, then I am sorry. But I will have my own blood as my family, do you understand?"

Jillian looked at him and nodded. "I will be honest," she whispered. "I swear, I will tell you the truth when her time comes next."

He looked at her, and in so doing, was oddly touched. There must be something good in his rebellious bride to be if this woman could love her with such a deep devotion. "I'll trust in your honesty, sincerity, and the love you bear her," he said. "And you needn't fear. I bear her no ill will, I would not hurt her, unless she betrayed me."

"And then . . ."

"Then . . ." he repeated, looking at Jillian. The woman was worried and afraid. But then, someone needed to be. "Why then," he said lightly, "perhaps, I would beat her black-and-blue and throw her into the sea. Excuse me, I will let you know when you may be with your lady again."

He left Jillian and hurried along the corridor. He was tired, and he wished he hadn't left Mellyora MacAdin in his chambers. He'd had no sleep the previous night, but he wasn't going to sleep with her near now. He was far too fond of living. He'd speak with her and give Angus a respite now, then sleep in Angus's room while Angus remained on guard. When he woke, he would determine what to do until the wedding. She would be safe enough with Angus watching her—there was no way out of the bolted room from within. The windows in the knights' quarters were arrow slits, nothing more. Not even the slender Viking's daughter could escape through them. The only way out was through the bolted door, and Angus would die and destroy half an army before that would happen.

He wondered how far the king's decision had traveled. Did Eleanora know that he was to be wed to the Lady of Blue Isle?

He was sore and tired. He missed her touch. He wished that she could be with him then, stroking his brow, setting his flesh on fire . . .

Laird Lion did not return to his chambers.

Mellyora spent hours, pacing endlessly, jumping every few minutes, certain that he had returned. At one point, she tried to exit the room. The bolt was firmly in place. She swore, pacing again. The door opened, and the huge bald man smiled at her.

"My lady, is there something you need?"

"Could I possibly return to my own chambers?"

"I'm afraid not."

"I'm filthy, hungry . . ."

"We'll see to your needs."

"But—"

The door closed. She paced before the fire again. Soon after, she heard a tapping; the door opened. Angus was back, stepping into the room ahead of a small group of kitchen lads who brought with them a tray of food, a handsome hip tub, soap, towels, and endless pails of water. They came and went quickly, leaving the tray on a trunk, and the tub before the fire, steaming with hot water.

"Have I forgotten anything?" Angus asked politely.

"No, you're quite thorough, but I can't possibly make myself so completely at home in my Laird Waryk's chambers," she said.

"Ah, well, my lady, you shouldn't hesitate to make all that is Laird Lion's your own."

"I have no clean clothing."

Angus hesitated just a moment, then stepped into the room and opened a trunk at the foot of the bed. He drew a long white gown with delicate needlework from the trunk, offering it to her.

"Will this suffice?"

She hesitated, then said softly, "It's not mine."

"It is yours now, my lady."

She stared at him, amazed to realize that she was blushing because they both knew that Angus was offering her a garment that had been purchased for another woman.

"It's been worn by no one else," Angus said kindly. "I realize your discomfort, but you're not free to leave these chambers. Waryk remains with the king, lady. The day is wearing on, you do have a smudge of mud on your nose."

She lowered her eyes. "Well, then, thank you, Angus, for your kindness."

"To serve you, my lady, is my pleasure," he told her, and exited the room.

Once again, she heard the bolt slide into place. She moved uneasily about the room, looked into the flagon, and found it filled with a dark-brewed ale. She sipped it, found it rich and good, and looked at the tub longingly. He could return at any moment.

Then again, she'd already been down to bare skin in his presence.

Before she had known who he was.

Still, she was tired, anxious, and encrusted in mud. She would remain tired, anxious—even desperate—but she could do something about the mud. She began disrobing while she picked at the contents of the tray—smoked fish, bread, a sweet sheep's cheese. She drained a long swallow of the ale, and by then, had stripped down to crawl into the tub. The water was so hot it hurt at first, but then felt delicious. She soaked her hair, scrubbed away mud and river silt, and lay back, still encompassed by the steam. She opened her eyes and looked around.

The tub was rich, with hammered-silver trim. The tapestries that hung on the walls, warming the room, were crafted with care; they depicted hunting scenes, and she thought that they had probably come from the Continent, Flanders, perhaps Bruges. His bed was huge, piled with furs, bear, deer, beaver, more. There were numerous trunks about, and pieces of his dress armor leaned against the walls, or lay upon the trunks. A coat of shining mail was stretched over a rack not far from the fire, and she imagined a page had recently polished the mail to its shining glow. Laird Lion. Strangely enough, his standard was a bird, a falcon, she thought, very similar to her father's. She closed her eyes. Admittedly, he was not what she had expected. She'd heard of Laird Lion before the king had announced her disposal to him, all of Scotland knew of the king's champion, though he was a ruler with many strong knights loyally indebted to him. Still, she had heard that Waryk, Laird Lion, had ridden in with the Normans who had accompanied the king to Scotland when he had come with pageantry and strength to take his throne. She had thought him old, at least as old as the king. His feats in battle and tournament were beyond distinguished; he was, in fact, annoyingly perfect, according to the king's seneschal and the balladeers who entertained from great house to great house, through the Lowlands, Highlands, islands, and beyond. She had assumed that he would speak only the Norman French, that he would be . . .

Easier to escape, she thought woefully. He was not nearly so horrible in his person as she had imagined, but that didn't change the fact that he would take over her life, take her island, take her place. Destroy her happiness. She closed her eyes, remembering how she had assured Ewan she would love him forever. And what now? What mockery did this make of the tenderness and the friendship they had shared?

She heard the bolt sliding and sat up, hands gripped on the rim of the tub. If it were Angus, she had learned, he would politely inquire if he could enter.

And if it were not . . . ?

It wasn't Angus. The door was opening, and no one was asking her permission to enter.

She sprang from the water like lightning, sweeping a towel around her. In the corner of the room, with his armor, was a handsomely engraved claymore. She raced across the room, seized the claymore, held it in one hand and her towel in the other, as the door opened.

Waryk had returned.

She stared at him, cold despite the heat of the fire that burned to her back, plagued by hot tremors deep inside despite the cold that had seized her.

He looked at her, noting the bath, the towel, the claymore. He walked toward her with such a silent menace she felt a new fear.

Had the king been furious enough to tell him to kill her?

"Come no closer!" she warned, dropping the towel to wield the sword in both hands.

But he ignored her. Blue ice eyes on hers, he strode toward

her, despite the second warning she whispered as he came before her.

She didn't move, and he grabbed the blade of the sword, putting it flat against his heart. "Do it. Kill me."

"Stop it! I can, you know. I have the strength—"

"Then try it, if your hatred is so great—"

"I don't hate you! I don't want to hurt you, I—"

He thrust the blade away from his heart, then wrenched it from her hands and sent the heavy weapon spinning across the room. She felt her nudity keenly, but he didn't even seem to notice it.

"The king knows that you have returned, and you are in my keeping," he said. "And I am tired. Exhausted."

She didn't know what he was telling her, but she could feel her flesh breaking out in chills, her nipples were hardening to little peaks, her limbs quaking. She inched down to sweep up her towel again, so anxious for its cover that she quickly interrupted him, "Sleep, please, I don't wish to disturb you—"

"You won't. You may remain here, my lady. We'll talk later."

He strode to the door and paused, his back still to her. "Don't take a weapon against me again, Mellyora. If you do, you had best use it."

The door opened and closed. She heard the bolt scrape across it. She slipped to the floor, huddled in the towel, shaking. He hated her. Loathed her. Her future seemed more dire than ever. There just had to be some kind of escape! Not just because of her. Because of him. Because of his strength. His eyes. The way he looked at her. Because she could not wield a weapon against him, and because she was still shaking, so cold, and still, on fire . . .

Sleep was not easy to come by. He was exhausted. He tossed, turned. Dozed. Dreamed.

He allowed himself to dream of Eleanora. Gentle, a balm, a soothing ointment, she wrapped herself around him with her warmth, her whisper, her words. She lay beneath him, she rode him, hair teasing his chest . . .

Blond hair, golden blond hair. Long, thick, rich, luxurious, sweeping around him, entangling him.

Her hair was dark. Her eyes were sable . . .

Nay, they were blue. And in his dreams, he no longer lay with the mistress who so entranced him, but with the Viking's daughter, and she had risen above him, naked, a child of Wodin, her sword raised against him. He seized the weapon from her, struggling with her, and she lay beneath him. Huge, sky-blue eyes upon his, and he wanted to throttle her, take the sword to her throat, and he wanted . . .

He wanted to touch her.

Wanted . . . her.

Once again, she haunted his dreams. Only now, he knew her face, and her eyes, and she was tangible within his dreams, far too easy to touch . . .

# CHAPTER 9

Daro met Anne as planned. So much was at stake. He meant to share a few words only, but . . .

In the darkness of the night, his lips touched hers. In the richness of the shadows, he felt her love. He thought of battle, of bloodshed, of the times he had fought, of the king's anger, his wrath . . .

And still, he could not let her go.

It was later, several minutes later than he had intended, when they spoke, breathless once again.

"Have you heard anything new?" Daro demanded. "I've been told that she remains in Waryk's chambers, tended by Angus alone."

"Aye. They say that the king is furious with her."

"Are you afraid?" he asked her.

"Nay . . ." she lied.

He smiled. "Are you ready?"

"Aye, but I don't know my way in this part of the castle, or what it is I'm doing exactly . . ."

"Trust me. Come then, take my hand, courage!" He drew her with him to the tapestries, looking out on the hallway. No one in sight. They started down the corridor. Anne didn't know where they were headed; Daro did.

"Daro, this might be foolish!" she whispered breathlessly. "It would take an army to change the king's mind where Mellyora is concerned. Your brother's holdings were far too rich to be risked in any way. Oh, God, if they are afraid of my wicked ways if I were to marry a Viking, what would they think of Mellyora seeking the aid of her Viking kin? They will hunt you down. Once the king knows, he will want to kill you—"

He paused, pulling her into his arms, kissing her lips. "You are my life, well worth dying for."

"But I don't want you to die. I want you to live. I would rather become a novice and know that you lived, even with another woman—"

"We will work this out," he said, walking again. Then he suddenly pulled her against him, and they lay against the wall as he looked around the corner.

"Angus," he said softly. "Aye, it's Angus."

"You know him well?"

He inclined his head to her and offered her a wry grin. "The son of a nun from Iona."

"A nun—"

"And a berserker. His mother was raped by a berserker. He grew up in the wilds of the Highlands, where his mother lived out her days in happiness, it is said, with her barbaric laird," he told her. "Angus has followed Waryk since his family was slaughtered. A brave and loyal man, but a decent man." He paused, studying the situation. "Aye, a decent man!" he said. Then he smiled at Anne. "Give me a few moments, then—scream."

"Scream?" she said, looking at him as if he'd lost his mind.

"Scream," he repeated. "As if all the demons of hell were after you. When he comes to your aid, tell him you were startled by something in the shadows. Keep him talking for a few minutes, charm him, stall him, and I'll free Mellyora, and meet you at the southern archway, closest to the stables. We'll gather helmets and cloaks and ride out like drunken soldiers."

Anne moistened her lips. She opened her mouth to speak, but trembled instead.

"It can work, Anne."

"I know."

"One man—and woman—can often win where an army cannot."

She nodded again.

"Can you do it?"

"Aye. It—it can work."

He squeezed her hand, and slipped back down the corridor to approach Waryk's chambers from another direction.

"It can work, but what then?" Anne said softly aloud. But he was gone, and she had her part to play. She was terrified, wondering if she could manage to scream in all her fear. She tried once

. . . and all she got was a breathy sound that would not carry two feet. She tried again . . .

And her piercing cry echoed off the hallways.

She closed her eyes, listening as footsteps came pounding down the corridor.

She opened her eyes, her mouth dry, her lips forming words she couldn't speak.

Angus had come. Bald, scarred, as hardened a warrior as she could imagine. She didn't think she'd ever been so scared in her whole life. He would see right through her. They would discover that Daro had set out to free Mellyora, and they would all be accused of treason . . .

Racked, disemboweled, hanged, beheaded . . .

"Are you all right? What has happened? You are white as parchment, speak to me, lass, what has happened?"

The man looked like a maddened berserker, but he spoke with a gentle enough voice, and his eyes were full of concern.

"I'm—I'm so sorry!" she stuttered, and it was the truth. She was very sorry and very afraid. "I—I thought I saw something in the hallway. It was nothing more than my own shadow, an illusion created by the torch burning there."

The man looked around. "Aye, lass, there's no one about here." He frowned. "Who are you, and what are you doing up and about so late?"

"Ah, sir, I've been with an ailing friend, and now I'm making my way to my own bed. I tell you again, I feel a complete fool to have disturbed you." The lies were coming more and more nimbly to her lips. But did he believe a word she was saying?

"I'd see you safe to your room, lass, but I'm afraid I must remain here. You'll be safe enough. There's really no danger here in the king's hall at Stirling."

"No. No, of course not," Anne agreed. She smiled. "I scared myself, sir. A flight of fancy. My friend is Irish, and you know how superstitious the Irish can be, what tales they tell about pookas and ghosts and banshees wailing in the night."

"Go on, lass. There are no pookas haunting these halls."

She smiled at him radiantly and fled down the corridor.

Mellyora had been beside herself, trapped with a growing sense of fear and dismay, when she heard the sound of the heavy bolt rising from the door. Afraid that Waryk might be returning, she backed away from the door. But when it swung silently open and she saw Daro standing in the hallway, she uttered a little cry of joy. He quickly brought a finger to his lips. "Come now, niece, if you want no bloodshed—and not that I'd mind shedding a bit of blood in my present state of mind!—we must leave quickly and quietly."

Mellyora didn't need to be warned twice. She sped out the door and waited while he closed it and slid the bolt back into place. She started to ask him a question; he brought his finger to his lip once again and took her arm, indicating that they must move down the corridor. She nodded, and fled silently along at his side.

Long after the banqueting with the king's family, knights, court, acrobats, and musicians in attendance, Waryk spoke with the king again in his chambers.

He'd slept, but remained tired. He'd kept his distance from Mellyora, yet he'd begun to dream about Blue Isle, being laird of Blue Isle. Tonight the king looked more fierce, like a Highland chieftain, for he wore a rough fur coat thrown around his shoulders against the cold and he paced his room with a purpose, drawing imaginary pictures on the floor with his fire poker.

"This property can only be maintained by my most staunch ally, Waryk," David said, "for you see, here lies the island, and just across the water on the mainland lies the old Roman road connecting much of the Lowlands with the Highlands. The little bay is sheltered—the island creates a breakwater—offering excellent defensive positions against raiders and dockage for commerce ships. The castle on the island is impregnable; for the Romans, the legends say, it was their last bastion, the place they ran when they skirmished with Highlands tribes, but could fight no more. Troops under William the Conqueror seized it for a time, which was beneficial, since William's architects and masons rebuilt the walls and strengthened the structure. Mellyora MacAdin's maternal grandfather was the man who won the fortress back under my father's rule, and I do not intend to lose it again. If this fortress falls into the wrong hands, my enemies could spill into the country behind me—you'll note the proximity to my stronghold here." He paused, looking at Waryk. "I'm sorry. You've fought for me a long time. I had not intended to put an enemy into your marital bed."

Waryk looked at the king, started to speak, then hesitated. It seemed very strange. He could remember the night when he had first stood with a sword in his hand, while all around him, his kin and friends had lain dead. He'd expected nothing much from life except for the opportunity to avenge the deaths of so many. He had followed the king and become such a renowned warrior knight because he'd had a passion then to kill his enemies to purge the pain the night had brought. He'd known that one day the king would reward him, but he'd never imagined this. Sweeping lands, a fortress to defy the devil himself, cattle, sheep, artisans, masons, an entire feudal community. He was sorry about his bride as well, but for this great a prize . . .

Well, she could just rot in a tower, if that was what she so chose.

"We will come to an understanding," Waryk said.

"The wedding will come in two weeks' time now, for the night of the full moon. I want as many of my nobles and warriors—and even my enemies—present so that there is never any question about the legitimacy of the marriage."

"Two weeks' time," Waryk mused dryly. The night of the next full moon. When the lady in question had sworn to meet another man as payment in her quest to be free from him. "It seems a long time with the lady not my wife, and yet in my keeping. What do I do with her until then?"

The king was angry and his tone was as harsh as his words. "Chain her, drug her, tie her down!" he swore impatiently. "As I told you before, do with her what you will. Before the wedding, though, see to it that she is properly dressed and groomed, by her woman and ladies of the court. We will follow every tradition."

Waryk arched an amused brow. "Chain, drug her, cast her in a dungeon. Ah, sire! Would that be appropriate behavior for a bridal groom?"

"When she leaves your chambers for her own, I'll see that the windows are barred, no scaffolding is near, and that guards line the corridors." The king poured wine, bringing a chalice to Waryk. "To your future, sir. May God give you strength."

"You, sire, have given me power. May God help me wield it well." Again, he hesitated. "David, your ward is capable of being very stubborn."

"Of that I'm well aware. But I am stubborn as well. I'll drag her down the aisle to the altar."

"She may still refuse to wed."

"If she chooses to be that stubborn," David said, eyes narrowing, "she will suffer for it, as I told you before. If I'm forced, I will seize her lands and bestow them upon you. I will not lose land my father claimed back from William the Conqueror. I will not let it happen. Rather Mellyora should live out her days in a stone chamber in a deep, dark dungeon. And though I would be sorry, I do mean that."

David spoke with a gravity that was chilling, though Waryk could not believe that so just a king would deal so cruelly with a young woman.

"We might have difficulty there, sire. I'm certain the people of her homeland must be very fond of her. Her mother's family are the ancient rulers. Adin proved himself a just and mighty lord. To dishonor the rightful issue of those two—"

"It will mean insurrection, and it will mean that people will die, and that you will live a hell for years to come. But I will not let that property fall prey to any man who is not my loyal champion. Not with the English unrest, and certainly not when a Viking threat remains so close. You've seen why."

Waryk stared at David, and the king lifted his powerful arms in an expression of aggravation. "I wish the lady no harm, Waryk. But I am the king, and by God, she will honor me!"

"Aye, David. As you say."

"You may tell her where she stands in this."

Waryk decided that he must do so.

The truth of her situation might be the strongest weapon he could wield against her.

At the archway, Mellyora stood with her uncle, shaking, excited, afraid. She hadn't thought that he was coming, she hadn't believed that he *could* come. She had given up almost all hope of help.

She had spent so many hours alone! Waiting, terrified, defiant. She dreaded Waryk returning; then she grew angry that he did not. The hour came when she knew that all the fortress would have assembled for the evening banquet, and she knew that he would be there, while she remained a prisoner.

Then Daro had come. And his urgency had sent her into a burst of speed. Now, she waited with him, because they were not escaping alone, Anne was escaping with them. Theirs was a daring and bold plan, with no help available to them should they make any mistakes. They were on their own; she had to move with the greatest secrecy.

With each passing second, she grew more anxious. She was greatly relieved that they hadn't killed Angus.

She was terrified that they would be discovered, and that swords would be drawn.

And blood would be spilled.

"Why is she taking so long?" she whispered to her uncle, referring to Anne.

His face was stone hard, impassive. Then he bowed his head. "If she doesn't come soon, we'll have to leave."

"Oh, God, no, Anne is the one who made it possible for you to free me—"

"And you kept Anne from being discovered behind the tapestries," Daro said impatiently. He smiled as she stared at him. "Anne told me so," he explained. "If I leave here with you, I have regained some dignity. I have a right to a say in your life, while perhaps it's true that I have no right to Anne."

"Daro—"

"Mellyora, I'm going for the horses, cloaks, and helmets. Keep a sharp eye out for Anne. We have but one opportunity to escape."

"Aye, and we must escape now," she murmured. They had already fled Waryk's chambers, they were together, and on their way to the Viking camp.

Aye, they had to escape.

Escape, or die the death of traitors.

During the day, Waryk would never have noticed Anne MacInnish's behavior. He knew Anne, though not well, because she was distant kin to Michael MacInnish, the border laird on the spit of land where so many had been slaughtered by Lord Renfrew's greedy quest for greater gain. She had grown into a lovely young woman with large, doelike hazel eyes and chestnut hair, a lithe figure, and a talent for warmth and laughter. Tonight, however, she was behaving strangely, hurrying down the corridor with her head lowered and hands folded. Her eyes darted nervously side to side every few steps, as if she were certain she was being followed. He leaned against the wall, into the shadows, as he watched her approach.

It was ridiculously late—or far too early—for her to be up and about. And moving so furtively. He was both curious, and worried about the young woman, kin to his friend. And he was not anxious to return to his own chambers too quickly; he had kept his distance from Mellyora, but now it was time to explain to her that the king meant to have her disinherited if she didn't obey his orders.

He couldn't have her waiting in his chambers for two weeks, not unless he found somewhere else to sleep. He had mocked her, but was the one now paying a price. She was far too provocative, and he meant to keep his distance until he was certain that any child created within her would be his own. With Angus on guard, she was safe. From all men, he thought, including himself.

Indeed, the castle at Stirling was a safe place, yet it seemed that Anne was furtive, as if she was afraid. As she neared him, he stepped out of the shadows, politely accosting her.

"Anne."

She stopped dead, staring at him, her face parchment white.

"L—Laird Lion!"

"What are you doing out at this late hour?" Seeing a lover? It seemed the only feasible answer. She had always been a sweet, gentle young woman, but her family had sometimes treated her harshly due to the circumstances of her birth.

"I'm—I'm returning to my chambers."

"From?"

"From . . . visiting with a sick friend." She was lying, and she didn't lie well.

"At this hour?" he queried.

She lowered her head, then looked up at him. "I may not have much time left for the freedom to visit anyone at any time. Padraic has determined that I'm to be given to the Church."

She had definitely been seeing a lover, and, from the tone of her voice, he thought she had been seeing someone who meant a great deal to her. Young women were prone to fall in and out of love, and most often, inappropriately.

"You do not feel a religious vocation?"

"Nay, I do not," she said simply. "I wish to wed."

"Have you said this to your uncle?"

The white left her cheeks; color flooded them. She lowered her head again. "He thinks my father's blood has created something of a wanton out of me. If I enter a nunnery, I help purge the sins of the Vikings against the Church in this country."

"Men sin against other men, mostly, so it seems, and a man

who was not a Christian and didn't understand the meaning could not have been said to sin against the Catholic Church."

Anne gasped. "Laird Lion! That is all but blasphemy."

"I am not being blasphemous, Anne. I was raised in the Church. And many Vikings converted to Christianity; if your father had lived, he would have done so. But he was slain, and you should not be left to pay for his sins, real or imagined."

Her eyes were very bright on his, a glimmer of hope within them. "If you were to say such things to my family, they would listen. If only I could speak so to my uncle, make him understand . . . if only someone were to speak with Michael, since he is the head of the family. But he fights these days, and does little else, and he has left my future to Padraic. But he admires you so, if only . . ."

She broke off, as if she had said too much, as if she were suddenly confused.

Then her eyes widened with alarm as Jillian, Mellyora's woman, came rushing up. Seeing Anne, Jillian bit into her lip, standing anxiously at Waryk's side. "Laird Lion, I must speak with you. It's urgent."

"Aye, then, Jillian. Anne, we'll speak again. Perhaps, if you can convince me that what you're seeking is not against God or king, I can help you," Waryk said. He stepped back, allowing her to pass.

"Laird Lion, Mellyora is . . ."

The woman broke off as if she were choking. As if she couldn't quite draw in the breath to finish the sentence.

"Mellyora is what?"

"Gone again, sir!"

"How do you know?"

"I went to bring her some clothing. But—she is gone."

"That's impossible!" he said harshly. "A heavy bolt was slid across the door; Angus was on guard—" He broke off. Looking into the woman's eyes, he knew that she was speaking the truth.

"Angus would not let any man by him," he said, striding down the corridor with Jillian following behind him.

The door to his chambers stood open. Angus was within, knocking at the walls, searching under the alcove bed, swearing. He stood, facing Waryk, and looking very strange, for Angus was so huge, so fierce-looking a warrior, though a kind man. He had probably not looked so sheepish before in all his life. He had known the importance of guarding Mellyora, and Waryk had warned him that she was as slippery as an eel.

"Waryk, she's disappeared like mist on the moor. The bolt remained on the door when Jillian arrived, but she is not within, as you can see," Angus said. "I'd lay down my life for you, and you know that—"

"Aye, I do," Waryk assured him.

"She's slipped out of this room somehow."

"There are no exits," Waryk said.

"The chimney?" Jillian suggested hopefully behind them.

Waryk turned to her. She was a handsome woman with soft silvering hair, an oval face and fine features that would make her lovely no matter how many years passed her by. She was anxious now, and he thought that she loved her young mistress, but realized something Mellyora did not—the king had spoken. Her fate involved the defense and strength of Scotland, and, therefore, she was nothing more than a pawn.

"Jillian," he said, not unkindly, "if she went up the chimney, she is well charred, for there is a fire burning still."

Angus let out an oath of frustration. "The bolt remained locked when Jillian arrived!" he repeated.

"Did you leave the corridor?"

"Nay, ye know I'd not—" Angus began, then broke off. He shook his head. "I didn't leave the corridor, but I moved around the corner when I heard the woman screaming. It was a terrible sound; I thought we were being attacked—"

"What woman?" Waryk demanded.

"The lass, Anne MacInnish—" Angus began.

"Ah, Angus, we've been tricked!" he swore, exiting the room with long strides, his man following quickly behind him.

"Tricked? By a slip of a lass? She was alone, Waryk, I swear it—"

"Aye, she was alone. For her part in the charade!" Waryk hurried along the corridor, long strides carrying him toward the southern arch, the direction in which Anne MacInnish had gone when she'd slipped on by him at Jillian's arrival.

He burst out into the night, but saw no one. Rushing to the stables, he noted many empty stalls, which meant little, since the king's men were constantly coming and going, and were his guests. He saw Joshua, the groom who had taken care of Mercury earlier, sleeping in a bed of hay, and he stooped to shake the boy awake.

"Joshua!"

"Aye?" Slow to wake, the lad rubbed his eyes, then saw Waryk. "Laird Lion. I tended to your steed—"

"Lad, I'm not questioning your care of my horse. Has anyone been in here for horses?"

"Just the drunk Vikings, m'laird. Three of them, tumbling over one another, barely managing to get up on their horses."

"How long ago?"

"I . . . just moments, I think. I don't know. I slept," he admitted sheepishly.

"Where's Mercury?"

"There, Laird Waryk, I'll get your saddle—"

"There's no time." Waryk had already found the bridle and was striding for his horse. His affection for the animal was great, since the horse had taken him through many a dangerous battle and journey. "Once more this evening, my fine lad," he told the horse, slipping the bridle over his great muzzle. Then he leapt on his unsaddled mount and urged the animal forward. By then, Angus was standing with Joshua.

"Waryk! If you're going to the Viking camp, you can't go alone—"

"I don't intend to take on Daro's army of Norsemen alone," Waryk told him. "I hope to stop them long before they reach the camp. And if I do not . . . perhaps Daro's own means of abducting his niece is the one I should use as well."

"Waryk, wait!" Angus shouted, but Waryk knew that speed was all that could bring her back swiftly—and without incident—now.

At the gates, he called out his identity to the sleepy guards. He rode hard, knowing they were headed north along the river and that they would have to reach the bridge to make the crossing.

Twenty minutes of hard riding brought him to the woods that ranged around the bridge. The moon was dying, the first streaks of dawn were just a pink whisper against the gray of the sky. Breaking into the trail, he saw them just ahead. Three cloaked riders. Two were almost over the bridge. The third was falling behind just a little, and hadn't yet gained the bridge.

It was a woman, judging by her size and the way she sat her

horse. She had paused to look behind, to be certain that they weren't being pursued.

Mellyora. He couldn't see her face, but he recognized the cloak she had worn earlier.

He had her, he thought.

He nudged his heels against Mercury's flanks, and the stallion rewarded him with a renewed burst of speed. The thunder of hooves was so loud that she didn't hear him as he rode down on her. Accustomed to riding and managing the accouterments of battle and the joust, he had little difficulty overtaking her horse and maintaining his seat while reaching out—and dragging her from that animal to his own. She'd been too startled to resist, and held precariously in a side grip, she was quickly blinded as the voluminous folds of her hood fell over her face.

"Wretched witch! This time I'll chain you down!" he told her angrily. "You are far more trouble than you can possibly be worth, and if it were not for the king . . ."

He allowed his words to trail, his meaning clear. He reined in, quickly turning his mount as she gasped and stuttered her surprise. He ignored her.

Looking back, Waryk saw the other riders hadn't realized they'd lost her as yet. He nudged Mercury once again, and began his breakneck race back toward the fortress at Stirling. He wasn't a fool. He had her now. He'd have his arguments with Daro later. He wore no armor and was poorly armed, and he was almost in the lap of a Viking camp.

She was still sniffling and making strange moaning sounds— but not fighting. She was clinging to Mercury's mane, simply trying to stay perched atop the wildly racing stallion. Then, as they galloped, she suddenly twisted, trying to free herself.

"Sit still! Do you want to die beneath the horse's hooves?" he hissed to her.

"Please . . . ! Listen—"

He reined in, seeing that Angus had almost reached him. As he did so, she slipped from his grasp. He swore, reining in hard, dismounting, and racing after her. He caught her, tackling her upon a bed of leaves that lay between him and Angus.

"Mellyora, I swear—" he began.

"No, please!" came a tearful cry, and he realized, looking down, why his captive had suddenly become so submissive.

He had captured the wrong woman.

# CHAPTER 10

The fire burned with a bright, rich heat in Waryk's room; nevertheless, Anne MacInnish sat before its warmth, shivering. Waryk leaned against the mantel, watching her sternly. Jillian sat nervously by her side.

Angus leaned against the door as if he could add bulk and substance to it. He still couldn't believe that such a slip of a girl had earlier caused the same effect as if she had broken down the door.

"I—I knew that Mellyora was in trouble, that she was running from the guards. And she swore to me that she'd done nothing wrong . . ." Anne assured Waryk miserably. She moistened her lips. "I wasn't certain that you were the man the king intended her to marry. I mean, I'd heard such talk, but Mellyora said . . . well, she believed that she was to go to a Norman, someone no better than a second generation of William the Conqueror's men. We all know how horrible life became for the ancient Saxon nobility in England, and the Norman threat remains here against us at the border . . ."

"Anne, you've proven yourself quite remarkable tonight, but Mellyora knew just exactly from whom she was running," Waryk said quietly. "She has her own plans for the future, but they're not to be, and she's going to cause a war, and get many men killed—her uncle among them, if she's not careful."

Anne leapt up. "That's why you can't go to the king. Please, Laird Waryk, you mustn't go to the king. There will be a battle, men will die . . ." Her voice trailed as she looked at him, a true picture of misery, tears streaking down her face, her hazel eyes beautifully rimmed with red. "It would be a foolish war! Think how many historians believe that Harold Godwinson might have remained king of a Saxon England if he had not come north immediately before the Battle of Hastings to do battle with Norsemen! England is in such disarray, there are many English nobles possibly just watching and waiting for Scottish troubles so that they creep northward up our border!"

She suddenly threw herself to her knees at his feet. "Please, Laird Lion, I'm begging you, you're a wise man, a Scotsman, and you know people ... Daro loves Scotland more than his own home. Show mercy here, and reason, I will do anything, anything at all to keep this from turning into bloodshed, and I know that you ... that you have the strength to keep it from happening."

"Anne, get up," he commanded, catching her by the elbows and causing her to rise. He prodded her gently back to the chair where she'd been seated. "I don't want bloodshed either. I admit that I've watched Daro suspiciously, because he is a Viking. But he's a good warrior, an asset to the king against a common foe. I don't want to see hundreds of men killed and I, like the king, agree with your assessment—it's foolish to battle the wrong enemy. I don't want to see Daro dragged in for a traitor's death in retribution for the abduction of his own niece."

"Oh!" Anne cried, looking more ashen than she had.

She loved the man, Waryk thought. Really loved him. She would give him up before she allowed harm to come to him, and take any punishment herself. He'd seldom seen a love so selfless, and found himself eager to help the girl, despite his anger against Mellyora MacAdin's reckless determination and Daro's foolishness.

He stared into the fire for a moment.

"Perhaps there is a way to keep it all from the king," he mused.

"How?" she asked him.

He shrugged. "I'll have to go after her alone."

"Nay, now ye'll do nothing so heedless of yer own life, Waryk!" Angus said heatedly.

"I've no wish to die, not when great battle awaits!"

"Great battle ..." Anne said distressed.

"My marriage, Anne, is the battle to which I refer," he said wryly. "Angus, find someone we can trust to reach Daro with a message."

"Aye, Waryk, but I pray you'll set my mind at ease before starting out on such a venture!"

"Anne," Waryk said, "you return to your room."

"And do what?" she asked anxiously.

He arched a brow at her. "Go to sleep," he suggested.

"I will never sleep, I'm so worried—"

"Then go to your room and worry."

"But if the king—"

"I've told you that I'm not going to the king," he said harshly.

"But when he discovers that Mellyora is missing again he'll—"

"He won't discover that she's missing. He told me that I should do with her whatever I chose. We'll let it be assumed that she went with Daro with my blessing."

Anne looked at him, biting her lower lip, rose, and came over to him. She took his hand, and kissed it. "Thank you," she said fervently.

Waryk touched her chin, lifting it. "Don't be so grateful. I'm not promising you that I can make this work out, and, God knows, David has ways of discovering the truth of things that go on beneath his nose. Go to your room for now and stay there."

"What happens when morning comes?"

"Go about your business as if you're not involved in anything beyond being a guest of the king. And be patient. Give me time."

"Do we have time? If the king finds out the truth, if there is trouble . . ."

"There won't be trouble, Anne. Because we will be careful, and not let anyone know that anything is amiss. Trust me."

"That is what Daro said," Anne murmured.

"Daro is indignant about Mellyora, and in love with you," Waryk told her with a slight smile.

Anne studied him, then said softly, "She doesn't know what she's being offered. But you should know, Mellyora is loyal and has a courage I lack, she . . . she is only fighting for what she believes to be . . ."

"Her freedom and her lover," he said bluntly. "But it isn't to be. Go on now, I've much to do."

"I'll stay with Anne," Jillian said.

Waryk nodded, and the women left the room.

"Shall I follow them?" Angus asked.

"Aye, see them safely to Anne's chambers. I'll send to Daro, and speak briefly with the king—"

"Did you lie to the woman? Do you intend to tell the king

what has happened?" Angus asked, puzzled that Waryk didn't mean to keep his word.

Waryk shook his head, then smiled grimly. "I never give my word if I don't intend to keep it. I'm going to speak with the king, but mention none of this. At the moment, Anne and Daro have no greater friend than me."

Mellyora had been the first to realize that Anne no longer rode with them. She'd turned back, but been stopped by Daro. "No! We're nearly to the camp. I'll send men back."

"Her horse is coming, chasing after us. Anne must have fallen, perhaps she's been hurt—"

"She hasn't fallen."

"If she's been seized, we must seize her back!"

"If we ride back now, we could face an ambush," Daro said. "Then all would be lost. We keep going."

"Daro, we can't just leave—"

"Mellyora, we must keep riding."

"But Daro, you must—"

"Mellyora! I am not a fool, and I know how to wage battle, and when not to wage it! We ride to the camp."

She knew that he was deeply distressed, but he betrayed little emotion. Deep feelings of guilt and unease assailed her. This was her fault. She had made rebels of Daro and Anne.

As Daro neared the camp, he called out his identity, and two of his men, Ragnor and Thayne, came out to greet them, and help them from their horses. Daro gave quick orders in Norse for men to ride carefully back along the trail to the fortress at Stirling, then set an arm on Mellyora's shoulders, ushering her through the camp of makeshift wood-and-skin dwellings to the shelter he'd had built for himself. The Vikings were masters at temporary housing, using skills they had honed over centuries of invading foreign shores. There was a small room off the main structure of Daro's great room, and her uncle sent her there. A servingwoman brought her a small copper bowl so that she could wash her face and hands. The little room contained a handsomely crafted Celtic tub as well, and a pallet bed of rich, warm furs by a blazing fire. She wondered if he had meant this room for himself alone, or if he had believed that he might marry Anne at Stirling and bring her here. She longed to curl up on the deep pile of furs on the bed, but she knew she couldn't sleep yet. Anxious regarding Anne, she hurried out to Daro. He sat before the fire that burned in a large, stone hearth in his long room, deep in thought, a chalice of warmed wine in his hands.

"Have your men come back?"

"They have."

"What happened to Anne?"

"She is nowhere to be found, not lost or hurt along the trail."

"But no ambush awaited your men? There weren't soldiers out searching . . ."

"No. According to Ragnar, the prints show that a lone rider came and seized her. They were met by a second horseman while riding back toward Stirling."

Mellyora's throat constricted. "We were discovered missing just after we left . . . but your men met with no troops? They were not accosted? Daro, if the king is aware that you aided me in escaping . . ."

He looked up at her. "Then the king's troops should be headed this way."

She turned away from him, suddenly sorry that her world seemed to have escalated into such deadly drama. She really hadn't wanted blood shed on her behalf. But what had she expected? That she could hide behind Daro in her defiance, and the king would listen rather than draw his sword?

She hurried to Daro, coming down on her knees by his chair. "Daro, I'm so sorry, I was wrong, I shouldn't have come to you for help—"

His eyes, blue and clear, fell on hers, and he shook his head, smiling. "We're reckless, aren't we? You and I, it's part of what we are. You didn't involve me, I involved myself. I don't understand why we're not engaged in battle now."

"We've got to be ready. The king's men could be riding now—"

"I've men watching the roads. No one is coming."

"Then where is Anne?"

He sighed softly. "I'm assuming that it is Waryk who came riding alone, and seized her. He meant to take you, but I believe Anne is safely back at Stirling. Why David is not thirsting for my blood, I do not know."

"I've got to go back, Daro. Tell the king that what has happened has been my fault—"

"No. That will solve nothing. Men are watching the roads, and the bridge. I'll know if there is movement by so much as a gang of fishwives at Stirling. Get some rest. I plan to do the same."

"How can we rest—"

"We have to rest, because we can't reason intelligently if we don't. Please, Mellyora, go and get some sleep."

"I can't."

"You must."

"Daro, I've dragged you into this madness, no matter what you say. I've hurt you—"

"I made my own choices."

"I'm afraid," she said softly. "More afraid than I've ever been. I don't understand what's happening, why no one has come thundering down upon us—"

"We wait," he said, looking at her. "It's all we can do."

"All right." She walked toward the room where the inviting pallet waited for her, then turned back to her uncle. "But I will not risk your life for mine, Daro. I defied the king, and dragged you into it, and if there is a price to pay, I will pay it. I thought tonight, that if I could reach you, he would want to talk, that he would see strength. Well, the king knows your strength. I believed so fervently that he would have to barter. Now, I grow ever more afraid that there would just be slaughter on all sides."

"Mellyora, you are my brother's daughter, and that is something that the king forgot."

"Great Adin was his ally. And I'm his godchild."

"And I'm a Viking, while you're a Viking's daughter. Women are given, and that is the way of it, and once given, you are no longer a Viking threat. But I have been David's ally," Daro said passionately. "He has forgotten that as well." He studied his niece sternly. "It wasn't just my love for you that brought me into this, it was my outrage as well. Now we have begun this rebellion, and we can't go back. But you tell me now, and truthfully, what caused you to defy the king in such a manner?"

"I'm not trying to defy him, I just want him to listen to me—"

"Is this over your young chieftain, Ewan?"

She hesitated, but only for a second. "Aye. He's of that land, Daro. He's a Scotsman, ardently loyal to the king. If David would just listen to me—"

"He can't listen. Your Ewan may be all good things, but he isn't a trained knight, and he hasn't the strength to go against the king's enemies. He couldn't hold out against me if I chose to seize the isle."

"You underestimate me, and him as well—"

"Nay, Mellyora, I beg your pardon. The lad is brave and wise and many good things. Don't despair. Besides, I had heard that Laird Waryk was to marry elsewhere—perhaps he is no more eager for this match than you are. He has had a mistress for many years, a woman he enjoys and admires who, though not landed as you are, is of a good family. Maybe something can be done. I'm weary, and need rest. Please, go and get some sleep. There is nothing we can do until we receive some news from Stirling."

She nodded, and went on into the room. The servingwoman who had helped her earlier, a plump, middle-aged woman named Inga, came to her with another glass of wine. "It will help you sleep," the woman told her.

She lay down on the pallet, suddenly more afraid than she had been all night. She had believed in her own strength and will, and then she had believed in Daro's. Her uncle was strong, and proud, and that might mean that he would die to defend her. Viking legends were rich with tales of warriors fighting to the death, berserkers heedless of all odds, running naked into battle, determined to win or die . . .

Her own determination had been one thing. She hadn't the right to kill others, and she knew that the king could be kind, strong, and merciful—and she knew as well that he could be unforgiving.

How could she sleep?

But the wine worked wonders. She had lain there but a matter of minutes, certain her thoughts would keep her awake forever, when she found her eyes closing.

And her thoughts tormenting her no more.

That night.

But a day passed. And then another. And while Daro's men practiced at arms and Mellyora watched and waited and feared the worst, nothing happened.

Daro sent men into Stirling. Anne was well, and attending the queen, and went about her life as if nothing had happened. Banns had been cried for the marriage to Waryk. There was no word that the Vikings had done anything amiss, nor did the king have men preparing for war.

Mellyora was disturbed to find herself lying awake until near dawn, night after night. What was he doing? She was alarmed to remember his face too clearly, disturbed that images of him haunted her dreams. She could remember his voice too clearly, the way that he touched her, the way he spoke. And sometimes, she would be sorry that she had made such an enemy, and sometimes, she would even jolt awake, thinking he was near her. He wasn't a stranger anymore, she realized.

But what was he doing?

She took to practicing with Daro's men-at-arms as well, and Daro gave her an old sword, dug up from ancient grounds at Dalriada and said to have belonged to a Celtic princess during the time of the Romans. The sword was much lighter than the heavy ones she had practiced with throughout her life, giving her the advantage that she could wield it longer. It was strong as well, and unlike so many other such small weapons, she didn't think that it would snap as easily under an assault by a heavier weapon.

Another day went by. Stirling remained quiet, the people going about their business. There were preparations going on for her wedding. She had spent time with Daro, gotten to know more of his men, practiced, laughed, joined in their games, listened to the great Nordic tales of gods and goddesses and Valhalla. But while she had laughed and charmed and been charmed in turn, she had grown continually more uneasy. Some of Daro's men had suggested they move against the king.

"Nay, we wait," he had told them.

And Mellyora knew that they both believed they might have had a chance at Blue Isle, where the fortress could withstand months of siege. But if they made a move, they would be in open defiance. They would be at war against the king, not involved in any misunderstanding, and if all were lost, many heads would roll. It was better to wait.

She'd been with the Vikings almost a full week when she went to bed at night and realized that, while she had worried about Daro, she had been haunted by visions of Laird Waryk . . .

But not once had she thought of Ewan. When a man had entered her sleep, it had been Waryk. She had seen his eyes clearly, their piercing blue, she had seen his face, the way that he stood, and she had even felt his touch, over and over again, and a strange burning in the night . . .

\* \* \*

The messenger was first seen riding out along from the gates at Stirling at dusk, a single rider, unarmed, flying the banner of Waryk de Graham, Laird Lion, a great falcon flying against a field of blue.

It was late night when the messenger left Stirling, a curious time. Daro's men awakened him with the first news of the man leaving the fortress walls. Daro advised his men to follow the rider's progress and to report his movements.

The messenger might have been riding anywhere, but Daro knew that he was coming to him. What game was Laird Lion playing? Daro was aware that he did not need to negotiate, that if the king had commanded a marriage, Waryk had only to report that the Vikings had helped Mellyora escape, and every king's man would be at Waryk's command. A brutal loss of life would ensue, and even the king's strength might be compromised, but men were known to slaughter one another for less reason.

When the messenger crossed the bridge, Daro came to the front of his camp to meet him.

"I've come from Laird Waryk, unarmed, and seek your promise of safe conduct out of your camp," the man told him. He spoke the Norse language, not haltingly, but with assurance, and Daro was impressed that the Scotsman had chosen a Norwegian as his messenger. A courtesy in itself.

"You've come unarmed, lad, and you leave here unharmed, you've my promise," Daro told him. "What is your message?"

"I am to repeat Laird Lion's words to you alone, Laird Daro," the lad said.

Daro nodded, and his men allowed the messenger to dismount and follow him into his camp hall. Daro offered the man wine, which he accepted.

"Has Laird Waryk sent you to say that he has something—or someone—that he wants while I am holding the woman he is to wed? Does he seek an exchange? Tell him he puts me into a grievous position, for he asks me to deal with my own blood."

The messenger quenched his thirst with the wine and swallowed, shaking his head. "I am not here to threaten or bargain, Laird Daro. Laird Waryk acknowledges you as the Lady Mellyora's closest kin, and regrets the fact that you were not consulted. Naturally, your niece has the right to refuse to wed—"

"Naturally?" Daro repeated with a wry grin.

The messenger shrugged. "Ah, Laird Daro, she may refuse him. But the king intends that Laird Waryk govern the property, with or without a bride."

Daro started at that, surprised at the bold move to be made by the king. It would be an unpopular move—many men would grumble.

They would also be forced to realize that they all held their land of the king, and that power might be fleeting, and that all that was gained might be lost. The Normans might not have conquered Scotland, but their feudal ways had come here, and if Mellyora had been a male heir, as the eldest son of the laird she would have had far greater strength under the feudal law that had permeated much of their society, just as it had the English. But she was a woman, with few more rights than those of a child. She could not hold the land in her own name alone.

If she refused Waryk, the king would not choose a different husband for her, or allow one. He would simply seize the property.

Staring at the messenger, Daro exhaled softly.

"Does Laird Lion wish me to explain this choice to my niece?"

"That, Laird Daro, is your choice. Laird Lion will tell her himself, if you don't wish to do so. He intends to come here and retrieve her—with the king, he hopes, remaining unaware of the truth of her flight—and will do so. He awaits your invitation, and prays that it will come speedily."

Indeed, Waryk was awaiting his invitation. Daro's admiration for the man grew. He would avoid bloodshed—if he could. If he could not, he would come in full force, with all the power of a mighty king behind him.

"Laird Waryk wishes peace," the messenger continued, "and has no desire to start his marriage with the blood of his wife's kin upon his hands. He wishes to offer you a gift."

Daro arched a brow. "A gift?"

"Aye, the gift of a woman. Knowing your desire—and that of the young woman—he has been to the king, and to the MacInnish. He and Michael, chieftain of the family, have long been friends and allies. He has argued a case in your behalf, and so Michael has spoken with his cousin, Padraic, and with the king, and wishes you to know that you begin negotiations for a marriage contract with Anne MacInnish."

Daro was truly startled. Waryk was not threatening, blustering, or riding down on him with his sword unsheathed. He was besting him in a most unusual way—through a cunning form of decency.

"How do I know he is telling me the truth?" Daro asked carefully.

It could be a trick.

"Because he will bring Anne MacInnish with him when he comes," the messenger said. "And because he keeps his word; it is sacred to him."

Waryk had taken Anne, and he would bring her back, and the situation had remained quiet all these days while Waryk had spoken with the MacInnish and the king. Now, they could all go about their lives with the king none the wiser. Waryk wasn't demanding that Daro trade Mellyora for Anne, he was simply advising him that Mellyora would be disinherited, rendered penniless and bereft of her property, if she refused the marriage.

That would remain her choice. Daro didn't think that the threat of being stripped of wealth would greatly disturb Mellyora—he was not a penniless man, and she would remain welcome to his protection. But she loved her homeland, her island, even the cold, wild water that lashed the coastline between the isle and the mainland. She loved being the lady there, listening to disputes, settling petty problems, tending to the sick and wounded, and most of all, keeping art and tradition alive. Storytellers came often, though Mellyora could weave a spell when she chose to tell a story herself. It was said that though the Celts had once ruled and roamed Europe, it was in western England, Wales, Scotland, and Ireland that the survivors came after the great barbarian warriors fell to the superior strength of Roman weaponry. She knew the stories about the ancient warriors of her mother's people, Celts and Scotia, just as she knew the old Norse legends. She was Viking, but she was her mother's child as well. She could sing with a voice that was crystal-clear and enchanting, and poets and artists came to the isle just to see her. She was proud, Daro thought.

She would not give up her position as lady of the isle. No matter what it cost to keep her place. If she had run and defied the king thus far, it was because she hadn't realized that the king could and would take the isle from her.

"You may go back to Laird Lion," Daro told the messenger. "And tell him that I am grateful for the fact that he spoke on my behalf, that Anne will be my wife, and I will not forget his kindness. He may come here with his safety a sworn promise. I, too, keep my word; we are of different backgrounds, but my word is as sacred to me. I will look forward to greeting the great Laird Lion as an old ally in battle, as a friend, and as my blood by marriage."

The messenger nodded, pleased. "I will carry your words, Laird Daro."

Ragnar entered as the messenger left. "Threats? Demands?" Ragnar asked. "Do we prepare for battle?"

Daro shook his head. "Make sure that all men know that the king's champion, Laird Waryk, is coming here. He is bringing my future bride, and he is not to be molested in any way. Any man who accosts him will face my wrath and my sword."

"What of your niece?" Ragnar asked.

Daro shrugged and answered truthfully. "The king will confiscate the property and give it to Laird Lion without her if she doesn't accept the arrangement. David isn't planning on a great marriage between two noble houses—he is making a political maneuver, and he will not be stopped."

"Shall I have Inga awaken Mellyora?"

Daro shook his head. "Let her sleep, let her have what peace she can find now." He hesitated. "Sleep has been such a difficult state to achieve since this all began. We'll let her rest until he arrives. It will not take me long to explain the situation; she will not be happy, but at least, she may be relieved, because we have all waited now so long, expecting a battle which might kill hundreds, and make us outlaws forever, should we survive."

Word went out among the Viking camp that Waryk, Laird Lion, the king's man was coming. He was Daro's guest, a man many of them had fought with before, the king's champion arriving on a matter of personal and political expediency. He was to be greeted with respect and offered full hospitality.

Most of the men in the camp, aware since Daro's return with his niece that the promise of war had been in the air, were relieved. It was one thing to fight a border skirmish, another to put down open insurrection. But the world had already changed, and was still evolving. Daro had come here to speak with the king to grant them greater tracts of land. Though they were known for going a-Viking, at home, they were hunters and farmers, as fond of the warmth of a home fire against winter's cold as any man, as anxious for the simple abundance of hearth, wife, and family.

Most men, hearing the news, were relieved.

A man known to the Vikings as Ulric Broadsword was intrigued.

Born in Scotland of Nordic descent, he had joined with Daro's Vikings just days earlier with a small contingent of men. He could fight with the best of them, laugh easily, drink, and tell tales with bold, wine-sodden charm. He offered the group strength and hard work, and also, if necessary, the hospitality of his own home, southward toward the ever-disputed border with Norman England.

He had come to be close to the king and the events at Stirling. He had watched Daro arrive with Mellyora; he had seen how Daro's loyal men had set the camp on guard. And now, Waryk, Laird Lion, the king's great champion—risen from a snapping pup—was on his way. The implications were obvious. Waryk was to be given the property that had been ruled by great Adin through the heiress, Mellyora, the headstrong beauty made famous through the poems of many a roving *seneschal* or storyteller. Well, indeed, he'd seen the noble lass now, and the stories regarding her were not exaggerated—as stories often were to please the rich and noble.

The lass was a fair prize.

Aye, a fair prize, indeed. Delectable. And since they weren't going to war against Waryk and the king . . .

Seizing her would provide Ulric with infinite entertainment. Not that that even mattered. He'd have taken her if she'd been as ugly as a warted old hag. And he'd have had his way with her—even if he'd had to have blindfolded himself—simply because of who she was, and who she was intended to be.

But she wasn't ugly. She was as lovely as a goddess with her flashing blue eyes and sun gold hair. They said that she was proud, but pride could be broken. He had grown up with rage, and he had learned, and he knew how to break people—men and women.

Watching as the servants scurried about, cooking, selecting shaggy cattle to slaughter for a feast, he thought that his time to move was now. He motioned to one of his men, Han, and told him, "It's time to ride. Gather our men and meet me, with an extra horse, horses, at the southwestern entrance to the camp."

Han arched a brow. "What are we about, Ulric?" he asked.

Ulric waved a hand in the air. "Vengeance. Where is Adin's daughter?"

"In Daro's hall."

"With him?"

"I've heard that she sleeps in a little room to the side. She's not to be wakened until Waryk arrives."

"Is she guarded?"

"Daro's men walk the front, but this is a camp, not a fortress. She is not a prisoner here, she would not flee or fight her own uncle. She rests, in the side room, with only a servant woman to watch her. The hall is hastily constructed wood frame and skins, no more. I've seen the servant woman coming and going from a doorway of deer hide at the far left corner of the structure."

"Good."

"But what are we about? If there isn't to be a war with the king—"

"Then we will make one," Ulric told him. "We ride as I said. We go a-Viking tonight in a different way."

Mellyora thought that she should awaken; she felt a strange sense compelling her to do so, but she was so lethargic, she couldn't quite remember why. Sleep had been good, so very sweet. No dreams had plagued her, and she thought that maybe Inga had added some special herbs to the wine to help her sleep. The warmth of the furs had been delicious.

"Mellyora!"

The whisper of her name had such a sound of urgency to it that she was instantly aware of danger.

The room was still dark; though she thought that daybreak had to be coming. Beyond the small room, torches burned, and around her, in the camp, they burned as well, but the light filtering in was pale, and at first, all she saw was the form of a man at her side.

"Daro?" she whispered, fighting the lethargy that still held her.

"Nay, but I am your uncle's man, here to help you."

"What has happened?"

"The king has sent a negotiator. I am to spirit you away, until Daro can make his own arguments. We must disappear silently, do you understand?"

"Is it a pretense? My uncle is to be as surprised as anyone that I have disappeared?" she queried.

"Aye, lady, that is it, you must help me, we must leave in absolute quiet."

"Aye!" She rose, a little unsteady on her feet. He set an arm around her. She looked up. He was wearing a Viking helm, but no armor other than a leather breastplate. She thought that he was wise, for any mail or plate armor might hamper his movement and create a trail of noise to follow.

"Where are we going?" she asked.

"To safety, my lady. And we must hurry."

She could hear voices beyond the entrance to her uncle's long room; people were arriving at the hall, she realized.

"Aye, give me just a moment to dress."

He turned away. She swept a gown from the foot of the bed to slip over her linen shift, and reached quickly for her shoes.

"Wait. Wear this cloak. Pull the hood low, but walk tall. Come quickly."

She slipped on the cloak, and as she did so, she saw that her uncle's gift, the small Celtic sword, lay by her bed. As he walked away, she belted on the slim leather scabbard and slid the sword in place. The cloak blanketed her then, as she joined him.

He pushed upon a hide and she saw that it was not secured, but created a doorway. She slipped out ahead of him, wondering what Daro might have decided to say. Her uncle must have planned well, determining on agreeing to anything that was said, swearing that he would return his niece as he had been asked . . .

The camp stretched out before her. Fires burned in the night; men moved around them. Able builders, the landscape was dotted with their temporary homes, and wooden walls had been erected around the camp to keep out unwelcome visitors.

"Keep your head low."

"Surely, I need not be afraid. These are my uncle's men," Mellyora told him confidently.

"You never know who can be trusted, my lady. Fighting men come and go, and loyalties change. We are best to disappear with no one the wiser at all. These are dangerous times we live in."

Mellyora kept her head down, her face covered, and they were not accosted as they moved through the camp. They came to a breach in the wall where a group of men on horseback waited with extra mounts for her and her rescuer.

"Where is the guard? There should be a man on guard here," Mellyora said.

"My lady, the guard will return. It is expedient that I get you out of here quickly if Daro is to be able to talk."

"Where is Ragnar?"

"Ragnar is your uncle's champion in all things, and he is at Daro's side now, my lady. Please, you must trust in your uncle. He is fighting for you, don't fight against him."

"Wait, I will not have Daro going to battle over this. I don't want anyone fighting—" she began.

"My lady, I didn't mean that your uncle would be drawing his sword. He is fighting with his wits, but in order to do so, he needs to know that you are safe. Don't make this harder for him. You must hurry."

She looked around her; most of the men wore helmets with some fashion of faceplate, either metal or leather. A few wore surcoats over chain mail, some wore leather breastplates, as if they were prepared for war. There should have been a guard at the gate. She didn't know if she recognized these particular men or not because their accouterments were so concealing.

She stepped back. "I must speak with my uncle."

"There's no time."

The man who had come for her lifted her and sat her atop one of the horses. She was surrounded by them, she realized. There were more than a dozen men, they carried weapons, they were ready for battle.

"No—" she began.

The man who had come for her leapt up behind her. Anticipating his action, Mellyora spurred the horse. The Viking leapt up, the horse reared, neighing and snorting as he pawed the air.

But the Viking's leap was powerful and sure, and his arms were tight around her. She was certain for several terrible seconds that he would bring her crashing down to the ground with him, and there, together, they would be trampled and broken beneath the huge animal's hooves.

The Viking held his seat, and shouted to his men, "Ride!"

"No!" she screamed.

But the sound of her cry was seized by the wind, and carried away.

And they raced into the night, and away from her uncle's camp.

# CHAPTER 11

Waryk didn't expect any tricks from Daro. He rode to the camp with only a few of his most trusted men—Angus, Thomas of Perth, Rem of Wick, and Gerrit MacLyle—and, of course, Anne MacInnish. He had weighed the situation carefully. He might have returned Anne to Daro, and still been set upon by the Vikings, but he was certain that Daro wouldn't turn on him. Daro, he believed, was a man of his word. Daro meant to marry Anne, he wanted his children with her to be legitimate issue, and Waryk had offered him that chance. Pride and responsibility might have kept him from trading his niece for the woman he loved, but Daro was not a fool—he would not allow his brother's lands to be taken, as he now knew they would be, if Mellyora did not become Waryk's wife.

Waryk acknowledged the ingenuity of his Viking host as he rode through the camp to Daro's quarters within. History had proven the Vikings to be invaders, but where they settled, they were excellent builders as well. Most of the peoples who had emigrated across Europe and into the British Isles had brought with them their culture, their art, and their beliefs. The Vikings had traveled so many places that they had learned the best from many peoples. No one built ships like the Vikings, and they had transferred their building talents here, to this camp. Their temporary dwellings were finer than many a cottage he had seen upon a great estate.

Daro stood in front of his hall, framed in the light of a great fire which burned within it. He was a tall man, close to Waryk's own height, streaks of red flame in his blond beard and hair.

He waited while Waryk dismounted from his horse, then gripped his arm firmly in greeting.

"Welcome, Waryk, Laird Lion."

"Aye, Daro, I'm glad to come as I have," he said, nodding gravely. He could see that although Daro held his peace, he was searching through Waryk's mounted men for Anne.

"Anne . . . ?" Waryk said, turning back. At his invitation, she stepped forward. She tried to be circumspect at first, but when Daro let out a hoarse little cry, Anne rushed forward. Daro enveloped her in his arms, his eyes closing as he held her tenderly for a moment. Then he looked at Waryk. "I am in your debt."

Waryk nodded, acknowledging Daro's words. "I admit to being glad to seeing you together."

Daro smiled, looking down at Anne. "Your kin have agreed to our wedding?"

Anne smiled radiantly, flashing a quick glance at Waryk. "Aye, and we are indeed in debt to Laird Waryk. The king made the suggestion to my uncle that we would make a fine pair, and that he would bring your strength more tightly into his fold if we were to wed."

He kissed her forehead. "Anne, I can't tell you of my happiness. Ragnar will take you to your quarters while I speak with Waryk and Mellyora." He gazed at Waryk. "We are to be married soon?"

"Aye, the week following my marriage to Mellyora. Naturally, you are to renew your commitment to the Christian faith."

"Aye, that I'll do. If a Christian god brought me Anne, then I can bow before him. Ragnar?"

Ragnar offered Anne a hand. She cast Daro a last dazzling smile and departed with the huge warrior. "Laird Waryk?" Daro said, and bowed, indicating his hall.

Waryk entered ahead of Daro, aware that his back was exposed, but also that Angus and his men waited behind Daro. If there were any treachery here, they might die because of the overwhelming numbers, but they'd bring down a dozen or more of the enemy before they did so.

But Daro entered behind him and strode by him, pouring wine. "You'll pardon me?" he said, sipping from the wine. "I wouldn't want you to fear that we were trying to poison you."

"Not the Viking way," Waryk said dryly, accepting the chalice from Daro. "But I thank you for the assurance. You had promised my safety. I wasn't afraid of your men, or your wine."

"I didn't want the least suspicion to mar your enjoyment of my hospitality," Daro said. He drank from a chalice of wine he then poured for himself, watching Waryk. "What you have done is truly extraordinary, generous, and merciful."

Waryk grinned. "Not so, merely logical. I understand the king's fear regarding Vikings, since invaders do upon occasion continue to come from the Nordic countries, and create mayhem here from our own islands. But I don't see outsiders as our real enemy now. With the English schism creating so much bloodshed there, keeping our borders strong against Norman invasion seems the expedient course. And if David trusted Adin, then he should trust his brother."

"Ah, but he wanted you on my brother's property because he was afraid of it becoming a Viking stronghold."

"Your brother's property became very important with your brother's death. Vikings have too often ruled too many islands—they still do. David doesn't intend to lose Blue Isle. Its positioning is far too strategic. He needs it."

Daro nodded. "If the king had told Mellyora that she'd be removed if she didn't agree to the wedding, she'd never have tried to escape the arrangement. You might have been saved a great deal of aggravation."

"Have you told her yet?"

Daro shook his head. "But I will do so, now that you are here. She hadn't slept much for days, and last night—before I had received your message—I had herbs put in her wine to allow her to rest. But I will get her now, and explain the situation before she meets you."

"Inga!" he called, walking to the opening. A middle-aged woman with long braids entered at his bidding. "You must waken Lady Mellyora now and tell her that I'm coming in to speak with her."

Inga went to do as bidden.

"I'm curious," Daro said. "After all Mellyora has put you through, you might have chosen to have her set aside. I had, in fact, heard rumor that you were to marry the widow of a border lord."

"If I take the property without your niece, Daro, we both know that some men will revolt, and I'll have to kill them. I don't wish to kill people for their loyalty."

Daro nodded, and lifted his wineglass. "Well, Laird Waryk, I welcome you then, I thank you for your intervention in my life, and I pray that you'll remember, I do love my niece. And I hope that you won't want to kill *her* either."

Waryk hid a grin. "I intend no violence," he assured Daro, then added, "other than in self-defense."

Daro shook his head. "You don't know Mellyora."

"I feel that I am beginning to know her very well."

"Aye, well, she can be headstrong. But once she realizes her position, her home will mean more to her than anything. You'll see. Ah, there's Inga now. Is Mellyora ready to see me?"

The woman was obviously distressed. She glanced at Waryk, and spoke in her Norwegian tongue. "Mellyora is not there."

"Not there?" Daro said, frowning.

Was it a trick? Waryk wondered. Daro looked completely surprised and confused, but that could be part of an act.

"What do you mean, not there?" Daro demanded then. He didn't wait for the woman to respond, but walked across the hall, throwing open a partition to a smaller room with the personal trappings of a woman's sleeping quarters. Following behind Daro, Waryk saw that the side room was empty. He felt a curious tightening within him. An ivory-handled brush lay on a dressing table along with two dragon-headed, hammered-gold bracelets. He could almost breathe in her scent; the bedding was disturbed, as if she had just risen. He hunched down and touched the furs and linen sheeting on the bed. Still warm.

"Perhaps she has gone . . . to see Anne, maybe she heard you arrive, went for a walk around the camp," Daro said with lame confusion.

"Perhaps it is a trick?" Waryk suggested very softly.

Daro paused, his mouth pursed, as if trying to decide whether to draw his sword, or deny the accusation.

He opted for the latter, though his teeth gritted between words as he spoke.

"I swear to you, as I gave you my word, that it is good. I have not sent Mellyora away, and I am not hiding her. To what avail? You will gain your riches with or without her, and the death of a few men may be regrettable to you, but it will not change the fact that the king has given you the estate."

He was telling the truth, Waryk determined, even if the slightest suspicion still plagued the back of his mind.

"Ragnar!" Daro called.

The Viking's man quickly entered the hall. "Mellyora is missing."

"Missing?" Ragnar seemed as perplexed, as if he didn't comprehend the word.

"Aye, gone!" Daro said. "Search the camp, find out who has seen her, or any activity, she cannot have simply disappeared."

Angus had entered behind Ragnar. Waryk bowed his head just slightly, indicating that Angus and the others should follow the Vikings, and ascertain if the search was real.

Daro stared at Waryk. "I did not do this," he said. "Perhaps she heard talking . . . maybe she awoke when I didn't know it and heard people saying that I had invited you here. She may have thought that I was simply trading her to you for Anne, though that was a suggestion she had given to me. She's proud and reckless herself, but she never meant to put me at war with the king. She said that she wanted no bloodshed."

Waryk made no comment. He was of the opinion that Mellyora would have loved to see Daro shed a great deal of his blood, slicing and dicing him to pieces.

"If she ran within your camp, surely your men would have seen her. And from here, where would she go?"

"I don't know," Daro said quietly, and he sounded more concerned than he had before. "It would not be like her to run from me."

"Umm," Waryk murmured.

But at that moment, Ragnar came into the hall, heavily burdened by the bulk of the bleeding man he carried. Waryk and Daro quickly made way, and Ragnar laid the man down before the fire. He had been run through with a sword, and was bleeding profusely and was barely conscious.

"It's Oso, who was guarding the gates," Ragnar told Daro quickly. "He was attacked earlier."

"By whom?" Daro demanded.

Ragnar shook his head. "He couldn't say. The men were helmeted, and he was taken so quickly, he didn't recognize any emblems on the helms, cloaks, or shields, or surcoats."

Oso inhaled in great, gasping breaths. He clutched Daro's arm. "Men . . . many men. Rode . . . south. Heard . . . the crags at the loch. From there . . . want to reach the . . . border."

The man's eyes closed. He lay back, ready to die with his

message told. Waryk could see the fierce loyalty the man had given Daro.

"Inga! Staunch his wounds, call for help. Ragnar, guard the camp." Daro was quickly on his feet. "Laird Waryk, we ride," he said.

Waryk was already striding out, whistling for Mercury. Damn her. He didn't like the fear he felt. Had she gone willingly with a pack of fools pretending to be her uncle's men?

Had she known that they were false?

And had it mattered?

"Waryk, we'll find her," Daro said.

"Aye," Waryk said, mounting his horse, his eyes on Daro. "We ride together."

"I've ordered men to follow—"

"Aye, but we've little time. My men will follow as well, but we'll ride now, immediately, you, Angus, and I."

"Aye, we'll waste no time."

Was she in trouble, or simply creating more mayhem? Waryk didn't know. But if he got his hands on Mellyora this time, he was going to see to it that she didn't escape again if it meant chaining her hand and foot and casting her into the deepest dungeon.

The moon was high in the sky when they finally slowed their wild rush across the hilly countryside. Mellyora saw that they had come to very rocky countryside where great crags and boulders rose above a small, shimmering loch. The cliffs and caverns here, she thought, offered a natural protection against attack and a maze of hiding places.

"See to the horses," Mellyora's rescuer ordered, dismounting from the horse and reaching up to her. "My lady?"

"Don't touch me."

"Get down." He reached for her despite her protest, bringing her to the ground. Her instinct was to run. There were perhaps twelve men surrounding her. Now was not the time.

She surveyed her surroundings in the night. Caverns opened to the rocky shore of the loch. Men, and even horses, could disappear within the wild terrain of rock and crevice.

"Come," her unknown captor told her, reaching out a hand to her, "there's a place I know you'll be safe from the king's lackey."

"Where will I be safe from you?" she asked.

He smiled. "You don't know the Norman, do you?"

"I don't want a war. Who are you?"

"Your uncle's men, my lady."

"You're lying."

"Come with me."

He reached out, grasped her arm, and thrust her forward. She felt her sword against her thigh, covered by the enveloping cloak she'd been forced to wear. She didn't draw it now; it wasn't the time.

He prodded her along the bank of the shore to a rough path that led upward along a rugged crag. In the darkness, it was an eerie place, but she was accustomed to such wild outcroppings; the landscape could be very similar along the ocean where she lived. She knew this kind of crag. The rock could be jagged and then smooth; the formation might be riddled with little caves, some barely large enough for a fox, some wide and never-ending. A cool wind was whipping around her, and the clouds covered the moon. The sense of her own peril filled her, along with dismay that she had been so easily duped into helping with her own abduction.

"My uncle had nothing to do with this."

"Again, I tell you, you didn't want to marry the Norman lackey."

"You are trying to force a war," she said.

"There is always a war," he told her. "Take care, the going is getting rougher. Here, give me your hand. We can move more swiftly—we wouldn't want you to fall."

She pulled back, trying to stare at him, but his head was covered by his helm, and she realized that she would not know him if she were to see him again.

"No, I'm going no farther. Who are you? What are you trying to do? If my uncle is hurt or held responsible for anything in this, I swear, you'll die—"

"Ah, so speaks great Adin's daughter! But Adin is dead, my lady, and you are a girl, at my mercy."

She narrowed her eyes. "Don't make mistakes. I am my father's daughter!"

She was instantly aware that she should have thought more carefully. He pulled his sword, setting the point of it against her throat.

"I think, my lady, you will do as I say."

What a fool she'd been, believing in a man she'd never seen, and so furtive an escape from her uncle's camp. Who was he indeed, and did he dare kill her? Was she a pawn he needed for his own game?

"You're going to kill me?" she inquired, fighting her fear and speaking contemptuously.

"If you force me, my lady."

"Well, I don't wish to die, so I'll move on," she said impatiently, pushing the sword aside. She gathered the skirt of her gown and swept quickly on, her heart pounding ferociously. The ground was precarious here, but he might not be prepared for the fact that she was as surefooted as a goat and could manage the terrain—given half a chance.

She quickly kept going, up, searching the cliff. There were numerous trails surrounding it, some going higher, some lower. The rock formation stretched like a trail of giant boulders cast down from the sky. They lay in the shadowed streaks of moonlight like strange white, jagged teardrops.

"Are you even a Viking?" she asked sharply.

"Ah, well, yes and no, lady. Viking, Norman, Scotsman, what difference? I am my own man, first and foremost."

"You are a coward, stealing a woman, leaving Daro to take the blame."

"What difference does it make? He is betraying you, that is true enough."

"How?"

"Laird Waryk had arrived for you, my lady. That is the truth. Your uncle intended to hand you over in exchange for Anne MacInnish."

"He wouldn't make such a trade. If Waryk had come—"

"At your uncle's invitation."

"Then there was a reason."

"It doesn't matter. The lion may roar forever. You are one prize he will not be seizing. God knows, lady, he may be dead already. He comes for you in good faith, and you are gone. A Viking trick. Accusations fly, swords are drawn! Perhaps I've done you a greater service than you will do me. Ah! I can see it in my mind's eye, a wondrous picture. The great Waryk arriving with his part of the bargain, Anne, as promised. But alas, the Lady Mellyora is gone—vanished once again. A treachery, played out by Daro! Two such great warriors! Daro the Viking, Waryk, the Scottish king's great champion. A sword will be pulled in anger, they will each accuse one another of deceit and treachery and . . . one will lie dead. The Scotsman must surely die, even if he slays your uncle first. Because if he kills Daro, Daro's men will kill him."

She had moved carefully ahead a few feet at a time, feeling more and more sick at heart and desperately worried. She didn't dare dwell on what might have happened. She had to somehow escape this situation. She was grateful for having spent so much time growing up under her father's influence. The only time she was completely unarmed was when she was naked. She had taken her sword, and she carried a knife, as well. The Viking hadn't thought to make any attempt to disarm her.

"Why have we come here—if they will all be dead and accusing one another?" she asked.

"Ah, lady, we are away from the camp, but close enough so that we will know the outcome. Eventually, we'll head to the border. Perhaps, in time, I'll even take you home. And then again, perhaps Waryk will survive. If so, I will still have you. His prize. The lady of the land. To be bestowed on him for all the services he has rendered—all the deaths he has brought about. So why else would I take you into the cliffs alone? Dear Lady, that I may plunder all your riches—and take what would be Laird Lion's."

She was ahead of him now by several feet, and saw a trail leading downward that crossed onto a second crop of rock. She hurried on up a few steps, allowing him to come nearer, and when she knew he was on a bluff with an edge, she suddenly turned, shoving him fiercely.

He swore, stunned, and staggered back, his sword clanking and falling against him. She knew she hadn't done him any real damage, but she had given herself precious moments with which to run.

She did so.

Scampering over rocks, cliffs, outcroppings of grass, weed, dirt, and tenacious saplings, she kept moving. Downward first, upward as she saw that the rock just a few feet from her was riddled with dark caverns. She climbed higher, then cried out, pulled back as he seized hold of her cloak. She was captured, pulled inexorably downward. She clung to the rock above her at first; then, realizing that she was losing her hold, she allowed herself to fall. Her weight sent him flying backwards, but he quickly recovered, trying to straddle her. She reached for the knife sheathed at her calf, a small, ornamental weapon her father had given her, but—she prayed—sharp enough to throw him off once again. She had never felt so desperate, so sickened, and so afraid. When he leaned into her, she took careful aim at his side, knowing that she hadn't the strength to pierce the man's leather breast armor with her small blade.

She caught him in the ribs. He bellowed with pain, pulling back. She shoved him, and he rolled, and she was up.

He staggered to his feet, drawing his sword. She cast aside her cape, and drew her own. For long fierce moments, she fought for her life. He was powerful. She parried his every thrust, but she didn't know how long her strength or her slim blade would hold out. He raised his weapon for a lethal blow; she saw the movement, and swirled and swung upward, cutting his thigh, ducking his blow. He bellowed, hunching down with the impetus of his own attempted strike.

She shoved him, and he fell.

She ran, knowing that she hadn't the strength left in her arms to keep fighting. She headed swiftly along the rock.

"Lady, now I cannot tell you the torment I will inflict upon you, you will not begin to know mercy, I swear it. There will be nothing left of your pride and spirit when I finish, by all the gods!" he roared after her, and she was very afraid, knowing that he meant the threat.

If he caught her again, she'd have to kill him.

Or die.

She ran, escaping him for some distance. Then, praying he did not see her, she raced into one of the caverns. The darkness was, at first, overwhelming. She stood dead still, getting her bearings.

Then she moved more deeply into the shadows.

They followed the trail of the unknown outlaws to the crags by the loch, and there the trail ended. Waryk dismounted, and saw that someone had tried to erase the tracks by brushing the dirt with a branch. But the work had been hastily, carelessly, done, and he could see that the horses had been ridden toward a cave. He raised a hand for silence from those who followed, and mounted Mercury once again. He nudged the great horse, and they started for the cave. He was nearly there when he heard the high-pitched scream of a berserker battle cry, and suddenly, men on horseback stormed out into the night from the cavern by the water.

His mace swinging, a huge bearded man bore down on Waryk. He judged his opponent's speed and strength, and drew his claymore, ducking the blow of the mace and countering with his blade. The man went down on the wet earth. A second man charged him; as they clashed swords, he was aware that Daro and Angus, behind him, had taken on opponents. The enemy outnumbered them greatly; Waryk thought briefly that if he had been tricked, and if Daro turned and fought with the Vikings, he and Angus would be in serious trouble. He couldn't dwell long on the thought; staying alive was too fierce a preoccupation.

One after another, the enemy bore down on him. He used only his claymore, swinging right and left with all his might. The man he fought was wearing leather chest armor, but he wore a plate himself beneath his shirt and woolen tartan—he'd never trusted any man far enough to be defenseless. His opponent nearly found his mark, but Mercury was swift and sure, the horse's dancing steps sweeping Waryk just out of range before his enemy's great blade could slit his ribs. He nudged Mercury, and the horse's impetus allowed him to slice through his foe's leather armor, straight to the heart. The second man fell dead.

Waryk turned within his saddle to see that Daro was engaged in deadly battle; if he had been a party to this abduction, he was willing to slay his coconspirator. Angus, too, was involved in hand-to-hand combat, but just as Waryk determined to come to the aid of his friend, another man burst forth from the cavern.

Waryk nudged Mercury carefully, urging him hard to the cavern. Was Mellyora within?

He didn't reach the cavern. He clashed with the man just outside. The waters of the loch rose into the cavern and as their horses jostled for position, the cold water of the loch soared and sprayed around them. He thought that Mellyora must be inside. Anxious to reach her and determine if she'd been harmed, he fought with a renewed strength. His opponent fought with battle-ax and sword, but Waryk gave no quarter in return, slashing with a fury. He split the battle-ax, and his opponent threw it to the ground. Their blades next clashed; the ring of steel seemed louder than thunder. His next blow felled the man, catching him in the neck. He caught at his throat from where his life's blood gushed, and fell into the water. Waryk dismounted from Mercury, rushing into the cave, his sword still ready. "Mellyora!"

There was no answer, and he wondered wryly if she would come to his call, but though there were more horses in the cavern, there was no sign of Mellyora or any other men.

He rushed out, seeing that Angus had just slain his opponent and that Daro was bringing his sword down on the man he battled.

"Keep him alive!" Waryk roared, but he had cried out too late, and Daro managed to just slightly deflect his blow. The man fell, and Daro leapt down from his mount as Waryk rushed forward. Together they hunched over the dying man.

"Where is the Lady Mellyora?" Waryk demanded harshly.

"Who are you? Where is my niece?" Daro demanded in Norse. The man, aware he was dying, smiled up at him.

"Join me in Valhalla!" he cried, pulling a knife, and trying to slam it into Daro's chest.

Daro caught the man's wrist, deflecting his blow. The man stared at Waryk. "A prize no more, tarnished gold, taken, alas, me laird ... Viking's daughter, Viking's prize ... she'll not be yours, Scotsman."

"Where is she?" Waryk demanded, catching the man by his hair and lifting his head by it. "Where—"

The man didn't reply. He coughed blood, and died.

Waryk rose, swearing in frustration, and fighting the suspicion that Daro just might have killed the man to keep him from talking. "Waryk, there are more horses than there are dead men," Angus said, and indicated the cliffs.

"Aye!" Waryk cried. "The cliffs. The caverns in the cliffs."

"Shall I start here?" Angus asked.

"I'll move to the east," Daro said.

"And I to the west," Waryk agreed.

"Mellyora!" Daro called, but Waryk caught him suddenly by the arm, and shook his head.

"But we must find—"

"We must find her carefully. There are more men out there. We may need to see them, before they see us. They have Mellyora."

Daro fell silent, his lips pursed grimly. "Aye, then," he murmured softly. "We'll search carefully and quietly, until we find her. And the rest of the traitors within my own camp!"

"And when we find them—" Waryk said with tight anger.

"They are dead men," Daro swore. "They lived in my camp,

they broke bread with my men, and then they betrayed me—and seized my niece!"

"Aye, they are dead men," Waryk agreed. "But not until we know who they are, and why they have seized Mellyora."

Mellyora didn't know now just how far she had moved into the cavern. There was scarcely any light seeping in, but she moved back as deeply as she dared, wondering what kind of varmint might frequent the area. Wolves? Could they climb so high? She didn't know. What other manner of creature? Bears, possibly? If only she could see . . .

When daylight came, she would be in a better position. In this darkness, she couldn't see her enemy, and neither could her enemy see her. But daylight might serve her well, since she was nimble and agile in these crags. She could move swiftly while watching for the man. He could not move so well as he searched for her.

She sat against the cavern wall, knowing that he walked the cliffs, knowing that he sought her, that he longed to kill her.

Knowing that there were more of them out there.

She barely dared to breathe.

Eventually, she realized that she could dimly see the entrance to the cavern. Moonlight had escaped cloud coverage now, and she could at least see form and shadow at the entrance. She blinked, then stiffened as if she had been pierced through with steel—there was someone there.

She heard nothing. She waited, her heart racing. Had he found her? No, now there was nothing, nothing at all. Had she imagined the bulk of the man at the cave's entrance. Had it been a trick of the night, of the moon, of the fear she was feeling?

She closed her eyes, listening.

There, just the slightest sound . . .

Someone . . .

Moving. Near her. Carefully, furtively, in the darkness. Coming closer and closer . . .

If she didn't breathe, didn't move, would he see her, or know that she was there?

She caught her breath. She strained to see against the darkness. There was a shape . . .

Yes, there was someone in the dark space with her, she could hear his breathing, his pulse, the pounding of his heart. Closer, closer; this time, he'd kill her.

She could make out his shape. A man, hunched just a few feet from her. He was staring at her through the darkness. Could he see her, had his eyes adjusted so quickly? Oh, God, did she still have an advantage?

In seconds he would be upon her. She knew that she had to strike, and strike surely this time. Fear raced through her like lightning. She had but one chance. In the darkness, she might aim too wildly with her sword. She needed her knife. She reached for it, knowing that she had to sail at him with strength and impetus. If she wounded him, and did not strike surely enough to kill . . .

He started to move. He had seen her, sensed her, smelled her . . .

She leapt up with a bloodcurdling cry, her arm raised high for the strike. She flew at him, stabbing downward with all her strength.

He swore, rising opportunely. She missed his throat. Chest armor deflected her blow. She heard a ripping of fabric, but knew instantly that she had missed flesh. Swearing, shrieking, insanely panicked and certain she was about to die, she kicked, scratched, pummeled, and fought. But no matter how powerful and vicious her fight, he managed to battle her down and capture her wrists, and the knife was wrested from her. She was thrown to the ground, and he was over her, straddling her. She couldn't move, couldn't breathe . . .

"Damn you, be done with it!" she spat out. And she waited for a blade to slice her flesh.

# CHAPTER 12

No blade fell.

"Damn you, be done with it?" came a deep, husky query.

The voice stunned her. She wasn't about to die—she didn't think.

She inhaled on a deep breath, shaking. She hadn't known how dearly she wanted to live.

"Laird . . . Lion?" she whispered. She still couldn't see in the darkness, but she was growing very familiar with the sound of his voice, his touch . . . even his scent.

"Ah," he murmured dryly, and the suspicion he bore her was heavy on the air. "You didn't know?"

"Nay, you fool," she charged him, shaking. He was angry, yes, contemptuous of her, but she was going to live. "I didn't know it was you, and you should have said something, told me, warned me—"

"Ah." Now there was the slightest touch of amusement in his voice. "And you would have greeted me differently, knowing it was I? Pardon my confusion, but didn't you run here to escape me?"

"I thought that you were—that Viking."

"Which Viking? There are Vikings everywhere. I've even been told that I do have Viking in my blood as well, m'lady. And then, of course, we all know that you are Viking."

"And Scottish."

"A Viking's daughter," he acknowledged.

"Damn you, I thought you were the man who—"

"Abducted you. You didn't go willingly?"

The sound of his voice was humiliating. "Please," she murmured, coolly, politely, "if you're not going to kill me, will you let me up?"

"Soon. You've not actually answered my question. If you'd known it was I, would the greeting have been different?"

She didn't know how to tell him that yes, there would have been a tremendous difference. She wanted to live her own life, but she knew that he was a powerful, compelling man, the king's man, and he wouldn't hurt her unless forced to do so, while with the other man . . .

She had felt something that was mean, frightening. Evil.

"Aye, it would have been different," she said wearily. "I never tried to kill you."

"No? Not even when you struck me with the oar?"

"I've been fighting for my own life. I don't wish death on anyone."

"Really. What an enlightening thing to learn about you. But when you left Stirling with Daro, didn't you imagine the two of us engaged in mortal combat, swords clashing, cries of vengeance on our lips?"

"Nay, I did not!" she swore.

His sniff in the darkness was insulting, but she had no chance to tell him so because she heard movement from behind him.

"Waryk . . ." she warned in a whisper.

He was instantly up. He didn't seek to help her to rise because he had moved forward to use his body as a shield for hers. She leapt to her own feet, not knowing who came now, but aware that there had been enough of the enemy for her to want to take care for her own life. Inching backwards toward the wall, she found her sword. Just as her fingers closed around it, the first man burst into the cave, a deadly battle-ax swinging. She was amazed to see Waryk's deftness as he ducked the swinging death, swinging his sword around to catch the man in his midsection while his own impetus with the ax brought him inexorably upon the deadly sword, where he was impaled.

Two men followed the first, and as Waryk withdrew his heavy weapon from the dead man, she surged forward, meeting a sword thrust meant for Waryk's throat.

"Get out of here!" Waryk bellowed to her.

" 'Thank you, m'lady,' might have been appropriate!" she cried in return, but the man she fought was lifting his broadsword and striding toward her, forcing her backwards. She would soon be pinned to the wall . . .

A blow to the fellow's back turned him, and Waryk was fighting both men, his sword clanging again and again as he met every thrust of steel. The enemy were not fools; they braced to strike together, and despite his strength, Waryk's sword was tossed into the air by the strength of the blows. Mellyora stepped quickly forward crying out to him, "Here, Waryk, my blade . . ."

He caught her sword midair and turned, taking the unwary attacker on his left midsection and ripping him to his throat. He spun again, and his second attacker was split through the center. Both men had fallen.

"By God, damn you!" he swore, unreasoningly, Mellyora thought, to the dead men. She was shaking; the carnage was horrible. But she hadn't wanted to die herself. She had done nothing to them, and they had meant to torture and kill her.

"Why—" she began, but she suddenly heard her uncle's voice from beyond the cavern's entrance.

"Waryk?"

He was silent for a moment. She couldn't see his eyes, but she felt him staring at her, as if he could see her.

"Here, Daro, I've found her!"

"Alone?"

"Aye, she's alone now!" He reached out to Mellyora. She was shaking so badly that she couldn't have taken his hand if she'd been able to see it. He caught her hand, and drew her to him, and she was still trembling so wildly that she had to lean against him.

Impatient, he swept her up into his arms, striding the distance to the cavern entrance.

"You're shaking now—when you stepped by me to attack those men?"

"Aye, well, at the time, it seemed expedient to do so!"

Moonlight touched the entrance, and she saw that her uncle and Waryk were both covered in blood.

"Daro!" she gasped, afraid that he might have suffered some mortal wound. Waryk let her down, and she rushed to her uncle. He set his arms around her.

"You're injured!" she said.

"A few scratches," Daro assured her.

"A few scratches, nothing more. Yet there are many dead men down by the loch," Waryk said.

She felt dizzy, uncertain, afraid. She didn't know who the men were. She was truly relieved that Daro and Waryk weren't killing one another, and she didn't want her answers to cause an argument to break out.

"Dead men," she whispered.

"Aye, who are they? Who brought you here?" Waryk demanded. "How did they get you here? Willingly?"

Her lips were trembling. "The man—the man I thought to be coming after me again—said that he came for me at my uncle's command. He and his men were to slip me away while the two of you engaged in negotiations. But when I didn't see a guard, I knew something was wrong. He said—"

"He—one man spoke to you all the time?" Waryk demanded sharply.

She nodded her head, looking at her uncle. "Aye, one man. I'd not seen him before, and I—I wouldn't know him now. He wore a helmet. I'd know his voice—or his eyes."

"Traitors amongst my men!" Daro swore. "Living among my people."

Waryk was watching him, and Mellyora wondered if the king's man believed her uncle, or if he thought that this had been a trick played on him by the Vikings.

She inhaled on a sudden gasp, staring at Waryk. "He—wanted vengeance against *you*," she said. She felt a strange, hot tremor snake down her spine as she looked at him in the moonlight. Towering in height, spattered with the blood of his opponent, his eyes hard and bright upon hers, he seemed as indomitable as the rock around them. She tore her eyes from his and looked at her uncle. "I fought with him. And I cut him, and he said that Laird Lion wouldn't have his prize, that he would ... that he would torment me until nothing was left of me. He wanted the two of you to go to battle and cut one another down."

"After you fought ... ?" Waryk asked.

She looked at the blood covering them both. "I eluded him. I thought that he'd found me again ... You fought men by the loch—"

"Aye, but we've more horses left than men dead," Daro said.

"Some have escaped, on foot. Someone knows the truth of what has happened here," Waryk said.

"In these rocks, we could search forever," Daro said.

"Let's get down the cliffs, back to Daro's camp," Waryk suggested.

She felt cold, and still afraid in a way that she hadn't before. "What of the other men?" she whispered.

"They are gone by now, Mellyora. We'd have found them, between the two of us and Angus if they were not," Waryk said.

She was still unnerved. "So they are free somewhere. But who were they? They had to have known your camp well—"

"Aye," Daro interrupted angrily, "bands of warriors sometimes come and go from loose alliances such as the Vikings who fight with me, but I've never known of such a treachery. I don't know any of the men we killed, though they certainly may have been at the camp. I'll send men to retrieve the bodies. Perhaps someone will know more about them."

Mellyora was still shaking. She was afraid to look at Waryk, though she felt his eyes, watching her, studying her, probing her soul. Determining that she and Daro were both liars?

She realized then that she'd been rescued by the man she'd been trying to escape. She'd also tried to stab him, and must surely have come close to his jugular. She had tried to beat him away with an oar, and she'd drawn his own claymore against him. Not that much else she'd done since they'd met could be construed as nonviolent.

He'd formed a friendship with her uncle, and she was glad that they hadn't gone to battle, that they hadn't killed one another, or that her uncle hadn't died for her honor.

But she was very afraid that Daro had agreed to trade her for some boon from the king. He wouldn't do so! she told herself passionately.

But her uncle and Waryk had ridden together after her.

"Fine, let's go down," she said nervously. She turned away from the men and started to descend, hurrying with greater speed as the downward trail brought her closer and closer to the level ground below.

She was fast, but Waryk moved with equal speed. He didn't speak, and she didn't intend to, but finally, as they neared the ground and the loch, she could bear it no longer. "Have you traded Anne for me?" she queried bitterly.

"Hardly an even trade," he murmured.

"She hasn't vast lands."

"She hasn't a knife for a tongue," he returned sharply.

"Did you make a trade?"

"No."

"Then where is Anne?" she demanded.

"At your uncle's camp."

"Then you're lying, you did trade—"

"Nay, lady, I did not. Anne and Daro have nothing to do with you."

"Oh?"

"We can speak later," he told her, seeing Angus before him with the horses.

"Thank God, the lady is safe!" Angus called.

"Aye," Waryk agreed briefly, turning to Mellyora. "Can you ride?"

"Of course."

Could she? She walked to the horse she had ridden, but before she could mount, Waryk was at her side. "Let's not take any chances, shall we? Ride with me."

She lowered her head, then took a deep breath and spoke in a whisper without looking at him. "I don't intend to run again. I'm exhausted, and there's nowhere left to go. And you would only run me down again."

"Perhaps not. You'll be given a choice of what actions you may wish to take, but until then, ride with me. I am only thinking of your exhaustion, and your well-being, my lady," he said. When his crystal gaze touched hers, she knew that he was lying. He didn't trust her. He never would.

But neither did it matter. He lifted her in his arms and set her upon his horse before mounting behind her. She was tired and unnerved, cramped, sore, and cold. She closed her eyes, and she would not admit it in a thousand years, but she was glad to rest against him, to feel his warmth and strength at her back.

They made the ride back to Daro's camp in silence, and there they were greeted warmly by Daro's men, Waryk's, and Anne. She was anxious, dying to demand of Waryk and her uncle just what was going on, but she was given no time with Anne, or her uncle or Waryk, who were both ready to bathe away the blood they wore. Mellyora realized that she was muddy and bloodied herself, sore from her fight and flight. Inga ushered her into the side room and again saw to her needs. Hot water filled the copper tub, and despite her anxiety and concern, she sank luxuriously into it. She washed her hair, and Inga helped her dry it. She was bathed and soothed, re-dressed in soft linen and warm wool, and given wine to drink.

And then he was there.

Bathed and refreshed himself, resplendent in his tightly knitted wool and sweeping cloak, he stood before her, a handsome, hardened man who seemed incredibly impatient now, and would give no quarter. "It was my choice to bring Anne here, and no part of any bargain. As to you, Mellyora MacAdin, you are not required to marry me."

"What new taunt is this? You've pursued me mercilessly, and now we're not to marry? Are you jesting?" she inquired.

He shook his head gravely, then a slight smile curved his lip. "In fact, should you wish to marry me now, you'll have to ask me, and nicely, m'lady."

"I will never choose to marry you," she said, stung by his hard tone.

She didn't know if his smile became more grim, or if she imagined it. "But this is the king's edict—the island and property formerly held by Adin are now to be held by me."

"I—don't understand," Mellyora said.

"Ah, well, m'lady, lands are held of the king—of course, a laird's might and heredity do come to play in all situations. Adin held that land *of the king*. The king now chooses that I shall hold that land. With or without you, m'lady. And my dear, precious, beauty, without you seems to be my personal preference at the moment, I do assure you. I leave in the morning. If you've anything to say to me, do so before then. A wedding is planned, but alas, God knows, many such events never occur. Good night, Lady Mellyora."

He inclined his head and departed, dismissing her completely.

Waryk joined Daro in the hall by his fire. Daro had been seated in one of the carved chairs positioned before the fire; as Waryk joined him, he rose, offering Waryk a chalice of wine.

"You've told her."

"Aye. The choice is hers."

Daro nodded. "There's only one choice my niece will make. If she had only realized how far David would go . . ." His voice trailed away. "The bodies of the dead men were brought here to camp. My men tell me that those we killed joined our group less than a month ago. One of my men told me that he found them an odd group, that their language was slightly different."

"You mean they were not Norwegian?"

"Perhaps not, or perhaps they had been living among the Normans or elsewhere. They spoke Norman French, our Norse, the old Gaelic, even the old Saxon, but there was an accent on their Norse, as if they were not accustomed to being among only their own kind. It's very strange."

"Indeed," Waryk agreed, drinking his wine. Interesting. If this were all true—if Daro and Mellyora were both completely innocent of conspiracy in her last flight, then something was strange—and dangerous. She had said that the man meant to take her—possibly kill her—to deny him a prize. Someone, perhaps, who did not realize that he would take the property with or without a bride. Few men knew that—Angus, himself, the king—and he had told only Daro, and now Mellyora.

"It's very unusual for Vikings to betray Vikings," Daro said.

Waryk arched a brow. He'd known Vikings to take mercenary positions with the troops of numerous men.

"Not in this manner!" Daro explained. "Danes have gone to war against Norse, Norse have fought Swedes, and so on. Men have had battles over land and women. But it's unusual for Vikings to live among Vikings and betray them without a word." He swore softly in his effort to explain. "We are warriors, our battles are open, we challenge one another with our strength, we are not men who plot and plan and undermine."

"Aye, leave the treachery to us!" Waryk said, lifting his cup with a wry smile. He finished his wine, and rose. "I'll accept your hospitality and get some sleep, Daro. It's been a long night—and a strange one, as you say. I might well have enemies; it would be good to discover them."

"The leader is gone, the others are slain. I wonder where to look from here," Daro said.

"If I have an enemy, he will show his face again," Waryk said.

"What will you do now?"

"Well, I will return to Stirling tomorrow."

"What of Mellyora?"

"I will return with or without her. I've told her the king's command. She may now do as she chooses."

"Aye, then," Daro said and nodded, and Waryk left, eager for a night's respite. Mellyora had made the last few days busy and wearing.

Daro was a fine host; he'd offered Waryk the use of pleasant sleeping quarters, an old stone sheepherder's cottage which, though not large, had been cleaned and repaired by the Vikings. A pallet heavily laden with furs had been left for his use, the chimney cleaned. Wine, bread, and cheese had been left for his comfort, and with Angus and his men gathered beneath a lean-to that stood not far from the cottage, he dared sleep while awaiting the morning.

Angus and the others were ranged around the fire in front of the lean-to. He bid them good night and entered the old cottage, a place of privacy. He shed his cloak and stretched out by the fire, laying his sword at his side. He helped himself to the food, then studied the flames in the hearth as he drank the wine. He wondered what move she would make next.

Strangely, he had never seen her appear more vulnerable than when he had left her now. Freshly bathed, she smelled sweetly of roses. Her hair, newly washed and dried, glistened around her like a halo of gold. Her eyes were luminous, large, brilliantly shimmering as well, caught by the light of the fire. She had seemed weary, delicate, feminine, gentle, even fragile . . .

Umm, fragile as rock, gentle as a kiss of steel, he thought. Did he dare trust her after all that had happened, after she had told him that she was desperate to elude him? Had she really suspected that he was an enemy out to kill her—or did she consider him equally as wretched as any outlaw, and had she hoped to slice his throat in that cavern tonight? For that matter, had any Viking ever threatened her? Had they been with her in her quest to escape him all the while? The questions were endless. They all involved truth, and trust, hard commodities to come by. Was Daro involved, had the leader simply run when he had seen that his fellows were falling dead?

He didn't know.

But the next play was up to the lady. He had done all he could. Now, in truth, the choices—whether she liked them or not—were hers. He closed his eyes, listening to the snap and crackle of the flames. *Aye, the choices were hers, the king had made it so. Whether she did or didn't choose to marry, he'd be engaging in battle, either with her, or the people on the island, and at that moment, he didn't know which he'd prefer. He could assure himself that he had made the right moves, stepping in for Daro and Anne, giving Mellyora the cold hard truth of it. Could he ever really sleep in his own bed without wondering if he'd wake to a knife at his throat? Yet he kept seeing her as he'd left her, a snow queen with her glittering hair and eyes, and the look of an angel. . .*

He rose with an oath of impatience and poured himself more wine.

After assuring herself that Waryk was gone, Mellyora burst out on her uncle. "It can't be the truth, Daro, it can't be. The king can't just take what is mine—"

"Mellyora, the king is strong enough to take what he chooses. And you have forgotten the Norman way. You are a woman. You can't hold that property."

"It was my father's. If I can't keep it because I'm not a male, then it should be yours—"

"Ah, but Mellyora, he held the land because of your mother, not because of his family. Your mother could not hold the property, the king granted your mother and the property to your father— admittedly, your father had a fair hold on it when the king granted it to him."

She stared at him a long time, then sank into one of the chairs before the fire. Two huge tears formed in her eyes, and fell upon her hands, like diamonds in the light.

"What am I to do?" she whispered.

"Make a choice," Daro told her softly. "Ewan loves you, I'm certain. You will not be without recourse if you choose not to accept the king's ultimatum."

"People will revolt—they won't just accept the king's Norman ways!"

"Aye, they will," Daro agreed. "But I imagine that a revolt will be put down quickly and harshly to prevent any further insurrection."

She rose, spinning before the fire.

"If you love young Ewan enough, your choice is clear," he told her.

She hunched before the fire. "I love the island as well. It's been my life, it is my heritage. He knows nothing about it. He has never seen it! How can the king so blindly and blithely give away what is mine?"

"He sees the country as his, Mellyora."

She stared at him suspiciously. "And Waryk simply decided to bring Anne here—to you. Her family would happily have burned all Vikings to a crisp, but Laird Lion speaks, and she is delivered with full blessings!"

"He has a way of making men see reason."

"Not women!" she said angrily. She wondered if most of her wrath at this moment was directed at him, or herself. If she'd loved Ewan, really loved him with all the poetic nobility she had thought, she would give up all hope of heaven for him. And she did love him. But not with the blinding fervor she had believed she had. She knew that she would not give up her island. She would never watch another woman take the chamber that had belonged to her parents, see another walk the halls with their exquisite tapestries and hangings. She clenched her hands into fists, hating herself that these things meant so much to her. But she loved the chapel and the market, and she was glad to settle the little disputes, watch the children grow . . . The people would be hurt, some men, loyal to her, could protest, and in their protesting . . . die.

She stood. "What do you advise, Daro?"

"Does it matter?" he asked her. "I think that you've made up your mind."

"You don't dislike him," she said sharply.

He walked toward her. "Did you want to see the two of us engaged in battle for your rights and honor?"

Her eyes lowered. She shook her head. "Nay."

"So you would have my advice. Marry him. Young Ewan is a fine lad, but he isn't the man the king needs. You hate Waryk not for the man he is, but for the manner in which the king ordered him to command you. He is in a strong position, but a pawn as well. No, I do not dislike him. I admire him. He has played this game well, and might prove himself the real victor."

"How can he lose? He holds the power. The land—with me, or without me."

"Aye, think on that. With or without you. He could easily choose *without* after all that has happened."

"We were not guilty tonight!"

"But try to prove it."

"You know the truth!"

"I know it, as do you. But try to prove it."

Mellyora stood very straight, agitated. She paced before the fire, then, with an oath, she started to leave the hall.

"Mellyora, where are you going now? There's no need for you to run, if you say that you do not want to marry—"

"I'm not running. I'm going to Waryk."

"Perhaps you should wait, and give yourself some time. Think about what you're doing—"

"No matter how long I think, my choices will remain the same," she said desperately.

"Mellyora, I must admit, if I were the king, I could not think of a better warrior to hold Blue Isle than Waryk."

She swallowed hard, wondering why it seemed that this logic worked for everyone but her. "I must go. If I tarry any longer, I'll never go," she said softly, and she hurried on her way.

He still sat surveying the blue flames that leapt in the hearth when he heard a tapping on the door. Then his name was called, and he knew her voice.

"Laird Waryk?"

He rose, opening the door. She stood there, still as angelic as she had been, lustrous hair free and cascading down the length of her back. Staring at her, he admitted again to himself that Adin's daughter was a fair prize. She possessed a rare beauty, flawless skin with no pockmarks, and all her teeth. She stared back at him, and he knew why she had come. Daro had known her well. She would not give up her homeland. But now, though she had come here, she still seemed unable to speak.

"Come in," he told her, not at all ashamed to feel pleasure at her discomfort after all the tumult she had caused. "I'll pour you wine. It will help you swallow down your pride."

"You're wretched," she told him.

"You don't want the wine?"

"Aye, I want the wine!"

He poured it and indicated the furs on the floor by the fire. "Sit, join me."

She didn't sit. She took the chalice from him and swallowed the whole of it before sinking down to sit and stare at him blankly still.

"More?" he inquired. "You do have a great deal of pride to swallow."

"You are being detestable."

"Not at all. I'm trying to help," he said, refilling her chalice.

She accepted the second serving of wine, swallowed quickly. She closed her eyes, and said, "I'll do this thing."

"Oh? What thing?"

"Oh, what thing!" she repeated bitterly. "Marriage." She sipped more wine, staring into the fire. "You must understand, I had other plans. It is my homeland. I know it, I love it. You are a usurper."

"I am a warrior," he said huskily. "Such a land needs a warrior."

"There are other warriors," she murmured. Then she forced her eyes to his and made a great effort to be civil. "Perhaps we can learn to be civil to one another. The fortress is a very big place. We can fulfill the king's wishes, and keep our own souls. You'll have your chambers, I'll have mine. It can work, we can do it."

He watched her incredulously. He stood, placing his chalice on the rough stone mantel. He turned and looked at her, crossing his arms over his chest. "No."

She stood, wobbling a little as she rose, staring back at him. "What do you mean, no?"

"No. I'll not have such a marriage."

"But . . ." She let her voice trail; then she inhaled deeply. "You have a mistress, a woman whom you love."

"Aye, and thanks to your refusal, I could marry her if I choose."

"The people would despise you."

"Ah, but I am a patient and reasonable man. In time, they would not. *Now,* you, my lady, you had other plans so you say. Have you taken a lover?"

Her cheeks flushed to a rose color and her lashes fluttered and fell.

"You know that there is someone else I wanted."

"Well, then, have him."

Her lashes rose, her eyes met his. "You say that you are a reasonable man. You have been clever. You've delighted Anne and Daro, and my uncle now believes that you are the right man to be laird of my property. Fine. We need only stay out of one another's way—"

"No, Mellyora. It will not be that way. If you want this young man, have him, but you'll not have me as well."

"But—but," she stuttered, "you said—"

"I said no. First, milady, I told you that you must ask me—and nicely—to wed you. You've not made any real requests—you've certainly not been nice—and you've attempted to dictate what you'll have."

"I've been reasonable under the circumstances—" she protested.

He shook his head, both amused and determined. "The circumstances are that you're at my mercy. An interesting position after all the trouble you've caused. So ask me nicely. And I'll consider your request."

Pale as ash now, she stared at him, speech refusing to flow from her. She spun around ready to exit the cottage, but he caught her arm and dragged her back, amazed himself at the savage determination that suddenly filled him. She was not going to best him. He would not allow her to complicate his life. "Humility, my love, is an excellent quality. A touch of it will do you very well."

She cast her head back, hating him with her eyes.

"You are a despicable Norman lackey, no matter what clothes you wear, no matter how you speak."

"That's not nice at all," he said politely, but a warning was in his tone and grip.

She lowered her head, bit her lower lip, and stared back at him, her eyes still on fire. "Indeed, noble sir! Will you be ever so kind as to marry me and allow me to remain on my own birthright?"

"Better," he said, his eyes as hard on hers as the touch of his hands. "Not exactly humble, but better."

"Well?" she cried.

"Never."

"What?" she cried, outraged. She tried to jerk free from his touch. He pulled her closer.

"Maybe. But not on your terms."

"Oh, God, if you'll just listen—"

"No, milady, you listen. A marriage, legal and binding, creates legal issue. I will have sons. So you will marry me, you will be my wife, and there will be no bargains, terms, or conditions. It will be as I say."

He felt her shaking, and he almost felt sorry for her. Almost. He could too easily remember her very real attempt to kill him tonight—even if she claimed she had thought herself facing a different enemy.

"Well," he repeated harshly.

"Aye . . ." she whispered, barely finding breath.

"Aye—what, milady?"

"Aye, it will be as you say!" she snapped angrily.

"Fine." He released her, and turned away from her. "I wish to leave by midmorning. The wedding is planned for the following day—king and countrymen in attendance. Go and get what sleep you can."

"Aye, m'laird, just as you say, m'laird!" she cried, spinning away from him. She stumbled, as if afraid he would reach out and touch her again. He did not. He let her go. Yet as he did so, he suddenly realized that he, too, was shaking.

It would not be a terrible hardship, taking her as his wife. Indeed, anticipation grew hotly within him, and he was disturbed to realize just how much he did long to touch her again.

He'd have to watch his back, every minute of his life, he warned himself harshly.

Aye . . .

Indeed, he'd have to take care. But he was suddenly anxious to have her as his wife, whether she chose to be friend or foe, and whether he found himself forced to house her in a tower, dungeon, or cell.

After all, he didn't care where he visited with his bride. As he had feared, it seemed that battle had begun.

# CHAPTER 13

At midmorning, as they prepared to ride, Waryk warned her that the king was unaware that she had fled the fortress at Stirling with Daro. If she hadn't been quite so angry, she might have thanked him for the courtesy of his silence, but she did not. Daro had surely done so. And her uncle was as irritating as the man to whom she would shortly be shackled by vows of marriage. He was so pleased to be with Anne. They were to be married in the chapel at Stirling the following week, and were so blissfully happy that they were entirely annoying. She was the only one left to suffer the teeth of fate, she thought.

Yet she couldn't help but wonder about Waryk, and she was curious about his mistress, if he really loved the woman, and how he had managed to accept the king's commands without protest. She bit her lower lip, aware that he probably intended to keep his relationship with his mistress. He was simply separating his life. He would have his wife, his title, his land, and his family. And he would have his woman on the side.

Yet, Mellyora thought, it was true that he could have rid himself of her—if the king thought she had conspired with a Viking enemy, she'd be lucky to keep her life, much less her title and land. She didn't deceive herself that Laird Waryk was intrigued with the thought of her as a bride, but neither did she want to accept the fact that he'd been willing to set aside his own desire to marry elsewhere for the peace of the people he would govern.

As they rode back to Stirling, he kept his distance from her. Watching him, she felt a tremor snake down her back. She was the one who had been adamantly opposed to him as a husband. He had accepted her as a wife. He had come for her again and again—but he avidly disliked her. Marriage seemed a more and more chilling concept.

As they neared the walled fortress, she urged her horse forward, closer to his. She knew he saw her, but he didn't speak to her. "Waryk?"

"Aye?"

"Where does the king think I've been?"

He glanced her way. "What?"

"Where does the king think I've been? If he was unaware that I left the fortress with Daro—"

"He knows that you have been at the Viking camp. With Daro. I told him that you left with my blessing to spend time with your father's brother before becoming my wife."

She didn't reply, thinking that he was a clever man, he had weighed this situation, and he was even capable of being decent at times. He was not the Norman she had expected, no matter what words she used against him.

Nor old or decrepit in any way. Yet his very youth and prowess made her nervous now, and she wished with her whole heart that the wedding might be planned for sometime in the far future. He wanted sons. Most men did. For all the courage she could sometimes display, she was dismayed by the prospect of intimacy. She knew that Anne did far more than chat with her uncle behind the tapestries, but she'd never envisioned such a relationship herself, not even with Ewan. They'd laughed, they'd kissed, they'd lain in the grasses with their heads on one another's laps, touched, and dreamed. But she'd never felt the stirrings of a great, earthy passion, and had likened her love for Ewan to something finer, like the romantic love of the poets.

She knew so little. He was experienced, a warrior accustomed to battle, different places, many women—and a mistress with whom he had been deeply involved.

"Well?"

She felt color flush her cheeks as she realized he was looking at her.

"Your pardon?" she murmured.

"A 'thank you' might be in good order," he told her.

"Thank you," she said flatly.

He studied her a moment longer, then urged his horse ahead. She bit into her lower lip, wishing she didn't become so defensive with him so quickly. It occurred to her that she should be a bit more politic herself. She could still find that she no longer belonged to her homeland.

*Yet what of Ewan? What of their hopes, what of their dreams, the vague beauty of a relationship founded in the deepest friendship, respect, love, and belief?*

Ewan would live on, remain chieftain of his family, marry elsewhere, and be gentle and kind and all wonderful things with another woman. They would sit before their fire, he would prosper. While she . . .

While she paid the price to remain lady of her isle. That was the way of it. She had made the choice.

They reached Stirling; the guards hailed them. In the courtyard, she politely allowed her groom to help her down. To her dismay, David came from the castle, every inch the warrior king in his Scottish wool. "Mellyora!" He reached for her hands, taking them in his own. He spoke with the affection of a father, yet she sensed an edge to his voice, and she knew that he had not forgiven her. "You look well and rested. Daro will arrive for the ceremony? It is just two days away now."

"Aye, sire."

"And you and Waryk are well met?"

"Oh, aye, well met," she murmured.

"Then all is well. Ah, and here is Jillian, ready to escort you to your chambers. We'll have your meal sent, and you can spend the evening resting and readying yourself for the wedding. Father Hedgewick will be your confessor, and will attend you this evening as well. Run along now, my dear. Tomorrow will be a big day for you."

The king set his hands on her shoulders and kissed her forehead. "Go now."

She did so, longing to look back and see Waryk's expression, and what exchange might come next between him and the king. Somehow, she kept from looking back.

At least she would be away from him for a while. She wouldn't need to argue, to attack, to bite back defensively. She could rest in peace.

Yet she wasn't to have a chance at the peace she had hoped to achieve.

"Sweet Jesu, child, but you have been reckless!" Jillian told her. "Heedless of consequences—"

"I thought I could win. If I had won, I would have been brave and admirable. But I did not win."

"You were not brave and admirable because you fought a battle you could not win."

"I didn't know that the king meant to disinherit me entirely from my own ancestral lands!"

"Then you should learn to judge your opponents better," Jillian warned her. Then, looking at her, she sighed softly and put her arms around her, hugging her. "Oh, Mellyora, it will be all right, believe me. I have come to know him, it will be all right . . ."

She hugged Jillian in return. She didn't say what she was thinking. She was coming to know him as well. And he had come to know her. And he didn't like what he knew. And if it weren't for Ewan, and for the fact that the circumstances had made them such enemies . . .

And if it weren't for the woman he loved . . .

There were too many "ifs." It wasn't going to be all right.

She survived the next day with dignity. It was late when she sat next to Waryk at the king's table in his great hall. His friends and fellows teased and congratulated, ladies of the court admired her knight and wished her well. They would all think her insane, she realized, for trying to run from such a fate, and married, and unmarried, they flirted boldly with Laird Lion, and she found herself disturbed to realize that though he might have loved his mistress, he had probably known a number of other women as well.

In turn, she did her best to be dazzling and charming. She flirted with the young men, and the old. She didn't even distinguish between men of the ancient Scottish races, or of the new Norman aristocracy. She didn't eat. She drank too freely. She knew her eyes were bright, that she moved like a hummingbird, afraid to be still. At the table, she felt him watching her. She refused to meet his gaze. She saw him smile at others, watched his hands as they curled around the chalice that sat between them. His features were striking, his fingers were long. His voice was deep, and she felt strange tremors each time he spoke. She was miserable. She wanted her life back. Absurdly, at the same time, she was haunted by thoughts of his life. She wanted to run more than ever; he fascinated her. She was strangely afraid of his touch, yet she was dismayed to realize she was wondering what it would be like. They had never been together as they were tonight, speaking civilly, surrounded by others. She had never watched him laugh and talk with others before, never seen the respect he drew from men, or seen the way that women looked at him.

Finally, the awful night ended. Thankfully, she had drunk enough to sleep. The next morning, she had a headache. She prowled her room, until the day grew late. She stared longingly out a window.

Jillian, far gentler that day, came to her. "There's a bath for you by the fire, the water is hot, I've tended it. It's filled with rose oils from the Mediterranean, and will soothe you. I'll bring you warmed wine touched with cinnamon. Rest tonight, ease your soul. Tomorrow will be a difficult day."

Mellyora was glad to settle into the steaming water, breathe its fragrance, and while doing so, close her eyes and drink the hot, sweet, subtly flavored wine. How was she going to endure the days to come? How could she get through a wedding ceremony with a man with whom she'd done nothing but violent battle since she'd first encountered him? No matter the strange rush she felt when she was near him, how could she bear to let him touch her when she would know that he would be wishing himself with another woman?

Dear God, could she really be jealous? Of a woman she didn't know?

"Mellyora, I'm going to the kitchen for more wine to mull," Jillian told her, adding anxiously, "You'll be all right? You'll be . . ."

"I'll be here when you return," Mellyora assured her, and she laughed, feeling like crying. "Where would I go now? The great Laird Lion would probably be delighted to see me disappear again."

She was dismayed that Jillian did not argue with her, and she closed her eyes once again, draining the remaining wine. She had drunk too much, too quickly; she wanted more. She had to sleep tonight . . .

She closed her eyes. The water was growing cold. With a sigh she rose, wrapping herself in a large linen towel and hunching down before the fire to dry. She combed through her hair, and slipped into a blue-linen gown hemmed with soft, rich fur. She heard the door, and saw that Jillian had returned. She looked pale as she reentered the room. She had not returned with wine, and she busied herself with unnecessary tasks, folding clothing that had already been folded, straightening what didn't need to be straightened.

"Jillian, what's wrong?" Mellyora asked.

"Nothing more than is wrong already!" Jillian said matter-of-factly.

"I don't believe you."

"Mellyora, you're not happy now, but you must believe me, this time will pass—"

"Jillian, you will please tell me what has happened now!"

Jillian was incapable of deceit. She met Mellyora's eyes. "The king is very angry."

"So . . ." Mellyora said. She couldn't breathe. She was suddenly terrified that it was all out of her hands, that the king had decided that she was to be punished by being removed from her lands no matter what. "The wedding is . . . off."

Jillian shook her head. "No, no, nothing so awful."

"Oh?"

"He knows how defiant you were, that you were with the Vikings for some time, that you wanted to marry elsewhere. He has suggested to Waryk that there be a public bedding."

Mellyora sat, sinking to the floor in horror. Such events were not uncommon, especially among noble families when a bride's parents wished to impress upon her groom her youth and innocence, or when the married pair were actually in love, and heedless of the ceremony. Though she certainly knew of the practice, Mellyora had never attended such a spectacle. The couples she had known to wed had enjoyed their wedding feast with family and friends, and gone on to the privacy of their marital chamber.

"Oh, God," she breathed.

"I shouldn't have told you," Jillian said, distressed. "Yet, perhaps it was best that you were warned . . ."

Mellyora stood quickly, heading toward the door. Jillian rushed before her, trying to stop her. "Mellyora, you mustn't run again! There will be no—"

"I'm not running."

"Where are you going?"

"To Waryk," she said. Jillian still barred the door. "To Waryk, I swear it, let me by."

Unhappily, Jillian stepped away from the door. Mellyora wasn't surprised to find Angus standing guard outside. "My lady?" he inquired politely.

"I need to see Waryk."

He hid his surprise. "I'll escort you."

It was good to rest in a bath, even if the biggest of tubs was somewhat tight. The tub in his chambers was his own, an import from Bruges with hammered-silver designs of guardian gargoyles and winged angels. He soaked in water that all but scalded him but also soothed his old battle wounds, all the little aches and pains that plagued him, and even his mind somewhat as well. He lay there, feeling the steam that rose and shimmered just above the water's edge. His last night as an unmarried man. Yet tomorrow, he became laird of Blue Isle, so called for the crystal beauty of the sea and sky around it, David had told him. And in a matter of days, he would reach and settle the isle. He'd be given time, he thought, before being called to serve the king again. He now had a home. And a wife.

Ah, yes, a wife. Well, almost.

If his bitter bride didn't have another trick up her sleeve. He lay back, eyes closed. Perhaps he was a fool not to have rid himself of her—the king was angry enough to have meant what he said. She was dangerous. But he would not be in danger, because he was wary of her, he would not make the mistake of trusting her. She had declared herself his enemy, there would be no peace. Yet he admitted to himself that he was growing as eager for his bride as he was for her land. Watching her last night had been . . . irritating. She had smiled for others, teased, laughed, charmed. He had seen young men all but trip over themselves to be near her, to hear her voice. She had been a stunning, golden beauty. Every man there had envied him. Indeed, she had gotten into his blood somehow . . .

Surely, he could quench the fire she ignited without forgetting that she was dangerous. Nor would he risk his soul. She was bewitching, he'd seen that from the beginning. She'd intrigued him. A thankful situation, since she was to be his wife. His *dangerous* wife, a beauty far too reckless for safety.

Reckless, and yet . . .

He had to admit, she had handled herself well in the cavern, when he had tried to shield her from the Vikings and their bizarre attack. She knew her weaponry—he had firsthand knowledge of that! She was strong; he had to prove himself stronger. He had no intention of feeling too much sympathy for her, nor would he ever allow himself to need her. Wanting was something else. Pure instinct. Fascination. But once curiosity was met, she'd be the same as any other woman. She'd no longer haunt him, as thoughts of her did now. Lust, he thought wryly, could be a cruel sensation. Pure wicked torment on the body, more cutting than a knife.

The king remained furious with her; David was not accustomed to women defying him with such energy. David had suggested a public bedding; Waryk was opposed to the idea. In fact, he had determined that not even his increasing hunger for his bride—which must obviously be appeased if children were to be achieved—would allow him to have her as yet. He wanted his own family, not another man's child, and the king had become informative with his will now being fulfilled. David had told Waryk that Jillian, while trying to make the king understand her young mistress, had inadvertently admitted why Mellyora had been so determined on her own choice—the lad's name was Ewan MacKinny, and though a fine youth, he was not a strong warrior, and hadn't the power to keep invaders from the door. So there was definitely a flesh-and-blood man she had wanted herself.

And she had not denied having taken a lover. He didn't particularly damn her for easy virtue; men and women were both capable of the need to love. It was simply that he was the man she was marrying, and, therefore, she was betraying him.

Yet he had made the decision to marry her. There would have been those determined to honor her, no matter what the king had commanded, and he wanted a strong, united homeland. Having her was certainly not going to be a hardship; she was young, supple, sensual, beautiful despite her temper. When she was his wife, she would learn he gave no quarter. But there was the past to be considered. He wondered what he would do if he discovered his wife was to have another man's babe. Could he take a child from its mother? Leave the child an orphan, alone, and the mother grieving? No, he could not do such a thing.

Ah, but could he accept it as his own? No.

Would he have to know? Aye, beyond a doubt. That was the entire point he mulled now. He could remember too clearly what it had been like, standing among the carnage and the dead on the battlefield, and knowing that he was alone. He would create his own kin, David had told him, and since then, family, his family, had been a dream, one he was determined he would live. So, no matter what the future, he had to know about the past.

He started, ready to leap from the tub, as he heard a tapping at his door. To his amazement, the door opened before he could say a word. He tensed, ready to grab his sword if danger threatened.

Danger seldom knocked, he reminded himself.

"Laird Lion—" He heard Angus begin, the great bald man's head just jutting around the door.

"Please, I can announce myself!"

The feminine voice was Mellyora's, and she stepped quickly into his room, leaning against the door as it closed behind her, leaving them alone together. He eased back, watching her. So at times, danger did knock. He kept his eyes warily upon her, wondering if he should be going for his sword in self-defense. He held very still, and realized that for once, she was extremely agitated, but not angry. She was upset. She didn't even seem aware that he was naked in a tub. She remained against the door as if she had been nailed there.

He lifted a hand from the rim of the tub. "Ah, my love. Welcome. This is definitely a surprise visit."

She didn't move.

"You've come, my lady, to speak with me, I imagine. So . . . aye?"

She inhaled, exhaled, her eyes brilliant, her pulse throbbing against the white perfection of her throat. Her lips moved. Had she been another woman, he would have thought that she had come in humble entreaty. She had agreed to the marriage, and he had spoken very plainly about what he expected, so he couldn't begin to imagine what argument she might have now.

She stayed so long by the door that his steam evaporated. Her breasts heaved against the softness of a blue gown that emphasized every tempting curve and form of her figure. Her hair burned in the firelight like spun gold, and his body quickened as if he'd been stroked. She might be a treacherous Viking's daughter, but the mere sight of her made patience an all-but-impossible virtue.

He lifted a hand again. "Mellyora, the wedding is not until tomorrow. However, if you wish to stay and speed things along . . ."

"Please!" She pushed away from the door. He saw that her eyes were so brilliantly beautiful because they were threatened with tears. To his amazement, she flew across the room and came upon her knees at the side of his tub. "Please, don't do this to me. I beg of you."

"Mellyora, you were given the choice not to marry. There is

nothing I can do about the king's edict; if I were to refuse him and lose my neck, he'd choose another man. But still, if this marriage is so horrible to you—"

"No, it's not the marriage."

He lifted his hands. "Then what, Mellyora?"

"Oh, God, please, don't humiliate me in public!"

He arched a brow. She'd heard. Rumor raced around a fortress such as this! And, it appeared, rumor raced with what was most sweetly, wickedly decadent, for she hadn't heard that it had only been a *suggestion,* and a suggestion with which he hadn't agreed. No matter how he might want her—and he was aware that wanting her was becoming a painful issue—he wanted to know that any child born of their marriage was his.

"Please, please, don't allow this!" she whispered.

"Ah!" he said softly. *This,* of course, was the king's public addendum to the ceremony.

"Please."

He'd never seen her so vulnerable, so elusively beguiling. He reached out, touching her cheek, smoothing a wild lock of golden hair from her face. He felt as if he stroked silk. He was tempted, God was he tempted, to reach out and drag her into the water with him, and there end the idea of anything public . . .

And his own determination.

Ah, but then again, the lady had put him through hell.

"The king is very angry," he told her gravely, watching her.

"You can stop this."

He hesitated, meeting her tumultuous eyes. "I'll admit the concept has disturbed me. Especially since there is a question regarding your past. But then again, you see, I've stated my feelings regarding family. It is my own blood I want, my lady, and not another's."

"Is it revenge you want? You've agreed to this because you think you'll be able to say at some later date that the marriage must be annulled because I was previously engaged and in another relationship? You want me to be humiliated, and then you wish to use it all against me!"

"I've not agreed to anything," he said, still watching her intently.

She closed her eyes tightly for a second, then opened them. "Don't do it."

"As I've said, the king is very angry. I think you hurt him, wounded his pride. Maybe he just wants the truth known. You mentioned that you'd taken a lover."

"No, I did not. You suggested that I had."

He shrugged, as if how the matter had been discussed was of little importance.

"It's not true," she whispered.

"What's not true?"

"I've never taken a lover. I swear on my father's honor."

He watched her for a long moment, feeling every muscle in his body contract while he tried to keep his face impassive. She remained so distressed, and spoke with such desperate urgency. She hadn't noted his touch, didn't pull away as his fingers stroked her face.

"Do you remember what tomorrow is?" he asked her quietly.

"Indeed, how could I forget? The wedding."

He shook his head. "Tomorrow night will be the full moon. Don't you remember? The time when you promised to meet me— a stranger you barely knew—at the hunter's cottage in the woods if I let you escape my room that night."

She lowered her head. "Aye, I was desperate."

"You swore that you'd be there."

"I was *very* desperate."

"I told you that you'd keep your promise."

"Did you?"

"So you shall. There will be nothing public between us. What I want will be in private. The perfection of my bride proven to me alone. When the ceremony and banquet are done, we will leave. And you will keep your promises to me, sweetly, gently— and for the love of God—quietly, with no arguments, taunts, or disagreement at all."

She tried to keep her temper, he saw. She had come here, meaning to do so. She simply couldn't. "How dare you be so wretched—" she began.

"Ah, but my love! There is the king's way . . ."

She exhaled, shaking, meeting his eyes. Now upset and angry, she suddenly realized that she was at his bath, looking at his naked body in the water. She pulled back, face softly flushed.

"Just what do you want?" she demanded.

"To know what I'm getting," he said sternly.

"A lot of land!" she reminded him angrily.

"I get the land with or without you," he reminded her bluntly.

"I told you what I wanted," he said, wearily. But she had caused him endless torment, and if he were being cruel now, there was little else he could do. Long years ahead were at stake here, his son, his family, his dream of life itself. Besides, she deserved a little torment. "You, soft, sweet, perfumed, pleasant—and silent. Listening avidly to my every word."

"And then—" she broke off, swallowing. "And then there will be no public . . . entertainment?"

"Aye."

"You swear?"

"Aye, and I do keep my word." He had no intention of letting his wife be anyone else's entertainment.

She sprang up, anxious now to flee his room.

"Mellyora," he said, calling her back, "you haven't lied to me."

"No, I swear it."

"I warn you, my love, don't ever lie."

She shook her head again, turned, and was gone.

He sank back into the tub, thoughtful, curious. She was going to be in for a surprise on their wedding night, and she might even be furious for the anxiety he had caused her. He also meant to carry on his charade until she realized just how serious he was about the future, but then . . .

Well, then, she would probably be quite grateful for a while. She would be reprieved. For a time.

And he would be the one in torment.

# CHAPTER 14

Mellyora slept most of the following morning, having fallen asleep very late. Father Hedgewick had come to her so that she could give him her confession, and she'd struggled long and hard deciding just what was and wasn't sin. In the end, she begged forgiveness for the sins of pride and disobedience, and left it at that. She'd then paced her room endlessly, certain that God couldn't really expect her to be *obedient* to the king when he was asking her to defy the laws of love, or how she could possibly *honor* a husband who disliked and distrusted her—even if she had possibly caused a bit of that distrust. She was angry with everyone, even her father. He'd had no right to die, and leave her to the mercy of others.

When she slept, she prayed she'd wake up and it would have all been a nightmare. When she woke at last, she knew instantly that it was not. Jillian had been anxiously waiting for her to awaken. She had to prepare for her wedding.

By early afternoon, preparations were fully under way. Three of the ladies of the court had come to help her dress—it was the way such things were done, though she would have dearly loved to have been alone. Among the women, however, was Lady Dougall, once her mother's friend.

"Oh, dear girl, if only your mother were here to see you!" she exclaimed when Mellyora was dressed in the fine, ermine-trimmed linen she was to wear for the ceremony. Lady Mary Dougall was slender and elegant, beautiful in a sad way, for she'd lost her husband and daughter to a sweating sickness, and her eldest son had died fighting in the king's service. Her youngest child, Darrin, served the king now as well, and she seemed constantly afraid that she would lose him, too.

"Thank you," Mellyora told her. "I wish my mother were here, I wish I remembered more about her."

"She was not so tall as you, and her hair was auburn, her eyes were greener, but you have her smile, the shape of her face . . . she was beautiful, full of laughter, and she captured your father's heart."

"Aye, and tamed a beast!" said Lady Judith Rutherford, coming forward with a necklace, a jewel-studded cross dangling from a delicate link chain.

"Now, Judith," Lady Dougall protested. She looked at Mellyora with a smile that warned her Lady Rutherford was prone to gossip.

"Well, it's the truth," Judith Rutherford said with a sniff.

"Mellyora adored her father," Lady Dougall said warningly.

"What are you trying to say?" Mellyora demanded.

Judith didn't reply; she pursed her lips. Sarah MacNiall, the youngest of the women, a sensuous beauty recently widowed, softly laughed.

"She's saying that your father was a savage beast when he first came here, and that's the truth of it."

"My father was a warrior, a Viking, but a decent man. Kind and gentle—"

"Aye, he butchered with a smile!" Sarah said.

"In the king's name!" Judith reminded her Sarah.

"Oh, do stop, Laird Adin was a Viking, but he became a good man, a king's man, loyal to his newfound country. And your mother adored him," she told Mellyora.

"Just as you'll adore your husband," Sarah said. Mellyora didn't mind Lady Rutherford, she simply said what she thought and meant no harm. Sarah was quite different. She had a malicious cast to her eyes, and Mellyora wondered why she had come to taunt her. She seemed to be laughing at her, goading her with every word, no matter how lightly spoken. "Ah, well, with a warrior, it doesn't matter if he's kind or decent. In fact, it rather goes against the concept, doesn't it? Your father was fierce; he had his way of winning your mother over. So with all warriors, it doesn't matter if they're kind or merciful. What matters with a warrior is . . . prowess."

"Laird Waryk is the king's champion," Lady Dougall said defensively. "A man could not have more prowess."

Sarah leaned against the mantel and the slow smile that touched her lips and the look in her eyes when she gazed toward Mellyora clearly stated that she hadn't been referring to the battlefield. "Oh, of course. Well, many ladies, landed and no, have dreamt of the great Laird Lion! Some have seen him in their sleep. There is Lady Eleanora of Tyne. It's said that she had true hopes of marrying again, but that if she could not wed Waryk, she'd not marry any man, for she'd never find another knight of his power and prowess."

Well aware that the other woman was stretching her claws, Mellyora determined that she wouldn't betray herself the least upset by any comment the other woman might make.

"Lady Eleanora sounds like a sensible woman. Marriage doesn't always seem to be a desirable state for women. She'll keep her independence, something very precious. Since so many marriages are arranged, she is a lucky woman. No one is stepping into her life to tell her what she must do," Mellyora said.

"Ah, well, it seems that those who wish independence, lose it. Eleanora was told to marry once, and she did so dutifully. Now, she may continue to do as she chooses. See whom she chooses, when she chooses," Sarah said, and smiled. "You do look beautiful, Mellyora. And it's nearly time." She walked close to Mellyora, and said softly, "I pray you'll be all right, Mellyora. The whole of the fortress whispers of the way you attempted to escape this arrangement and humiliate Waryk. Most people think you should be whipped and cast aside. I assure you, besides Eleanora, there are many who would gladly take your place."

"It's a pity that the king will not allow them to do so," Mellyora said sweetly.

"Men marry when they must, and yet seem so free to do as they choose. You're right. I shall cherish my independence," Sarah told her. "So many husbands die, battles never seem to end. Wives are left widows, and then alas, wives die, too. Childbirth, disease, accidents, and then the husbands are left to seek new wives." Again, she smiled.

Mellyora felt chilled to the bone. It was as if Sarah were trying to will her to die.

"It's nearly time for the ceremony. We must get on over to the church. Come along now, Judith, Sarah," Mary insisted. She winked at Mellyora as she ushered the other two out of the room, and Mellyora decided that she wasn't at all as innocent as she had imagined. She stopped and kissed Mellyora on the cheek. "Eleanora is a close friend, Sarah is being bitter, and nothing more. You're quite lovely, and I'm sure your groom will forgive you anything!"

She didn't know how much there was to forgive, Mellyora thought, but smiled, and bid her thanks.

Left alone at last with Jillian, Mellyora shook her head. "I can't go through with this."

Jillian nearly snorted aloud. "You've never been a coward. You're not going to let that evil witch beneath your skin! You can't possibly be afraid of her!"

"I'm not afraid of her. I'm not afraid. I feel ill." She gripped Jillian's hands. "I can't do this," she whispered.

"You have to do this."

"Help me, I need something, a drug, a drink, anything, strong ale, wine—"

Jillian cleared her throat, looking over her head. Mellyora realized that the door had been left open. She turned slowly, with dread.

Waryk stood there, resplendent in his tartan, a length of the wool fashioned over his shoulder and held firmly by a falcon-crested brooch. Angus stood behind him.

"What are you doing here?" she asked him. "I wasn't supposed to see you until we were at the church—"

"Ah, but it's good that I'm here, isn't it? I can help you actually make it to the church. Angus, see what we can find for my lady. There, on the trunk. A carafe of wine. That will do for now. Bring it quickly." He lowered his voice, speaking to Mellyora alone. "We can't have you gulping down the communion wine at our wedding mass, can we?"

She didn't know if he was amused, or simply contemptuous. She didn't care. Angus brought her a chalice of wine. She offered him a smile of gratitude, and felt her soon-to-be husband studying her still.

"Drink it, and let's go," he said impatiently.

"Take care, Mellyora, you don't want to lose all sense and reason," Jillian warned.

Mellyora continued to stare at Waryk. "Aye, but I do," she said softly.

His eyes remained locked upon hers, and he betrayed no emotion. He took her arm. "Shall we, my love?"

It wasn't an invitation. He was moving, and she was going with him.

"The church is quite full," he said lightly. "The king has seen to it that this is a spectacle for many to witness."

She felt a moment's deep unease. "You—you haven't—"

"I haven't what?"

She moistened her lips. "Reneged on your promise?"

"Are you reneging on yours?"

She shook her head.

"I always keep my word. I told you so."

He was walking quickly, his long strides were difficult to keep up with, and she was tall, and accustomed to moving quickly. "Tell me," she said, slightly breathless, "is your mistress in the church?"

To her astonishment, he stopped dead, staring at her.

"What?"

"I asked you if your mistress was in the church."

She didn't know what he saw, or thought. He studied her so long that she wished she could take back the question. She realized that she was taunting him on purpose, that she was disturbed. There was so much in life that was simply done, or simply expected. Men had wives for gain, mistresses for pleasure.

And, she realized, she did not share well, could not meekly accept such a fate.

"Let's go, shall we, it makes no difference!" she exclaimed, aware that Angus and Jillian were behind them, and though they hadn't heard her speak, they were hovering awkwardly some feet away.

She started walking. He held her arm, and walked as well. "Would it matter?" he asked her after a moment.

"What?"

"If she were here. If Eleanora sat in a pew just beyond the altar?" he asked casually.

"Nothing seems to matter, does it?" she said.

"Trust me. The future shall matter," he promised her.

They had reached the entrance to the church. She didn't remember exiting the corridor to the courtyard, walking through the twilight, and coming here. The wine had helped, she thought. Somewhat. Candles burned brilliantly within, hundreds of them, so it seemed. The light cast an eerie, shimmering glow, and it seemed as if everything within that glow were part of a dream, and not real. She was grateful, feeling that she could rise above the light and watch what went on, as if she were not real, nor was anything that happened.

The king waited impatiently at the rear of the church, ready as her guardian to escort her to the altar, anxious to give her into marriage and be done with her. She was amazed at the number of people there. She would have been touched that the king had gone into his own pocket so deeply for her wedding, except that she knew he had not done it for affection, but for effect. She and Blue Isle were now Waryk's, Laird Lion's, and all should know it.

The walk to the altar seemed interminable. She was glad again of the wine she had gulped. She kept telling herself that she was above the glow of the light . . .

A chorus sang hymns, the bishop was there, a skinny, taciturn man, stern to the extreme. He spoke endlessly, so it seemed. She was on her knees, head bowed, when he came to her with the communion cup. She felt a wild urge to seize the cup and gulp down the wine, as Waryk had taunted, but managed to refrain. It didn't seem like a good time to tempt God, king, or Waryk.

She was amazed to realize that she was standing again, that she didn't realize she had come to her feet. There was a silver inlaid band upon her finger, and the bishop was announcing them man and wife before God and all witnesses gathered there.

Then she felt him, touching her, his fingers threading into her hair, tilting her head. His mouth closed over hers, molding to it, his tongue forcing her lips. She had expected a chaste kiss . . . not this. His lips encompassed hers, his tongue invaded, and she was filled with the warmth and taste of him in a way she had not imagined. She'd kissed before, known pleasure, a subtle excitement . . .

She couldn't breathe. He seemed overwhelming. She couldn't escape his hold, the tangle of her hair around his fingers, the forceful pressure of his lips, his body against hers. A warrior knight, she thought desperately. Hard as steel, unyielding as rock. She breathed him, felt him; he seemed to be within her, stealing her air, seizing her strength. Tremors seared along her spine, heat danced before her eyes. She struggled to free herself, hearing the bishop clear his throat, hearing the laughter and the roar of approval from the gathered guests . . . Her eyes were closed, her breath was gone, she could barely stand, her knees were giving, she would taste him forever . . .

He lifted his mouth from hers. Her lips felt damp, swollen, so tender . . .

She was shaking, and wanted to wipe his touch away. She would never be able to do so, she thought. He had somehow made certain already that she would never be able to forget him, ever. She need only close her eyes, and her senses would remember.

"What are you doing?" she whispered frantically. She was aware of the crowd, the good-natured laughter, the cheers.

"There has to be some show," he responded.

He had her arm, and was turning to leave. She stumbled, he caught her. He led her from the church, and the guests spilled around them.

Lady Dougall came to her, embracing her. "I've never seen a more beautiful bride!"

"I've never seen one more ready to pass out!" Sarah said, kissing her cheeks, as if she spoke with empathy and affection.

But it didn't matter, she didn't reply, because Anne was hugging her next, and the affection was genuine. "You were beautiful, spellbinding. The two of you make the most handsome, most noble couple. You're so golden, he's so dark, and you're both as tall as the gods . . . what beautiful children you will create together!"

Her jaw clenched, she hugged Anne back, unable to respond at first.

"Well, it will be your wedding next," she reminded Anne.

"I'm so grateful. To you and Waryk. If it weren't for your husband, something dreadful would have happened. Daro might have defied the king for you, for me, and David might have fought him, and Daro might have died, and the king's forces might have been so weakened that an assault from an enemy might have devastated him. But your husband has the strength to be merciful, and so we shall all live, and be happy."

She didn't have the heart to remind Anne that she hadn't wanted any part of this.

"Ah, Mellyora, your father would be proud!" she heard the king say, and she was turned about, and he held her in his arms, kissing her on the forehead. Aye, she'd been dutiful now, with no choice. She was in his favor again, so it seemed, or she was being chastised.

"Would he?" she queried softly.

"Trust me, lass, in time, you'll thank me," he told her.

She arched a brow, but smiled, wary of the king at the moment. When she was gone from here, even with her new husband, she would be relieved. She wasn't going to argue with David, not when wine was flowing freely from barrels in the courtyard and servants were bringing tables and food out under the moonlight for the wedding feast. The crowd could too easily grow raucous, and demand more entertainment than Waryk had already chosen to give them.

David beckoned to a servant for wine, and when it arrived, he gave a chalice to Mellyora, and kept one for himself. "A salute!" the king cried, and the crowd fell silent. He lifted his chalice. "To the power and strength of unity, to this marriage, combining great houses, peoples, and strength of our country; to my warrior and his bride, and to our united Scotland!"

Cheers surrounded them. Mellyora drank her wine, and accepted good wishes from more and more of the king's guests, friends, acquaintances, and those she hadn't known before. At one point in the evening, she felt an uncanny sensation of unease, and she turned to see that she was being watched. Sarah stared at her. She didn't turn away when caught, but gave her a slow smile that was in some strange way a threat. Mellyora turned away from her, laughing at something a young knight said.

In time she wound up seated at the banqueting table with her husband. Still, there was so much activity around them, they were not forced to talk. The king had ordered entertainment: jesters, dancers, magicians, jugglers. The hour grew late. Lady Rutherford sat with her husband, face flushed from wine, cap askew. Sarah sat next to a drunk knight, teasing him, laughing with him, goading him, Mellyora thought. She was right. Sarah smiled at her, then whispered to the knight. The young man rose suddenly, stood, and shouted cheerfully, "To bed, Laird Lion! You've taken the bride purported to be the fairest in the land, sir! Shall we see to it?"

Mellyora had known Sarah was determined on her discomfort. There was a vicious streak in the young woman. She felt her cheeks flood with crimson, and she prayed that Waryk would remember his promise and do something quickly. If the crowd got too wild, there would be little anyone could do. She and Waryk would both be seized and stripped and thrown together, and it would be horrible.

She didn't dare look his way, but she felt him rise beside her, lifting a chalice to the young man. "Why, sir, so the hour is late! So if you'll give us a moment . . ."

He had reached out a hand to her. Mellyora took it, and he drew her to her feet. He led her from the table, taking all the time in the world, stopping here and there to speak quickly and casually with one person, and then the next.

"What are we doing?" she whispered.

"Running," he told her.

They came to the far end of the banqueting table, and he whistled. His great warhorse Mercury made a splendid entrance upon the scene, loping across the courtyard, attracting everyone's attention, and coming to an obedient halt directly before his master. Waryk lifted her and threw her atop the horse, and hopped up behind her.

"They're getting away!" someone shouted.

"Catch them!" someone else cried good-naturedly.

"Get them, come, the fun is just beginning!"

But they would not be caught. No one else was mounted; the horses were in the stables. And Mercury was as swift as his name. They rode through the gates, and out into the night, and hard along the northern trail that led to the forest.

Waryk had kept his word, and they were gone from the castle. She closed her eyes and felt the wind, and, relieved of much tension, she rested against his chest. Then she felt his heartbeat, the power of his every movement. She had been so desperate to escape the fortress that she had thought about little else; she certainly hadn't thought ahead about the night.

Now suddenly, the cottage deep in the forest seemed too close. They were moving far too fast, galloping toward the inevitable.

They rode hard for the first twenty minutes; then, mindful of his horse, Waryk slowed their gait. When they came to a stream, and he allowed the horse to drink, Mellyora asked for water. He lifted her, and let her slip down to the ground. She rushed to the water. It was icy, sweet. It cooled the fever that burned within her. She drank deeply, bathed her face, drank some more. She cooled her face and throat again, bound her hair slowly to keep it from getting soaked, and started the ritual all over again, tarrying long and deliberately.

He was tolerant for a while, then spoke impatiently. "We need to move on."

"The water is delicious. The moon is full here. We've the night to ride."

"Now, Mellyora."

She didn't want him coming for her, so she rose reluctantly. She didn't look at him as she returned to Mercury. He reached down for her, easily hoisting her back upon the horse before him. The moonlight was very strong, guiding them in a slow lope toward the cottage in the woods. It seemed that they reached it in no time. It should have been much farther.

Waryk leapt down and reached up to set her on the ground.

She felt him behind her, his whisper husky and warm against her ear.

"We're here, my love. Time for debts to be paid and bargains to be fulfilled!"

She longed to break free from him; she didn't need to do so.

He stepped back, tending to Mercury.

And she stood in the clearing in the forest, staring at the cottage with dismay. Nothing had been a dream; no sweet warmth of wine or candle glow could now keep the edge from the truth.

She had married him; they were man and wife.

Everything in life indeed had its price.

# CHAPTER 15

She walked ahead of him, not daring to look back. Suddenly she found herself remembering the madness with which she had suggested this place. She hadn't known who he was, she had been willing to sell her soul to escape the king's edict. She hadn't known the simplicity of his power. She had been certain that she could say or do anything at that moment, and it wouldn't matter, because she would escape, and all would be well.

It had all been madness, and she didn't know how she had come to this. She should have been so much smarter. But she had been mourning her father, consoling herself with the belief that she would go on as he had done, creating a haven within her own country. Then the king had sent for her, and she had come to Stirling believing that she had only to speak with him, make him understand . . .

But here she was in a cottage in the woods, afraid and miserable. Ruing the fact that she had been so naive from the beginning. She had believed that Daro's strength could save her. She had risked her uncle's life. Because he was part of Scotland now, even if the king did not realize that it was so. Like her father, her uncle had chosen his homeland, and this was it. He wouldn't have called upon Scandinavian mercenaries to help him fight the king. He would have fought himself had it come to it, and he would have died. Seeing so clearly in hindsight was painful. She did owe Waryk her gratitude that he did not allow her rejection of the king's plans to create warfare. Owing him her gratitude did not make the situation easier, but rather all the more difficult.

But he didn't understand. The old ways in the isles had been so different. Women had been given rights, there had been laws, different laws. She still wanted to shriek out that the Normans had not conquered Scotland, that the feudal laws were not fair, that once upon a distant, better time, she'd have had a right to own property, to govern it, to live her own life.

He was the king's man, trained in the art of war, a Scotsman, he said, but a warrior familiar with Norman building, Norman law, armor, swords, and power. There was a prize he was to receive for risking his neck for the king; her land was that prize.

"Mellyora, go in."

Her mother had told her stories about the woods. There were sprites and nymphs living in great oaks. Magical creatures who played tricks, who hampered mankind, and helped as well.

If she could just disappear into the air, melt into an oak . . .

"Mellyora."

She shivered and opened the door to the cottage. Someone had come there before them. The place had been cleaned. An open door separated an outer room from a bedroom. In the outer room, on a large, rough-planked table, food had been left, smoked meat, cheese, bread, wine. Warming fires had been set in the hearths in the outer room and in the bedroom. Through the doorway, Mellyora could see that a tub had been left for her with snowy towels, soaps, perfumes. A large kettle heated water over the fire, water to be added if the other had chilled before her arrival. A sheer white gown lay on the bed which had been laden with pillows and furs. She didn't realize that she had frozen in the doorway until he entered behind her. "Forgive me for presuming to know you so well, but I imagine you would like some wine?"

"Yes."

He poured wine, handing her a chalice. "Veritable love nest, isn't it?"

She didn't reply, but gripped her chalice tightly, swallowing down the contents.

He took the chalice from her. "One more. Then you keep your word."

He poured her a second serving of wine, then indicated the doorway. "Do you need help with your clothing? I wasn't sure if you would want your woman, Jillian, here at first, but I decided discretion meant more to you than assistance."

"No. I don't need help with anything."

He bowed to her, his eyes bright with amusement as he indicated the bedroom. "Your bath awaits. As do I. You do intend to keep your word?"

She stared at him, absolutely hating him for finding the whole travesty so amusing. "Yes, I keep my word!" she told him furiously, then strode by him, slamming the door behind her.

In the bedroom she saw that steam was still rising from the tub. She downed the last of her wine, stared at the water, and cast her clothing off in a sudden frenzy. The fire burned warm around her. She filled the tub with the last of the heated water, wrapped her hair into a knot, and stepped into the tub. She sank into the water. *Yes, she kept her word. This was marriage. It wasn't so terrible. She wouldn't die, women married every day, women fell in love, Anne was in love with Daro . . .*

The warmth of the tub was good, lying there was good, being numb and trying not to think while minutes rushed by was good as well, and yet . . .

It wouldn't be so terrible. She remembered his touch, his kiss, the feeling it had evoked in her, and she realized that she was feeling that strange heat again without his touching her, just thinking, remembering. And she recalled the taste of him, his scent . . .

"My love?" There came a tapping on the door. "Are you alive in there? It's been some time, and I wouldn't want to criticize, but surely, you must be pruning to a pit?"

She gritted her teeth. Just when she thought he might be bearable, he opened his mouth.

She stepped out of the tub, wrapping herself in the towel. She clung to it. Jillian had been here: She'd set the linen towel over a chair by the fire, and it was deliciously warm and comforting.

"Mellyora?"

"Wretch!" she murmured angrily. But she realized he might open the door any second, and so she dived for her gown, pulling it quickly over her head. She loosened her hair, and it fell around her. She heard the scrape of the door as it began to open, and she dived into the bed, covering herself with the furs. She couldn't dim the firelight, but just as he walked in, she leaned over and blew out the candles that burned bedside.

She stared at him in the pale firelight of the room. "You may come in now," she said imperilously.

"I am in."

"So I see. And I am here. As I gave my word I would be."

He perched on the end of the bed, staring at her. "Well, not exactly as you promised you would be."

She frowned, holding a fur cover close. "What do you mean?"

"I mean that this will not do at all."

"In what way?"

He lifted a hand vaguely. "Well, had we remained at the fortress in Stirling, a goodly group of drunkards would have led us about, stolen our clothing, gaped over our good points and bad, and I would have been forced to take the initiative in their voyeuristic debauchery or forever lose face before my friends and countrymen. And women, of course. The crowd would have shown me first the absolute perfection of the king's great prize, his ward, great Adin's daughter. But we are here, and I didn't ask for you to be cowering in bed beneath the covers—"

"I'm not cowering, I'm simply here."

"But it's not what you promised."

"What did I promise?"

He smiled, crossing his arms over his chest. "To start, my lady, get out of the bed."

"Why? Isn't it where you wish to end up?"

He arched a brow, still smiling slightly. "Up, my lady."

Gritting her teeth, she rose. She stood nervously by the bed, glad she had doused the candles. She felt as if the gown she wore were completely diaphanous, and she was grateful for the shadows. She felt his eyes rake over her. He rose, and she braced herself, certain he was coming for her.

"What now?" she murmured.

"Umm, more wine, I think," he said. He collected her chalice from the mantel and strode to the outer chamber. "My love, do come out here."

Where there was more light.

"I think you should come back here."

"I think you should keep your word."

She walked slowly through the doorway to the outer room. He beckoned to her, and she walked to the table before the great hearth there and stood before him. He sipped from a chalice and she noted that he had meant more wine for himself—not her. He hadn't poured a second chalice. He leaned against the table, drinking, and made a motion with his hand. "Spin."

She controlled her temper and did so. He beckoned her closer, setting down his chalice. He slipped an arm around her, pulling her tight against him. With his free hand he lifted her chin, and touched her lips with his own. She was instantly aware of the power of his body heat again, a warmth and vitality in his touch that seemed to sear from his caress into the length of her. His lips moved slowly over hers, with an amazingly gentle force. Her mouth parted. She tasted and breathed him again, felt her heart thundering to great new heights of speed. Her limbs felt liquid, and she was glad that he held her, for she couldn't stand. She had expected this to be terrible. No, perhaps she had wanted this to be terrible. It should have been duty, and she should have never felt this sense of searing excitement, of wild heat, racing throughout her, touching her limbs, touching within . . .

His lips broke from hers. "This won't do," he said.

She straightened, stunned, then finding strength not to waver, and to step back from him, back to sanity.

"What won't do?" she demanded distractedly.

"That gown."

"My gown—"

"Off with it."

Once again, she felt her temper soar. He was playing with her.

"My love," he murmured, picking up his wine again, "you might break your jaw, you know, if you clench your teeth any tighter. And you do have wonderful teeth."

"Do I?" she breathed. "How convenient. Yours are wondrous fair as well!"

He smiled, black lashes lowering over his crystal gaze for a brief moment. Then he was looking at her again. "So you've noticed that my teeth are decent."

"For a Norman's." She knew, instinctively, that there was nothing she could say or do to irritate him more. And she was floundering. Afraid of his touch, longing for it, so afraid of the way he could make her feel, so afraid of what she would feel when they had taken it even farther.

He maintained his casual smile. She knew that it was forced. "Off with it," he told her softly. Even his voice touched her. Burned within.

She shook her head. "This isn't fair at all. I—"

"You swore to meet me here, in payment for your freedom. Then, you promised to keep that first vow in return for the courtesy of escaping the fortress. Come, my love, be bold, be reckless, be daring. Gentle, sweet, sensual—and silent, as you promised."

She wasn't silent. Beneath her breath she began to revile him with every cutting word and oath that would come to her mind. But as she swore, she wrenched the gown over her head. It fell to her feet, and she was left with the cloak of her hair as her only garment.

He stared at her a long while. His eyes seemed black, but his expression remained impassive.

Then he smiled. "Now. Come to me."

Again, she began to swear.

"Great Adin's daughter, afraid?" he queried, arching a brow. "But then, you're missing your knife and sword tonight, you're without your weapons."

"So are you."

"Never," he told her gravely. "Come ..."

She stood before him. He took her hand and brought it to his face. She trembled as he moved her palm, and kissed it. It seemed a surprisingly tender gesture, and it took her off guard. Naked, she was very aware of the steel structure of his body, of the supple ripple of muscle as he drew a line down the length of her spine, bringing her closer.

"Feel free to seduce and repay me at any time," he murmured.

She tensed, ready to slap him. He laughed, fingers gentle upon her jaw, lifting her face to his. "M'lady, you kiss me ..."

She wasn't certain if she managed the act, but their lips were touching. She didn't feel the kiss so deeply, for she nearly jumped a mile at the touch of his hand. Moving over her, the length of her, breasts, ribs, waist, hips, belly, breasts again ... she nearly shrieked aloud, she felt as if she shook inside and out, the heat that filled her was unbearable, she couldn't breathe, couldn't stand, couldn't move, could just *feel* him ...

Then he suddenly set her from him. She willed herself not to waver, stumble, fall. He was staring at her, eyes almost black in the firelight again. "Well, so you do know how to pay your promises," he said flatly, adding softly. "And you are very near the absolute perfection legend claims you to be." He lifted a hand, incredibly, dismissing her.

She just stared at him for a moment. Then it dawned on her that he didn't intend to demand any conjugal rights that evening. He had forced her to do all this just to prove that he was now the great laird and master. It was revenge, indeed.

"You bastard!" she said quietly.

"Maybe. Maybe you've simply run me ragged, and I don't choose to wear myself out wondering where I shall be looking for you next. Go to bed."

Teeth grating, she didn't move. Her fists were clenched at her sides to keep them from flying. She couldn't have moved had she tried.

He let out an oath of impatience. "Don't you ever simply accept something that you want in silence and good grace?"

"Accept your kindness, in silence?" she queried. "You're right that none of this is kindness or consideration. You've chosen not to believe or trust me—"

"Surely, you can see my point!"

"You think that I might be carrying another man's child, and you will annul this marriage without blinking if it is so."

He didn't reply.

"Well, you didn't wish to be married, did you? You have your mistress. God alone knows what other women. But tell me this, my great Laird Lion, what is to stop me from seeing other men in the future?"

He straightened from his stance against the table, ice as crystal as glass. He took a single step toward her, and she would have backed away from his menace had she time. He reached out and lifted her chin with a touch so forceful she nearly cried out. He lowered his lips nearly to hers and spoke in a controlled whisper that frightened and chilled her more than any shout could do. "The past, my lady, is the past; it is what has happened already, before I was in your life. I would not condemn you for it, indeed, I have, at times, almost felt sympathy for your longing to be free. But if I ever suspect you of a lover, m'lady, I promise you, he will be dead within the hour, and should you survive my wrath, you will live forevermore with all the independence and freedom you might desire—alone in a stone tower."

She stood dead still, returning his stare, not fighting his grip. Perhaps he realized his own force. He released her and stepped back. She longed to leap forward in rage, rip into his face, pummel it into little bits and pieces. She was afraid to touch him. She clenched her jaw again until it hurt and controlled her fury.

"Well," she murmured, "I shall revel then in the independence you have given me now, my laird husband. And naturally, sir, I do thank you for this time, and of course, for refusing to allow us to be entertainment for the king's drunken guests."

"Don't thank me for refusing that spectacle. It was not so much a kindness to you; I simply didn't intend on humiliating myself," he said irritably. "Go to bed, get some sleep. I am anxious to reach Blue Isle."

There were more things she might have said. She remained furious with the game he had played, and furious that he thought her a liar. But her anger was impotent. He had what he wanted. He was laird of Blue Isle. And he would have his children. But the children would wait, because he wanted to be certain she wasn't carrying another man's child. She wondered what had so convinced him that she'd been with another man, when she had sworn that she had not. *He doesn't trust me. That much is obvious. And painful,* she thought suddenly. *What a way to begin a new life.*

And still, she tried to tell herself, it was, at the least, a respite. The thought didn't soothe her; she simply felt empty. And he no longer seemed amused or pleased with his own quest for the evening. His temper seemed sharp, ragged as the edge of a saw. Perhaps it was time to retreat with a final word, if possible.

She stared at him coolly, determined not to show her fury, or any emotion regarding him whatsoever.

She smiled.

"Fine, m'laird. You've had your amusement. You've mocked and teased me, and taken revenge. Tormented me, when you knew the outcome of this evening from the beginning. As it happens, you've arranged the very marriage I wished, one in name only. Good night, Laird Waryk. Sleep well."

She spun about, not bothering with her gown. She was furious, bizarrely hurt, and close to tears. But it was her turn to taunt his senses, if nothing more. He had taught her much in a matter of moments. She walked slowly through the doorway to the bedroom and straight to bed, swaying her hips confidently as she did so. He would not touch her again. Not tonight.

She lay upon the bed, closing her eyes tightly in the near darkness. She brought the furs around her then, as she shivered with the cold. She closed her eyes. She feigned sleep. *She should have been so glad, happy enough to lie here gloating . . .*

She wasn't happy at all. She had gotten what she would have wanted most, had she been asked, but she felt strangely bereft, and she found herself wondering what it would have been like had he been lying beside her, had she slept in his arms, felt his strength, his warmth, his protection. Far from pleased, she was keenly aware of being alone, cold, and wretched. He hadn't wanted to marry her; he had done so because he was the king's man, and because he wanted Blue Isle and the power and position that went with it. He had never lied.

She lay very still, and was more wretched when she heard him go out and whistle for Mercury. Sarah's words came back to haunt her, and she wondered where he was going, and in whose bed he would spend his night.

When she was certain he was gone, she rose. A fur wrapped around her, she walked to the outer room. She moved the heavy skin that covered one of the window vents and looked out onto the moonlit night, wondering why she still felt so tumultuous, so wretchedly awake and unhappy.

She wasn't alone, she saw. Good loyal Angus sat out by an old oak, chipped at a piece of wood. Was he protecting her from whatever dangers might lurk in the woods?

Or was he her prison keeper, seeing that she didn't disappear into the forest, seek a different escape?

She silently returned to the bedroom, desperate to sleep.

Such sweet oblivion would not come.

She was still awake, hours later, when he returned, though she continued to pretend to sleep when she heard him cast off his sword and boots, and walk quietly to the bed to look over her.

She couldn't see him. She felt him watching her. Felt his eyes. Felt the strange warmth that invaded her, and again, she could too vividly remember the taste of his kiss, the scent of the man, the vital heat of his body.

She nearly jumped when he touched her, his fingers light, moving down the length of her hair. Somehow, she remained still.

She didn't dare breathe.

With a brush of his knuckles, he smoothed a lock of her hair from her face. And strangely, again that night, his touch was so gentle it might have been tender. She wished that she had curled more deeply beneath the covers. He watched her, and she didn't know what he saw in her, and she wished that she could hide far more of her body, her mind, and her soul.

She had made him her enemy, and it was too late to go back. He didn't trust her, she couldn't trust him. She had said and done things that she couldn't change now. She had meant to hurt him at times, and she had hurt herself.

What did he see? Why did he stay so long, his eyes upon her, just the brush of his fingers touching her still . . .

At length, he turned away. The door to the bedroom closed, and she heard him moving in the outer room. Pouring wine, drinking it, pouring more.

He remained in the cottage. And still, she lay awake.

Eventually, she did sleep, and it was in the midst of the peace and rest she had so desperately craved that a nagging realization woke her.

He knew too much about her. In her anger and rebellion, she had given away far too much.

He knew that the man she had wanted as her husband was Ewan MacKinny. Someone had told him. She had always thought that it would be bitter enough, painful enough, to see Ewan again as it was. And now . . .

Oh, God. What would he do with Ewan?

He had threatened to kill at the slightest provocation.

She suddenly felt very alone.

And very afraid.

She was coming to know him so well.

She didn't know him at all. Yet it was disturbing to realize that the evening would have ended better if only she'd slept in his arms.

# PART II

## Laird and Lady

# CHAPTER 16

From the time he was a boy, Waryk had possessed land. He'd received an inheritance through his mother, and his father had been given lands as well. It was all good land, if not densely populated or boasting great castles. It didn't matter: He loved the wildness, and the peace to be found in different parts of his own holdings, and in all, he had a passionate love for his home, Scotland. He found the hills and valleys as beautiful as the rugged cliffs; the Grampian mountains were majestic and humbling, the rolling Lowlands were gentle and welcoming. He had ridden into England with the king, he had fought and been feted by the Norse; he had traveled to Brittany, Normandy, Paris, and into many of the Spanish and German kingdoms for tournaments; he had seen many fantastic things. But he had never seen anything so wonderful as his first glimpse of Blue Isle.

A week's ride from Stirling had brought them here, to this high mainland cliff. They might have traveled much more quickly, but they were accompanied by pack animals and wagons bearing wedding gifts and his personal belongings from his rooms at the king's court, so the ride had been a long one. Ten servants accompanied them, eight strapping young men and two maids, and ten men-at-arms, including Angus. Jillian rode at Mellyora's side, her constant companion and protector. Though what Mellyora might need protection from now, he didn't know. Certainly not him. He had purposely kept himself as busy as possible, and as far as possible from his wife. In turn, through the entirety of the long journey, his new wife had been polite, cool, and aloof. To him. He couldn't begin to fault her behavior.

He longed to pick her up and shake her—or, with far less chivalry—send her flying.

She was coldly courteous to him; to others, she was charming. She spoke sweetly, properly with all his men, and was equally gentle and courteous with the servants. She raced her horse alongside Thomas, teased Garth about his stubble of beard, set flowers in Sir Harry's hair. At night, she sang while strumming lightly on a small harp, or moved about, telling more of her tales. She told of the great Pictish war chiefs facing battles with their flesh all painted in blue, told tales of daring Vikings, and a long story, surely taught her by the king's *seneschal*, about Kenneth MacAlpin taking the throne of a united Scotland. She was wonderful, captivating. His men-at-arms, just like the servants, sat around the fire in stone silence, watching, listening, with all the enthrallment of little children. She was natural with her stirring tales, she could sway men and women with her words and her passion. *So she must be on her isle,* he thought. *Revered.* She was her father's daughter—the child of a Celtic heiress as well. She was bred to this, she was good at this, and he realized that he hadn't been generous at all in standing by the marriage even when the king had said that he would set her aside—he had been smart. Taking this isle without her would have meant slaughter.

The thought did not help his temper where she was concerned. Battle lines had been drawn, and it didn't matter that he had drawn them. She was waging her war all too well.

The first few days, he had managed to ignore her, riding hard to see that the wagon wheels made it over cliffs and through water, slush, and mud. At times, he'd silently taunted himself regarding this land he loved so much—it didn't seem they had come one flat mile. He was ready to discard his precious bathtub and half his mail, plate, and instruments of war. If he were not in the king's service . . .

But he was. And he would be called back into service, because he knew David, and David would press his boundaries against England. David had given him time to establish his hold here, and then he would be called back.

Sometimes, he stood back in the trees as she wove her tales around the campfire, and he watched her, and he thought about the first night he had seen her. Sometimes, he turned away. She had made them enemies. If so, he would see their war to the finish. But it seemed that something painful had begun to plague him, and it made him all the more angry with her, even as she continued with her perfect politeness. Wasn't courtesy more than he had ever expected? He asked himself at times.

The days had been long; the nights endless. Camping had been wretched. Each night his men had erected them a shelter in the woods. She had gone in first, and he had walked the forest trails before joining her.

She had slept.

He had lain awake. Beside her. He had never touched her. Always, a breath of space remained between them.

And each day, it seemed that his temper simmered to a greater degree. Still, he thought he leashed it well. But how could he yell at her, and long to throttle her, when she had been soft-spoken and entirely courteous?

But now, this . . .

Atop the ragged, tufted cliff above the place where the land met the water, he could see far across the horizon. At first sight, all seemed peaceful.

Below him, dozens of farmers' cottages with fencing and barns and stables lay strewn over a wide area of land that was abutted by the rocky cliffs and naturally protected by them. Shallow waters stretched out, with huge outcroppings of rocks here and there, to the isle itself. Like here on the mainland, long stretches of sandy beach gave way to rich green grasses; then the rock seemed to rise to the sky, and the castle itself seemed to be part of the rock, and part of the sky, the high towers all but meeting the clouds.

Angus had ridden beside him.

"I told you, Waryk. It's a place as beautiful as your bride. As wild, as well, perhaps. Sometimes, the sea rages, and beats against the rock. At low tide, a man can run across the water to reach the isle, and yet, to the protected southern side, there is no finer harbor."

"No one is about," Waryk heard suddenly, and he turned to see that Mellyora had ridden to join them at the precipice, and that she stared down the distance between them and the shoreline with distress.

He frowned. "Dusk is coming—"

"There is no one about!" she repeated.

Then Waryk saw the smoke, rising from the thatched roof of one of the cottages below. "Angus, alert the men, we've visitors," he said calmly.

"Visitors," she breathed. "I have men-at-arms—"

"Aye, lady, and they are atop your walls, yonder, see?"

Indeed, once alerted, they could all see that men lined the high parapets and towers of the castle. Small boats could be seen northward to the shoreline, and a man in simple mail, waving a staff, came from one of the cottages, dragging with him a young woman whose hysterical cries could suddenly be heard rising even unto the cliffs.

"My God!" Mellyora breathed. And before he could stop her, she was racing down the cliff toward the shore.

"Mellyora!" he cried, and charged after her. He was glad that no horse was faster or more adept than Mercury. His wife had drawn her sword as she charged down the cliff, and he swore, furious that his first action would have to be to subdue her when his newfound home was under attack. But he would not allow her to charge against an unknown enemy, and so he shouted to Angus to lead the attack while he brought Mercury galloping hard in front of Mellyora to cut her off, and when he had so succeeded, she stared at him as if he had gone mad. "Waryk, they are killing my people—"

"My people, my lady, and they will not kill you."

"I can fight, you know that, I am a Viking's daughter—"

"You were a Viking's daughter. Now you're my wife."

She was frantic, he saw. All the worse. Fighting he had learned, despite his own successes as a passionate and desperate lad, was best done with a cool head. She pulled back on her horse, ready to race by him, and he swore, spurring Mercury on so that he could leap from his own mount and bring her down.

Tears stung her eyes now as he straddled her, tears of utter frustration. "Waryk—"

"Lady, you know I can best you, and you know that I can best whatever enemy strikes your doors. By God, will you leave me to it?"

"It's my home, Waryk, we can both fight, we can both die—"

"You are to be the lady, the bearer of the heirs, and I the protector, madam, it is the way it is done."

Her lashes covered her cheeks. "That is hardly the situation at this moment."

"Then practice allowing me to be the one to lead the charge against our enemies!"

He rose, swiftly helping her to her feet, then leaving her there.

She wasn't helpless, she could swing a sword, and he knew it. That frightened him more than anything.

He leapt back on Mercury and stared down at her. She watched him with frustration still in her eyes. "My lady, allow me to die for you!" he said, and whirled his horse about. He saw that Jillian, on her gentle gray mare, had almost reached Mellyora, and so he dared spur Mercury onward. Clumps of mud and grass flew as he covered the distance to the shore, where he discovered his men engaged in pitched battle with a small, fierce army of attackers.

Boats—Viking longboats, so it seemed—had come ashore on the isle as well, and quickly assessing the situation, Waryk realized that the inhabitants of Blue Isle and the shore had been surprised by a whirlwind attack that had come strategically from the sea— the boats had crept dead close to the shore until the attackers could come in force and first overwhelm the inhabitants of the cottages, then turn to the business of the castle with its people demoralized by the slaughter of their land mates. Men hastily prepared counterattacks at the parapets of the great stone castle. The gates had been closed against the attackers, and he saw that no troops had left the walls to fight because opening the gates to allow warriors out would make the castle vulnerable to the attackers.

Many of the attackers were in mail. They carried shields and wielded axes, maces, swords, and more. The farmers on the shore were fighting back with nothing more than shafts and pikes, knives, and an occasional small sword. Men lay scattered about; women screamed. A baby sat in the midst of the melee, crying and muddied. An attacker bore down upon the infant, his mace raised to swing at the child's head.

Waryk raced Mercury toward the scene, gripped with his thighs, swept up the babe, and turned just in time to avoid the mace. Angus, quick to fight in perfect unison with him, saw the action, and rode in where he had been, his blow against the man so ferocious that the would-be child murderer was nearly decapitated.

His men, trained warriors, had turned the tide of the attack at the cottages. The invaders were shouting to one another, turning toward their boats. Waryk saw the young woman who had been seized and torn from the smoking cottage; he passed the crying babe down to one of the women who had come from a burning home, and tore after the offender. He rode the fellow down; he and his captive fell into the dirt. His claymore drawn, and swinging the double-handed weapon with all his strength, he felled the Viking before he could be axed down himself. The young woman was screaming and shrieking; the dead Viking fell at her feet. Waryk drew her to her feet, and directed her back toward the village on the shore. "Go!" he commanded, and she turned and fled as told. He leapt back upon Mercury, turned his attention toward the men trying to escape now in their longboats. They had already shot away from the shore. They were experts in their boats, and pursuit would be futile.

He stared across at the castle, looked at the water, and judged the tide.

"Cross the water!" he cried, as he saw Angus riding to join him. "Divert the attackers so that the castle's warriors can open the gates to join in the fighting!"

"Aye!" Angus cried, and turned to do as told.

Waryk urged Mercury into the sea. The water rose up two feet, three feet, four feet . . . and then no more. White foam spewed around him as he forced his great warhorse toward the isle. The others followed in his wake. He burst upon the shore, and immediately took advantage of his mounted position, charging the Viking foot soldiers and bearing down on them with a fury. Men fell down before them. He heard cries from the walls, and then the sounds of the mechanism as the gates opened. Others would be joining him.

Suddenly, men-at-arms from within the castle burst from it. Ten mounted men were followed by a score or more of foot soldiers. Waryk paused, seeing that the men were led by a helmeted horseman in a distinct tartan. The MacKinny, he thought briefly, but could give the matter little thought. The man was an able soldier, so it seemed, warning the warriors behind him that they must circle the enemy before they could escape.

The attackers began to take flight. Still enraged by the destruction and wanton carnage he had seen among the village on the mainland shore, Waryk rode in hard pursuit. He caught up with one boat before it could shoot out into the water. Three men were aboard. He weighed his odds, furious but intending to live, then dropped down from Mercury, stepped out into the surf and rushed the few feet to the boat, and leapt into it like a berserker himself, claymore swinging hard with all his strength behind it. He sliced through the middle of one unarmored man, dodged a battle-ax, and rose to rip into a second man, catching him beneath his metal breastplate. He met the last in a grim, hand-to-hand battle, steel clanging against steel again and again. The fellow was burly, huge, well muscled, and missing all of his front teeth. He kept grinning as they fought. Finally, Waryk caught him in the throat; he caught hold of his neck with both hands and stared at Waryk in surprise as he died.

He felt the air as someone lunged at him from behind. He turned, ready to fight his attacker, but before he could raise his sword, the man fell.

He looked to the shore and saw the man who had led the others from the castle walls. He was still mounted; his horse stood in perhaps two feet of water. He held a crossbow, which he had used against the fallen man. He was a somber, serious-looking young man with tawny hair and hazel eyes. Still a wee bit green, perhaps, but steadfast.

Waryk stepped from the Viking boat to the water and walked through white foam turned red with blood toward the mounted man. The fellow dismounted as Waryk approached him. He bowed, inclining his head. "Laird Waryk." He looked up, a slight glint of wry humor in his eyes. "Watching you, sir, I did not know if you needed the help or not, but it seemed that such a man being dead sooner than later would not be a bad thing."

Waryk grinned in turn, surprised and not entirely pleased to sum up the man and determine that he certainly had his merits. "You're the MacKinny?" he said, though he did not need to ask the question.

"Aye. And we do beg your pardon, Laird Lion, for such a homecoming, but the raiders came from nowhere. Such an attack has not occurred here since . . ."

"Since Adin took the isle himself, I imagine," Waryk said.

Ewan MacKinny shrugged. "Strange. We've guards on the walls, always, as you can imagine. Such a fortress as Blue Isle is only strong when her gates are closed. In times of trouble, naturally, we bring our people and livestock within the walls of the fortress. This assault began, as you surely saw, with incredible stealth. They came from the bend, around the cliffs, and straight to the village. We were sickened within the fortress to watch, but I couldn't order men out—"

"You would have jeopardized the entire isle, aye, man, I could see that."

Ewan nodded, relieved, apparently, that Waryk didn't think he should have risked all to dive into the fray.

"Your coming as you did saved many people. We're grateful. We didn't expect you until tomorrow—as your last messenger had estimated your arrival." He inhaled and exhaled on a strange sound. "My own sister was among those you saved," Ewan said.

"Aye?"

Ewan smiled. "The great bearded giant stealing the woman from the cottage. She was Igraina, my sister."

"Shall we see to the damage?" Waryk suggested.

"None here, sir. We were able to bring in those on the isle; it was only across the water where the villagers were at the mercy of the attackers."

Waryk nodded and whistled for Mercury. His horse came obediently, and he mounted the animal. Angus was almost instantly at his side, nodding in acknowledgment to Ewan and waiting for Waryk's instructions. "Cross the water; we will see what ails we can fix."

Across the rising water, they met with Thomas, who quickly gave a report. "We did arrive most opportunely. Two dead, four injured, five houses sacked, three burned."

"The injured are—"

"Being tended, sir. Lady Mellyora has seen to them with her priest, a man called Phagin, who is well versed in healing herbs."

Waryk dismounted from his horse. "Where is my wife?"

Thomas pointed toward one of the cottages. Waryk nodded, then instructed, "Much is in stone here, the burned-out homes can be rebuilt. Have the masons and workers come and do what repair can be done before the night."

"Aye, sir, these are all MacKinnys, MacAllistairs, and Mac-Mahans here, Laird Lion. They'll work together for one another."

"And their overlord," Ewan added quietly. "Especially when he is a warrior prepared to risk his own life's blood for his people."

He looked up at the young man. His eyes were impassive. Waryk wondered if he wanted to kill the fellow here and now for knowing his wife, or if this loyalty meant that he had accepted the king's word and would be an asset Waryk could not afford to lose.

The man was a good warrior. *He could be trained to fight for the king,* Waryk thought. He didn't think that he'd be leaving the fellow behind on the isle when it came time to depart himself.

"See that there is a guard set on shore as well as at the castle tonight," he said, and strode toward the cottage where Thomas had said he would find Mellyora.

The place was in disarray, but already, something boiled upon the hearth, a slender, middle-aged woman worked there, and Mellyora indeed sat by the bed of a man with a huge gash on his arm. An ancient man with a long white beard held the gaping wound tightly together while she sewed it closed with tiny, expert stitches. "Aye, there will be a scar, but I will make it pretty, as fine as my needlework, Joshua," she said, teasing him, soothing him, as she worked.

"I killed the man who came with a staff—" Joshua began, then broke off, wincing.

"You were brave, indeed. Margot, bring the poultice, and your strongest ale; he needs to sleep."

"Aye, son, rest is the strongest healer now," the white-haired man said.

The woman who had worked at the hearth bobbed to Waryk and hurried to the bed with the poultice she had heated over the fire. Mellyora stood and turned to him. She quickly colored, and he realized that Angus and the MacKinny had come to stand behind him, and that she was seeing young Ewan for the first time since her marriage.

"All is well here?" Waryk inquired.

"Aye," Mellyora murmured, lifting a hand and indicating Joshua's carefully tended wound, and the way that his wife served him now.

Waryk stared at the man with the white beard.

"Laird Lion, arrived most opportunely!" the man said, and bowed, watching him with open curiosity. "I'm Father Phagin, Laird Lion, but since it's rumored my father was a Viking rune-master and my mother a Celtic witch, my flock just call me Phagin. I advise, I heal, I communicate my very best with Heaven."

Waryk thought that Phagin might turn elsewhere when he didn't feel that Heaven was answering, but he instinctively felt that whatever his ways and means, Father Phagin was a spiritual man, and probably did commune more closely with God than many a more orthodox man. "There are two dead, Father?" he asked.

"Aye, young Avery, the smith, and old Joseph, a mason."

"Let the women prepare them tonight; we'll hold services tomorrow."

"Aye, Laird Waryk. And sir, welcome to Blue Isle." He smiled somewhat grimly. "We are not so incompetent, sir, as it might have appeared when you first arrived. You must be weary from your journey. If you wish to settle into your new home, I can promise you that we will take care of the houses here, our people, and all that needs be tended to from this heinous attack."

Waryk watched him, and nodded. Mellyora still stood across the room, silent for once, and appearing stricken.

He reached out a hand to her. "Come, my dear. Indeed, show me my new home, I've a need to reach *our* chambers."

She was ashen, and he wondered if she would fight him, as she so often did—especially since he had emphasized the fact that they would share quarters and that he had done so in front of MacKinny. If she did, it might be well—he'd make the point immediately that he was laird of this castle.

But apparently, she didn't want any points made.

"Father Phagin, we'll speak later. Margot, pray, take good care of Josh."

"Aye, lady, he's my life," Margot said passionately, and she sat at her husband's side, taking his hand. They were neither young, nor especially pretty people, but there together, the tenderness they shared, despite whatever hardships in life faced them, seemed to cast a beautiful glow upon them both. Their lives were simple; poor perhaps, but in Margot's eyes, he could see that she believed she had everything, for her husband had survived.

Waryk found himself pausing. "Don't worry in the days to come, Joshua. You bravely withstood an enemy. Whatever you need that we can give, you will have."

"Thank you, me mighty Laird Lion," Joshua said humbly. "Thank you fer that boon, and thank you fer arriving in time to kill the heathens!"

"Aye, well, that thanks belongs to God, for we could not have planned it so, Joshua," Waryk said. "Mellyora?"

At last, she found motion and strode from the bedside. She hesitated just briefly, teeth clenched, before she accepted his hand and let him lead her from the cottage. "The tide is rising—" she told Waryk as he led her toward Mercury.

"Mercury can manage."

"The water is cold," she murmured.

Perhaps the water was cold; he had not thought so charging into battle, but then he had to admit to himself, he had been wild with rage. This, *this* place was his. His property had been attacked. And he would fight any man to the death.

"Aye, lady, then—"

"There are boats on the shore. My people will see me across," she said smoothly, intending to walk right past him.

"Really? Tell me, were those *your* people who just attacked?"

She stopped dead, turning furiously to him. *"What?"*

"Vikings. We were set upon by Vikings."

"Outlaws. Many Vikings are now as much a part of Scotland as you or I," she insisted.

"Umm. Curious, my lady, that you have so much Viking kin. Your father was Viking, and with the least invitation, surely, there are Vikings who think that this isle should be theirs."

"How dare you! If you're referring to my uncle—"

"I dare, because Vikings attacked."

She turned from him, starting away. He caught her arm, pulling her back. "And I'm referring to no one. I just pray you realize that such Vikings are your enemies, and not your saviors!"

"Let me go. I'm tired. It's been a long ride, and a long way home."

She jerked free and started walking again. He mounted Mercury, then decided that they would reach the isle together—he didn't give a damn if the water was cold, or scalding. He urged Mercury forward. She turned, hearing his approach, but before she could protest, he reached down for her, drawing her before him on the great warhorse. Mercury obediently plunged into the surf, and though the water rose, the horse didn't falter. They touched ground again, and together, rode onto the shore of Blue Isle. He urged the horse into a lope, and they entered through massive gates into a portcullis, through a second set of gates, and into the great courtyard of the fortress.

For several long moments, Waryk held his seat, staring around him. The huge stone walls housed marketing tables and merchants with their wares. Animals brought in during the attack still roamed about in large number. There were five tower sections connected by five lengths of thick wall; parapets lined the uppermost region, by way of the towers. The expanse of the courtyard was huge, and suddenly, all the people who had come into the walls for protection from the attack began flocking around them.

They called greetings to Mellyora, welcoming her home, and they welcomed him as their new laird with a warmth and passion that he realized could not have been his had they not arrived to such tumult.

People crowded Mercury; the horse accepted the adulation well, as if it were all for him. Finally, a man broke through the crowd. Mellyora spoke softly, using the Gaelic term for the master of the household.

"This is Donald, *ard Ghillean an-tighe.*"

"Aye," he murmured.

"Lady Mellyora, Laird Lion, welcome, come, there's wine by the fire, your chambers are prepared."

"Aye, Donald, I'm most anxious," Waryk said, and he eased Mellyora to the ground before leaping from Mercury. He saw a groom come for the horse, and Donald's presence had created a trail through the crowd. As they followed Donald, Mellyora greeted people, and people watched him, their eyes bright with curiosity. He nodded here and there, accepting the homage given him.

They entered the northernmost tower and immediately came up a flight of stairs; as with many fortresses, Waryk saw quickly, the lower floors were kept for livestock, arms, and other supplies. Donald told him that the men were quartered in the western walls, guests were given the eastern sector, and the northern tower and halls had always belonged to the laird. As they moved, Waryk rested a hand against the small of Mellyora's back. She walked very quickly. He kept pace.

The tower itself was the great hall of the fortress; Donald escorted them to the left to reach the master's chambers. They were vast, taking up the entire length of the seaward section of the hall. A huge bedchamber was separated from an anteroom by a draped arch, and while the bedchamber boasted the bed, a great hearth, a table by an arrow-slit window, a number of trunks, a washstand and an elaborately carved dressing table, the ante-chamber was equally comfortable, with large, leather-bound chairs, furs upon the floor before the hearth, a large table laden with books and plans, and walls hung with all manner of weap-onry.

He had best be careful, he thought. His wife could choose many a blade to use against him at a moment's notice here.

While Donald pointed out the view from the arrow slits and

the door that led to a balcony with stairs to the parapets, Mellyora stood still and silent in the center of the room.

"M'laird, what is your pleasure?" Donald asked.

"My belongings from the wagons will take time to load on boats, I imagine," Waryk said. "Is there a bath?"

"Of course, Laird Lion," Donald said indignantly. "They say that we are ruffians, barbarians, perhaps, but we've a fondness for water, here, sir, as it were. You'll find that the Scots—"

"I am a Scot, Donald."

Donald froze, embarrassed. "Your pardon, sir. Word had it that the king would choose a Norman laird, and—"

"I'm a Scot. My lady will have a bath now. She's cold. From the seawater, you know," he said, staring at Mellyora. She looked as if she was ready to take a weapon from the wall to use against him. "I'll see Phagin, Angus, and young MacKinny in the great hall."

"Aye, m'laird."

Donald left. Mellyora remained silent. Waryk stood before the hearth watching her, and knowing that she wished him dead.

"Well, is the prize worth the effort?" she asked.

"I don't know," he told her.

"You don't know? You've seen the land, and the castle."

"Aye, 'tis fine land. The castle is exceptional, and I can understand why David refused to let it go to anyone he didn't trust."

"Like a Viking's daughter."

"Again, I say, it was Vikings who attacked."

"Vikings are not all one people, they are not one happy set of countrymen!" she reminded him angrily.

"Pity, no one of the enemy survived to tell us from where they had come."

"I'm not the one who slaughtered them," she reminded him.

He shrugged.

To her surprise, she took a step toward him. "Daro did not do this. Daro would not do this!" she said angrily.

"I did not accuse Daro."

"You accused me."

His brow shot up. "You think that I should trust you?" he demanded.

She hesitated, and he could see her effort to control her temper. "When I thought I could escape you, no. But I do find this prize worth the effort. It is my home. These are my people. I love them.

I depend on them, and they depend on me. To me, it is everything. I find this prize well worth every effort, even if you don't."

"I didn't say I didn't find it worth the effort."

"You said—"

"I've yet to really explore the whole of the prize," he told her pointedly, and he bowed to her and started to exit the room.

"Waryk," she said, rushing forward to stop him.

She touched his arm, coming before him, then quickly withdrew her hand. He paused, staring down at her. She waved a hand around, indicating the room. "I've never slept here. These were my father's rooms. They are quite well decorated with his weaponry. Since you don't trust me, perhaps you'd be happier if I kept my own chambers, they are just opposite from here, facing the courtyard rather than the sea—"

"Your father is dead, Mellyora," he said. "And you may honor his memory, but this is the king's fortress and not a shrine."

"I didn't intend to make it a shrine—"

"You're the lady of the castle. You'll sleep here."

"And where will you sleep, Laird Lion?"

"Milady, I will sleep here."

"Will you? But do you dare? Have you decided that you can trust my past?"

She was taunting him, he thought. Her eyes were bright, challenging, touched with a humorous fire. Pity he was so damned determined. He was tempted to sweep her up and see how quickly her good humor faded if he chose to act like her *sainted* father then and there.

But he smiled at her, shrugging as if the nights were of no difference to him. "Fine, my lady, I will sleep wherever I choose."

He pushed her aside and exited the room, slamming the door.

In the great hall, he found Phagin, Angus, and Ewan seated at a huge carved table. A fire burned in the hearth, and wine had been served. He helped himself to a chalice of the wine and took a seat at the head of the table. He looked from Phagin to Ewan. "No one knows from where this attack came?" he demanded.

"Nay, Laird Waryk. They came from out of the clouds. I told you, we've not seen a Viking attack in years and years. What Viking would come against Adin?"

"But they were Vikings," Phagin said, and sounded distressed.

"Aye, that they were," Waryk agreed.

"Mercenaries, perhaps . . ." Ewan suggested, looking puzzled.

"Maybe it isn't so strange," Phagin said. "While Adin lived, Vikings would not attack."

"Ah, but the longboat attacks have been infrequent for a long time," Waryk reminded him. "What would the Vikings hope to gain?"

"They couldn't have hoped to scale the walls," Ewan said.

"And in the village . . ." Phagin said. He stroked his long beard, then looked at Waryk with dark eyes. "Nothing. No great riches. Just hardworking farmers and craftsmen and their women. Women . . . Vikings have often stolen women, but . . ."

"Not enough reason for an attack."

"Perhaps they just hoped to weaken our defenses, tear us up before . . ." Ewan began.

"Before what?"

Ewan looked at him curiously, then shrugged. "Before you arrived. I'm not certain what I mean." He hesitated, then added, "There are men who enjoy destruction, rape, and death for the sake of no more than cruelty."

Waryk sat back. He didn't believe that Daro would come against him. But someone had used Daro's camp. First, to take Mellyora. And now . . .

He had an enemy. Not strong enough to reach him yet. But with enough power and money to buy men—many men. And to frighten them. Frighten them into dying before telling him the truth about what was going on.

He rose. "Double the guard. MacKinny, Angus has been my right hand for many years. You'll share that with him, just as you served Adin. For now. Tomorrow, you'll show me every nook and cranny of this castle. And when we're done, we begin."

"Begin?" Ewan asked.

"Training. I've brought ten men, but I'm to have twenty ready when the king asks me to ride again, which will happen. And under such circumstances, we'll need more men here to be even more aptly trained—these attacks, I believe, will come again. And we will lose no more lives, no more livestock. We will not allow attack."

"Aye, sir!" Ewan said, rising.

Phagin rose as well. "I'll see to our injured again, now that night is falling, m'laird. And we'll bury our dead come the dawn."

"I'll see to the men," Angus said.

"Aye," Waryk agreed. The men started from the hall. "Mac-Kinny!" he called sharply.

Ewan came back. He looked sheepish, and even nervous now. "Aye?" he queried.

"I never condemn a man for the past, Ewan. I know that Mellyora once had hopes for a union—"

"I told her it would never be," Ewan interrupted softly.

"You seem a fine man, and a good warrior," Waryk said evenly. "Serve me, as you served Adin, and you'll do well."

"Thank you."

"I give you fair warning, though. Touch her, and you'll probably die."

Ewan hesitated, his head down, then he looked at Waryk. "Sir, I'd not cause her trouble now. I love her very much, you see, and, therefore, would not hurt her in any way."

Watching Ewan, Waryk felt strangely sorry. He needed work, training, but he might have been a man who could have held this fortress for the king.

"I'm sorry," Waryk told him.

Ewan shrugged. "Be good to her, sir. If she rants and raves, let her talk, and her temper eases. She's strong, and courageous, and—"

"Ewan?"

The man flushed. "Your pardon. I've known her since she was a child."

"I'm aware of that, and I don't want to be reminded."

Ewan smiled and nodded.

"Go on about your business tonight, MacKinny," Waryk said. "It has been a long day for us all."

"Aye, Laird Lion." Ewan started out. He paused, turning back. "You are, sir, more than I expected. It will not be such a hardship, serving you."

He walked on out. Waryk drummed his fingers on the table for several long minutes, then shivered, and remembered he was cold. He rose, and returned to the master's chambers. His rooms now, to be shared with his wife.

He entered quietly. She wasn't in the bedroom, and he walked to the archway. A bath had been brought as he'd ordered. It was old, of Celtic design. The heavy oak was carved all the way around with Celtic faces. It was deep, and even longer than the one he had brought for himself. Steam rose above it.

Mellyora rested within it.

Her hair trailed over the rim of the tub, and she lay back, her head laid upon the wooden rest. The water smelled pleasantly like a newly mown field. The water covered the length of her, yet it was startling to realize just how cruelly such a sight of her tormented the length of him.

She opened her eyes suddenly, as if she sensed him there. She sat up, staring at him.

"The water certainly appears hot," he told her.

"Aye."

He sat upon a trunk and discarded his scabbard, weapons, hose, and boots, then did away with his surcoat, the short mail he had worn, then his tartan. She looked away all the while, at the fire, at the soap, at the water. Then she was forced to stare at him, her eyes widening with alarm or incredulity, as he stepped into the tub with her. She gripped the edges, ready to fly.

"No," he told her, catching her wrist.

He could see the way her heart was pounding in the vein that thundered madly at her throat, and no matter what torment he was in himself, he wanted her where she was. He smiled. "I just had a conversation with young MacKinny," he said.

"Oh?" she inquired, but the sound of her teeth gritting—meant for him to hear, he thought—didn't take away from the concern he saw in her eyes.

"I like him."

"Do you? How generous."

"Here, take the soap. Wash my back."

"I thought you meant to sleep elsewhere."

"I'm not sleeping; neither are you. Wash my back."

He gave her the soap, and turned, amazed at the size of the tub. *The Celts must have had strange rituals within the thing*, he mused.

She didn't touch him. He wondered if he were being wise, sitting with his back to her. "Mellyora, if you please . . . ?"

The soap touched his back. He lowered his head, knowing the meaning of agony and ecstasy. Her fingers worked upon him, covering the expanse of his back, lightly kneading muscle and flesh. "Indeed, I actually admire young MacKinny."

"He is admirable."

"Aye, I like him very much."

"Good."

236 / Shannon Drake

"I did, however, do the fair thing, and warn him that I'd kill him if he so much as brushed by you."

Her fingers ceased their movement. He remembered the weapons displayed on the walls in the room. He turned suddenly, and saw that her fingers were vised tightly around the soap.

He took it from her.

"Turn around."

"What?"

"Turn around. I'll wash your back."

"It isn't dirty anymore."

"I'll just make sure . . ."

He manipulated her around, catching the length of her hair, curling it into a ball at her nape. Then he touched her flesh with the soap, and his fingers. She tensed against him, but didn't protest. He worked the soap over her shoulders, her neck, and moved his hands down to her ribs. He could feel her shaking, and after a moment she said, "You don't want anything to do with me right now, remember?"

"Aye."

"Then . . . then what are you doing?"

"Exploring the prize," he said dryly, and he inched closer; he couldn't help himself. He gently ran his hands down her shoulders again, over her back; then he slipped his hands forward with the soap, covered her belly, then her breasts.

She didn't breathe.

He didn't breathe himself. He cupped the fullness of the mounds, rotated the soap over them again and again, felt the pebbled hardness of her nipples, and the erotic depth of the valley between them . . .

Sweat, having nothing to do with the water, popped out on his brow. What the hell was he doing? He didn't give a damn about the future, a dynasty, his name . . .

His name. His father's name. A child's name.

He closed his eyes and dropped the soap.

"Get out!" he told her hoarsely.

For once in her life, she did as she was told. She was up and gone in an instant.

And he was left, trapped in . . .

Trapped in the great prize he had coveted so dearly.

Time, he told himself.

He had only to bide his time.

# CHAPTER 17

Father Phagin was an interesting man, one obviously beloved of his flock.

His voice was that of a storyteller; Waryk thought that in that aspect, he was much like Mellyora himself. Phagin spoke the Latin Mass in a pleasing tone that carried beyond the walls of the church, a structure built into the south tower of the castle, to the many people who listened from the courtyard. He eulogized the men killed, and in his speech, Waryk gained insight into the people here. He wondered vaguely if most of these people had ever realized that David had brought feudalism more firmly into Scotland, or if they simply went about life the way they always had. They were protected by the lords of the castle, and in turn, they gave the lords a portion of all that they built, created, or grew. The lords were responsible to them in times of trouble, and they were responsible to serve in a military capacity when necessary. Feudalism might have added more titles to the system, and kept many a freeman on the land where he was born, but in all, life had changed little. The men killed had been good Christians, good fathers, good providers. Beloved of the people, they were deeply mourned. The older man followed his wife to the grave by a few scant months, and there was solace in that thought; even with all the evils of the world, it was hard to accept the death of a young man.

Throughout the service, he stood beside Mellyora. When it had ended, the dead, in their shrouds, were carried with great ceremony and reverence to a cemetery beyond the walls of the castle. It was on a high mound that rose above the sea, an ancient place, strewn with beautifully carved Celtic crosses. More words were said, then the men were gently lowered into the ground. Dirt fell upon the dead.

Mellyora went to the younger man's widow, and spoke softly with her. Waryk followed her, bringing the woman a small linen satchel, filled with coins. "Times ahead may be hard," he said softly, then turned away, intrigued by a place on the high cemetery mound where it appeared that a space perhaps fifty feet by fifty feet had been dug and covered. He walked to it, frowning as he looked over the expanse. He turned back and saw that Mellyora was still with the young widow, but looking at him. Moments later, he realized the others had begun the trek down from the high mound, but his wife stood behind him.

She spoke before he could. "It's my father's gravesite."

He turned. "Aye, I'd heard he was a big man."

She flushed slightly, and he realized that she was being defensive. "He is buried with a longboat, and many of his belongings. It's the Viking way."

"But he had converted to Christianity."

"He was buried in a Christian ceremony. A knight may be buried with his sword; my father was buried the same."

"I see." He turned and started by her.

"Waryk."

"Aye?"

"The silver coins you gave the widow were an impressive kindness."

"She will not have her husband to support her."

"It is something my father would have done."

He hesitated. "Is that a compliment? I compare with great Adin?"

She stiffened slightly. "No. You will never be my father."

"Perhaps you should thank God for that."

He started walking again. She hurried after him. "What do you mean by that?"

"Nothing, Mellyora, nothing more than should be perfectly obvious."

"Wait—"

"I can't wait. I have business."

He left her there, upon the mound. He was anxious to find Donald, Ewan MacKinny, and Angus. The fortress was huge. He wanted to know all of its defenses, and its every weakness. He didn't intend to be taken from without . . .

Or within.

Days trailed into more days in a most unnerving manner for Mellyora. Their first night home, she didn't know where he slept. Nor did she the second. On the third night she lay awake so long that she discovered him crawling into the farside of the expansive bed to sleep. He lay still, and she didn't dare breathe.

She awoke late, and he was gone.

They were days of unease, but days in which they settled into a strangely comfortable pattern as well. Her father had been a Viking, but this castle had been her mother's holding, and many ancient offices remained. Donald was *ard Ghillean an-tighe*, Alaric of Iona was *as seanachaidh*, the sennachie, or bard, Mallory Mac-Mason was *am fear sporain*, accountant, or treasurer, and Hamlin Dougall, older than Phagin even, Mellyora thought, was *an Clarsair*, the harpist. Ewan's position with her father had been *an Gillecoise*, or personal attendant to the chief of the isle, a bodyguard as well, though Adin had needed little guarding. Since Angus filled that position for Waryk, Ewan became known as the most important of the *an Kuchd-tighe*, fulfilling much of the same function, and continuing to lead the men within the boundaries of the estate. Jon of Wick served as master of the guard, as *an Gocaman*, the warder. He had sharp eyes, and kept the night watch from the eastern tower, always on the lookout for danger.

Waryk made no changes to the way the castle had been run, appreciating the honor of the titles given the men. To Mellyora's sheer annoyance, Waryk didn't seem to need her at all; he learned the domestics of the castle from Donald, and the defenses from Ewan and Jon, and the expenses from Mallory. From his second day at Blue Isle, he began hard training with the men he had brought and the men-at-arms from her people. She knew that many of the isle's fighting lads were pleased to have so renowned a knight to teach them, and she was glad to hear as much laughter from the training grounds as she did the sounds of clashing steel. He trained men at cavalry, and he trained them to be foot soldiers. They worked with claymores, swords, axes, maces, pikes, Celtic and Viking weaponry, and farm implements.

At first, she kept her distance, and watched. Then, determined to keep her foothold upon her own authority, she spent time with Donald and Mallory, budgeting and planning household expenses and rents. In the great hall, during the day, with Waryk gone to the training field, she settled any disputes that had come up among the farmers, craftsmen, and merchants. She spent time on the mainland, tending to the injured, and to the needs of the homes burned in the Viking attack.

At dusk, the main household—Waryk, Phagin, Ewan, Angus, Jillian, Mallory, and herself—sat to dinner. Hamlin played his harp or another instrument, and Alaric usually entertained with a family tale. He learned Waryk's family history, and told it eloquently, and she was intrigued to see that Waryk was pleased with his effort. When the meal and entertainment ended, Waryk always had some business, and would leave the hall with Mallory, Phagin, Jon, Angus, or Ewan.

At first, Mellyora fled as well. As the days passed, she became more comfortable. She played chess in the great hall with Ewan. She played the lute, or the harp, invented songs with Hamlin, laughed and enjoyed her home once again. She knew one night that he was in the adjoining counting room, and so she played chess with Ewan, laughing, teasing, trying to tell herself that this was what it might have been. Yet she didn't feel the poetic anguish she should have known, she simply felt an emptiness, and she wondered whether she was angering Waryk, or taunting him. He seemed to show no interest in her at all.

A pattern had been established: He avoided her. He seemed to need very little sleep, and he came to bed late, and rose early. At first, she stayed to her own side of the bed. Then she realized that she could do whatever she wanted, and he would keep his distance. She no longer crept to the corner. He came in upon her bath, and ignored her; she backed her length against him in bed, and he lay still and stiff for hours.

She was amused, and yet irritated—and worried. When she spoke with Donald or Mallory about a matter concerning *her* castle, they would tell her that aye, of course, it must be done, if Laird Waryk agreed. By dusk, before the evening meal, she started to stand sentinel on the mound where her father was buried with his dragon-pronged longboat. Why had he died, why had he left her? She was even angry with her father.

She felt someone watching her, and turned. Waryk. He stood

higher upon the crest, his tartan mantle waving in the breeze around him. "Mellyora, come back to the tower," he said.

She turned away from him, stubbornly determined that he wouldn't tell her what to do. She thought that he would wait, argue with her, make some command again, and she could fight it out. But he didn't wait, he turned, leaving her there. The wind suddenly felt cold. It whipped around her, biting into her. Still, she remained upon the mound. At long last, she turned to walk back to the great hall.

Jillian greeted her at the second floor arch to the great hall. "Where have you been?" she demanded in a heated whisper. "A messenger came from the king—"

"Why?"

"You'll not know now. He's been with Waryk in the counting room for some time."

"Who came?"

"Sir Percy Warring," Angus whispered, joining them. As Angus spoke, the door to the counting room opened, and Sir Percy exited with Waryk. "You know my wife, Mellyora, Percy?" Waryk said.

"Aye, indeed!" Sir Percy said, taking her hand, gallantly bending over it. His lips just whispering against her flesh. His eyes touched her with a pleasant appreciation she hadn't known in a long time.

Married to a Yorkshire heiress twice his age, Percy had the reputation for being a reckless ladies' man, seducing countesses and chambermaids. She wasn't a fool; she knew him. But since he'd had a private meeting with Waryk, and neither of them seemed inclined to share the message he had brought, Mellyora determined to be a charming hostess, and play upon Percy's nature.

"Sir Percy, welcome, how charming to have you here, though I don't know to what we owe the pleasure?"

"King's business, my lady, and thankfully, quite finished now."

"Ah, well, Sir Percy, I insist you sit at my side and tell me what you know at court?"

She whirled about the room in a charmed manner, speaking to Donald about the best food, telling Percy about Ewan's bravery against the enemy, seating Percy on her one side and Ewan on the other. She flirted sweetly with them both. She brushed her fingers against Ewan's time and again when she reached for his chalice, apologizing, telling him she thought it was her own.

She didn't know what she was doing.

It was frightening, but she couldn't seem to stop. She sang with Hamlin, danced, played, teased, entertained, laughed, dazzled. She felt her husband's eyes on her the long evening. But then Percy suddenly remembered to present Waryk with a gift, a Viking longboat intricately formed in gold, a thank-you from her uncle who had legally wed Anne MacInnish.

"How wonderful, the wedding has occurred!" she said. And she was happy for her uncle, and for Anne. And she looked at Waryk, wanting to make sure he was aware that Daro had been with the king—and not attacking her property.

"Aye, lady, not at court. Daro brought Anne to Skul Island, and there they were wed, two days ago. I witnessed the ceremony for King David, and came straight here with my retinue from the nuptials. They are both quite happy and very grateful to your husband."

"Is that why you have come, Sir Percy?" she inquired.

"That, and other business," he said.

"What other business?"

"Business that is settled between us, my dear," Waryk said with harsh finality. She felt as if she had been slapped. Every man stared at her.

"Ah, well, I wouldn't interfere with business!" she said, and rose, and staring at Waryk, she swung around Sir Percy. "Good sir, I'll bid you good night, in case some other matter of the king's business comes up."

"I'll escort you to our chambers," Waryk said.

But she had already paused behind Ewan's chair, and insisted, "Ewan will escort me, laird husband. I'd not have you miss the king's business."

Ewan, crimson, had little choice but to rise and escort her. She fled the hall quickly, in a rare fury. Ewan left her at her door; she was in such a state that she barely said good night. Then she turned and kissed his cheek, apologizing quickly. "Forgive me. I'm not the same since—my father died."

She fled into the room.

Jillian had left her warm wine, and had prepared a bath. She drank down the wine in a single swallow. She poured more, allowed it to burn its way down as well. She cast off her clothing heedlessly, and stepped into the bath. When Waryk arrived while she still bathed, she ignored him. He strode to the table by the fire where the wine carafe and chalices were placed and poured himself a drink. She felt his eyes, but refused to look at him. She pretended he had never come to the room. She stepped naked from the tub, dried before the fire, slipped into her gown and left the anteroom to curl into bed without acknowledging his presence.

What did it matter?

Yet that night, it mattered.

As she lay there, she suddenly felt his hands on her. She nearly screamed out loud, for his fingers bit into her waist, dragging her against him. She felt the full, hard length of his body at her back, and the harsh contempt in his whisper as he spoke to her. "I could hardly kill young Ewan for being tempted by the behavior of such a whore, milady, and I warn you, milady, if I see the likes of it again, I'll beat you black-and-blue before Sir Percy, so that he'll understand that in no way do I tolerate your games."

She tried to jerk away from him, burning, furious, and close to tears. She had behaved outrageously, she knew it, and she was dismayed by her own actions; she hadn't been able to help them. Still, she lashed back, "How impressive! The king's great champion, the laird to take great Adin's place, must beat his wife into submission!"

Beat her—he would break her if he held her any more tightly! she thought. She couldn't breathe. She was crushed against him. She closed her eyes, aware of the shape and form of him against her as if her thin linen gown did not exist. She felt shaken, hot, angry, afraid, and still determined to goad him . . . His arms were so powerful, his scent, subtle, musky, sensual, the feel of his breath against her nape, her ear. The feel of his sex, hard, searing, cleanly delineated against her . . .

She opened her mouth, to speak, to protest, but his voice was suddenly so harsh and cutting in the darkness that she was silenced. "Compare me to your father one more time, and you will have him as he came to this isle, milady!"

He released her so suddenly that it seemed she was enwrapped in a chill wind. He rose, and swept up a rich fur and wool rug from the foot of the bed.

"I—I don't know what you mean—" she whispered in protest.

"You don't want to know what I mean. You're so immersed in legend and storytelling you can't see a truth known by the rest of the world. Adin was a Viking when he came here. He raided, plundered, killed—and raped. And then he stayed and married your mother."

"That's not true! My father wouldn't—"

"Your father *did*, milady," he said, and he was gone, slamming his way out of the room.

Mellyora lay there for a long time after he had gone, shaking. Then she rose, found shoes, and a fur-trimmed robe herself. It wasn't true. Adin had fallen in love with her mother. He had come here, he had seized the isle, but he had loved her mother, her mother had loved him.

She left the bedroom and started for the great hall.

But Waryk would be there.

She turned and hurried down the corridor in the opposite direction.

He was grateful, exceedingly grateful, to find the great hall empty.

A few of the huge hounds still roamed in front of the hearth. When he settled into one of the large carved-wood-and-leather chairs before the dying fire, the hounds settled around him. He absently scratched the ear of one, staring at the flames.

She was making him insane.

For other men, she burned as brightly as the fire. For others, she charmed, she smiled, she moved with tantalizing grace and sweet wicked appeal. By God, it was as if she taunted him to see how far she could shove, how great her power might be. And yet . . .

She stood over Adin's mountain of a grave with tears in her eyes. He was all things good, while the king had given her a wretched, decrepit Norman.

And he couldn't touch her.

He just didn't dare touch her . . .

He heard a sound, and he was up, spinning around, a fire poker in his hand for want of a better weapon. But the person who had come upon him in the night was Jillian, and she had turned white, staring at his face, and the poker.

"Laird Waryk . . ."

"Aye, Jillian, what is it?" He replaced the poker, taking his seat again, rubbing his forehead. He was acquiring a monumental headache.

"This is your home, sir. You needn't fear the people around you."

"I've been fighting a long time, Jillian, and I've reason to fear enemies within."

She held silent for a long moment. "Fewer than you think, perhaps."

"Perhaps. Why have you come here? Why aren't you sleeping?"

"I felt I had to see you. After tonight . . ."

Her voice trailed. "Aye?" Waryk said angrily.

"You can change things, Laird Waryk."

"Oh?"

"You spend hours each night, pacing, staring at the fire. You sit there late, night after night." She lifted her hands, at a loss. "Sir, there is no reason for you to do so." Next, she sounded just slightly aggravated, as if she could not properly explain herself. "Laird Waryk, you can count, can you not? 'Tis well over a month since you first met Mellyora."

He arched a brow, staring at her. Poor Jillian. She was so uncomfortable, wondering if she should be loyal to him, or to Mellyora, and if she wouldn't be doing her mistress a lesser service if she didn't speak truthfully with him.

"Meaning?" he said, a slight smile tugging at his lips. He was pretty sure he knew what she meant, but . . .

"I can promise you that she carries no other man's child," Jillian said, then turned, and fled.

He stared at the fire a while longer, then rose so suddenly that the chair fell behind him. One of the huge hounds jumped, whimpering nervously. Waryk barely noticed. He strode from the hall, and down the corridor.

Her father had been buried in the mound with his longboat, in a Christian ceremony, but in a Viking manner.

Her mother had been buried in the crypt of the small chapel in this, the laird's tower. She lay in the stone crypt with her father, her mother, and those who had come before them, preserved in the cold stone, ghostly in their linen shrouds.

Mellyora slipped down the stairs to the ground floor, then across the room to a corridor parallel to that above. Taking a torch from the wall, she moved in the shadows until she came to the chapel. It was small and simple: a Norman arch had been built over the altar, the pews were basic oak, and no more than twenty-five people could comfortably sit in the room. A winding stairway led to the crypts below, but she hesitated, staring at the single religious symbol in the chapel, the beautiful gold Celtic cross that hung above the altar. She walked down the hall, then started, thinking that she heard movement.

"Hello?" she called softly. "Hello . . ."

Unease filtered down her spine. "Hello! Come out!" she whispered heatedly.

She'd heard a rustling from the stairs. But now, she thought that she heard something from behind her.

She spun around.

Waryk. Still in his fur-trimmed robe, arms crossed over his chest, eyes narrowed in the dim light.

"Waryk!" she cried nervously.

"Who are you meeting here?" he demanded.

"What?"

"Who are you supposed to meet here, who are you calling?"

She shook her head. "No one!"

His expletive cut the night like a blade, and despite herself, she winced, moving backwards, hands clenched into fists. He started down the aisle toward her, strides long, eyes sharp. "Then why are you here?"

"I just came to—to—"

"To what?"

"See my mother's grave."

He stopped, just six inches from her. She had to hold her ground or trip over the dais where the altar stood.

"In the middle of the night?" he challenged. "To commune with her? To ask her if your father hadn't been a plundering, thieving, raping conqueror when he first came here?"

"Aye, maybe!"

"You're a liar," he told her.

She opened her mouth to protest, but his hand suddenly shot out. His fingers entwined in her hair and he dragged her toward him, tilting her head. He stared into her eyes, then lowered his mouth to hers, covering it, encompassing it. His tongue moved into her mouth with a coercive, invading force. His lips punished, and yet seduced with a strange, wild, fire. She struggled against him, unnerved by his mood, and his sudden actions. He had touched her before, and pushed her away. Time and again. Yet now it seemed that something exploded within her, liquid, like mercury, dancing in her blood. She wanted to free herself, she wanted to go back, she had taunted him too far, and she knew it, and she wanted the evening to start over, she didn't want to feel this cataclysm of scalding heat sear through her with such wicked design . . .

"Stop, we're in a chapel!" she whispered, breaking from him.

"So, confess your sins. Who were you meeting?" he demanded against her mouth.

"No one!"

"You're a liar," he said, and his fingers, threaded into her hair, tightened their hold so that she nearly cried out. She didn't think that she'd ever seen him so incensed. "You were expecting someone to be here. You wretched little fool. You'll bring about the deaths of a dozen men yet."

"No!"

"You're right. Because I won't let you," he said suddenly, and he ducked, picking her up, hiking her over his shoulders.

"Waryk, what are you doing. Waryk, let me go, I can walk, someone will see us—"

"Oh? Who?"

"Let me go, let me walk, let me stand on my own feet, I will go where you want me to go—"

"Aye, that you will."

He was very angry, and she was flopping against his back as he moved with long, heedless strides. "Waryk, you're tossing me about like a sack of flour—"

"Aye, and I've only just begun."

He carried her back to the main stairway to the second floor apartments, and down the corridor to their rooms.

He laid her down upon the bed, and was with her, over her. Firelight played in the room, catching the ice in his eyes, and it seemed that they gleamed red, and gold, a demon's eyes, eyes of fury, relentless. She started to speak, to protest, to fight; but once again, his mouth covered and consumed hers, and the taste of him seemed to fill her, even as she felt as if he raided her soul with his kiss, the force of his lips and tongue sweeping thought and reason, protest and strength away from her. Her robe was split open she realized, as was his, and she felt his nakedness pressed to her. Her linen gown was shoved high to her waist; she felt his hand on her flesh, fingers brushing her nakedness, touching, probing. She couldn't breathe; she was pressed deeper and deeper into the bed, she wanted to jump, to scream, to leap atop the walls as she felt him probing, and then shifting, and then . . .

She did scream, into his throat, against his lips. Her nails dug into him. Conflicting sensations tore into her, warmth, unbearable warmth, filling her, blood seeping into bone, overwhelming. She wanted to cling to him, she wanted to throw him away. Something seemed wonderful, touching, feeling, breathing him . . . his lips, still so close to hers, his scent, still so subtly sensual, compelling, tantalizing, even while . . .

The pain seemed to knife right through her. She wouldn't cry, she thought, wouldn't whimper. Would never falter, allow him to see, to know, how he had hurt her . . .

But he would see, he would know, because he was dead still, and even in the shadows and darkness he was staring down at her.

"Why didn't you tell me?" His voice was harsh.

"Oh, you idiot, I did tell you, you didn't want to listen, you didn't want to believe! I swore on my father, and—"

She broke off. He'd made some sniffing sound of impatience and begun to move again, and she gasped, fingers clinging into his fur-clad shoulders and a cry escaping her no matter what her promise to herself. "Quit, quit, quit . . ." she pleaded, eyes locked on his in serious entreaty, but his mouth covered hers, and some-thing . . . began to change. His lips moved with such subtle persua-sion, his tongue caressed, beckoning as much as plundering, his fingers moved down the length of her, tips stroking her flesh . . .

The pain faded slowly . . . and she was numb. No . . . not numb. She could feel him, the taut constriction of his muscles, the increasing fever of his movements, the heat that threatened to overwhelm her. His breathing came like a north wind, his heart beat like thunder. Enveloped in his arms, she suddenly felt as if he impaled her to the bone, and she twisted in his arms, amazed at the shuddering force it awakened within her. He moved again, and again, and she was still just clinging, feeling broken and split . . . and amazed, and strangely gratified by the feel of wet, steaming heat that seemed to fill her, permeate her body, and her being . . .

He withdrew slowly, and lay on his back. She was cold, and instantly sore once again, keenly aware of what had taken place.

Of course, she had known what it was to be married, expected what had come, and yet . . .

She'd never expected to feel a strangely awakened hunger. With him. When she still hurt, yet felt a need to touch his flesh, lie against him, bury herself within him. Be held by him, and soothed by him, caressed, and . . .

Wanted.

It was one thing to accept all this.

*It was another to long for it, for him . . .*

She turned away, curling to a ball at his side, tangled in her gown and robe.

"I'm sorry," he said after a moment.

"You should be."

"Well, milady, it's really your fault—"

"My fault!"

"You liked the game you were playing. You played it well, you taunted me, and enjoyed my discomfort."

"I never!" she lied. "I told you the truth, and you chose not to believe me."

"I was wrong."

His answer surprised her so much that she lay silent for a long moment, then whispered, "What?"

"Obviously, I was wrong."

"Obviously," she said, surprised at the tears that stung her eyes and glad that her back was to him.

"Glad, too, of course. I really do like Ewan."

She swung around at that. He wasn't looking at her, but up at the ceiling, and he seemed annoyingly complacent. "You're glad because you like Ewan?" she said.

"Aye."

She rose up in her tangle of clothing, raising both hands to pummel him at that, but he caught her wrists, surprised. "Now, what, madam—"

"You should be glad, sir, to discover that your wife had told the truth when she swore to you—on her father's honor—that she'd not taken a lover!"

"Ah!" he said, and suddenly she was swung down upon her back, and he was straddling her. "I see, you didn't want me to like Ewan, you wanted to see us both ever tormented and suspicious, ready to tear into one another at all times."

"No!" she cried. His robe still clung to his shoulders, but that was all, and she was so newly aware of his scarred and muscled body that she felt as if her own reddened at the simple contact. "Oh, will you get off of me, please, you refuse to understand, you are simply wretched, you—you—"

She broke off because he was staring down at her, smiling.

"What do you find so amusing?" she inquired.

"Not amusing. Pleasing," he said softly.

Again, she felt her flesh flame.

"Waryk, get—"

This time, she didn't finish because his lips were on hers again. Once more, his touch had changed. His kiss was slow, a caress with mouth, lips, and tongue, subtly tasting, exploring, tantalizing. She wanted to remain untouched, offended, and indignant; he had far too much patience at that particular moment, savoring the kiss with such determined leisure that she felt a trembling begin deep inside her, blood and bones, heart and mind. His fingers moved over her cheek, he broke away and the tip of his thumb traced the dampness on her lips while his eyes studied her. "I never wanted to hurt you," he said softly. Then shrugged. "All right, perhaps upon occasion, I have been truly tempted to beat you black-and-blue. But not in this . . ." Again, his mouth touched hers. Briefly now. He straightened, shrugging out of his robe. She longed to reach up and spread her fingers over the broad expanse of his chest. Scars crisscrossed his shoulders. She wanted to trace each one, and hear the tale that went with it. She kept very still, suddenly afraid not so much that he would touch her, but that he could become a need greater than any she had known. She lay very still, and he tugged upon the robe tangled around her. "Off with this now . . ."

"Now, wait, we've—"

"We've been introduced, my love. Now we become better acquainted."

"You've just apologized for mistrusting me, for hurting me—"

"Nay, dear wife, only for hurting you. You were highly instrumental in the mistrust."

"But—"

"I've been exploring the prize; I thought myself insane at times that I agreed to marry you when I had been offered the land without the bride. But the land, of course, is nothing without the heart, and now I am discovering even greater wonders."

"But it did hurt—"

"It will not hurt again. Come now, you didn't suffer so at the end."

"Oh, but I did—"

"Then I'm so sorry, and wretched, decrepit old knight that you've been saddled with, I'll still do my best to see that you want me."

"I came with the land; I was not what you wanted!" she reminded him as he eased her up, discarding her robe, pulling her gown over her head.

His eyes touched hers then, cobalt, as deep a blue as a tempestuous sea, and the smile he offered her was an honest one, not touched with mockery or amusement. "Ah lady, don't be so modest! Tonight, when I watched you seduce the household, I saw that you knew your own power. You're beautiful, Mellyora MacAdin, and you know it well, and the lads around you might well trip over their own hearts—and other regions!—since you would so cruelly rip them out and so carelessly cast them about."

"Oh, aye, and this is what you feel?"

"I'm not such a fool, my lady."

"That's right, you had no desire to marry me."

"It's not such a hardship."

"I shall lose my head with such ardent declarations of your desire."

He smiled, watching her. "Do you question my desire?" he demanded, and pushed her back against the pillows, continuing to speak with intensity. "Nay, lady, I was not fond of the idea of marriage with you because I am too fond of the idea of living. But as to desire, well, just what is it that you want? You know that there are poems about you, songs that range Highlands and Lowlands, you're aware that scores of men came to your father and the king, wanting you—"

"Coveting Blue Isle."

"Aye, the land is important, lady, when is land not? Fine. I'll not turn your head. You're dangerous enough as you are."

She wanted to protest that, but he shifted quite suddenly, moving against her. She felt his lips against her throat, his tongue tracing a pattern along her vein. He surely felt the wild speed of her pulse within it. His kiss went on, forging a trail to the valley between her breasts. She realized she had ceased to breathe; her fingers fell upon the richness of his dark hair. His mouth covered her nipple, and she burned with the lightning bolt it created, a shaft of heat that seemed to radiate within and without, tearing through her limbs, centering somewhere low in her abdomen. She remained very still, wishing she could protest, hating that he could do this, and yet suddenly wondering if she did have the power to please him. She wanted that, wanted him to want her, to feel the strange compulsion and longing that she felt, no matter how much she had wanted to deny him any part of her life.

Why did she want so much to deny him? she wondered vaguely. Simply because he had taken her life, been given her life . . .

The question, at the moment, faded. She had to breathe. She gasped in a tremulous breath, fingers tightening in his hair as he continued to move against her. His hand moved against her hip, his lips continued to lave her breasts, a slow assault, teeth and tongue teasing, touching, the heat of his breath whispering . . . he moved lower again, kisses brushing her navel, her abdomen. Her fingers remained gripped taut within his hair. And still he moved, bathing her with his touch, his kiss, everywhere, thighs, stomach, hips, thighs, and then, between.

She gasped, a startled scream that barely touched the air. She ceased to breathe again, she writhed in protest, and then . . .

She writhed.

She seemed to pulse within, body, blood, bone. Sweetness, heat, hunger, filled her; she ached, she longed. Mercury whirled within her, molten steel, sweet, explosive. She couldn't bear it, she couldn't stop him, she would die if he did cease . . .

Then suddenly he was atop her, lips against hers, whispering, "Lady, you need never question my desire for you . . ."

He brushed her lips with his kiss, caught her palm, kissed its center, drew her hand down the length of him. She trembled, and he taunted, "Ah, lady, you may touch a man. Such a region is vulnerable, and does not bite."

He closed her fingers around the fullness of his manhood. "Nay, it does far worse!" she murmured. "It . . ."

"Aye?"

"Robs breath, steals the soul."

He smiled, and rose above her, and with a slow seduction of movement, impaled her. She shuddered, and his eyes touched hers, and he smiled slightly. "It's the heart, lady, that steals the soul, and nothing other can do it."

She closed her eyes. He began to move. And all that he had touched before took flight from the fire that had been, and this time, when she climbed and longed and reached, it seemed she touched the sun. And then the sun exploded at that touch, shattering within her, and bringing with it a million shards of perfect light to melt throughout her . . .

He lay at her side. Then his arms were around her and he drew her to him.

"The prize," he said softly, "is worth any fight." She was startled to realize that she couldn't speak. "Umm, that good, eh?" he whispered. "Ah, see there! I must be careful of how much I admit, for I don't dare confess that you're entirely fascinating, when you, of course, remain married to an old, decrepit Norman."

She was surprised to find that a smile could touch her lips.

"You are not entirely repulsive."

"Ah! Such words of encouragement will keep me forever captivated!"

"You have all your teeth, sir, and they're actually very good."

"Alas, after tonight, I may not have all my hair."

She knew to what he referred, and she twisted, ready to strike out with far more embarrassment than anger, but he laughed, and he caught her, and kissed her again, and that night, she had less sleep than ever.

And it was true, of course, that he was not at all repulsive, old, or decrepit.

Indeed, she didn't dare admit just how compelling her laird husband was proving to be.

# CHAPTER 18

For several days, Mellyora moved about in a state of happy oblivion. She slept far into the day, spent the afternoons on the mainland still tending to the injured, and enjoyed the company of Sir Percy at their dinner table. She felt somewhat awkward with Ewan, even somewhat afraid that everyone might realize just what part of marriage had given her such a renewed energy and optimism for the future. The rest of the world couldn't possibly know that her marriage hadn't been intimate from the very beginning, she told herself, and certainly, nothing showed in her face. But Phagin commented almost sourly on the cheerfulness of her disposition; she flirted as outrageously and charmingly at dinner, but did so standing by her husband's side, feeling his touch, and making her own relationship quite clear. She did challenge and taunt her husband, but knew that he was not displeased, for though he never said as much, the way that he swept her up the minute they reached the privacy of their chambers was eloquent in itself.

She had discovered power—her own, and that which Waryk wielded. Sometimes, she was afraid. Sometimes, she was glad simply to awaken with him by her side, arms strong around her, giving her a feeling of belonging unlike anything she had ever known.

Sir Percy didn't leave. One morning, late in the second week of his arrival, she finished breakfasting in the great hall and walked out to the parapets. From there, she saw that he was out on the hills beyond the castle walls with Waryk, watching while her husband worked with his fighting men, perhaps twenty-five of them, mounted on warhorses. The men were armed with maces, and one by one they raced across the field to a standing dummy to swing at its vegetable head. From the parapets, Mellyora viewed the proceedings thoughtfully. Sir Percy had been charming and entertaining every evening. Igraina, Ewan's younger sister, had joined them for a more equable distribution of the sexes, and the evenings had been most pleasant. But Sir Percy had come for a reason, and, of course, Mellyora realized now, it had to do with the fact that the king would never let Waryk rest; he would be called back to David's service.

They often talked about the king at dinner. It was natural, of course, that he take the side of Empress Mathilda in the English question. Mathilda was his niece, since his sister had been Henry's first wife. The English had loved Henry's sister; she'd been known as Good Queen Maud. She'd renewed the Roman roads, built numerous religious houses, and she had known humility. She'd washed the feet of beggars in the church, kissed those feet, and taught humility to others. She had borne Henry two children, their daughter, Empress Mathilda, and their son, William, named for his grandfather, the Conqueror. But William had died in a shipwreck returning from Normandy to England, and Stephen, the Conqueror's grandson as well, had managed to take the English throne. Mathilda had reigned for eight months, at one time, and now, though agreements had been made, civil unrest went on. And on. And lawlessness prevailed. Waryk, she knew, disliked the fact that Henry looked to stretch his borders into northern England. He felt it was most important to make Scotland stronger and more unified. The kings of Scotland already gave homage to the kings of England, and it seemed to him that the Scots suffered each time they tried to take advantage of any chaos in England. He said as much at dinner, even while Sir Percy speculated about the present situation; Stephen's wife was another Mathilda, and she, like the Empress Mathilda, was a cousin of Stephen's. There was rumor that while Mathilda and Stephen battled for England, they also shared a wild, passionate love affair, and that Mathilda's son, Henry, born of her second marriage to Geoffrey of Anjou, was in truth Stephen's son. But the older Henry grew, the more it appeared he carried the blood of none other than his great-grandfather, William the Conqueror. Speculation continued to rage among the English people, unhappy as their government deteriorated, left now to what was often a lawless land.

Mellyora knew her history, especially recent history, as it so affected them all. And she knew Henry, and that he would indeed, invade England. Yet the way Sir Percy talked, it seemed as if plans for his invasions were still under way, which made her wonder just exactly why Sir Percy had come, and why he and Waryk worked so strenuously, training more and more men. The goldsmith's son, once intended for the church, was now spending his days working with a crossbow. One of the master mason's three boys excelled with a sword, and had been taken from his work, repairing a wind-damaged wall. The sons of tenant farmers, household servants, artisans, and more were entering into the training.

She asked Sir Percy why he had come, but he refused to answer questions at night, diplomatically sidestepping answers. If Waryk were being called back, he could not disobey the king's direct command, and so it seemed foolish to her that no one would simply tell her what was going on.

Mulling the question, she wondered what she would discover if she just rode out to the field to watch the men practice at arms. So determined, she walked along the corridor to her room for a cloak, then paused as she heard talking within. Igraina was with Jillian, tending to the chamber, and the two women talked.

"Do others know?" Igraina asked.

"At this time? Well, Sir Percy, of course. He came with the news. And Angus because he knows everything, and—Ewan, because he will defend here."

"Perhaps Mellyora isn't aware—"

"Well, there's nothing to be done."

That was enough. Mellyora pushed open the door and entered. She stared at Igraina. "Aware of what?"

Igraina paled, and didn't reply. Mellyora stared at Jillian. "By God, what is this? Jillian, I'll never forgive you! Obviously, something is going on, and I don't intend to be a blind idiot, and if you make it so—"

"Waryk has to leave," Jillian said.

"Aye, I can see that," she said sharply. "The king has summoned him?"

Neither woman replied.

"All right, both of you, what is going on here?"

Jillian cleared her throat. "David intends to invade England."

"That's not a surprise."

"He has sent Sir Percy to Waryk because they are both good

friends with the English border lord, Peter of Tyne. They are to ride in force to visit, and suggest he accept a new overlord in King David of Scotland."

Mellyora held very still. In the few moments that she stared at the women, she wondered how she would have felt if this had come about earlier. Might she have been pleased that he was going to leave, and she would have her isle alone?

She felt a tightening in her stomach. No. She had been jealous from the moment she had known about Eleanora of Tyne, even when she had totally despised Waryk. She was foolish; she was living in a heedless, merciless world, and she had been given by the king to a man in love with his mistress. She had not simply accepted him at the king's command, but she had allowed herself to be seduced. To smile, to laugh, to bask in his warmth. To savor the feel of his arms through the darkness and the night . . .

And now he was going to his mistress.

She spun around. Jillian chased after her. "Mellyora, he has to go. It doesn't mean anything. After all, he thought you were in love with Ewan, he had to be afraid that—"

"I was in love with Ewan," Mellyora said curtly. "But he came here with me, and threatened Ewan's life. Can I do the same?"

"Mellyora, please—"

"Leave me be!" Mellyora told her, shaking off Jillian's gentle touch and hurrying down the corridor. She was feeling reckless, and determined.

She hurried to the stables. She was about to ask that her silver palfrey be saddled, then determined that she'd rather take one of the large warhorses. Dabney, a huge bay, had been bred from a massive draft animal and a fleet Arabian mare, a gift to her father from a caliph he had chosen not to plunder in his a-Viking days in the Mediterranean. Dabney had been one of her father's favorite horses, and she had made a gift of him to Ewan after her father's death. Ewan, however, was mounted on Pict today, his own sturdy favorite, and so Dabney remained for the taking. She quickly ordered him saddled. Mounted, Mellyora waved to the guard and rode out to the field. She reined in as she neared the men. They were now lined up across the hilltop. Waryk, comfortably seated atop Mercury, was speaking.

"I've seen many an unwary man, fully trained, fall to the fury of a farmer's hoe. You must have eyes everywhere, and remember that all armor has weaknesses. For yourself, you must recognize those weaknesses, and protect yourself against them. When fighting, you must find those weaknesses in your enemies' defenses, and be ready to use them, to use any edge against your foes. You've done exceptionally well against an enemy on a pole; live men do not allow themselves to be attacked quite so easily. Don't underestimate your enemy, nor should you overestimate. More battles have been lost by fear than through lack of arms or armor. Take care against a greater strength; there is strategy in retreat as well as in a hopeless confrontation."

She had come from behind. He had concentrated on the men before him, and it was only as Ewan and Angus saluted her that Waryk turned to see her coming. He did not seemed pleased to find her on his training field.

He could not be, she determined, any less pleased than she was.

"Take my lady wife, good fellows. A Viking's daughter, she is well trained, as I'm sure many of you know. It's her belief that she can battle warriors with her sword."

"Ah, well, sir, that is because she can battle warriors with a sword. I have defended myself in many a sorry situation, and will surely do so again."

"My lady," Ewan called to her, "we are trained to defend you, you must remember!"

Her resentment grew. It seemed that even Ewan had turned against her.

"Ah, well, Ewan, I do appreciate such loyal nobility from you all, but I'm afraid I've discovered that I cannot always count on a warrior being present when danger threatens." She stared straight at Waryk.

"Ah, but my dear wife, were you to remain safely within fortress walls, where you are protected, such danger could not threaten," he said pointedly.

"It's difficult to tell sometimes if danger isn't living within the same walls," she countered quickly, and equally as pointedly.

"But you must always have a protector!" Brett, one of her own young men, a MacKinny, and kin to Ewan, called to her. "My lady, it is a simple question of size!"

"Size is not so simple a matter," she said, and nudging Dabney, she circled around Ewan.

"Give me your shield, Ewan."

"Mellyora, no."

"Ewan, please—now!"

He did as she commanded, and she reached for the lance he'd been about to use in the next training exercise. He resisted, but then released the long lance.

"Your husband will spear me with this thing!" Ewan whispered.

She cast him a withering glance and rode on by him, looking quickly to ascertain that the tournament weapon, used here today to practice aim, was blunted. She turned Dabney quickly, challenging Brett. "Come, let's see how size affects the outcome of a joust."

"Nay, lady, I could not—" Brett protested.

"Then, sir, I have the advantage, for you will not defend yourself against me!"

"Mellyora!" Waryk warned, but she ignored him.

The other men had cleared away, and she had taken the requisite distance between the two of them, then spurred her horse onward. Dabney was expert, and fearless. Brett's mount betrayed his rider at the moment of impact, and though Mellyora was severely jolted, she held her seat while Brett was unhorsed.

There were cheers for her, and shouts in defense of Brett. "Ah, lady, now, Brett is a gentle fellow and would not take aim at your fair form!" cried Angus.

"Then he'd best take care to guard himself!" she said firmly. Dismounting, she dropped her lance, and seized a sword from the arsenal of weapons brought to the field. Shield in her left hand, taut to her body, she strode determinedly toward Brett, her eyes pinned on his with steely purpose. Waryk, she was certain, was an excellent trainer of men, but he had not had enough time yet to teach young Brett the finer rudiments of swordplay. "Today, sir, I will help with Laird Lion's lesson." Brett lost his sword after her fourth swing. He fell to a knee, bringing his shield up to deflect her final blow. "Milady—" he began, but as he spoke, she swung around, aware that Waryk had come behind her. She had expected him.

"Another lesson," he said firmly, eyes furiously on hers. "There is seldom just one opponent on a battlefield. Just when you might feel that you've triumphed, there will be another man ready to skewer you through!"

"Well, then, that is life, isn't it? It seems that there is, indeed, always another man ready to skewer you through! All the more reason to be ever on the defensive, and never underestimate your opponent.

"Aye, lady, don't underestimate," he warned softly.

"And don't take me for a fool!" she returned.

She swung at him hard in anger, and realized that he had planned on her doing exactly that. He came back at her with a staggering series of blows, so that she was forced down as Brett had been, raising her shield to deflect his blade. But when he would have brought his claymore down with such force that her blade would be torn away, she suddenly rose, swinging with her shield, and left him slamming his claymore with full force into the ground. She quickly flew back at him, ready to strike, but he drew his blade from the ground just before she brought her sword against him, and she struck his steel with a shattering force. Stumbling to recover, she retreated to regroup, ignoring the fierce pain in her shoulder from fighting to hold the blade.

He came after her. Grimly. She moved behind Dabney; he followed. She backed away, watching for his least movement. She stepped backwards upon a rock, and missed her footing. She wasn't hurt, but she cried out as she fell.

"Milady—"

He lowered his sword, reaching for her.

She swung her sword to his throat. He held still, eyes flashing, staring down at her. "Treacherous witch," he said softly.

"Use any edge," she retorted.

"Any edge." He caught hold of her sword, heedless that he cut his hand, and wrenched the blade from her. The weapon flew across the field.

"There, lady. Advantage taken."

"You were already a dead man, had I chosen."

"Is that a threat?"

"I no longer hold a blade."

"Life is full of weapons, isn't it?" he queried.

"And dangers," she agreed.

He bowed to her, reached down, caught her hand, and drew her to her feet. The men had heard none of their exchange. There were cheers for them both. She wanted to shout out that it was all a lie, that there was nothing gallant or charming between them, that she was indeed hurt, and that her cry had been a cry of pain.

"Ewan, Angus! Carry on, will you, please? The way she has

wielded her blade makes me think my wife has something to say to me. In private."

"Aye, Waryk!" Angus said, and he was instructing the men again even as Waryk drew her along to Mercury. She knew him enough to know that her resistance was futile, but she remained stiff and cold as he lifted her atop the horse and mounted behind her. She remained cold and straight as they rode back through the gates to the courtyard, and kept her teeth clenched as they entered their tower and strode the steps to the second floor.

He all but threw her through the bedroom door, and when she found her balance, she spun back on him, defiantly staring at him. He stared at her in return, striding to stand before the fire. He didn't take his eyes off her, but stretched his hands before the blaze to warm them.

"Mellyora, I don't know what it is you've got to say, but I promise you this—if you ever decide to perform such a foolish stunt again, I'll have you locked in these rooms, and you will not so much as step into the great hall for a meal without my precise permission."

"What?" she demanded incredulously.

"You just risked your life—"

"No man would have killed me!"

"Your limbs, your flesh!"

"Don't be absurd; you train daily, there is—"

"There is always risk, even in training."

"But if you—"

"I risk only myself."

"And I risk myself—"

"And maybe a child."

She gritted her teeth, regrouping her argument. Here she was the furious one, and he was going to chastise her! And, she thought, dismayed by the anguish it caused her, they were back to where they had always been. She had never been his choice. She came with Blue Isle, she was important to it, and he wanted children. Legitimate children. She was, as his wife, crucial to that aim as well.

"You're leaving," she accused him.

"Aye."

"For *Tyne*," she said.

"Aye. The king—"

"The king did not order you to go to Tyne! The king is preparing to invade England, and when he is ready to fight—"

"Peter of Tyne is a friend, and has long been my friend. His property will be the first to come under David's dominion, and I intend to give him every chance to bow to David before the king sends troops to strip the property from him."

"So, how gallant you all are! Sir Percy came to tell you that your dear friend Peter is in trouble, and so you will train your troops and bring them quickly to Tyne, where Peter will be politely warned, and all will be well!"

"Aye."

"And what of dear friend Peter's sister?"

He wasn't surprised by the question. "What about her?" he asked bluntly.

"You tell me."

He arched a brow, a slow smile forming on his lips. It was all the answer she needed. She turned, starting to exit the room with fierce speed and determination. But he could move with equal speed, and before she could reach the door, he had blocked it. She didn't try to barge past him; she didn't want to touch him. She stood dead still.

"There were many times when I had thought that there was nothing you would like better than to have me leave. You'd have your precious isle back—without me upon it."

"Fine. Leave."

"I must go."

"Fine. Do so."

"It's a matter of honor."

"Of honor! Oh, you bastard, let me by—"

She tried then to drag him from the door; a futile effort. "Mellyora—"

"What? You have to leave, leave. You're going to your mistress's home, fine, but get your hands off me!"

He suddenly released her, but didn't step away from the door. He folded his arms over his chest, watching her, a deep frown furrowed into his brow. "So that's what you want?" he said softly.

"Aye, now let me by—"

"I am riding to a friend, to avoid what bloodshed I can, because God knows, there is no way to tell the king he shouldn't invade England. There will be real battles soon enough. Hard-fought battles, and God, but I am sorry to say, he will push so far that we will have little chance for victory. But here, I can see a friend, and change things, but you're determined that I am on my way to see my mistress, nothing more."

"No."

"No?"

"No, I believe you will be delighted to see your old friend Peter, you will laugh, you will drink, you will thump one another on the back, and you will be great warriors, and greater allies of the king! Then you will see your mistress."

She didn't have to exit the room. He stared at her another moment in pure fury, then slammed from the room himself.

Igraina had stayed long enough. She lived in one of the cottages on the mainland with Gwyneth, their grandmother, and Lars, their grandfather. The two had raised Ewan and Igraina since their mother's death at Igraina's birth, and though Igraina was an exceptionally lovely young woman who'd received numerous marriage proposals, she had determined on caring for her grandparents before accepting any man's offer. She had, of course, been charmed by Sir Percy, just as Sir Percy had intended, but she knew as well that as a chieftain's sister, she had a certain social stature, but not enough to be a wife to such a man, even if his elderly bride were to pass away. Since she did find him very charming, however, she thought she might be better off at home. She often traveled from the isle to the mainland by herself, but that afternoon, the tide was low, and Ewan was anxious to see his family, and so she rode with him to the cottages.

"Do you ride with Waryk?" Igraina asked him. "Or are you left home, to guard the castle—and Laird Lion's bride?"

"I stay home," he said carefully.

He felt his sister's disapproval.

He sighed. "Igraina, I do not lust after the laird's lady—"

"You're a liar. She's my friend as well. You've loved her forever. She's beautiful, willful, passionate—"

"And you're right, I love her. But you needn't fear for me. I knew when Adin died that the king would never let her go to me. I'm glad the king chose the man that he did, for God knows, matters might have been much worse!"

Igraina turned to look at him. "Aye, that I can see. He is a fair laird, a fierce defender. He saved me, and I remain grateful. We may have Viking in our blood, but my blood, at least, is settled here, and I'd not be a Viking's slave. He will hold this land for the king, of that I'm sure. But brother, he is leaving, and I promise you this, Mellyora is upset."

Ewan looked down at his sister's tawny head. "Ah, I see. And you think that she will be furious that he's gone to his mistress, and so she will think to use me against him?"

"She loved you—"

"Aye, sister, she did."

"You think that she loves you no more?"

"I think that she will always love me, a bit differently, perhaps. And because she loves me, she will never use me."

"I hope that you are right."

"Indeed, because I would be so easily seduced to adultery?"

"It's not that you would be easily led! You loved one another—"

"Aye, but again, things have changed. She would not use me, and—"

"You would not use her?"

"I wish it were that simple. The truth is, she would not want me anymore."

"What?" Igraina said incredulously.

"She loves him, you see."

"No, I don't see."

He sighed with mock distress. "Women are so blind!"

The fortress at Blue Isle sat atop high rock, cast against the cliffs, hills, crags and water with startling majesty. Even when night came, her towers seemed to reach to heaven. Candle-and firelight gleamed. Blue Isle glittered like a priceless gem set in a sea of gold. Watching the isle, Ulric Broadsword contemplated his actions. On the border, his Norman ally was creating havoc, but Ulric had been given much in the way of arms and men, and surely, he was expected to provide more in return than he had thus managed. Actually, he'd performed magnificently, but since his attacks had thus far proven less than effective, no one would know. That in itself was frustrating. But there was a great deal offered, not the least being the satisfaction of revenge. Becoming part of Daro's camp had been a stroke of brilliance, but Adin's daughter had escaped from them. He thought crossly that he really would enjoy taking a horsewhip to the girl—or slicing her throat. Adin had trained his daughter to be a warrior, and he'd done well enough at the task. But though he now found himself more anxious than ever to get his hands on Mellyora MacAdin, it was the complete downfall of his enemy that he craved. Blue Isle. Adin had taken it. Adin had held it. Just like other Scottish isles, this land could be taken and held by the Norse. That would indeed be retribution. Yet so far, plans which should have succeeded had failed. He had seized the Viking's daughter from a Viking camp, only to lose her and a number of good men. He had staged an attack which should have laid waste the mainland, but Waryk had arrived with his armed and mounted troops at least a day before he should have come. So now . . .

Now, word came, the great Laird Waryk was riding again— to bring an Englishman into the Scottish fold before the king seized lands which had fluctuated back and forth between the two countries for more than a hundred years—and would surely continue to do so. David of Scotland would have his way. While Mathilda and Stephen fought, the powerful barons in northern England did what they would, creating their own little kingdoms, their own form of law. Ulric knew this well himself, and was grateful for the situation.

Waryk rode with well-armed, well-trained troops. Many of them. He'd learned his first battle tactics from descendants of wild, barbaric Celtic tribes; he knew to use the forests, the trees, the cliffs, the hills, to attack and retreat, to repulse an ambush. Attacking his troops as he moved across the countryside would be suicide. Any major action now against the mainland would be seen; the masons and carpenters had erected a tower from which guards would see any assault from the sea, and any large movement from the forests carpeting the hill to the east . . .

His impotence suddenly enraged him. He could remember the past. His father had often told him of a time when Vikings set out in their great longboats, and the people screamed in terror as they came. The fury of the Norsemen! Monks prayed, women wept, men died. The Christian God was cast down, His nuns were raped, His churches violated. The Vikings took what they wanted, and they left, and they fought so well and so fiercely that they conquered half of the land they invaded, they ruled, they were the power. They were such great warriors that indeed, they brought their prowess to their enemies, they interbred, and even when they did not, they were so powerful and indomitable that their enemies hired them at great prices to do their fighting for them and with them, and many a great alliance was born.

Han came to him where he stood on the hill. Han had become sour. While escaping after they'd taken Mellyora MacAdin from Daro's camp, Han had broken bones in his foot, and he still limped. He'd been injured during the assault on the mainland off Blue Isle, and he was weary of their encampment here, northward of the isle.

"Word has come from the south," Han said, sounding bitter. "You are not causing a great enough disturbance, and the Scottish king is beginning to move. There will be an attack on Tyne, but whether it can be rallied quickly enough . . ."

Ulric scowled and stared back at Blue Isle, glittering on the coastline. "Tyne is no one's objective," he said contemptuously.

"Tyne is perfectly good land, and the fortifications and manor there are fine enough. And with King David so staunch a supporter of his niece Mathilda, any land or estate we seize we can take in the name of Stephen, and history will say that we were but loyal supporters of a king over the prospect of a queen. The Normans brought this form of primogeniture here—they understand that a male must inherit. History may well exonerate us, and Stephen himself reward us. Vengeance and rewards. The fortress here will be weakened again with Waryk gone. If there was but a way for you to seize Mellyora MacAdin again and keep her . . ." Han said, his voice trailing.

"Aye, now more than ever!" Ulric said, trembling with the hatred that had grown and festered through the years so that it was now something almost tangible. "Aye, take what he most desires. Hold her just out of his reach . . ." He started to laugh. "Kill her, not kill her. Hold her and see if she carries his child at this point, and let the child be born . . . then return his son to him, piece by piece. Aye, great Laird Waryk, here is your boy—his heart! Or let him wonder. Take his wife, his legal lady, and make of her a Viking concubine, and let him wonder year after year if he raises his own son, or a Viking's bastard! His pope may not allow him to disavow the grandchild of the man he murdered! Or . . . capture the lady, bait the great laird. And if he can be killed, then keep the lady and the isle, and resurrect the power of the Norse jarls here on the coasts! Whatever comes, I will see that a knife twists into his heart. His father was killed; he should have lain on the field with him. His line will end with him, I swear it!"

Han made a strange noise. "For you, Ulric, there is passion and vengeance in this! We must begin to take care. Some of your own men begin to doubt your wisdom. We're warriors, we fight. Fighting men win, and fighting men die. We fight for gain, to seize land, for power."

Ulric spun on Han. "Don't you understand as yet! Aye, Waryk killed my father, but more, don't you see! The wretched Scots were beaten, they were dying one by one, it would have been over before King David arrived. The ancient MacNee land would have been ours, the MacInnish would have perished, and all the riches would have been ours long ago—"

"Maybe. You must remember, your father was a mercenary with the Norman lord. Would he have proven trustworthy? Will your great friend in this vengeance provide us land and power as he has promised?"

"Aye, his bitterness is greater than mine."

"But we must take care. We lose more and more men—"

"We will find more and more men."

"Aye, we call out to the isles, we bring in Danes, Norse, Swedes, younger sons, men who must make their way. They aren't enough. We call on the Norman peasantry, on those with bitterness themselves, old Saxons, disgruntled Scots. Soon, someone will betray us, and when the cause of these skirmishes is known, the whole force of the king's army will come down on us—"

"We will not be discovered, Han."

"One day, an injured man will talk."

"No man will talk when he knows that his death will reward his family, while a betrayal will cause us to slay his sons, daughters, and wife, and further kin."

Han held silent. Ulric brooded for a moment.

"We need Mellyora MacAdin," Ulric said.

"The fortress is impregnable. Perhaps, as well, she will accompany her husband when he rides."

"She will not do so. She fought the marriage. She will be glad of his leaving."

"But tell me, Ulric, do you really think that he will leave her."

"He goes to his mistress."

"I ask you again. You've had Mellyora MacAdin within your grasp once before. Do you really believe that he will leave her?"

"He must! And aye, the walls may be impregnable, but if she can be drawn outside the walls . . . where is Daro's camp now?"

"Fifty miles to the east, I've been told. He has been the guest of the king now on many an occasion, and I believe he is to receive more lands near Stirling."

"He married Anne?" Ulric persisted.

"Aye, that he did."

Ulric smiled. "Perhaps I will pay a visit to my little cousin then."

"And again, I tell you, perhaps Mellyora will accompany Waryk when he rides."

Ulric looked at him sharply. Then he smiled. "We will have to see that she doesn't ride with him."

"And how—"

Ulric suddenly laughed. "Two men will succeed where dozens of berserkers have failed!"

"Are we out to murder—"

"Nay, we're out to wound a man. And to cast the seeds of doubt and suspicion into the ground! Aye, the lady will stay. We shall see to it." He set an arm around Han's shoulders. "When you cannot tear down walls from the outside, you must tear them down from within. The more I think about it, Han, the more it seems there is a greater prize than even I imagined here. I will find a way to take the old Viking's daughter. To slay the man who murdered my father. I will rule Blue Isle, and pay homage to a Norse king, and make peace with Stephen of England. David of Scotland will pay to travel his own land. Aye, I will rule Blue Isle. An old Viking laird, a new Viking laird. Waryk dead. Not too quickly. I would have him see me take his wife, and know that if she carries his child, I will kill his child very slowly before making the isle and his woman my own."

"You'll need to take care."

"Aye, Waryk is a fierce warrior, well trained, lethal. I will take care."

"I did not refer to Waryk. If you try to take his wife, she might well kill you."

"Indeed. But I'll never give her the chance. Perhaps there's even a way to have him die believing that she was the one to betray him. She is a Viking's daughter."

# CHAPTER 19

Darkness came, and Mellyora remained upon the hilltop where her father's body had been interred. He'd been buried with one of his longboats and his weapons, but she knew where he lay himself, in a wooden coffin carved by the finest of his countrymen, old Oginwald, who still lived in a cottage down the hill. The Celtic cross she leaned against marked his actual burial site. She thought that she might feel closer to him here, that she might be able to close her eyes and go back to a time before he died, when it had seemed that the world would always be hers to command and she would never, never have to feel this awful hurt and jealousy.

But even as dusk came, she couldn't seem to bring her father's memory as close as she wanted. He had been huge, golden, red-bearded; his laughter had run in the hall, he'd changed languages twice in every sentence, and he had loved to move among the people. His battle tactics had not been so trained as Waryk's, he had called upon distant friends when serving the king, and he had sat here often, as she sat now, high upon this hill, and stared out to the sea. He'd loved the sea, but he'd loved Scotland more. He had seen this land through her mother's eyes, and he'd still talked about her mother until the day he died. To him, her mother and the sea had become one, ever fathomless, ever beautiful, offering storms, offering peace, never still, always changing, always fascinating.

Mellyora rested her head upon her arms, closing her eyes. Adin had seen the world that he'd wanted, and he'd made it his own. She'd always believed that she could forge her own life as he had done. But the king had taken that.

She felt the thunder of Mercury's hooves against the ground

long before she saw the horse. She stood, surprised and somewhat unnerved that he had come for her; she had not expected him to do so.

He reined in on Mercury across the expanse of the burial ground, and stood, looking at her for a long moment. Then he nudged the horse and walked him slowly to where she stood. She didn't move, but waited. He stared down at her, and she wondered if he meant to be as imposing as he was atop the warhorse. To counter the way he towered above her, she reached out, patting Mercury's nose. The horse was loyal to his master, but for all the bloodshed the animal had seen, he was an affectionate horse. He responded to her touch as she moved her palm over the softness of his muzzle.

"So here you are. Among the dead again."

She looked up sharply. "I came here often long before my father died. It is usually a pretty and peaceful place to come."

"Aye, as I said, among the dead."

"They are sometimes far more agreeable than the living."

"Because they can't argue with you? Ah, but then, do you think that great Adin will rise up, return to run the wicked from his land?"

"It's quite a pity that he can't."

"Alas, most unlikely. It's late, it's dark, and Adin is gone, and you have guests in your hall, milady."

"My hall? But I've been told that it's your hall."

He reached a hand toward her. "Come up."

She backed away. "I think not."

"Let's not do this, milady."

"Let's. You're the great laird, the mighty hero—I was expendable in it all. Sir Percy came to see you with news regarding the doom about to befall your very good friend. Go and discuss your gallant rescue with him. If I'm not there, you'll need not take the least care with what is said. Sir Percy had tried so hard not to state the truth of why he has come. He will have a far more pleasant evening without me."

"I leave tomorrow, and you are coming back with me."

A strange ache twisted in her stomach. "Tomorrow? You leave tomorrow. And I find out here, now. As I see it, sir, you are gone now. Leave me alone, and have Blue Isle to yourself before you leave it on your great errand of mercy."

"Mellyora, you fought me for this isle, and you married me

for this isle. Alas, I would not be so cruel to forget that this is your isle. You're the lady here—"

"Aye, fine. And when you're gone, I'll tend to domestics, Laird Lion. I know that you can suffice magnificently on your own. You are, after all, the king's great champion. My father, the Viking, managed on his own for many years."

"Ah, yes! Your father. The great man."

"My father, aye, he was a great man, he served the king, but he didn't bow so low to the floor that he could no longer see anything other than the dirt!"

"Mellyora, I'm sorry for your father's death, but I am weary of hearing of his greatness with every move I make."

"My father kept peace here, every move he made—"

"You think I should be more like your father? Kinder, more gentle, make every move as he made it?"

"You refuse to understand what I'm saying."

"Damn you, lady, if you want me acting like your father, you shall have it."

She started, backing away as he dismounted with determined anger, striding toward her. "I don't know what you think you're doing. My father was not a tyrant—"

"A tyrant. No?" Waryk demanded, striding toward her until she was backed against the large stone Celtic cross that bore her father's name. "Dear wife, perhaps not—when you knew him. That was after he had come here, seized this land, then married your mother and made his peace with David." He set a hand upon the stone, leaning toward her. "Adin was not always gentle in all things. He came here in a dragon-prowed longboat, the son of a jarl, come out a-Viking. And he raided this place, laid it low, and took your mother, and I'm delighted things went so well for them both, and he was blessed, surely, to have a child with his lady to so adore him, but my love, he came here just as Alexander came across Europe, he came, he saw, he conquered—"

"That's history as you heard it—"

"That's history as it happened!"

"You weren't here!"

"And neither were you. In the flesh, of course. I've heard you were conceived during their very first encounter."

"You've heard!" she cried. "So it is truth! Well, I'd heard that you were a Norman, an English upstart, grabbing up whatever crumbs you could gather from the Scottish king's floor! I've heard this and so, indeed, it must be true."

"Shall we stop now, milady?" he inquired tightly.

"Stop? I didn't begin this fight. I came to this place to be alone. You intruded."

"I came to bring you home, milady. It's growing dark, and we've a guest who awaits, not to mention our own household."

"I'm sorry. You so often accuse me of games. This is one I cannot play. If you're going to your mistress, sir, don't expect to visit first with your wife. Eleanora is Norman, I understand, and I'm sure you have much in common."

He smiled slowly. "I've many different strains in my blood, so I've been told. Viking through both the Scottish—and the Norman. You want a man like your father, milady? Let me oblige. I'm terribly sorry, I must be disappointing you so, I have to change, I have to be the man you want me to be."

"No!" she cried, startled as he reached for her. She tried to dodge around the Celtic cross, but he came after her relentlessly, his features grim.

"Waryk . . ."

He caught her arms, drew her hard against him. It was as it had been at the river; he cast her impatiently over his shoulder and strode back toward Mercury while she struggled to rise and speak some sense to him.

"Waryk, I swear, I never saw my father treat my mother so—"

"And did you ever see your mother rude to the guests in her hall, or refuse to take her place at the table, especially with a guest in residence?"

"Aye, she missed meals! When she was ill—"

"You're not ill."

"I'm terribly ill. You've made me quite sick to my stomach—"

"Then I'll keep you by my side and make sure that you are well."

She gritted her teeth, tightening her hands into fists, slamming them against his back. "Put me down now, Waryk. You cannot do this—"

"How amazing! I believe I can. Just like the old laird."

"I am going to dig deep gouges into your back."

"I don't suggest it, or else I will create big blisters on your derriere."

"Put me down! I will not go to dinner and pretend that all is well—"

"Then we will miss dinner together, my love."

He mounted Mercury with her cast so over his shoulder, causing her a jolt when her chin slammed against his back. He kneed Mercury, and when the destrier began to race back toward the castle, stable, and his own food, she quit fighting to hold tight against the wild, hard motion. She was mortified when they rode through the gates, aware that the men in the gatehouse watched. She slammed her palms hard against his back again, furious that he seemed not to notice. She demanded, "Let me go, this has gone far enough!"

"Let you go?" he queried, slowing Mercury's gait. "To walk freely, have your way, turn your back on me when we have a guest in the hall? Would Adin have allowed your mother such freedom had she determined to humiliate him in this way? I think not. If the lady refuses to appear in the hall, then she must be in the deepest distress, and a kind and gentle laird would not leave her side for a minute!"

"Waryk—"

"Ah, lady, here we are. A beautiful ride, a pleasant night."

They had passed by the gates and into the center of the courtyard, and she knew that the men on guard around the parapets were watching. His men, her men. Were they amused, or angered? Many of the people, men and women, had always known what she had not—that the king was Norman in his ways, and that he would never simply allow her to have her father's power on her own. And those who had known that one of the king's men would be given Blue Isle were probably grateful of the man who had come, and thus they probably watched the spectacle below thinking her the willful one to cause trouble for such a powerful warrior laird.

"Aye?" he queried as Mercury trotted to a halt.

"Put me down."

He dismounted, allowing her to slide to her feet before him, but not releasing her. She saw that his young armor-bearer, Geoffrey, was there, ready to take care of Mercury.

Waryk's eyes locked with hers as she found her feet.

"What shall it be?" he said softly.

"Let go of me. The guards are watching."

"Aye, they are, aren't they? So, if I agree, what will you do?"

"Walk into the tower."

He arched a brow, and released her. She spun around and started toward the tower, entering through the arched doorway, nodding to the guard there, and heading directly up the stairs. She came to the corridor. He was behind her, she felt his presence, his breath, his being, so close that she nearly screamed.

The concept of a pretense of domestic tranquillity suddenly seemed appealing; she wanted only to reach the great hall.

"Ah!" he cried mockingly from just an inch behind her. "Would great Adin allow dinner now, in the face of such obstinate disdain and total rejection? I think not." He reached out, catching her arm, spinning her around.

"Waryk, we've a guest—"

"And you are concerned for him now? I imagine that since Sir Percy might have managed on his own without you, he can fare on his own without me as well."

"We've a household—"

"Aye, and the household can entertain our guest. I like being like Adin, my lady."

"You're not like Adin!"

"Fine. I shall be like me." Alarmed by the look in his eyes, she tried to wrench free. He drew her to him, sweeping her into his arms. He turned in the corridor. Angry strides brought him to their chambers, and he kicked the door open with a power that made the wood groan and shudder. Inside, he closed the door in much the same manner.

"Waryk, stop this, leave me alone!" she cried.

"Nay, lady, I will not."

She struggled in his arms, writhing like a fish on a hook, then slamming her palms against his chest. She realized after a moment that he was just standing there, letting her beat against him, and then he walked with her to the furs before the fire, eased to his knees, and laid her there, his eyes locking with hers once again.

"Listen to me," he told her.

She shook her head, staring at him, trying to keep the tears stinging her eyes from falling. "No, I will not listen—"

"You will." He reached out, drawing his knuckles down her cheek. "You may believe this or not, but I've no desire to go to Tyne."

"I don't care—"

"You do, that's what this is all about."

"But you will go to Tyne. And you will see her."

"You see Ewan daily."

"That is different. We were never . . ."

"But did that matter? You did love him. Enough to fight for him, to defy the king for him! I can't deny that Eleanora and I were lovers, and in truth, I must either see her or blind myself, a rather drastic measure to take."

She turned her face from his, staring at the fire. He caught her chin, and drew her back to look at him. "I admit as well, in marrying you, I felt myself wed to a double-edged sword, albeit an enticing one at that. But then, since, I have also admitted that I find you quite beautiful, while you have discovered me only slightly less than repulsive."

"Waryk—"

He set his palms upon her face, and lowered his mouth to hers. She tried to twist free, and could not. His kiss was engulfing, forceful . . . seductive . . . relentless. She fought hard not to respond, yet was breathless when he raised his head from hers.

"Ah, yes, a mistress. Well, she never fought me, you know."

"I've never fought you."

He arched a brow.

She set her jaw. "I know that I'm your wife," she said tightly.

"Duty, eh, my love? A mistress seduces—there is a difference."

"Well, sir, you'll be seeing her soon enough, since you've chosen not to blind yourself."

"Ah, well, it was a try . . . then I shall have to do the seducing myself." He set a hand upon her bodice, fingers tangling around the embroidered lacing there. She caught hold of his hand, amazed that despite her anger and determination, she could still want him so. His scent seemed to permeate her senses, his touch created fire, his eyes danced with the blaze, and his power seemed to be all around her.

"No," she murmured, fingers curled around his.

"Duty," he reminded her dryly.

Soft fur lay beneath her; the light was simply a glow of the blaze. She opened her mouth to protest again, but his kiss consumed her ardent and demanding, and his fingers were deft as he dealt with the lacing of her gown. Her heart ached, she couldn't submit, and she tried to twist upon the soft fur, escape his touch. Her gown came free, and even as she turned, her very movement bared her shoulders and back. His arms came around her, and she bowed her head as she felt the liquid flame of his caress against her nape, down her spine, lower and lower. His palms moved over her breasts. In a tangle of clothing, she was turned within his arms, meeting his kiss once again. His fingers stroked between her legs, slid deeply into her. Caressed. Enticed . . .

His tartan needed little effort to cast aside.

In seconds, he was within her himself, and she closed her eyes, clung, and felt the fire cast gold and crimson upon her, and rage with its fierce, all-encompassing flame. She swallowed down the cry that would have escaped her when it was over. It seemed impossible that she could feel such acute physical pleasure one minute, then such a wave of abject misery the next. She had known that she must never want him, need him. She had *known* . . .

Then she heard his whisper.

"Since you are my wife, lady, there is the solution that you ride with me."

"What?" she gasped.

He rolled her to him. "Ride with me. Be with me. Sleep with me."

"You want me to come?" she said, amazed and skeptical.

"Aye, lady. Did you think me happy with the thought of leaving you behind when I know that your mind is ever busy?"

"Meaning?"

"God knows, you disappear far too easily."

She had no idea, searching his eyes in the fire glow, if he teased her or spoke with serious intensity. She only knew that she could think of nothing she wanted more.

"Well?"

"Aye, sir, if you wish it, I will ride with you," she said primly.

"Aye then, we will ride together," he said, drawing her into his arms. She leaned back against his chest. They lay upon the furs in the fire-shadow, watching the lure of the flame. Then she closed her eyes, setting her fingers upon his arm as he held her, and she was afraid to be so happy.

Igraina stood just outside her home, seeing that her grandfather's shaggy cows had come into the enclosure for the night. And as she did so, a strange sense of fear, of unease, swept through her. She turned, and there was a man.

Tall, burly, yet with a middle just beginning to run to fat. He had the size and stature of a Viking, yet something about him seemed not quite right. He was clean-shaven, as a Norman might have been. His hair was clipped, yet . . .

He'd been sleeping in the woods. His neatly cut hair was laden with grass and twigs. His clothing was torn, and he looked hungry. And he was coming toward her, smiling . . .

"Lass, 'tis been a rotten time I've spent in the woods, but with the boats gone, and me cut off from my fellows, well it seemed there was nothing other to do. But all is calm, now, eh? The guards sleep, for the master is in his house. I'll have food and plenty tonight, eh? A fire to feed me, a woman to warm me, and more . . ." he said. He spoke to her in Norman French, and she thought that perhaps he didn't realize she could understand his words.

A massive sword hung from a scabbard at his waist.

His grin deepened as he stared at her. He switched to the Gaelic tongue, accented as if he had learned the language farther to the southeast. "You. I will have you. I am hungry, you will sate me. We'll be warm and full, and if you please me, I will spare the old Norseman and his aging bride. Come now, come to me."

She stared at him, thinking that hunger and living in the wild had given him an edge of insanity. She backed away from him, and a scream tore from her lips.

Instantly, Ewan was outside. He saw the man, and ran to her, casting her behind him. "What's this?" the burly man demanded. "A farmboy turned warrior, a shepherd in his master's clothes? Come, come on, lad . . . you may feel my kiss as well, ah, boy, the kiss of my sword, the kiss of death. Or, you may step aside, and I'll take the woman, and maybe you'll live with the old folks."

"Who are you? Why did you come?" Ewan demanded.

"Who am I? A man who lives by the sword, willing to die by the sword, to sit in Valhalla, heaven, or hell."

"A Norman? A Norseman?"

"Norman, Norseman . . . a hungry warrior. Maddened by the smell of the meat within. The old woman cooks well. I've learned to eat the meat of a beast with the blood of a man on my hands, so move aside, farm lad, or I'll slice you gullet to groin."

"I am the—"

"The MacKinny, eh?"

"Who sent you?" Ewan demanded again.

The man started to laugh. "Ah! How fight an enemy when the enemy can never be clearly seen? Suspicion is a fierce weapon, tearing upon a man. You'll not know, MacKinny. Come, fight me if you will."

Ewan beckoned to the man. "Aye, you mercenary dung. We'll meet, and see who it is who kisses death!"

Igraina shrieked as their swords clashed.

Again, and again, and again.

The men moved around the yard, one taking the offensive, and then the other. Ewan leapt upon a stand of rolled hay, his strange foe dropped and rolled just in time to miss the plunge of his blade.

The man was speaking. Quietly. Threatening Ewan, taunting him.

But Ewan would not be put off guard.

The burly man spun, ready to slice her brother in the middle; Ewan jumped back just in time, and the sword slashed through the air. Then the men rushed together, and they were locked in the moonlight and the shadows.

The Viking shouted, calling upon his gods, Igraina thought. Because he was losing. Ewan was going to kill him. Or . . .

Keep him alive. And they would know why the Vikings were attacking.

But the burly Viking wasn't calling the gods. He was calling for help. He knew that someone was near. Someone who had been watching all this time . . .

"Ewan!" Igraina called, trying to warn her brother.

As the burly man fell, another man suddenly came from the shadows. He stepped forward, fresh, rested, ready. His sword came clashing down upon her brother's; they locked in deadly combat.

The man drew back, turned, and ran, disappearing into the shadows.

"Ewan!" she cried, and raced for her brother.

He turned to her.

"Ewan?"

"Igraina . . ."

He smiled sheepishly. And then she saw that he clutched his middle. Blood streamed through his fingers.

He fell, clutching her. "Get help, don't be with me, don't be alone. A man remains out there. They are with . . . Daro," he whispered.

"What?" she cried, looking around, confused, afraid. Oh, God, he was bleeding. So much blood.

His eyes found hers. He moistened his lips to speak. "He told me he was with Daro as we fought. He told me we will fall like Rome, from within."

"Daro, but Ewan—!"

"Get back inside, get help, shout for the guard in the tower . . . they have to know, don't be alone. He is gone, but could come back."

"Ewan, be still, I'll get help, I'll be safe."

"Someone has eyes within, and tells them what goes on in the fortress."

"Ewan, hush, please!"

His eyes closed, and he lay limp against her.

"Ewan . . ."

A low, moaning sound came from her, and then she began to scream.

And scream . . .

# CHAPTER 20

M ellyora awakened to the pounding on her door.
At her side, Waryk rose. The fire burned low. He moved quickly, drawing a fur from the bed with which to cover her and sweeping a robe around his own shoulders. He opened the door. Angus and Phagin stood there, grim and anxious.

"The MacKinny is downed by a Viking sword, and lies in his family's cottage, sorely wounded," Angus said.

Hearing those words, Mellyora leapt to her feet, gasping. "Ewan . . . is killed?"

"Nay, lady, he hangs to life by a tenacious thread," Phagin said.

"A Viking sword?" Waryk said. "Another attack?"

"A survivor from the woods," Phagin explained quickly. "He appears to have been alone, driven from his hideout by hunger."

"The water is high. A boat awaits," Phagin said.

"I'll be quick," Waryk said, and closed the door. He moved with swift competence, redonning his tartan, scabbard, boots, and mantle. Mellyora watched him for a moment, numb with worry. She tossed aside the fur, fumbling as she tried to dress as quickly. She felt his eyes on her.

"What are you doing?" he asked.

"I'm coming with you," she said, keeping her eyes lowered on the laces she tied at her bodice.

"Perhaps you shouldn't," he said, and his voice sounded harsh.

She looked up at him. "I could make the difference, Waryk. I have to come. Please."

He shrugged, but she still felt a peculiar heat in his eyes. "Hurry then. I don't mean to sound cold, but if he is to die, I must speak with him first."

Her fingers felt too large, like ice. They refused to respond to the commands of her mind. Waryk came to her, tying the gown, reaching for her cloak and sweeping it around her shoulders. He caught her hand, leading her out of the room.

Angus and Phagin awaited them in the corridor. They hurried down the stairs together. Geoffrey, Waryk's *an Gille-mor* or armor-bearer, awaited them with horses ready to ride to the boats at the shore. Her father's boats, they were Viking-built, swift and maneuverable.

It seemed to take forever to cross the water, yet they came at last to the mainland. Waryk stepped from the boat, boots sloshing into the seawater; he reached for her, lifting her to the dry sand. The cottages were all alive with firelight and many precious candles burned. The people lined the outside of the house, waiting for their laird to arrive at the bedside of one of their loved chieftains. Mellyora hurried along behind Waryk, frightened and numb. Ewan. She had thought herself so loyal. How quickly she had fallen out of love. How loyal and fine he had remained. And now, in defense of her homeland, he was dying.

She followed Waryk into Ewan MacKinny's grandmother's cottage, and there saw him stretched out on a high pallet, his features white as death. He had been stripped of arms, armor, and clothing. His bare chest gleamed in the firelight, punctured by various fresh stab wounds, while a linen cover was swept to his waist. Igraina was by her brother's side, dabbing at his wounds. Waryk paused in the doorway. Mellyora swept past him, coming to Igraina, Phagin close behind her. "Igraina . . ."

His sister, face tear-stained, moved aside. "Mellyora, I've tried to staunch the blood, some are flesh wounds, no more. Here, I think, is the worst, against his side . . ."

Mellyora quickly examined her fallen friend, finding that most of the wounds were not so deep; easily sewn, and packed with salt water and the healing weed that littered the shore, some would not even scar. She moved the sheeting, exposing the length of his body in search of a mortal wound. She caught her breath when she saw the great gash just above his groin. Blood still seeped from it. She pressed her fingers hard against the wound, and the blood slowed. She carefully felt the area, trying to ascertain what organs might have been damaged below the flesh and muscle. She prayed that he'd torn muscle, nothing more. Pressure, quick sewing, and a poultice was needed. But she was so afraid.

She couldn't look at Ewan's face without feeling a terrible guilt. And she was aware as well that her husband watched as she tended the naked body of the man she had intended to marry. A moment's great sorrow filled her. Stretched out so, unconscious, brutally torn, he was still a fine sight. Lean, hard-muscled, young, handsome. A brave man, a good man, in his prime. She couldn't make a mistake. She dealt with Ewan's life.

"Pressure, here," she said quickly, and, stepping back, she anxiously asked Phagin, "I think that it is flesh and muscle torn, no more. I want to stop the blood, sew, and poultice the tear with the sea salt and weed, and prevent swelling from within."

He stepped by her, studying the wound as she had done, his long fingers incredibly gentle and delicate upon Ewan's flesh. He nodded after a moment. "Aye, Mellyora." He turned suddenly. "Laird Waryk, you've the strength in your palm, I believe, sir, if you would . . ."

Waryk stepped forward, placing his hand on the wound as Phagin told him, "This is difficult, to bring such pressure here where the blood vessels cannot be tied . . ."

"I'll bring the needle sutures," Igraina said. "Grandmother has gone for the seaweed and salt water to make the poultice."

The flow of blood decreased to a trickle. Ewan remained white. Mellyora stood waiting, feeling as if a million years passed. The trickle of blood ceased. Phagin carefully placed his fingers where Waryk's had been.

Mellyora knew that Igraina stood at her side, ready to bathe the wound again and offer her the needle and thread. Her fingers still felt so cold. She'd worked with Phagin all her life, she could sew with deft, tiny stitches, and she knew that she had a healing touch. But she could barely move now, she was so afraid to touch Ewan, so afraid that he was going to die. He'd lost so much blood. How could any man live, when he had lost so much blood?

"Mellyora."

It was Waryk who said her name sharply. She met his eyes, then stepped forward. Igraina cleansed the area again; Phagin gripped flesh and muscle. She stepped forward. The light was flickering. She couldn't see. The night was cold. Sweat beaded her brow. The light was suddenly better. Waryk held a candle at an angle that gave her far better vision. She bit into her lower lip, and began to work.

Ewan never moved. She looked at his face again and again,

certain he had died while she worked. He lay so still. But his chest rose and fell, rose and fell. He breathed; he lived.

She expertly tied off her last stitch. Ewan's ancient, tiny grandmother moved in. She muttered prayers beneath her breath, soft incantations in Gaelic, as she plastered the freshly sewn wound with a poultice of the healing seaweed. Mellyora turned. A basin of water had been left. She soaked and wrung a cloth to put upon Ewan's forehead, then she cooled his neck, shoulders, chest. Night was becoming morning, and as they had all expected, a fever was setting in. He had to be kept cool, and it would take a constant vigil to see to it that the fever didn't claim him.

The sun rose. They had made it through the first night. Stretching and straightening as Ewan's grandmother brought her fresh cool water, she realized that Waryk was gone. She didn't know when he had left the cottage, only that he was gone.

Phagin remained with her. His eyes were on her, and he seemed to read her mind. "He left some time ago, Mellyora."

She nodded. "I see."

He was still watching her. Igraina, who had gone outside, came over to her brother. She touched his forehead, changed the cloth there.

"When will we know?" she asked Phagin softly.

"Each day he survives, he will grow a little stronger. If he can shake the fever for a full week, well then, I believe he will live. Unless he has bled too much inside, and then . . ."

Igraina let out a soft sob. She lowered her head, then suddenly looked across at Mellyora as if she were fighting to remember that Mellyora was lady of the isle. But she suddenly spoke with tremendous bitterness. "Mellyora MacAdin, you are lady here, but by God, I swear, if you are a part of this . . ."

Stunned, Mellyora stood. "A part of what?"

"It is Daro."

"Daro!"

Igraina angrily wiped tears from her eyes, staring at Mellyora. "The Viking claimed that Daro had sent him when they fought."

"That's a lie—"

"It's what my brother said. My brother doesn't lie."

Mellyora shook her head. "I didn't accuse Ewan of lying. But the Viking lied, or whoever or whatever he was. Daro wouldn't do this—"

"Why not? This was his brother's little jarldom. Adin left a daughter, perhaps he feels that the land is rightfully his. God knows, enough Vikings have ruled Scottish islands!"

"Daro would not do this—"

"Wouldn't he?" Igraina accused very softly. "Perhaps with your blessing. Someone knows what is going on here. That Ewan came with me to the mainland. That any major attack would be seen, but that a man or two could slip quietly through the trees to assault a cottage."

"So someone saw!" Mellyora cried indignantly.

"You swore that you'd keep this place alone, that you'd be independent, that the king would see your strength. You said there would be no Norman laird here. The only way this fortress could fall is from within."

Mellyora tightened her fingers into fists. "I've known you all my life, Igraina! I wouldn't do this, I didn't do this! Would I risk Ewan? *I love him!*" she reminded Igraina.

Then there was silence. A dead silence. And she turned around to see that Waryk had come back; he stood in the doorway.

He stared at her with more than suspicion.

She knew that he had taken Igraina outside sometime while she had worked on Ewan, and that Igraina had described the attack to him, shown him the body of the dead Viking, and made every accusation she had just made to Mellyora. And now she stood there, stricken by what had happened to an old friend, yet accused of causing the travesty—while having just stated before her husband her love for another man.

"The men are searching the hills, crags, cliffs, caves, and forests for the second man, any other survivors of our recent attack, Igraina. The carpenters and masons have begun work on a wall around the dwellings here so that there can be no such surprises again. We've every able pair of hands at work, and we'll bring a permanent guard here so that the mainland no longer lies vulnerable."

"Did any man recognize the body?" Igraina asked.

Waryk shook his head, looking at his wife. "Mellyora . . ."

He stretched out a hand. She felt a fierce trembling in the pit of her stomach. "Waryk, I—" she began, but it seemed she had no voice. "He remains in danger," she said lamely.

"Mellyora," he repeated firmly.

She couldn't leave Ewan, but Waryk wouldn't understand why.

He had been her friend forever, he was the MacKinny. He had always been willing to die for her.

"I don't question your healing talents," Waryk said sharply, "nor the tremendous value of this man's life. But you will come with me now."

She swallowed hard, staring at Igraina. If she didn't walk across the room, Waryk could come and take her, and she was very afraid of his temper and suspicions should he have to do so. She lifted her chin, angrily staring at Igraina for a moment, then turning to her husband. "My uncle didn't cause any attack here, Waryk. You may say what you wish about my father being a conqueror who raped my mother, but she conquered him in the end, he became Scottish. This is a Scottish isle, day by day, we have followed the ways of the old Scotia, and all that my father ever forced upon this isle was better boats—and himself. Daro respected my father; he has fought with you, he fought with you for King David."

"Mellyora," he repeated. "Come with me now."

"I have not betrayed you or anyone to any Viking forces."

"Mellyora, come with me now." His tone was very sharp. She felt ill. He was suspicious of her. Igraina had simply accused her without doubting the word of their enemy.

Behind her, Phagin urged, "Go, Mellyora."

"I will tend my brother with Phagin," Igraina said, coming to her and setting a hand on her shoulder. Perhaps, hearing Waryk's tone, Igraina was sorry, and perhaps she at least believed that Mellyora was innocent in what was happening, if Daro was not.

"He will need constant care, someone by his side every minute, hour after hour."

"Aye, Mellyora, I will take this hour!" Igraina said. "Phagin will be with me."

Mellyora lowered her head. She was alarmed when she realized that Waryk had lost patience with her, and was coming across the room. She found life, hurrying toward him. His fingers bit into her arm. "You may return to tend this man you love, my wife, but at this moment, you will come with me!" he said with quiet menace.

She bit into her lip, very aware that he was furious with her. They exited the cottage together. Angus waited just outside.

"The lad?" Angus inquired softly.

"Lives. And may survive."

"There is, just arrived, a messenger from David. There is more trouble breaking out at the border."

"At Tyne?"

"East of Peter's lands. They will surely try to draw him into whatever action is taking place."

"Ready our forces. We'll ride with the morning."

He urged Mellyora toward the dragon-prowed boat, her father's boat, a Viking boat, that waited to take them across the high tide. She was reminded painfully of the night they had first met as he seated her, stepped into the water and pushed the boat from the shore, then took his position center to row.

They shot across the moonlit water. She felt him staring at her, and she still felt numb. She wished that she could explain that she loved Ewan like a brother now, that things had changed. But she was accused again, for being what she was, and she knew her uncle, and knew that he was not guilty, just as she knew her own innocence. He had no right to accuse her.

"I am not guilty of anything! I didn't—"

"Don't talk. I don't want to hear it right now."

"But I—"

The hard crystal look in his eyes silenced her for the moment.

They came to the isle. Mercury awaited. She made no protest when she was seated on the great destrier with Waryk behind her. She knew the path they were taking. Back to the fortress, to the tower.

Angus had preceded them. Already, the tower was filling with men, wagons, horses, implements of war. They moved grimly, a man here or there pausing to ask quietly after Ewan, then go about his business again. She knew that Waryk needed to ride with a force, and she knew as well that he had to leave Blue Isle guarded. Jon of Wick stood his post at the gatehouse, and she knew that Jon would remain. No man could see as far as Jon, none knew the defenses of the fortress walls nearly so well.

Indeed, when Waryk left, the fortress would be guarded.

For her . . .

Or against her?

He didn't have to urge her to the chambers they shared. She walked ahead of him, pushing the door open, striding to stand before the fire and then turn and challenge him. "I have had nothing to do with this. I didn't agree to this marriage to plot and plan with Daro for the downfall of my property and my people."

He came into the room and closed the door, taking off his mantle and his scabbard, laying his claymore, his father's weapon, on the bed.

"Are you listening to me!" she cried out.

He looked at her, crossing his arms over his chest. "Ewan is your man," he said. "And Igraina is your friend."

"Aye, that's true! Why would I wish them hurt—"

"These men, it appears, were left behind when the Vikings retreated after their attack. But were they? Or has someone figured out that the fortress really is impregnable, and the way to kill those who guard it is to pick them off, one by one. Interesting."

She exhaled, furious. "So you are really accusing me of sleeping with you—and planning on my uncle seizing this place?"

"Are you sleeping with me by choice?" he inquired politely.

She turned away from him, gripping the stone mantel at the hearth. "I agreed to this, to all of this, your terms!" she reminded him.

"And even that might make good sense. There was no choice for you. Marry me, or be disinherited. You were furious, you defied the king. You hated me. You might well have gone to your father's kin with a plan."

She inhaled sharply, so angry she could scarcely endure it. "I do hate you, you bastard, how dare you accuse me so!"

"I didn't accuse you; I said that the plan might make sense."

She walked over to him, so incensed that she couldn't think. "One word from anyone else and you are ready to accuse me! Let's not doubt the whispered words of an enemy we can't even see, let's just accuse Mellyora—it makes sense. You—bastard!"

She tried to strike him. He caught her arms. His fingers were vises, she was drawn against him. Desperately, she wrenched free. She couldn't bear his touch, his scent, his closeness, reminding her of all the intimacy, of the way she had begun to feel, of wanting him, needing him, feeling jealousy, and fear. She spun around, striding across the room again.

"And Ewan lies dying."

"Damn you, I would never plot with anyone to hurt him—"

"I know. You love him," he said dryly.

She spun again. "He is a friend, a good man. He has served you, you said yourself that he was a good man—"

"You don't need to defend him to me. Only your own words and actions."

She lowered her eyes, inhaling. "I said, he is a friend—"

"But you aren't planning on riding with me to Tyne anymore, are you?"

She lifted her eyes to his, feeling an emotional tug of war within her that was agony. "He might die!" she whispered softly. "I am the best here, I might be able to save him."

"And I should leave you because you wish it?"

She stared at him a long while, then lifted her hands. There was only so much she could admit when it seemed that she stood accused again. She spoke softly. "You may believe this or not—I don't want to stay. I wanted to ride with you. But now . . . I must stay."

"If I allow it."

She caught her breath. In her heart, she wanted him to disallow her, to insist that she accompany him, as she had said that she would. But she could make a difference at times, she knew it. For all of Phagin's knowledge, and for all the love Igraina bore her brother, Mellyora knew that she was the one with the greatest healing talents.

"You have to allow it. He might die. And he has served you well."

"And you love him."

She shook her head. "There is nothing between us. Was nothing between us. You know that. There was never anything more than words and false promises, and dreams that could not be."

"Dreams, my lady, can be far more dangerous than sins of flesh," he told her.

"You are going to your mistress. With whom you shared numerous sins of the flesh," she reminded him bitterly.

"You can still come."

"But I must stay."

"You must?"

"You know that. He could die! Please, you cannot forbid me—"

"No, I cannot, or will not, forbid you to stay, Mellyora. It's your choice."

She turned from him suddenly, alarmed by the tears that welled in her eyes, and slid down her cheeks. She was startled when she found him suddenly behind her, turning her into his arms. His fingers moved down the length of her hair, and he tilted her chin toward him.

"I am not in league with a contingent of Vikings against you!" she said passionately, and she was surprised when he smiled.

"I never said that you were."

"But—oh, you did! You suggested—"

"I merely said that there might have been good reason for you to turn to your Viking kin for help. The man Ewan killed claimed that Daro was responsible. I've no proof of that, nor can I believe it so easily. Perhaps someone believes that I will be quick to accuse you, and Daro. And perhaps even wage war against Daro—and my own wife."

She exhaled on a long breath, amazed. She trembled, relieved by his words, yet still angry that he had tested her so. Yet she knew that her words of affection for Ewan, spoken so passionately, had angered him. Not that there had been secrets between them. But because she had said what she had in front of others, and perhaps, even, because of the emotion in her voice when she had agreed to marriage with him—and all its terms.

And when it had seemed that there might even be happiness in that marriage.

"Don't wage war against me!" she pleaded softly. "I have not betrayed you. I swear it."

"Tell me, why would you no longer fight me?"

"I married you."

"Aye?"

"I promised to love, honor, and obey."

He laughed suddenly. "My dear, I don't think you're familiar with the meaning of the word *obey*."

"I agreed to the marriage," she said softly.

"And . . ."

She swallowed hard. There was only so much she dared admit when it seemed that someone, somewhere, was working against her.

"I am resigned."

"That's all? Resigned?"

"I'm finding marriage to be . . . more than palatable."

"I've made it to palatable, and now I must leave."

He was speaking lightly, teasing her, but she was suddenly afraid, and miserable. "Yet, if there is any fear . . . shouldn't you stay here? If the isle is in danger, can't the English wait? If you were to go later—"

"I must go today."

"If you could just wait . . . a few days. Time will tell quickly with Ewan. Perhaps, in very little time, I could come."

"I don't have time."

She lowered her head again. He cradled her skull with his palm, holding her to his chest. "I have to go, and you have to stay. So tell me good-bye."

She was silent. He lifted her chin again. Her eyes met his. "Good-bye," she said painfully. "Godspeed."

He smiled, fingers gentle as they moved down her cheek. "I'm glad that you would have God with me. But I'd wanted something a bit more memorable in the manner of a good-bye. Especially since I've gone from being not entirely repulsive to actually *palatable.*"

She was amazed to realize that she could smile through her tears. And more, she was amazed to find herself on her toes, delicately, with a whisper, brushing her lips against his. Then she threw her arms around him, and the kiss she gave next was anything but delicate. Her body pressed to his, she teased his mouth open with her tongue. Passionate, hungry, angry, afraid and trying to hold on, she slipped her hands beneath the linen shirt he wore beneath his wool, running her fingers along his flesh. She kissed and teased, stroked boldly with her tongue. In seconds, his shirt was open, and she worked down his body, her fingertips brushing flesh, her lips and tongue feathering after. He hastily began ripping clothing from his body, and hers, and while linen and wool were strewn, she scarcely missed a brush, a taste, a touch. The fire burned very low, the dawn just crept into being. She tended each scar upon him with a stroke of her tongue, the brush of a kiss. She lowered herself against him. Stroked him, cradled him, took him into her mouth. His fingers curled into her hair, hoarse cries escaped him. He came down to his knees before her, captured her lips in a kiss, found her throat, shoulders, breasts . . .

They lay before the low-burning fire upon the soft furs. And he kissed her and tasted her, caressed her, touched her, imprinting sensation upon his mind. The dawn came inexorably, light filtered through arrow slits in crimson and mauve, subtly changing, playing upon their flesh in shades that slowly changed to gold and yellow . . .

He made love to her, she rose atop him. No matter how hard she tried to hold on to the moments, they slipped away. She could not be passionate enough, fierce enough, tender enough. She had never been so aggressive, so hungry, so desperate. She ached to reach the promised pinnacle, and she drew back each time it threatened. His eyes touched hers, his rich dark hair brushed her flesh, his skin was fire, his arms were all powerful, holding her, he moved like lightning, like the wind, like thunder, with all the sweet promise and violence of a storm at sea. Then it seemed that the world itself was ripped asunder, climax seized her in a final, wild tempest, and she lay with him drenched and shivering upon the furs, and realizing that the fire had died, and that dawn was breaking to the full light of day.

He rose after a moment, walking toward an arrow slit, looking out at the sea. Sunlight poured over his body, and she watched him, thinking that she loved the way he moved, the tall, muscled length of him, even the scars, pale white lines here and there on his shoulders and back. He was at ease with her, she thought, and she loved that, too, and she was afraid, and wondered if it was the same with his mistress, if such a way of being was simply easier for men. She closed her eyes, and heard him moving again. He poured water from a pitcher to a bowl, and washed. Then he moved about, dressing. She could hear him, and she knew each piece of clothing he donned. Shirt, hose, tartan, boots . . . no armor now, for Geoffrey would be carrying his armor as he moved out, Thomas would be *am fear brataich*, or standard-bearer, carrying his banner, and he would be unencumbered as he rode until he was ready to take on his mail, shield and lance, and other weaponry.

Perhaps he would never wear it. He went to the household of a friend, to warn that friend that his land would be seized were its lord not to pay homage to the Scottish king. And perhaps, very soon, he would shed his clothing again as he had done here, to be with the woman he had loved, rather than the woman who must bear his legitimate heirs.

Yet, when he was dressed, he came to her again. He hunched down, and swept her up, furs and all, and held her very close.

He smoothed back her hair and kissed her lips. "Keep our home free and safe," he said softly.

"You believe in me, that I will do so?"

"Against any enemy," he said, a slight smile curving his lip.

"But of course, I'll have your men with me."

"Angus is staying."

"If he stays to watch me, to see that I guard my virtue against so sorely wounded a man, his presence is wasted, I fear."

He shrugged, apparently aware that she could not be unfaithful with a man who might well be dying. "Angus stays, because he is my right hand, and he would guard you with his life."

"Who will guard you, if Angus is with me?"

He caught her hand, kissed her palm. "Do you doubt that I'll return?"

She shook her head. "Nay, Laird Lion, I would not doubt you."

He was silent for a moment. "Don't doubt me, lady. Don't doubt me, ever."

He straightened to leave, easing her back down to the furs. She watched him stride away, dismayed that she could feel so disconsolate, so alone. When he reached the door, she could not help but call him back.

She rose to her knees, drawing furs with her. "Waryk?"

"Aye?"

"Don't doubt me!" she whispered. "Please, don't doubt me!"

She was startled when he came back to her, drawing her up and to him once again. He kissed her forehead, then her lips, and whispered against them, "Aye, you're the Viking's daughter, Mellyora, but *my* wife."

Then he turned, and exited quickly, and she knew that far more time had passed than he intended, and the dawn was just a memory.

She lay back down, closing her eyes tightly. Day had come. Waryk was gone, Ewan lay near death. She had to rise. But it was so hard to do so. She could hear the men below, the preparations for the army to ride out, to take the boats, the horses, all the implements of war.

The noise ceased. It grew later and later.

She had to rise; she had stayed to tend to a wounded friend. At last, she did so, wishing that she did not feel such fear for Ewan.

Nor that her was heart was breaking with fear and jealousy.

She washed her face, her hands, her throat. The cool water splashed over her. She was so tired. She turned, and saw his scabbard and sword on the bed.

A strange panic seized her. She dressed quickly, and took the scabbard and mighty sword and hurried out to the courtyard. The men were gone. There were guards on the parapets, but even Angus had ridden out partway to say his good-byes.

She mounted her mare bareback, rode hard to the shore. The horses, wagons, and men were regrouping on the mainland. She saw Waryk atop Mercury, directing the movements of his men.

A small boat lay on the shore. She slipped from her mare and into the boat, and she called to Waryk. He saw her and frowned, and she knew he was disturbed that she had come out alone and was taking the boat alone. He left his task, riding to the shoreline. There he dismounted from Mercury and watched her curiously, and she realized that it appeared she might have decided to come with him rather than stay, yet she thought that he might have been disappointed in her had she made that choice.

"Lady—" he began.

"Your sword, Waryk. Your father's claymore," she cried across the water.

He smiled suddenly, coming to her. He took his sword as he stood in the shallows, buckling it on, low on his hips. He dragged her boat on in, high on the sand, and lifted her from it.

"Thank you, milady," he told her.

"Aye. I know that you fight with your father's sword. That it may—that it may bring you back to me."

"And you want me to come back?"

"Aye." She hesitated, meeting his eyes. "Actually, you're more than palatable. You're quite handsome, striking, rather magnificent. But I . . ."

"Aye, lady?"

"I . . ." Her voice faded. She spoke in a whisper, giving all that she dared. "I'm finding that I need you and that . . . I . . ."

Her courage faded. It seemed that she had said enough. His eyes touched her with a strange, dark passion and tenderness she had never expected, and his words were equally comforting. "My love, I will return. And perhaps then . . ."

He kissed her, before the troops, and there went up a mighty yell, and she knew that they had the full approval of the men.

But then Waryk mounted Mercury, and with a last bow to her, he turned and rode to the front of his troops.

And as a breeze swept in from the Irish Sea, he was gone.

And she was left behind.

With a dying man . . .

And her deepest fears.

# CHAPTER 21

For five days straight, Ewan hung between life and death. Mellyora had known a fever would come, and she had known that the fever was what they must battle. She, Phagin, Igraina, and Ewan's grandparents tended him constantly, and no one else. She and Igraina grew close again, as they had been as children, cooling the whole of his body with ice brought down from the top of the hills when he burned too hotly, blanketing him with furs when the chills set in, changing the poultices on his many wounds every few hours, trying to draw whatever poisons tormented him from his blood.

For five days, he lay silent. They forced water and thin porridge between his lips. They sat in silence, they talked quietly, they prayed.

Angus remained constantly at the door to the cottage. Jon of Wick remained ever vigilant at the great wall of the fortress, while men now stood guard at the wall still being constructed around the residences.

Angus would never leave her, she knew.

And she wondered sometimes if he had been left to watch her, or watch over her. Yet the great, scarred, bald old warrior could be gentle in a way that completely defied his appearance. When other hands were busy, he would assist her. Though Ewan remained unconscious, Angus talked to him as if he could hear, and in time, despite her fears, Mellyora found herself doing the same. "Treat him like a dead man, and he may well die," Angus told her. "Speak to him as if he were needed among the living . . ."

"And he will live?" she finished.

"He will have a good chance," Angus told her.

Day after day, she sat with him. Held his hand. Tended to him. And she thought of him with tremendous affection, yet she remembered the days when they had been together now as if they had all happened very long ago. Theirs had been a strange time of innocence. She had loved him, just as she loved him now. It was a deep love, and aye, she did love him. But that love had shifted so! She thought often, in her long vigil, that she might well have made him a miserable man; she was far too willful, too demanding, too determined. She had been lady here, great Adin's daughter, and she had meant to have things her way. She would have pushed Ewan to the wall time and time again, while with Waryk . . .

It was all so different. Her emotions regarding him—hate, anger, fury, passion, and even hunger—were stronger than anything that had ever ruled her before. She didn't know quite what it was he had done, or when it had been, that had made him so predominant in her every waking minute, in her dreams, in her soul. She knew that it was not simply that he had married her, no matter how great that bond was meant to be under God and the law. The king's command had not made her want him. Or love him.

Aye, for she did, she realized. The last thing she had wanted. Aye, to have a husband she loved was a painful thing, how ironic, and she had never known before that love could hurt as badly as this, that it could come with so much fear and longing . . .

She watched Ewan, and she was glad to do so, and she prayed daily that she could help keep him alive. She told God that He had taken her father too soon and too cruelly, He had taken her mother, He must have mercy and leave Ewan. But even as she prayed, her mind would wander, and she would worry. Had Waryk reached Tyne? What was he doing, was there battle, was there peace, *where was he sleeping at night? She could have been with him, except that Vikings had attacked again, and everyone, her own people, friends included, thought that she had invited them . . .*

On the afternoon of the fifth day, Ewan took a turn for the worse. Igraina was in tears, wondering where they had failed. Phagin was frustrated, Mellyora was at a loss herself, so disconsolate that she could give thought to nothing else as the hours passed by. Ewan burned with a new fever. Riders brought back ice, and they packed him with it. Angus suggested he should be bled, Phagin was against it, saying that the poultices drew poisons from the blood, and with what Ewan had shed when he'd been injured, it was doubtful he had enough left that he could be bled. Hour after hour, they soaked him with wet linen sheets, and when the sheets drew the heat from his body, they soaked him again. One of the wounds had become infected; they lanced it and drained it, and covered him anew with the sheeting. At dusk, Phagin touched him. Ewan was very still, and Mellyora thought that he had died. "I think . . ." Phagin said. "I think he has cooled a little. We must keep up our work."

Ewan lived. For hours, they worked over him again. Finally, the fever seemed to break. Ewan still hadn't opened an eye, spoken a word, and Phagin was very grave. They had covered him in sheeting, now they made him clean and dry and blanketed him with furs against the cold. Near midnight, Phagin and Igraina slept, and Mellyora, holding vigil, laid her head upon her arms where they rested on his bedside, and she dozed.

*Mellyora . . .*

She heard her name as if she was dreaming, felt a touch upon her hair, and for a moment, she thought she was at the fortress, in her chambers, lying before a fire, and Waryk was there. Then she started awake and she realized she was in a MacKinny cottage on the mainland, where she sat with Ewan. And his eyes were open, and he was looking at her, and he'd tried to say her name, but didn't really have a voice as yet.

She let out a cry of simple gladness, leaping up, seeing that his eyes remained open, then bending down and kissing his forehead. Her cry awakened Igraina and Phagin, and then Ewan's grandparents, and they all kissed him and gave him water to sip, and then Phagin said that they'd smother him now that he was alive if they didn't find some decorum, but even Angus came in and kissed Ewan, who couldn't protest, on the cheek. He was weak as a kitten, and Phagin was right, they still had to take care.

But once Ewan started recovering, he seemed to have a firm grip on life. He lay in his bed, raising his head a bit more each day, flexing his arm muscles, finally managing to stand and then to sit. It would be a long road back to good health, Phagin warned him. But it did seem that he was on his way.

One afternoon when Mellyora sat with him, she felt that he was strong enough that she could question him, and so she did. "Igraina told us you said that Daro caused these attacks on us. She implied as well that I might have been involved. Ewan, I cannot believe that Daro could be involved, or worse, that you could believe that of me."

His eyes touched hers with a soft sorrow. "Mellyora, the man I fought and killed told me that they'd been sent by Daro, that this was a Viking stronghold, and he would have it again."

"But Ewan—"

"I was cut to pieces, Mellyora, certain I was dying then and there. I wanted my sister to get help, and to be safe. I'm very sorry that I involved you, I know that you would never cause death or injury to anyone you loved, to anyone in your care."

She closed her eyes, grateful to hear his words.

"Has Waryk gone to rout Daro?"

Her eyes flew open, she shook her head. "No . . . I don't believe so. He was ordered to Tyne, he was riding there."

"I must have caused tremendous trouble for you, Mellyora. I'm truly sorry. I hope that Waryk doesn't think you would betray your own people."

"He did point out the logic of my seeking Viking aid," she murmured dryly.

"But he didn't . . ."

"Beat me? Throw me into a dungeon? No, not as yet. He has said that men might falsely accuse others."

Ewan smiled at her, closing his eyes wearily. "Thank God he didn't beat you. I'm in no condition to defend your honor against such a man."

She laughed softly, and kissed his cheek. "Oh, Ewan, thank God that you are alive and doing well now. I could not bear it if I were to lose you—"

"Ah, but I have lost you, haven't I?"

She caught her breath, looking at him, and he shook his head. "It's all right, Mellyora, it's as it should be. I just pray that Daro is innocent in this, that Waryk is riding for Tyne, and that we can all find some peace."

"I'm sure that Waryk is riding for Tyne . . ."

Her words trailed as she suddenly realized that Waryk had gone to Tyne, aye, but he was riding with an army, and there would be little to stop him from going after Daro if he did believe her uncle guilty.

"Oh, God . . ." she breathed.

"Mellyora, what is it?"

"Nothing, nothing, I'll be just outside, your sister and Phagin are here, resting—"

"I'm all right, Mellyora."

She stood, nodding to him, and hurried outside where she knew that Angus would be waiting. He was sitting on a wooden bench in front of the cottage, whittling a piece of wood. He started to rise.

"Nay, Angus, sit. Please, tell me, where is Waryk now?"

"At Tyne, lady, you know that," he said unhappily.

"Where is my uncle, have you heard?"

Angus hesitated. "I've heard he remains camped outside Stirling."

"I need a man to bring a message to Daro for me. I'm writing to Daro, Angus, and telling him that I believe the person responsible for my leaving his camp before my marriage is trying to cause trouble and bloodshed between my husband and my kin. I want him to hear the accusations so that he can defend himself."

Angus looked at her. "Defend himself, or prepare an army," he said quietly.

She knelt down by him. "Angus, my uncle is not guilty. I am not guilty. I swear to you, I have no desire to oust my husband, or have any other man as laird here."

She felt his eyes on her, and knew the loyalty and love he bore Waryk, and she touched his scarred cheek. "I swear to you, Angus."

"Why?" he asked her quietly.

"I love him," she told him.

He smiled after a moment. "Aye, write your letter to your uncle. We'll send a messenger. Daro can bring this matter before the king, and the truth of it all will be learned."

"Thank you," she said simply, then asked him, "Angus?"

"Aye?"

"How long will Waryk be gone?"

Angus shrugged. "Some campaigns last for months, lady, you know that. But if all has gone well, he will be heading home soon."

"Ewan is well. Growing stronger every day."

"Aye," Angus said gravely.

"Take me to Waryk, Angus."

"Ah, lady, you should not be out of the fortress—"

"Please. You will be with me."

Angus rose, and she stood with him, her eyes on his. "A messenger is due today or tomorrow," he told her. "Let's find out if Waryk remains at Tyne."

Mellyora threw her arms around the bald warrior. "Aye, Angus!" She kissed his cheek, and spun away. As she did so, she suddenly felt dizzy. The world threatened to turn black. She set a hand upon the wall to steady herself. Angus was immediately at her side. The black cleared away.

"My lady?"

"I'm fine, just tired, I imagine."

"Tired, eh?" he said, looking at her peculiarly. "Tired—or?"

"Well, I do imagine I'm just tired. I'm hardly fragile, Angus, and I never falter or feel in the least ill or queasy or ..." Her voice trailed away. She'd given so much time and attention to Ewan, and she'd been so worried about Waryk being ...

With Eleanora.

She hadn't thought about herself at all. If she'd been thinking, or paying attention at all, she might have realized how many days and nights had come and gone since ...

She couldn't be.

*Yes, actually she could.*

At the thought, her stomach seemed to pitch and toss. Fear and excitement swept through her in a swift wave.

"Oh, no, I don't think so," she said to Angus.

He arched a brow, and she knew his silent question.

*Why not?*

Why not. It was what Waryk wanted, or so he had said. But of course, she didn't really know, she wasn't certain ...

Angus seemed certain. "We'll go to Waryk, lady. If you promise to rest."

"Ah, now, Angus! Who is the lady of the castle here?"

"You are the lady here. But I am to guard you for the laird of the castle, and I mean to do so—even against yourself!"

"Angus ... if so ... he will be pleased?" she asked anxiously.

"Oh, my lady, I cannot begin to tell you just how pleased."

She sank to the bench, wanting to see Waryk more than ever.

Waryk was aware, aligned with his men atop the hillock that led to the gates of Tyne Castle, that his troops cut a formidable picture. He'd ridden with his own contingent of cavalry, and the king had sent archers and foot soldiers, men to leave behind when either the negotiating or the fighting was done, because once the castle was taken in the name of the Scottish king, it must be kept. He had spent five days reaching the king to swell his ranks, and when they had arrived here, on the outskirts of Tyne, he had ordered the men to set up camp, stretching their numbers across the hillside so that Peter would have no doubts as to what strength the king meant to put into this enterprise. This morning, two weeks to the day from the time he had left home, he was ready to force his old friend's hand.

He knew where Peter would be, along the wall, watching his arrival, and whether his friend damned him or was grateful that the king had sent a friend to offer terms, he couldn't be certain. But Peter had told him often enough that he felt a strong loyalty for whoever was in power, and here, now, David was the power. For centuries this region had been tossed back and forth like a child's ball, and there were many in the area who considered themselves Scots, many who thought themselves English, and many who didn't really know or care to what king they bowed as long as they were left to till the fields for an overlord who didn't starve them, beat them, or drive them from their land. Feudalism had come in with the Normans, but service for protection had begun with the dawn of man.

At his side, Thomas said, "Now, Waryk?"

"Aye, Thomas."

Thomas, acting as *am Bladier*, would bring his oral message, offering terms in the name of David, King of Scots. He rode out with only Tyler of Dumbarton, *am fear brataich*, who carried not only Waryk's banner, but that of the king. Waryk watched, uneasy for a moment, thinking how easy it would be for archers on the walls with their crossbows to pick off the two men. Peter, he thought, would not be so foolish. This was the way that things were done, and those seeking any terms did not kill a messenger.

The gates opened; two riders came from Tyne, and the messengers met upon the field. Horses whinnied, stamping their feet. Waryk heard the sound of a buzzing fly. Along his ranks, except for the occasional sound of a man shifting position, there was silence.

But then Thomas and Tyler broke with the messengers, and rode toward him. Thomas, who had accompanied him here many times before, was relieved.

"Sir Peter of Tyne sends his welcome to you, Waryk. He has

always known that his land lies in dispute between two great countries, and he is equally aware that his refusal to surrender to the king's forces would bring about death and destruction, destroying Tyne for any man, or any king. He hopes, if David intends him to hold Tyne against the brutal factions vying for power in the battles between Mathilda and Stephen, that he intends to fight such rebellious factions with him. Some of the great northern barons have armies themselves now as powerful as those of many a king."

"Go back to his messenger. Tell him, aye, David knows he will be vulnerable to English attack, and we have come with strength. And tell him we'll enter his gates with a party of one hundred men, while the rest of our party camps here, on the field, just outside the gates."

Thomas did as he was bidden. He waited on the field while Peter's messenger and standard-bearer rode back through the gates. Then the gates opened, Peter's men returned, and with perfect courtesy and not a drop of blood shed, Tyne was taken in the name of David of Scotland.

Waryk gave orders for men to camp, and for men to accompany him. Peter wouldn't betray him—not out of loyalty, but out of good sense. There would be too many armed men inside his walls for him to decide to make a protest then. If there had been a fight at Tyne, it would have been a siege, and one quickly put to the test because the walls were wooden and easily burned and it was only Peter's easily vacillating nature which had kept Tyne standing thus far.

He rode through the gates with Thomas and Tyler flanking him, others of his immediate guard surrounding them, and ranks of cavalry, and the foot soldiers, behind them. Peter was mounted in the courtyard with Eleanora at his side. Brother and sister were handsomely dressed, prepared for pageantry rather than battle, and Peter's speech, on meeting Waryk, was a mastery of diplomacy, accepting the Scottish while reiterating his inability to do anything less—he was satisfied to surrender, but should the English monarch retake the land, he might not retain his lordship, but he could, at least, hope to keep his head upon his shoulders.

Waryk graciously accepted Peter's words, telling him that he was a wise and just lord, that his decision saved the lives and livelihood of his people, and that surely God in his infinite wisdom saw that they all stood on Scottish soil. As he spoke, he felt

Eleanora watching him, saw her smile, and knew that nothing had changed with her, that it didn't surprise her that David had arranged for him to take a wife. She appeared amused with the proceedings, anxious for formality to be done with and the day to continue.

"Laird Waryk, as newly sworn Scottish subjects, we invite you and your men to sup with us, that we may drink a toast to David of Scotland."

Waryk accepted the invitation on behalf of himself and his men.

He, Thomas, and another four of his retainers would actually dine in the great hall—the great hall at Tyne being rather small. Entering, Waryk remembered the last time he had come, and how he and Peter had talked. As the king's representative he was seated between Peter and Eleanora. As was often done, one chalice was set between him and the lady to be shared. Her fingers brushed his continually, and her eyes touched his with warmth and humor.

"So, sir, tell me about your wonderful new property. Blue Isle. Naturally, I have heard about the place. It is legendary, in story and song," Eleanora told him.

"It's quite fantastic. Sheer rock rising from the sea in some places, yet there is beach, and a deep harbor to the one side. At times, you can walk to the isle from the mainland, getting a bit wet, perhaps."

"And the fortress?" Peter asked from his other side.

"Built on rock foundation. The Romans claimed it for a time, I'm told, and they built the first walls on top of the rock. The walls are twenty feet thick in some places. Even the proud Celtic inhabitants admit that Norman building techniques added to the strength and beauty of the fortress in the day of the Conqueror."

"It all sounds quite beautiful," Eleanora said, her fingers brushing over his as they both held the chalice. "Is it?"

His eyes met hers and he knew that she wasn't asking about the fortress, but rather his wife.

"Very beautiful," he told her.

"Enough to hold a man's interest for a lifetime."

"Aye," he said gravely.

She watched him without rancor, a slight smile playing at her lips. Musicians entered the hall, the sounds of merriment began. *An Cleasaiche*, the hall jester, arrived, and there was laughter all around at the little man's antics. Peter rose, lifting his chalice, saluting David of Scotland. The evening wore on.

Waryk excused himself early, having had Tyler make sure that he be given sleeping quarters in the castle. When he had retired for no more than thirty minutes, there was a tapping on his door, and he knew that Eleanora had come.

"So you are here alone," she said, looking around.

"Aye," he told her.

"Well, I suppose there is no way for me to be delicate, is there?" Eleanora said softly. "You're a married man, the king has arranged it. I expected this day to come, and yet . . . I always knew that it would make no difference to me. Adultery is a sin, so they say, but there are so many men and women guilty of it that the halls of hell must be quite crowded. I can't find it to be a sin. They also say that God has given us free will, but none of us seems to have free will to marry where he or she will. But your wife is young, isn't she?"

"Aye, that she is."

"With long golden hair and eyes bluer than the sea."

"Aye," he said simply.

Eleanora crossed her arms over her chest, looking at him. "Beauty itself cannot bind a man."

He went to her, caught her, brought her gently into his arms and smoothed back her hair. He knew the feel of her, the scent of her, he'd known her so long. It would be so easy to be with her; the time he'd been gone from Blue Isle already seemed so long . . .

Yet . . .

He had wondered himself how he would feel when he saw her again. They had been together, when possible, for years. She was as familiar to him as his own hand. She had not changed in any way, she remained a beautiful woman, one who had cared for him, one he had loved. He had wondered if human nature would rear itself here, and if he would see her, and want her. But he realized, holding her gently now, that he had wanted Mellyora with him. Aye, he wanted her with him now, for many reasons, yet one more important than any other.

No matter how rational he had forced himself to be where Ewan was concerned, he had been jealous. Afraid to leave her with a young man who had proven himself brave, daring, resourceful—and moral.

Then . . .

He had watched her tend her would-be lover's naked body, and before his injury, the MacKinny had been strong and fine, and he was somewhat amazed that the two never had culminated their love for one another. She had flatly stated her love for the man, and still . . .

But he hadn't invited Mellyora to be with him because of anger, fear, jealousy, or any other such emotion. He had wanted her with him . . . simply because he wanted her.

And he had been able to leave her simply because it had been the only right thing to do. Because, against all odds, he believed in her.

He didn't know how his emotions and desires had changed so swiftly and surely in the time they had been together. Eleanora remained beautiful. It wasn't that he had now been with another woman—there had been other women over the time they'd been together, too. He had simply done the most outrageously foolish thing: He had fallen in love with his wife. And he knew, quite suddenly, holding another woman, just how much he loved her. His passion was overwhelming; he would die for her, not because he was a knight, a warrior, her husband, or the king's champion, not for nobility, honor, or any other chivalrous concept. He would die for her, because she had become his life. So much was etched into his heart already. He would never forget her, coming across the water in her father's dragon-prowed boat, bringing him *his* father's claymore. He would never forget her face, her eyes, so many times, the way she had looked at him, defying him, loving him . . . if only just a little.

"Eleanora, you are a beautiful woman, you've meant so much to me, you've been peace and sanity to me over the years, but . . ."

She drew away from him, studying him. "You love your wife?" she whispered.

"I'm sorry."

She smiled. "Don't be. It's a miraculous situation."

"I care for you, Eleanora. You know that. I have never meant to hurt you—"

"I know that you care about me, Waryk. I know what I've meant to you. And of course, now, well, I am hurt, of course. Because I want you. Except that I don't want to be with a man who wants another woman. And still . . ."

"Still?"

"If you ever fall out of love with your wife, please, my fine laird, come back to me. I'll be here."

"You may not be, you know. You may find yourself wed again."

She shook her head. "I've been promised that it's my choice from here on out. And I don't see a marriage in my future."

"The future can change. It remains elusive."

"Aye, that it does." She touched his cheeks, lightly kissed his lips. Then she slipped from his arms and left the room, and his heart felt very heavy.

The Celtic custom had been to shave the cheeks, but grow the mustache. Normans tended to be clean-shaven. The old Anglo-Saxons, to Ulric's mind, were simpletons, growing hair everywhere, but then, the Vikings, as well, tended to long hair and full beards, and he had been bearded when he had last been at Daro's camp. Therefore, he shaved, and had his hair close-clipped in a Norman fashion, then surveyed himself in a hand mirror and decided he had changed his appearance enough. Those who had been with him before, except for Han, were dead. An acceptable loss of life. As Han had said, Vikings fought for riches and honor. Death in battle was noble. They had made their choices, fighting with him. Perhaps the peasants and farmers he forced into service had not realized the honor of dying in battle, but as they sat in Valhalla, heroes from the field, they would understand.

He dressed handsomely to pay a visit upon his cousin's daughter, Anne Hallsteader, now wife to Daro Thorsson. The old family in Denmark were nobility; they had ruled areas of Northumberland in Britain, and had Renfrew only seized the MacInnish land and more a decade ago, Ulric's father would have ruled on the border now, and Ulric would be heir to vast estates. But because of the intervention of one incensed young boy, Ulric's father had been killed, Renfrew had been killed, and all had been lost. Their followers had been left to eat dirt. Renfrew's son, Etienne, had spent the last decade rebuilding what his father had lost. It had only been in the last few years, since the trouble between Mathilda and Stephen in England, that barons in the north of England had begun to flex their power again with real force. And though Etienne had been a slim, cowardly youth to Ulric's way of seeing things, he had grown to be a cunning man, gaining aid from his neighbors through false promises and innuendo. Through marriage, Etienne had gained the rich lands to the west of his homestead. His wife, poor thing, had died after giving birth to their only son. The birth had weakened her and she hadn't recovered. Some, said, of course, that she had been poisoned so that Etienne could take his second wife, who had brought him the manors of Fiffen and Hoar, and with them, their incomes. Tall, thin, handsome, clever, Etienne wasn't much of a warrior—he could barely wield a sword—but he could buy hundreds of swords, and through the deaths of many of the knights in his service, he gained ever more property, confiscating that which belonged to the men in his service who left no widows or children, and sometimes managing to take homes and land anyway, insisting that the knights had owed him for their expensive destriers or trappings. Etienne watched and waited. He kept Ulric constantly abreast of what went on at the border; Ulric was aware of every military movement by Stephen, David, or Mathilda. Etienne found the right time and place, and Ulric led sometimes unwilling armies in rebellions that caused David's forces to remain on the move. Any fighting man worth his salt knew that harassing an army could cause great damage. Draw soldiers south, then plot an attack in the north. Harry the coastline in the north, and wage a major attack in the south. Chip away at morale, kill the bravest and the best.

Ulric had always been a warrior. He had been contemptuous of Etienne, but he'd been eighteen, in the fighting himself, when his father was killed in Lord Renfrew's attack on the Scottish border. Etienne, seventeen but with his tutors back at his father's manor, had become Lord Renfrew, and therefore, Ulric had made his bond. Aye, the old Lord Renfrew had hired on Viking mercenaries. Just as the Scots had hired on Norman mercenaries; MacBeth, when king, had hired Norman mercenaries to fight Malcolm and the *Norman* knights who had come to take his throne during the last century. Men and women, like all other commodities, could be for sale. Almost all had their price.

But though he still thought of Etienne as a poor excuse of a man and respected many of his enemies more, Ulric had learned from him. The Viking way was to attack, to fight hard, to win on one's own bravery and prowess, or so to lose. Etienne was a thinking man who knew he hadn't his father's fighting power. Etienne had taught Ulric the power of chiseling away at his enemies through treachery from within.

And so, this time, when he entered Daro's camp, he sent a messenger ahead, telling Anne that he had heard of her marriage, that he was delighted with her choice of a Viking husband, be he a Norwegian rather than a Dane. He wished to come and bring a wedding present.

He received an effusive reply from Anne. Of course, she was very happy to see her father's kin. She was sorry that her mother's MacInnish family had been so bitter against all Hallsteaders, but they'd heard that Hallsteaders had fought the MacInnish with Renfrew years ago. Since she was now full-grown, a woman and a wife, she was happy to welcome him—as she would continue to welcome her MacInnish kin, as well.

He came to Daro's camp with a retinue of six men, all splendidly attired, well mounted. Men who had not been near Stirling with him before, but who had earned glory in their skirmishes at the border. They ransacked English villages and laid the blame on the Scots just as they ransacked Scottish land and claimed that the English were guilty. What Ulric could not accrue himself, he demanded of Renfrew, and Renfrew gave him. Thus, to get into Daro's camp, he brought his young distant cousin Anne a beautifully forged silver bowl with elegant silver chalices to match.

Greeted outside Daro's great hall, Ulric was chivalrous, charming, polite. He kissed Anne, and welcomed Daro into the family. He was welcomed into the great hall as kin; he was kin. Vikings supported family, they were loyal, welcoming to one another. He was brought the best food, the sweetest wine. They spoke, they laughed. Anne told him excitedly how Waryk, now laird of Blue Isle, had brought her case before the king himself, and talked Michael MacInnish into allowing the marriage. "It's a new time, a new age. There will be peace now. We're all Scottish, even if we've come from different places!"

Ulric lifted his cup. "To peace," he said, and he smiled, knowing that he was lying through his teeth.

This time, he would see to it that Daro Thorsson and Waryk Graham came at one another with their swords drawn.

In truth, he would very much like to kill Waryk himself. The man who had killed his father and Lord Renfew. But he'd learned a lot from Etienne. He wanted Waryk dead, and he wanted Waryk's wife—and he wanted Blue Isle. Not only would Daro serve him by coming to death blows with Waryk, but he would die himself, and thus would be a possible contender for Blue Isle be taken from the competition as well.

"To peace!" he repeated, and he drank deeply.

Then, of course, he wanted to know about their friendship with Waryk.

"He has married my niece, great Adin's daughter," Daro told him.

"I heard the lady was less than pleased with the prospect."

"Oh!" Anne said, and laughed. "Perhaps at first . . . but I think she's very happy now. I've just received a message from her, and we'll see her quite shortly."

"Oh?"

"Well, she is quite anxious to spend some time with Daro, and talk with him. Daro and Waryk must meet again. There are vicious attacks occurring in which Daro's name is being cast about, and the problem must be solved!" Anne said passionately.

"Anne!" her husband warned sharply.

Anne waved a hand in the air. "That's all nonsense. But we'll see them both soon. Mellyora received word that Waryk is coming north with Peter of Tyne so that Peter may pay homage to the king. And so she plans to come out and surprise him in some special way, and for a wife to plan such a surprise . . . well, I believe that she must care very much. I knew that she would once she knew him."

"I can believe that anyone knowing the man would have strong feelings, one way or the other."

"Oh?" Anne said curiously. "You know him?"

"By reputation, of course."

"Oh, of course."

"To Laird Lion!" Ulric toasted, and then he looked at Daro. "And to your niece, as well, great Adin's daughter, Mellyora."

"To them both!" Anne said happily.

He was a guest in the hall through the night. In the morning, he left with Daro's banner secreted in his bag, along with one of his host's surcoats, knives, and, most importantly, his antlered bascinet or helmet. *Very Norman attire,* Ulric thought. But it will do nicely.

Of course, it would not be that much longer that he would make use of such trickery. He'd heard from Renfrew. Etienne's troops were on the way to the meeting point. Ulric would shortly be creating havoc throughout Scotland—and all in the name of King Stephen.

Vengeance could be played out, and all in the name of justice. It was a wonderful irony.

David sent orders that Waryk was to come to him at Stirling, where he remained at court, and that he was to ride with Peter of Tyne, who would swear his new allegiance to the Scottish king and, therefore, retain his property, and be strengthened there as a Scottish laird.

David, Waryk thought, must be delighted, thinking that Stephen would be fuming at the loss of Tyne.

Waryk, though Peter's friend, knew the man well. He wondered if David had ever thought that a lord so quickly willing to swear allegiance to him would be equally willing to foreswear that allegiance if it became expedient.

But he was glad of the orders to ride north, and anxious to return to Blue Isle. There was new rumor of a planned English attack, but where it would take place, no one seemed to know. To reach Stirling from Tyne, they traveled northward on the western trail. He would come very close to his home, and it was possible that he might be able to ride there and collect his wife before riding on to Stirling. The last messenger to come from Blue Isle to Tyne had brought the news that Ewan lived, that he appeared to be gaining strength.

Waryk was glad. Ewan had proven himself a decent man.

But Waryk still haunted himself with doubts. Would she feel such gratitude and relief that Ewan had lived that she might find herself alone with him, by his side? Where he lay in bed, naked, regaining his strength? He'd taught her himself the simple ecstasy to be had between a man and a woman. Had she learned that lesson far too well, and now, knowing what it all meant, with Ewan simply there . . .

Despite the tortures he cast against his own mind, the ride was not unpleasant since they moved slowly. Eleanora, anxious to see the Scottish court, had decided to accompany her brother. She had also decided to haunt him as well, he realized. She was always with him. She needed a hand up on her horse, a hand down. She sat with him at meals, shared his cup, laughed pleasantly. She never chastised him, she simply remained close, teasing his senses, if not his heart. He wondered if he hadn't gone completely insane.

He was tormenting himself, sleeping with anguished dreams, and Eleanora was always so near, and so available. It would be easy to forget, easy to reach out and touch this woman who had given years of companionship and pleasure, and who asked nothing in return. So easy . . .

But he did not. And it was baffling at times to admit that the golden vixen who had fought him with the dogged determination of a berserker could have brought him to this point. And when memories of the things she had done, the things she had said, would taunt him to no end, he would recall the night when he'd told her he must leave, and the way that she had touched him, the look in her endlessly blue eyes . . .

She had brought him his father's sword. And prayed that he would return.

Still, he didn't want to hurt Eleanora more than he had done; he spent time with her, and allowed her to know that she did tempt him, that she was beautiful still, and that he suffered the tortures of the damned, staying away from her.

At night, as they camped along the way, he took his place between her and Peter at the table they would erect in the woods. He shared his chalice with her, broke bread with her, enjoyed what entertainment came along.

On the night when they neared Blue Isle, he sat next to Eleanora, laughing as she told him a story about her brother's horsemanship. There had been good game and fishing along the way, and they dined well on pheasant and fish cooked over open fires. They had just passed a small village in the valley, and an old man there had come to him earlier, offering entertainment for their evening meal. A sennachie came, and told a rousing tale about King David, then a harpist played, and acrobats performed. Then, the harpist came out again, and in his wake, a masked dancer. She began to tell a tale as well, about a great warlord with a mysterious past, the Gaelic bride he married, and the son they produced. A king's champion, a laird to right all wrongs, who, even as a youth, roused himself from a sea of the dead to avenge his king, to fight for his country, his family's honor, his king.

She moved with a curious grace. Her voice was crystalline, enchanting. When she had begun her story, the group had been chattering. As she continued, all voices fell silent. She was lithe, and shapely, and when she danced, she seduced. And of course, as she continued, he realized that she was telling his story—

enhancing it all very nicely. He had grown several inches and had muscles to rival those of the Greek gods.

*What was she doing here?*

He didn't know whether to be angry, amused, or pleased.

"Dear Lord!" Peter breathed at his side. "The lass is pure temptation! I must know who she is. I'll marry her. My God, I've never felt such pure . . . lust."

"Peter, you cannot wed the lass," Waryk murmured.

"Because she's a village lass? Aye, I would marry her. I'm not a greedy man, I need no great dowry. Lust is reason enough for me!"

"Peter, you've had way too much wine," Eleanora said, amused, then she leaned over to Waryk. "Tell me, truthfully, Waryk. Is lust so strong among all men? Would the golden sprite before us tempt you from your loyalty to your wife?"

A broad smile touched his face as he whispered back to her. "Eleanora, the blond sprite before us is my wife," he told her. "And Peter, you cannot marry her, for she's already wed, and if she brings about any more lusting here and now, she's going to be seriously sorry!"

# CHAPTER 22

With that, Waryk rose, uncertain as to whether he was so delighted to see his wife that nothing mattered, or if he should be angry since she had obviously come to see him with Eleanora, and find out exactly what he was doing. Seeing her here also frightened him; he didn't like the idea of her outside the domain of Blue Isle. He knew that she'd be on the mainland, tending to Ewan, but he knew as well that Angus and the other men would guard her like hawks, and that now, on the isle and the mainland, she would be well protected against a surprise attack.

But outside their own realm . . .

He felt as if they were vulnerable to some strange evil he knew existed—but not how or why. With men attacking the isle and claiming to be there on her uncle's orders, she must surely recognize the danger she was in.

Eleanora arched a brow, reaching for his hand.

"Steady, my lo—friend. You look as if you're about to take her head off."

"She shouldn't be here."

"But she is here. She came here for you."

"Perhaps . . . perhaps she came to see you."

Eleanora smiled. "Still, that is for you. I had not been jealous before. I am now."

He closed his fingers over hers. "You need be jealous of no one, Eleanora. You are a rare beauty and you know it." He squeezed her hand. "Excuse me . . ."

"Only if you've controlled your temper."

"It's controlled."

"Waryk . . ."

"I swear it."

He rose, and started across the clearing. Mellyora saw him, and stopped midstride. She stood poised and still as he approached.

He reached her, and stripped the painted linen mask from her face. Her eyes touched his. "So I am found out!" she said softly. "I meant to finish the story."

"My lady, I am sorely tempted to strike you senseless."

"How rude and ungracious!" she retorted, eyes alive with blue fire. "It was a good story, slightly embellished, excellently told. And it had an ending you would have liked."

"It was told far too well, and I'm afraid you might not have reached an ending! Poor Peter was willing to marry you thinking you a peasant lass and not even knowing your name for the privilege of taking you to bed. God knows what went through the minds of other men!"

She flushed, gnawing her lower lip, and he was pleased to realize that she hadn't known quite what her effect would be.

"It was a good story," she repeated.

"Aye, you do an excellent job. You could have survived nicely as a singer, dancer—or harlot."

"Waryk!"

"And you shouldn't be outside of the fortress." Anger edged his voice.

"I knew that you were coming."

"You know as well that there is danger all around. Did you come because you were so anxious to see me? I dare say that it was Eleanora who drew you here."

She lifted her chin. "That's she, I assume?" she murmured, indicating the table.

"Aye, that is."

"She's exquisite."

"She is," he agreed, and he smiled, taking her hand. "Eleanora and Peter. Come meet them both."

"Waryk, no, I—"

"You were curious, I insist." He drew her forward, to the table, and once there, he introduced her. "Eleanora, Peter, my wife, Mellyora. My dear, Peter of Tyne, and his sister, Lady Eleanora."

"My dear . . ." Eleanora murmured, studying her.

"Peter, Lady Eleanora," Mellyora murmured.

"Will you have some wine?" Eleanora inquired. "Your husband's chalice is there."

"Are you hungry?" Peter asked. "After dancing so . . ."

"Peter!" Eleanora murmured, rolling her eyes.

"Well, she was . . . spectacular."

"Peter, dear, don't let Waryk forget we're all friends. Would you like something to eat, Mellyora?"

She shook her head. "No, thank you, we dined in the village."

"We?" Eleanora asked politely.

"Angus is with me, of course. I wouldn't ride out alone."

Waryk looked across the clearing. Angus was indeed there, grave, heavily armed. Waryk tried not to smile. Angus did the same, but then shrugged helplessly and grinned. His nod indicated that he had been on watch, and would remain on watch.

"Well, if there's nothing you require . . ." Waryk murmured absently to Mellyora. "If you'll excuse us?" he said to Peter and Eleanora, suddenly entirely focused on his intent. "I'm anxious to hear about Blue Isle in my absence."

He steered Mellyora from the table and down a trail in the forest. The moon was full, high in the sky, casting down a golden glow to guide them. Waryk knew, from the resistance he felt from his wife, that she had come here, anxious to see him—and anxious to spy on him—and now that her performance had been carried out, she was slightly unnerved, and uncertain as to what his reaction would be.

"Where are we going?" she asked him.

"Down by the loch."

"Why?"

He smiled wickedly. "Because no one will hear you scream there."

She stopped, trying to tug free from him. "Waryk, you've no right to be angry, to throw out threats! You should be pleased that your wife came out to meet you and see—"

"If I was sleeping with Eleanora?" he inquired.

She flushed, and he knew that had been her plan exactly. She hadn't sent ahead any messages, she had wanted to catch him by surprise.

"You were very close."

"Aye. Let's go, come on."

He caught her hand. She tried to pull free. "Waryk—"

"Come, my love, down to the loch. And by the way, how is Ewan? Hale and hearty and strong, so I hear."

"Out of danger, at best!" she protested. "And I am here, hav-

ing left Ewan, while I arrive to find you head to head with Eleanora—"

"Ah! So you did come to spy, and for no other reason!"

The trail curved. They came upon the loch in the middle of
the night, with the full globe of the moon playing upon it. The
water rippled in a soft reflection, the earth beside it was soft and
redolent and the trees grew with great trooping branches that
cast gentle fingers upon the strangely glowing landscape. Soft
leaves carpeted the ground, and Waryk drew her around to stand
before him just at the water's edge. He caught both her hands,
lacing his fingers with hers, and pinning her arms behind her
back. "Indeed, my love, you came to spy."

"I came to—" she began, but he didn't really care why she
had come. She was there. He had wanted her. She had tormented
his dreams, left him lying awake and wanting, and now she was
with him. She couldn't finish speaking because his lips found
hers. Hard, hungry. He ravished her lips, plundered the depths
of her mouth. Searched and delved and tasted. And at last he
lifted his head, and she tried to speak again. "Waryk, she is
beautiful, and if you've been with her—"

"Aye?" He touched her lips again with his own, softly now,
seductively.

"Waryk!" she struggled to free her arms. He would not let her
go. Her eyes glistened with unshed tears. "If you've been with
her . . ."

"Aye . . ." He pressed his lips to her throat, teased her earlobe
with a brush of his teeth and tongue, found her throat again, and
again.

"Let me go . . . because . . ."

"Because?"

"I will not have it. I won't . . . I can't . . ."

He lifted his head, and her eyes were absolutely beautiful, and
he'd never seen her so vulnerable. "You will not have it?" he
asked softly. "Why?"

"Because . . . I have some pride, Waryk."

"Pride? Aye, well, we all have pride. Not good enough. Give
me another reason."

"Because . . . you're my husband."

"Ah, good, but still, not good enough . . ."

She leaned her head against his chest.

"Mellyora?" he persisted.

She murmured, "Because I want you myself."

He released her wrists, finding her chin, tilting her head upward. "Not completely what I had in mind, but . . . it will do for now. Because I cannot bear for it not to do!" he whispered hoarsely. He pulled his mantle over his head, casting it down on the spongy bank. Then he swept her up, kneeling down upon the mantle with her in his arms. She clung to him. "Waryk . . ."

"I've not betrayed you, my lady."

"But . . ."

He laid her upon the mantle. He leaned next to her on an elbow, his hands beneath her soft woolen knit gown. Her flesh seemed as soft as a rose petal, as hot as the sun. He cupped the fullness of her breasts, and they seemed fuller, her nipples seemed larger, harder. Her gown was annoying; he shoved it up, and dragged it over her head.

"Waryk, we're in the woods . . ."

"Angus is on guard, no one will come near us."

He pressed her back to the ground. She smelled like a field of flowers. He buried his face into her flesh, her breasts, reveled in the scent of her, found himself aroused to hardness in just wanting her, touching her. His body seemed to burn. He tried to hold back, not to want her so urgently, to touch and stroke and tease . . .

Her hands were on him. She fumbled with his clothing, his scabbard, the awkwardness of his sword. He stripped himself of scabbard and weapons, tore off linen and wool, hose and boots. The ivory cast of the moon lay upon them. Eleanora had called her a sprite. She was more like a goddess, made flesh from the lake, golden tresses silver in the light. She touched him with fingers as fevered as his own. He bore her down to the earth, breathed in her sensuous scent and the redolence of the earth. She cast her arms around him, but he drew back. He caught her knees, parted her limbs slowly, meeting her eyes. Then he drew his fingers down her inner thigh. He followed each touch with a kiss, the brush of his tongue, light . . . here, there. Her thigh, her knee, her belly, her hip, her thighs, one, the other, and then between . . .

When he came to her at last, she writhed and thrashed in a fierce fury of desire that enwrapped him with his every movement. She clung to him more tightly each time he thrust within her, and each time he thrust, he felt himself move deeper, harder, faster. He closed his eyes, gritted his teeth, staved off climax until he could stave no more ... it burst upon him, sweat beading his shoulders, his brow, the seed that burst from him draining him as if he were suddenly left lifeless, rendered helpless, as his very soul seemed to slip into her. His heart thundered, his blood rushed, and a feeling of sweet, saturating ecstasy swept over the length of him. Her nails curled into his shoulders, she cried out, and lay still.

At his side, she shivered. He drew her against him, taking his surcoat from the ground where it had been strewn and cast it over her as a cover against the sudden chill. She curled against him, and lay in silence for long seconds. Then she asked softly, "Must you go into Stirling with Peter and—his sister?"

"Aye. We will go into Stirling with them."

"We?"

"Aye."

She seemed pleased with that. She shifted, looking up into his eyes. "Waryk, I wrote to Daro and Anne, telling them that Vikings attack us—and accuse Daro. They remain just outside Stirling. I want to meet with them and the king, and let Daro proclaim his innocence."

Waryk frowned, suddenly uneasy. He shifted to an elbow to better see his wife. "You told them that you were coming to meet me?" he asked.

"Aye."

"I don't think that was wise—" he began, but even as he spoke, Mellyora suddenly screamed, looking over his shoulders.

"Waryk!"

He rolled, just in time. Where he had lain, a battle-ax thudded into the earth. Mellyora flew to her feet as he did, but they were parted by the width of the copse then, and Waryk suddenly found himself facing four men.

Vikings ... Normans?

Two blond and bearded; two reddish. They wore full beards. Their bascinets or helmets appeared to be Viking; their long, plated chain mail seemed more Norman. But looking at one man among them, he knew that he had seen the battle gear before.

On Daro Thorsson. Aye, and it was Daro's banner being carried by another of the men.

Four of them. One wielded a mace, two carried axes ...

Daro wielded a blade.

And he was naked as a newborn. His sword was ten feet away, his wife . . .

Clutching the surcoat to her breasts, she stood staring, frozen and transfixed.

Stunned?

He could not help the suspicion that crawled into his mind. *Was she so surprised? She had just told him that she had written to Daro, telling him they would meet with him, warning that his name was being cast about . . .*

*But why tell him?*

*Why not?*

*Just as Peter of Tyne took extreme care with the way he surrendered to the Scottish king, maybe she watched her every step with him. Maybe she pretended not to be involved in any moves against him, because if he won the battle, she would be lost . . .*

"At last, Waryk!" one of the men spat out. "The king's great champion, the boy murderer! Well, here we meet at last. And look, sir, there you are, milord, naked as a fish, without so much as a sword. How cowardly! We should give you a weapon, a fighting chance. But I think not! You may die like a dog, sir, cowering down in the dirt!"

The first man strode toward him, ax swinging. As he came Waryk dived in a roll forward, leaping to his feet across the copse again.

"Waryk!"

She was beside him suddenly, thrusting his sword into his hand. His father's claymore. Double-handed, he started forward, swinging at his enemies.

"Get behind me, Mellyora."

"Waryk, I can—"

"You can't fight without a weapon!"

One of the men with the axes took a swing. Waryk sidestepped and brought his claymore crashing down. The sound of crunching flesh and bone was terrible, but the second man let out a sound like a berserker, rushing forward.

He took longer to kill. Waryk lunged and retreated, lunged and retreated—spun around when he felt the man with the mace behind him. He was a fool. Threatening with his swing and harsh taunts, he forgot to watch for his own vulnerability. Waryk stepped swiftly forward, swinging. He sliced the man across his midsection, deeply enough to kill with the single motion. Yet he barely turned back to his other opponent quickly enough. He missed the man's ax blow by a hair; in fact, he felt shaven down the arm, the blow came so close. Yet he reacted quickly, bringing his sword up to catch the man from groin to throat, knowing full well that if he didn't kill then, and kill quick, the man's next move would crush in his skull.

But the man lay dead. Waryk spun quickly, expecting the fourth man to rush him. But he did not.

He spun again.

No one rushed him. The fourth man was gone. Along with Waryk's wife.

Daro. Daro was gone . . .

And he had taken his niece with him.

She had gone for the ax. That had been her mistake.

Bending to retrieve the weapon, she had found herself scooped up from around the middle. She had screamed in pure surprise as well as panic, but Waryk hadn't heard her, because two men had been trying to kill him at that moment.

Her fingers had reached out . . . .

And missed the ax. And she had been grappled, and dragged, and thrown over a man's shoulders, and taken swiftly atop a horse. She was tangled in her husband's surcoat, and she couldn't fight her assailant because he was clad in plates and mail. She wouldn't release her husband's surcoat; it was the only cover she had. Her only relief was in seeing that one man fell, and Waryk was swinging at the other as they disappeared from view.

They rode hard. Very hard, and very long. The night seemed unending. The wind grew colder. They came at last to a copse, near to the sea, and she realized they had come closer to Blue Isle. She was, in fact, now far closer to her home than to Waryk's camp.

The horse came to a halt, and she was dragged back over the man's shoulder. Because of his mail and plate, her flesh was scratched and bruised. He slid her to the ground, nearly dropping her, before dismounting from his horse. She clutched Waryk's surcoat with its flying-falcon emblem to her and backed warily away from her captor.

He wore Daro's helmet, Daro's emblem.

She narrowed her eyes, staring at him. "Who are you?"

"Daro."

She shook her head. "You are a coward, a liar. You're not my uncle. Do you think that I don't know my own uncle, my own kin? You bastard, how dare you use him, how—" she broke off, suddenly thinking that she did know the man. She didn't know his name, or why he was so relentless, but she did know him.

"It's you again. You think that you will convince Waryk that it is my uncle who is so determined to pillage, rape, maim, and kill our people. Well, he's not a fool. He knows better. And he will catch you, and find out who you are, and—"

"You'd best shut up, Lady Mellyora. Neither your uncle nor your husband is here, lady. Your husband is quite possibly dead already, and if not, he will never reclaim what is his."

She stared at the helmeted, nameless man who was her enemy and felt chilled. She pulled the surcoat more tightly to her.

"My husband is not dead."

"Oh? And why not? He killed one of my men, but two remained to kill him."

She shook her head, not wanting to tell him that she was certain his men had fallen.

"He has his father's claymore. He will not be defeated," she said.

"Well, other men carry their fathers' swords, my lady, and that does not keep them alive," he said sourly. "But no matter. We will reach Blue Isle before your husband—or his men, or the king's men, if he is dead. And you will order the gates opened to admit us. We'll have met with the rest of my men and Lord Renfrew's forces, and once we've entered Blue Isle . . . well, it will be a Viking fortress again, my dear. You should be quite glad."

The man's plan was easy to understand—enter Blue Isle, and the walls were so formidable that the fortress was almost impossible to take. But for him to believe that, even if Waryk were to be killed, he could reach the fortress without the king's men coming for him was insane. And how and why he had plotted so relentlessly seemed equally insane. When one idea failed, he seemed ready to go to another, no matter how foolhardy or reckless.

"We'll never reach Blue Isle."

"We will, but even that will not matter, as long as I have you. I want the isle, of course. But there are things I want more."

"What?" she asked warily.

He leaned toward her from his destrier. "Revenge, my lady."

"Against me, my father, Waryk—"

"Ah! There you have it."

"Why?"

"He killed my father, and worse. He killed Lord Renfrew, who would have made my family's fortune, and given us position for all the years to come."

"Your father fought Waryk?"

"You didn't know your husband was a murderer, eh, lady?"

"I don't believe that he is. I've seen him avoid bloodshed whenever he could. He's reasoned when many a man would have drawn a sword. He's not a murderer."

The man suddenly drew his sword and pointed it at her throat. "I tell you he's a murderer."

She shrugged, trying to ignore the blade. "Kill me, if you think that it will hurt him. He didn't choose to marry me."

"But I understand that you're carrying his child."

She started, wondering how anyone could have known such an intimate detail. Angus? She felt sick suddenly, wondering if Angus, whom Waryk had trusted with his life and hers, could be a traitor to him. Everyone, it seemed, had Viking blood.

She tried to lie, though she had become more certain every day. "I don't believe so."

He dismounted from his horse, coming toward her. "Mellyora MacAdin, wild as the crags and hills and the windswept sea! Such a fighter! Well, my lady, you're wrong about many things. No matter what comes, I will hurt your husband. He will bleed inside and out. I have you. And if you live, and he lives, he will wonder forever whose child you carried now. When it's born, it will die. But he'll have to wonder. He'll always have to wonder. If he lives. If he dies, it won't much matter. I'll have Blue Isle. And like great Laird Waryk, I'll keep you just the same. My wife."

"I'll never marry you! I have a husband—"

"Dead. Perhaps."

"If he were dead, I'd never marry you."

"Brave words." He came closer to her. She backed away.

"My lady, you will marry where you must. You didn't want Waryk; you grew accustomed to him. You will grow accustomed to me."

"No—"

"Aye. For I will beat you to within an inch of your life, lady, until you submit to me."

"You are more the fool. I grew much more than accustomed

to Waryk because he *never* hurt me in any way, because I saw him use reason with others, I saw him use mercy as well as strength. He's shown decency and—" she broke off, gasping, because he'd caught the surcoat with the tip of his sword and cast it aside. The blade was now placed against her throat.

"Get down right now, my lady. You're changing partners."

She stared at him for a moment, desperate. *She wanted to live, she wanted her child to live, was anything worth the hope of life?*

She closed her eyes. She couldn't. She grabbed the blade, bringing it closer to her throat, and she stared at the man's eyes through the slits of her uncle's helmet. "If you touch me, I'll kill myself. You're right; I'm carrying his child. But you won't use me against him, and if you're planning on murdering my babe when it's born, I would rather the child perish now. Because if I kill myself, you see, you'll never enter the gates of Blue Isle."

It was an incredible bluff; she didn't know if she really had the strength to thrust a sword through her own throat, or if she could kill herself, knowing that she carried Waryk's child. Life was hope.

Yet . . .

She was never tested on the matter.

To her amazement, he stepped back, letting the sword drop. "You will bring me into Blue Isle, Mellyora, daughter of Adin, a Viking."

She lifted her chin. "My father was a Viking. But he was a good man. He knew the difference between battle and slaughter, justice and murder."

He grabbed her by the hair, jerking her around, thrusting her toward his horse. She stopped, turning around to stare at him. "I need Waryk's surcoat. It's cold. And you will be noticed before we ever manage to meet up with your men if you drag around a naked woman."

Apparently recognizing the wisdom of her words, the man turned around and went back for the surcoat.

Mellyora looked at his horse. She bit her lower lip. She had tried this once before . . .

And it hadn't worked.

But then, Waryk's horse was well trained; Waryk had an affection for Mercury, and Mercury knew his master. Whereas this man . . .

He had reached the surcoat, he was bending over to retrieve

it. He was a good thirty feet away. She was freezing, stark naked. She leapt upon the man's horse and slammed her heels against the animal's flanks.

She heard him calling out behind her, swearing that he would catch her, and that he would make her pay.

She felt the cruel bite of the wind, the hammering of the horse's hooves beneath her. She prayed that the destrier would not turn back . . .

The animal apparently liked the man no better than she.

They raced into the moonlight and shadows.

Home and help were close. She was desperate to reach that safe harbor herself, and even more desperate to find a messenger to ride to Waryk with the truth.

Waryk retrieved his clothing and dressed while he walked and hopped from the copse, desperate, furious, and very afraid. He burst first upon Angus.

He shouted his friend's name, bending down. Angus lay in a pool of blood in the dirt. Yet when Waryk called his name and touched his cheek, he rose, groaning. "My God, man, you're alive!" Waryk breathed.

"Aye," Angus said, rubbing his head.

"The blood—" Waryk began.

"Nay, that came from the other man; it was a strike on the head that felled me!" Angus said, shaking his head disgustedly then. "I shouldn't have failed you, but when I saw that it was Daro—"

"Daro!" Waryk swore.

"Aye, I know Daro's armor, his helmet, his surcoat. I guarded you, but I knew that Mellyora had written her uncle, and was not surprised that he had come to meet you on your journey northward. But . . ." His voice trailed away. "They tried to kill you, too," he said huskily. "My God. The Lady Mellyora . . ."

"She's gone; he has her."

"He seized her?"

Waryk's eyes narrowed. "I can only hope. Can you stand, Angus? Are you injured? I've got to get to the men, and ride to Daro's camp. We're not far from the mainland off Blue Isle. I shall send Eleanora there, and you may accompany her—"

"Not this time, Laird Waryk. I am fine enough. When you go to battle, I go as well."

Waryk nodded rather than argue. "Thomas will take her along with Tyler and Geoffrey, I think. And Peter will have his own escort, I'm certain. Let's get moving."

Eleanora had just gone to her camp bed for the night; Peter had remained awake by the fire, and he was ready and anxious to move when he heard that Mellyora had been seized by her own uncle in a power play by the Viking. Waryk explained that they would send Eleanora with his men, and that she should go now, despite the night. The moon would be enough of a guide, and his men knew the exact trails to take.

"Waryk, I am so sorry," Eleanora told him as he said good-bye to her.

"Aye," he said rather curtly.

She shook her head, watching him. "Waryk, it was no trap. She has not planned against you, or betrayed you to her uncle, of that I'm certain."

"Oh?"

She touched his cheek gently. "You should have seen her face when she watched you. She loves you very much. More than I do, even."

He found that he could smile suddenly. He took Eleanora's hand, and kissed it, holding it tightly for a moment. "Thank you for that," he told her. "Jon of Wick guards the gates at the fortress; ask first for Ewan MacKinny when you reach the village at the shore. He'll see to your safety."

Eleanora nodded. She and her guard started into the night. Waryk turned grimly to his own horse.

It was time to fight Daro.

Mellyora didn't stop. She didn't have time to stop. She knew that she was killing the great destrier, but she had to force the horse onward through the night at breakneck speed.

Come the morning, she was frozen to the animal, exhausted, and very afraid. But just as dawn broke, she cleared the top of a cliff and could see the village below, and across from it, out across the foam-tipped sea, Blue Isle and her fortress. With a glad cry, she went tearing down the cliff, shouting for help.

It was Ewan, using a stick to help him walk, who threw open the new gates to the village enclosure so that she could race through. Other villagers burst from their cottages; Phagin, his robes flapping in the breeze, hurried out as well. Igraina was there, and when she fell, like an icicle, from the horse, babbling about what had happened, it was Igraina who wrapped her in her own cloak, and helped her to stand when she would have fallen.

"We must get something warm into her immediately," Phagin said.

"Wine, warmed on the fire, quick, Grandmother," Igraina said, leading Mellyora into the cottage. Ewan sat before Mellyora. She was wrapped in Igraina's cloak, and a wool blanket. She was warmed by the fire. A cup was placed in her hands. She drank deeply from it. The wine was good. It went throughout her body. Warmed her. Her lips ceased to tremble. She stared at them all, shaking. "I don't know the man's name . . . it isn't Daro, Ewan, we've got to get someone to Waryk fast, because it isn't Daro, but he stole Daro's clothing. His helmet, his—"

"How could this person steal Daro's belongings?" Igraina asked.

"I don't know!" Mellyora said. "He has to be someone that Daro—trusts." She drank more wine, then stared at Igraina. "That's it, it's someone Daro has reason to trust. He wants to kill Waryk . . . he tried to kill him. This man is meeting someone. Someone named Renfrew—"

"Renfrew?" Phagin said sharply.

"Aye."

Phagin started for the door to the cottage.

"Phagin!" Mellyora called, but he hadn't intended to walk out with an explanation. At the door he turned back to them. "Lord Renfrew attacked MacInnish land a little more than a decade ago. He slaughtered farmers, tradesmen, and peasants. He had an army of Viking mercenaries who were promised great riches when he prevailed. Renfrew and most of the Vikings were killed, many of them by a lad the king took on as his ward—your husband, Mellyora. Renfrew and his men had slaughtered his whole family that day. Waryk avenged his kin—this Viking is out to avenge his. His methods are as bloodthirsty and treacherous as those used by his father and Renfrew. I will reach Waryk and Daro. No one will stop a priest, and the countryside could be very dangerous now. Mellyora, get to the fortress immediately. You are your father's daughter. Renfrew and this Viking—his name is Hallsteader, by the way, Ulric Hallsteader, known as Broadsword—will be coming to attack Blue Isle."

"Hallsteader!" Mellyora cried, leaping up. "Hallsteader. Anne's father was a Hallsteader, he must have—"

"Aye, he must have used Anne. It's no matter now. She is surely as innocent as a babe in this, Mellyora. I'm going. Get to the fortress."

Waryk rode, with the full size and scope of his army plus Peter's armed men, to the walls of the Viking camp. Yet, even as he reached the camp—and he was certain that word had gone out that he was coming and that Daro would be prepared—he felt doubt working into his reason. Daro would have had no need to come to a camp in the forest. Daro could have visited them at their home. He could have murdered him in his own bed, and been inside the fortress walls—great Adin's brother, already known by many.

Yet as this plagued him, he saw that Daro—bareheaded—was riding out toward the gates, Ragnar and others of his immediate council at his side. As Waryk had suspected, Daro had heard that he was coming.

Viking archers lined the walls.

His men were armed and armored; he had archers, knights, and foot soldiers ready to fight beneath him. Messengers had been sent to the king; greater forces were coming.

As Daro rode out and Waryk saw his eyes, he knew that Daro would fight to the death.

"Tell your men to halt, Waryk. We will meet one on one in this!" Daro roared to him.

Waryk lifted a hand. Daro was riding outside the wooden palisade the Vikings had erected around their camp as protection.

He rode toward Daro. On a white destrier, Daro rode in a circle around Waryk. He spat on the ground. "I never did you harm!"

"Where is my wife?"

Daro shook his head. "*My* niece!" he reminded him. "I don't have her. You come to challenge me, while once again you have been careless with a woman who is my own flesh and blood!"

"Someone uses your camp. You have been careless!"

They circled one another once, twice, a third time.

Daro suddenly raised his sword in a fury, slamming it down. Waryk raised his shield in just enough time to ward off the blow. He nudged Mercury into a sideways dance, slamming his sword in a hard series of blows against Daro. The Viking deflected each one and went on the offensive again. Waryk went on the offensive also, returning the blows, and each time, they were deflected by Daro's shield.

"Bastard!" Daro cried to him. "You haven't the sense to see a friend!"

"Fool! You are used then, by those beneath your very nose!"

"Bloodthirsty Norman."

Waryk gritted his teeth. "Scot! I'm a bloodthirsty Scot!"

"You don't deserve my niece—"

"What we all deserve is truth!"

"I should kill you!"

"I should kill you!"

Waryk raised his sword again, hacking at Daro's shields, slamming sideways once again with Mercury. It wasn't so much skill that gave Waryk the edge, but luck. Daro's horse stepped into a hole; the animal tripped, and Daro went down with the great horse.

Waryk leapt from Mercury, approaching his enemy, his sword held tight in both hands. Daro lifted his blade from the ground, staring at Waryk. "Kill me if you would."

Waryk stared at him a long time. Then he lowered his sword, and reached out a hand. "God help us both, Daro. Where is Mellyora, what in God's name is going on?"

Daro hesitated, staring at him. Just as the Viking gripped his hand, a cry was suddenly heard. Both men looked.

Father Phagin, white beard and black robes whipping in the wind, was bearing down on them. "Stop fools, don't kill each other!" he shouted, reaching them. He dismounted, panting so hard that he had to lean against Waryk as he reached out to support him. "I'm too old; my heart can't take this. Daro, you've been used."

"Aye, I've been used! I've never been your enemy, Waryk!"

They were all interrupted by the sudden sound of a woman's screams.

Anne Hallsteader came running out on the field, screaming. "Stop, oh, my God, stop, I didn't know . . ."

Waryk looked at Daro. Daro shrugged. "I had men holding her in my long hall. She would have come between us."

Waryk smiled ruefully. "Aye."

"Daro, Waryk, for the love of God, I know what is happening—"

"Aye!" Phagin snapped. "Fine time for discovery, lass, when I've ridden to my death to reach these madmen with the truth! I will tell it. It's Hallsteader, out for vengeance with that fool son of Renfrew. Mellyora is at the fortress; she escaped Ulric Hallsteader, the Viking who dressed in your clothing, Daro, hoping you and Waryk would tear one another apart and weaken your forces when you finally realized the truth and came against him."

"It's all my fault," Anne groaned softly. "He wrote that he wished to visit me. He was my father's cousin."

"There is no one at fault!" Phagin said sternly. "But for the love of God, will you muscle-bound whelps listen to an old man? Fault be damned. Now is what matters. Don't you two understand? If the fortress isn't under siege now, it will be as soon as Hallsteader and Renfrew can reach it!"

Daro and Waryk stared at one another. "Anne, get back to the hall!" Daro commanded.

"But—"

"Do as I say!" he added fiercely.

Huge tears touched her eyes. Waryk touched her cheek. "You're not at fault, Anne, get to safety, or else we shall have to worry about you as well!"

He turned, leaping upon Mercury, while Daro strode quickly for his own horse. Waryk started to ride back to his troops.

"Waryk!" Phagin cried.

He paused, impatient.

Phagin came to him. "Pray God you will reach the fortress before he pulls another of his tricks. He has his ways . . . his father and Renfrew are men who find the weakness in others and prey upon them. The walls of Blue Isle are impregnable. The people within are not."

"Phagin, I need all speed. Catch up with us if you will. I will be wary. Now, you must let me go—"

"One other matter."

"Aye?"

"I believe Mellyora to be expecting your child. Bear that in mind."

His child . . .

As if he didn't feel enough terror in his heart. "Aye, Phagin," he said simply. He spun Mercury around, racing his horse to reach his troops. "We ride for the fortress!" he cried.

# CHAPTER 23

Eleanora was quite impressed. The village was charming, protected by a new wood wall, occupied by an intelligent and
clever group of people.

She was greeted by the man Waryk had said she should find.
She was welcomed politely, taken to a cottage, and given wine.
The MacKinny had obviously been very ill; he was still weak. But
he saw to it immediately that she was taken care of, and with
such courtesy! She was quickly assured that Mellyora was all
right, and had already ridden across low tide for the fortress. He
was arranging for a boat for Eleanora since the water was growing
deeper. It was very cold, and only those who lived here were
accustomed to riding across the sea.

"But Daro and my brother and Waryk will go to battle!" she
said, distressed.

Ewan shook his head. "Nay, lady. Phagin, our priest, has gone
to warn them. Whatever troops may be coming here to assault
the fortress, Phagin will make it through. If you've warmed yourself, lady, we should make the journey to the castle. No one can
touch you there."

He bowed to her, helping her to her feet. He had beautiful
hazel eyes she thought, gold in places, forest green in others. He
was grave, he had a quick smile. His hands were handsome, his
fingers were long.

"Thank you," she said. And she smiled. "I should be helping
you. You were so seriously injured."

"I am much better."

"Mellyora MacAdin is such a fine nurse?"

"Phagin, the priest, served in the Crusades. He saw the way
the Muslim doctors healed injuries with poultices rather than

amputations. He taught her all that he learned, and she took it a step farther, since her mother knew herbs, and the healing properties of seawater and grasses and such."

"I should love to learn," she said, as they stepped out of the cottage.

He looked up suddenly, instantly alarmed.

She smelled the fire.

The new wall had been drenched with oil, and set ablaze.

Ewan MacKinny put his arms around her, and they started to run. Outside the walls, Eleanora screamed as netting fell around them.

She struggled. She and Ewan were caught together, trapped and rolling, in the net. Captured and snared like flies in a spider's web, they went still.

"Courage, all will be well," Ewan whispered to her softly.

All could not be well. But, strangely, in his words, she did find courage.

Ewan struggled to his feet as the net was lifted. He came out with his fists swinging, striking two men. But another man stepped forward hastily, using the hilt of his sword to strike Ewan on the back of his head. Ewan fell. She cried out in alarm, ready to bend down to him.

But a man reached for her. He was helmeted and dressed in mail. She could see nothing but the curiously cloudlike shade of his nearly colorless blue-toned eyes through his visor.

"Ah, well, hello there, my beauty. You must be the legendary Eleanora. How I would like to get to know you! But alas, we've so little time . . ."

Mellyora knew how to defend the castle.

Reaching the fortress, she'd dressed swiftly in a linen shift and warm, woolen knit gown and immediately gone to the parapets to take charge.

The gates were closed, to be opened only at the command of Jon of Wick, and she would give that command to him herself if necessary. Jon and Mallory were with her, at her side, ready to advise her and give counsel. She wished that Ewan were with her, for he had worked most closely with her father.

She wished that Waryk was here.

And she was anxious that Ewan hadn't reached them yet,

and when she saw that the palisade was afire, she knew that Hallsteader had come.

Archers were prepared; they lined the parapets. The fortress was not at full strength since Waryk and so many men had ridden out, but the power of Blue Isle lay in the rock on which it had been built. She rose out of the sea with majesty and strength. Her walls were thick, formed of rock and stone that could not burn, that could not be rammed. In times of danger, a heavy portcullis was closed behind the main gate. Boiling oil could be poured onto any attackers who breached the first gates. Cauldrons bubbled now with oil to be cast down upon any attackers who neared the walls.

Weakness could only come from within . . .

She knew that well, and she didn't mean to be weak, but when she saw the fire burning across the water, she was sick at heart. Ewan hadn't reached the fortress; he was in danger. Or dead. And the others—Igraina, their family, their friends, the very old, the very young, the little babes . . .

*Waryk will come, Waryk will come, oh, God, he will come soon . . .*

She thought it over and over again, and it gave her strength. But she was afraid. So afraid. She had come to know Hallsteader. He'd been willing to risk any number of his own men. Had he slain those who hadn't managed to flee into the woods on the mainland?

The first assault came immediately after the fire. The water had been growing deeper, but Hallsteader's men came across it on horseback and afoot. He had been joined at the head of the troops by a second man. His banner was red, a dragon graced his surcoat. Renfrew, she thought. His armor was rich; his horse was huge and powerful and dressed in trappings every bit as costly. Behind him, his standard-bearers carried not just his colors, but those of Stephen of Blois, King of England, as well.

Hallsteader and Renfrew directed the assault, but were not part of it. They knew the death that would come, and still, they sent their first wave of men to test the walls, men with a ram to charge the gates, others with grappling hooks to attempt to scale the walls.

The archers brought them down with such speed that the ram was abandoned. The warriors regrouped, out of range of the castle's archers.

"What now?" she murmured to Jon of Wick.

He shook his head. "They can't come close; they know it. They'll have to give up and go away."

"They won't give up," Mallory advised with assurance. He gazed at her, his lined face stern. "They won't give up, ever. They want the fortress, or you."

"They cannot have Mellyora!" Jon said fiercely.

"Mellyora! Mellyora MacAdin, surrender the castle and yourself, and your people will receive mercy!" Ulric Hallsteader suddenly called across the green slope leading to the castle walls. "Surrender now, and all will be well. No one will die."

She walked to the wall. "Retreat, sir, and save your own life before the laird returns and slays you all!" she called back.

She couldn't see his face because of his helmet. She'd never really seen his face. He was still wearing Daro's helmet.

He suddenly took it off, as if he were reading her mind. He smiled. He had sandy blond hair, cool eyes, a clean-shaven face. He might have been a handsome man. He even had something of a look that reminded her of Anne. But there was something about him that wasn't quite right as well. Something in his eyes, in the twist of his jaw.

"Surrender, Mellyora."

"Leave, Hallsteader, or die!"

"Ah, lady, you'll be worth the fight!"

He rode to Renfrew and conferred with him. She heard his laughter once again. It held an evil twist, a sound that seemed to carry loud and clear on the air. She realized suddenly why he was so very frightening. Nothing meant anything to him, except his quest. He could take any risk, perform any deed, because he meant to have his way—or die. If he perished in his quest, he would sit at the high table at Valhalla. And if he did not . . .

His laughter rang out again. And once again . . .

Waryk rode with Daro at his side, Angus, Ragnar, and Peter close behind them. The fastest of their horsemen hurried with them; the foot soldiers would follow behind, they didn't dare wait for such troops to follow their lead.

He was afraid, deeply afraid. She was free now, Phagin had said that she was free. Strange, when she'd been in the deepest danger, he'd thought her Daro's prisoner. And he had known that Daro would never hurt her. He hadn't the sense to be terrified when she'd been seized because he hadn't realized that it had been a Hallsteader who had taken her. A clever man. Plotting and planning year after year. Causing irritation after irritation. Never betraying himself. And now . . .

*Mellyora had now escaped, but she had been Hallsteader's prisoner. He'd had her in his power. For how long? Where had he taken her, what had he done to her, had she really survived it in her heart, in her mind? Would she ever forgive him for the doubts he'd had which had cost them all so much?*

*He'd cast blame upon her. Upon the Vikings, upon Daro.*

*And all along, the enemy had been his, his from a distant time, a distant day. A man seeking vengeance, for the vengeance he had wrought . . .*

*"Run, Mercury, run, race, like the wind, boy, race like the wind!"* he urged, and, looking over at Daro, he spurred his horse to greater speed.

*What would Hallsteader do next?*

*Hurt her, use her, wound her, to wound him. Take her, because she was his. A Viking's daughter, he would think he had more right to her. To Blue Isle. Any man knew that she was the key to the power there, and any man would learn that the lady was the prize . . .*

*She carried his child. Hallsteader couldn't know such a thing. He would want to take her, use her, and if he could not kill Waryk, taunt him for as long as they lived with the belief that his wife might bear another man's child . . .*

*But, he realized, it had ceased to matter. He wanted only one thing. His wife.*

Ulric had dismounted. He stood on the green slope below the wall. His men dragged a woman toward him, and Mellyora bit into her lower lip, startled to see that the woman was Eleanora of Tyne. "Look who arrived here for safety, my lady! Now, I haven't time to ram the gates, Mellyora MacAdin. I'm well aware your husband is close behind!" he called.

"Is there no way we can reach him with a hail of arrows?" she asked Jon of Wick, standing at her side.

He shook his head. "He's just out of range."

"What is he up to? He has taken Eleanora . . ."

"Come out and ride with me that I can negotiate with your husband, Mellyora. If you do not, I will slit her throat."

*Slit Eleanora's throat? To what sense,* she wondered.

She hadn't asked the question aloud; he meant to answer her anyway.

"Peter and Eleanora are traitors to the English cause of King Stephen, my lady. I will not be amiss in such a simple execution!" Lord Etienne Renfrew suddenly cried out, joining in with Hallsteader's claim.

"You will die a slow death, Hallsteader!" she found herself crying in return. She winced. She hadn't intended to let them know she was concerned.

Waryk could not be far behind. Nor could Daro.

*Unless Phagin hadn't reached them. Unless they had already massacred one another and their troops ...*

"It's so very simple ..." Ulric shouted. He left Eleanora standing as she had been, hands tied behind her back. He walked back through the ranks of his cavalry and then reappeared, dragging a man behind him who wore Peter's colors of Tyne. The man was middle-aged, graying, dignified. He didn't glance at Ulric, but stood very straight. He brought the man next to Eleanora, whispered something to him, then looked back at the gates. "Mellyora MacAdin. This is Walter of Tyne. He has served young Peter and Eleanora since they were children. He has told me that he would gladly die for them."

Finishing his speech, Ulric smiled. Then, in a split second, he brought his knife to the man's throat, and ripped it open. At his side, Eleanora screamed, wrenching away in pure horror. Mellyora lived in a violent world in which she'd seen death far too many times; and still, she'd never witnessed so brutally cold an act in all her life. She choked, clutching her stomach, backing away from the wall.

Ulric had given no thought to the murder. None at all. It had meant nothing to him.

The dead man fell. Ulric reached out for Eleanora, dragging her back against him. "Traitors, all! I will suffer no ill fate, Mellyora, for I am an English subject, while all of these people are treacherous bastards, cloying to the Scot's king in times of trouble! I will give you just enough time to come out of the gates, lady. If I do not see your beautiful blue eyes before me in a matter of minutes, I will slash Eleanora's throat. Your husband's mistress, some say, eh? Will you let her die for such a sin? Or is the daughter of the great Adin too honorable to condemn her for such a reason?" he taunted.

Waryk would come, Waryk would come . . .

Aye, she could hold the fortress. The fortress could hold itself. She had always wanted to prove herself, and she'd had no choice but to do so, but now . . .

"You know that I will do this thing!" Ulric thundered.

"Aye, you'll do it, we've seen that, Ulric!" she called out to him. She tried to keep her voice as cool as his. "But you're right; Eleanora was long my husband's mistress, while I am lady here, and Waryk's wife."

"My lady! The ice in your heart makes me crave you all the more!" he cried out with mock gallantry.

"Nay, Ulric. I will come out—"

"Oh, madam, what a wise thing to do! Your charity toward those who have wronged you is most exemplary. I meant to give Eleanora one more chance. See whom I would have let die for her next!"

Mellyora bit deeply into her lower lip as Ulric motioned to one of his men.

Ewan, still weak, barely able to stand, was dragged forward. Her heart skipped a beat. Ewan, still loyal, still proud. To be dragged forward, threatened anew . . .

"You would kill a man half-dead already?" she demanded.

She could see Ulric's grin. "Aye, lady—"

"Let him!" Ewan cried out with a sudden burst of strength. "Don't surrender the fortress, Mellyora, don't—"

He broke off as Ulric spun around, striking him with a heavily gloved fist with such that he fell, knocked unconscious.

"Half-dead, all dead . . . what will it be, Mellyora MacAdin? The Lady Eleanora has a throat, so slim, so easy to cut . . ."

"I told you that I'm coming out. But I want Eleanora and the rest of your prisoners. The gates will not open unless you make this agreement. I will not come with you to watch others coldly murdered after I have surrendered myself."

Ulric grinned, amused. "The other prisoners are but added weight. In good faith, I'll send them toward the gates now. Eleanora comes when I see you through the gates."

"I will wait between the gates. When all your prisoners have entered past the portcullis and it has been closed again, I will come to you."

Mellyora backed away from the wall. Jon reached for her. "I can't let you do this."

She shook her head. "I can't let him butcher Eleanora or anyone else in cold blood like that, my God, did you see what he did to that poor man—"

"Aye, a warrior, willing to die for Eleanora of Tyne, he was so sworn. You cannot die for her, Mellyora—"

"He doesn't want to kill me, Jon. He wants to use me. Against Waryk."

"And that he will."

Mallory stood at the wall with them, brooding over the matter. "We'll offer him a ransom."

"He doesn't want money, Mallory. He is seeking vengeance."

"You can't go to him."

"But if I go to him, it will buy time. We have to have that time!"

"I can't let you go—" Jon began again.

"What do we do against this enemy? He will kill, and kill again. He will bring forth all our people, and slay them one at a time before these walls. And I don't really intend to go, Jon."

"Ah, Mellyora, he is dangerous—"

"Jon! I know that, but I am the lady here, and God knows who else he is holding, who rode with Lady Eleanora when she came here." She lowered her head. Once again, Ewan had been willing to die to defend the honor of his home. He was hurt out there. He was barely recovered from the last wounds he had received.

But she was carrying Waryk's child. Ulric knew that. She didn't think that he wanted her so much; he wanted the gates opened. His only chance to storm the fortress.

"Jon, listen, this can work. I can go between the gates, we can receive his prisoners . . . and then, close the main gates before he can come at us again."

Jon arched a brow. "You know that though he is saying that he will exchange you for the prisoners, he plans treachery already. When the portcullis opens to let the prisoners through, he plans to rush the gates."

"Aye, but we've more defenses than he knows. The oil is ready; our archers will set fire to their arrows, and his men will burn like tinder—they'll have to retreat. He will not gain access to the fortress!"

Jon sighed, looking down.

"Jon, I am my father's daughter, I know warfare. If I were laird here, would you question me?"

He looked into her eyes. "I don't question you. I fear for you."

She reached out, caught his hand, squeezed it.

"Be ready, be prepared!" he called out to their archers.

"Lady Mellyora! I will kill Ewan MacKinny if I do not see your lovely face very quickly now, and after Ewan, I slay the beautiful Eleanora!"

She saw him conferring with Renfrew once again. Renfrew lifted an arm, and she knew that he was directing different men to rush the gate.

She started down the stairs from the parapets to the portcullis, already being raised. It was heavy; the winches were difficult to man. "This must be closed quickly once our people are in. Have men ready to help them. They may be terrified and hurt . . ."

*May be. She would never forget Walter of Tyne, and the way that he had died, so coldly, so quickly, so mercilessly . . .*

The gates were open. She stood between the two sets, waiting. She stood very still, as if she were incredibly calm.

The tenant farmers, craftsmen, and villagers from the mainland came first. She saw their gratitude in their eyes as they passed her, and saw their pity as well.

The men came next. Garth, Tyler, Geoffrey . . . half-carrying, half-dragging Ewan along with them. Tyler spoke to her. "My lady, you can't do this!"

"Tyler, for the love of God, get in. Get Ewan on in, the others . . ."

She didn't recognize all the men. Eleanora's escort, she assumed.

"Send Eleanora, now!" she shouted to Ulric.

Ulric pushed Eleanora forward, and the woman came. Mellyora saw her eyes briefly, and saw her thanks, and her admiration. Small comfort. She shivered. She would make it back inside, she told herself. But, for a moment she realized that Ulric might seize her. She might die. And Eleanora would be here . . .

She closed her eyes, waiting.

"Come out, Mellyora MacAdin!" Ulric demanded.

She heard the sudden thunder of horses' hooves. Aye, they were ready to storm the gates!

"Close the portcullis!" she cried, and she raced for it.

She was startled when Mallory suddenly came running out of the gates, toward her. "Mallory, have you lost your mind? Get in—" she began.

But Mallory was grim-lipped. He gripped her hard by the

shoulders, and was powerful for a man who had spent his days counting rents earned and monies spent. She was so stunned that she didn't even fight back at first. Then, as she was thrust inexorably toward the front gate and away from the closing portcullis, she knew. She didn't know how or why, but Mallory had willfully and determinedly betrayed her. When Ulric had known about the movements of those in the fortress, it was because Mallory had somehow sent him the information. He had known when Waryk would ride, when he would return. And now . . .

"You bastard! Why?" she cried, aware that it was too late. The Vikings and Normans were rushing by. They'd be caught in the portcullis . . .

But she would never reach safety.

"For your father, for the Vikings!" he said.

"Not for my father! My father became Scottish!"

Mallory smiled at her ruefully while men rushed around them. "For the riches then, my lady. All these years, I have counted your revenues . . . all these years. So much . . . gold, silver, and coins. Now, lady, riches will be mine. I will go a-Viking."

Ulric himself came riding hard to where she stood. "I've delivered her!" Mallory said proudly. "I will be rewarded—"

She screamed as Ulric swiftly swung his sword, nearly decapitating Mallory. Blood sprayed over her. She tried to run, but the portcullis had closed. Ulric was on top of her. He reached down and caught her by her hair. She screamed again in pain, but he released her, grabbing her around the waist and dragging her up to the horse. He spun the animal around, racing away from the gates.

She heard the horrible screams of the men caught between gates even as they rode from the walls of the fortress. She struggled against Ulric, fighting fiercely.

She could smell burning flesh.

From atop the wall, her men were shouting. The archers aimed at Ulric, but Jon cried out in fierce command. "Nay, you'll hit our lady!"

And Ulric was free to take her up.

They kept riding. The scent of burning flesh seemed to permeate her nostrils. The screams of the dying rose all around her.

The fortress had been saved, she realized.

But she was lost herself . . .

# CHAPTER 24

They arrived too late.

With Daro and his men at his side, Waryk realized that he had probably never ridden with such a ferocious force of men before.

But it didn't matter. When they reached the mainland, he saw the burned ruins of the new wall, and of many of the cottages. But he saw no bodies strewn about, and as they headed for the water to the isle, he suddenly heard the cheers that were arising from the fortress at his arrival. He looked anxiously to the wall. Even at his distance, he could see Eleanora, Tyler, Geoffrey, Thomas, Jon, Igraina, Jillian . . . even Ewan.

But not his wife.

He nudged Mercury and tore across the water. The gates opened as he reached the land and continued across the slope. He rode into the courtyard, and he was surrounded. Jon of Wick, Ewan, Eleanora, all trying to tell him what had happened.

"A traitor within our own gates!" Jon cried to him furiously. "My lady was in command, she had a strategy, she could have saved those he intended to murder, and closed the gates upon him as well. But she was betrayed. By Mallory!" Jon spat on the ground.

Ewan was ashen. He leaned upon Tyler, looked up at Waryk, and shook his head in misery. "Her plan was good. It would have succeeded. And he meant to murder more people, she had no choice . . ."

Waryk felt as if ice swept his veins, as if he were cold beyond death.

"Where is she?" he rasped out.

And Ewan, pained, shook his head. "He took her. And rode

away. And he is in great force; Lord Renfrew has made it into a battle between the Scots and the English. He claims he rides against Peter of Tyne and Eleanora, for betraying King Stephen."

"Where did they ride?" he demanded.

"North, toward the settlements still largely Viking," Ewan said.

"I'll ride with you—" he said, turning toward the stables.

But he staggered, and fell. Eleanora gasped, rushing to his side. "Ewan, poor Ewan, I will stay with you, the others must ride now."

Waryk turned, and saw that Daro, Peter, Angus, and Ragnar and others had arrived behind him. He saw that Geoffrey, pained, stood in the courtyard as well.

"Water, lad," he said wearily. "We need water for ourselves, and the horses, and then we ride again. Northward."

Mellyora didn't know where they were when they at last stopped.

It was night, darkness surrounded them, but they had come to high ground with a natural stone boundary to the south, and Lord Renfrew commanded that it was the best place to make camp for the night.

"We should push on," Ulric argued.

Renfrew disputed him. "Men falling from their saddles cannot fight. We don't even know yet if Daro and Waryk have destroyed one another. If they have not . . ." He shrugged. "We can make a defensive stand here if we have to. Our troops are equal to Waryk's, and we could win a major battle here."

Ulric remained disgruntled, but he dismounted, and shouted out orders to camp.

A large command tent was quickly assembled for Lord Renfrew. Rugs were thrown over the bare ground, furniture was provided, a fire was built in the center so that the smoke could escape through the vents cut into the thick fabric of the tent.

Mellyora was beyond exhaustion when she was brought before Renfrew.

"So you are the Viking's daughter, Waryk's great prize."

She lifted her chin, and told him, "The property is the prize, Lord Renfrew. You failed to seize the property."

He arched a brow, comfortably taking a seat in a folding camp chair. He didn't invite her to sit. "Ah, yes, men desire property. But then again, most men desire women as well. And you, as a wife with property ... I imagine Laird Lion has the sense to appreciate his incredible good luck. As Adin's daughter, you created quite a stir. Men vied for you, offered your father fortunes for your hand. And now, among other things, you have driven Ulric quite to distraction."

"He is easily driven to distraction then."

Renfrew grinned. He studied her so long that she began to feel a greater sense of fear. "He said that you threatened to kill yourself if he touched you."

"It wasn't an idle threat."

Renfrew laughed. "Ah, but harder to do than you might imagine while the instinct to survive still rages within you. And I believe, my lady, that you are a fighter, a survivor. But then, Mellyora MacAdin, if I decide to explore for myself just what manner of prize you might be, I will not give a damn if you threaten to kill yourself or not. Of course, you won't. What woman takes her own life when she carries the child of the man she loves, eh?"

He stood suddenly, walking over to her, and around her. He touched her face, allowed his hand to fall to her breast. Her heart thundered, she longed to lash out at him, and she fought to control her temper. She carried a knife in a sheath at her calf. The knife she always carried. But she was surrounded.

"Ah, wouldn't you love to kill me, Viking's daughter!" he said. "You should take care. I am keeping Ulric from you."

Was that true? It didn't really matter. If she killed Renfrew, someone would kill her. And he was right in that she didn't want to die. Not while she lived with hope.

"You will not find me fascinating this evening, Lord Renfrew."

"Oh, and why not?"

"I am exhausted. And sick. If you touch me—"

"You'll kill yourself. I've told you what I think of that threat."

She shook her head. "No, my lord Renfrew. I shall vomit all over you."

As she had expected, he backed away. He waved a hand toward her. "You may sleep in the pallet in the rear. Don't try to escape. My men have been ordered to hack off your toes if they catch you so much as slipping outside. I will maim you, lady. I swear it."

She didn't doubt it, but it wouldn't have mattered. Whatever the morning brought, she would have to bear. She was too weary, and too relieved, to try to escape tonight.

The pallet in the back offered her a little privacy. She had been left water with which to wash, ale to drink, and bread and cheese to eat. She couldn't manage the cheese; she wolfed down the bread. She scrubbed her hands and face, and lay down to sleep, staring into the darkness, wondering how it was possible to be so numb and in such pain at the same time. She was just so tired. She prayed that Waryk was alive. That he and Daro had made peace.

*What if they hadn't? What if they had slain one another? How would she survive? How would she make herself care . . . ?*

Tomorrow, she would find a way to fight again. Tomorrow. He would come for her. He was alive, and he would come. Waryk would come.

She closed her eyes. Despite herself, she dissolved into tears. They were even more exhausting, and at last, she slept.

They found the trail that night and followed it—it was not difficult to track such a large party of mounted men and baggage. By the following morning, they were not far behind, but Waryk saw, with Daro and Angus, that the enemy had found a spit of land on which to make a stand which offered them a natural defense. They would be at a severe disadvantage if they charged in without preparing their battle tactics. "We need to make a large shield, so that our men can approach and have refuge against the archers who will have the advantage of height," Angus said.

"Aye," Daro agreed wearily, and Waryk, clenching his jaw in frustration, knew that they needed to take time and prepare. But he was desperately worried about Mellyora. She was a fighter, and Ulric was so brutal.

But though they had as yet to be seen by the Viking camp, there had been women among the Vikings who had returned to the valley, and from them, Waryk was able to learn that Mellyora seemed to be well. She was being kept with Lord Renfrew, and though she had no freedom to move about the camp, she had been seen, and she was well.

He lay awake, tortured at night, wondering if Renfrew had raped his wife. If he did, he prayed that she didn't fight him, that he didn't hurt her. He wanted her back. It was all that mattered.

In the morning, he supervised the building of their war machines, shouting, harrying, hurrying the men along.

By that afternoon, the Vikings knew that they had come.

A rain of arrows came falling down upon them just before sunset. Thankfully, the great, moving shields had been hastily finished, and they were protected from the falling death. Immediately after the arrows, a messenger arrived, seeking Waryk to surrender the castle at Blue Isle, and all the men would be allowed to leave the field.

"Tell Renfrew and Ulric they will be allowed to live if they return my wife now!" he retorted furiously to the messenger, approaching the man with menace.

Daro caught hold of him, drawing him back. "You can't let them know how worried you are!" he warned him in a whisper.

"If she comes back to me now," Waryk said calmly, "they will live. If she is harmed, they will die more slowly than even they, masters of brutality, can imagine."

"Ulric intends you to die, Laird Waryk. Then he will return with your wife to Blue Isle, and she will accept him as laird in your stead."

"I cannot oblige Ulric, and, therefore, he must die," Waryk said.

The messenger left them.

She lay on her pallet, aware that morning had come again. She still felt tired. She had been here two days now, she believed. Renfrew came to taunt her at times. Thankfully, he was too busy planning his battle to threaten her often.

Yet she lay awake, afraid to feel excitement, happiness, relief.

Because Waryk lived. And Daro.

They had not told her, of course. But she had ears, and she had heard.

Her laird had come for her. With his Scottish troops, with Peter of Tyne's English troops, and with her uncle's Vikings.

They had not slain one another. They had banded together.

And at first, just knowing that had given her hope and pleasure. But then . . .

Hours had gone by, and then days, and she had realized that Renfrew was smart, that he had put himself in a powerful place. Battle would not be easily won.

She had tried to step outside the night before; men had been there so quickly and so close that she had felt real terror, imagining that they would begin to hack off her toes with their razor-honed axes. She had lied quickly, pretending she had been seeking them, and asking if there was deep water somewhere near so that she might immerse herself in a real bath. Guards had been sent with her to a small stream; she had bathed in her undershift, but it had still felt good after the time on the road. This morning, however, she lay in desolation again, wondering how long this state of affairs could go on.

The linen screen suddenly moved. She sat up on her pallet, seeing that Renfrew had come, and that he stood over her.

He knelt. She half rose on her elbows, warily shifting away. "Are you feeling better?" he asked politely.

She shook her head.

He smiled. He was a slim man with an ascetic face, yet his eyes and his smile were bitter, cunning, and cruel.

"I don't think you're sick at all. I think you're a liar."

"I'm not lying."

"Well, I shall find out. I have grown bored, my lady, waiting. We'll see just how sick you are. I am repulsed by such things, so be warned, I will hurt you if you ruin my clothing or create a miserable smell."

He reached out, grabbing the material of her bodice, and dragging her to him. She struck him furiously, catching him in the face. He instantly returned the blow. Her ears rang, a blinding pain spread out before her eyes. He moved quickly while she lay stunned from the blow, straddling her. Her knife remained at her calf, if only . . .

"Ah, there you are, Lord Renfrew!" Ulric stated suddenly, and he was there as well, seething as he stared down at them both. "Leave the woman be until we know what leverage we need," Ulric said, mocking the command Renfrew had apparently given him.

Renfrew shrugged. "I've decided we don't need such leverage. You may have your turn."

"Aye, that I will," Ulric promised bitterly. "The woman, Renfrew, is mine. But not now. Waryk and his troops are marching up the hill. They are ready to attack."

Renfrew instantly rose, dragging her to her feet.

"We need to prepare for battle. What are you doing with her?"

"She is part of the battle, you fool, don't you see?" Renfrew demanded. "Our very best defense."

At the rise in the slope leading to the hill, Waryk assembled his archers. They let free a single volley.

There was screaming among Ulric and Renfrew's troops; then suddenly, a warning rang out.

"Be warned, Waryk! Arrows will pierce what you have come to retrieve!" Renfrew's mocking voice called out to them.

The forces at the crest of the hill moved, and Waryk caught his breath.

Renfrew had used his wife well. She was tied to a pole set deeply into the ground at the top of the hill. His men had blocked her during the first volley. If another rain of arrows fell, she would surely be struck.

"Fall back!" Waryk commanded.

And his archers, their shields lifted high, obeyed.

The sun rose, but the wind was cold. Her arms hurt, for they had been dragged over her head, and her feet barely touched the ground. She'd had no water, no food. As the hours went by, she began to wish that she'd been struck by one of the first arrows, she was in such pain.

But Renfrew had warned that she was there, and the Scots had retreated.

Renfrew and Ulric waited . . .

The Scots would regroup, come back.

But they didn't. The troops grew restless, and Renfrew rode by frequently, shouting that they must be prepared. His warriors would straighten in their position again, but warriors were meant to fight, not wait. As time passed again, their vigilance waned. She was vaguely aware of men gaming, of runes being cast on the earth, of drinking and conversation as time passed.

Dusk fell.

The Viking and Norman troops began to break discipline, moving about the camp. They were amused, certain that Waryk's forces were beaten back by the prospect of killing her.

She began to lose faith herself, in agony, cold, weary . . .

She looked out across the field. She thought that she was seeing things, for suddenly out of the shadows, shapes began to come at them.

Closer and closer. They blanketed the landscape.

She thought at first that the defenders didn't see them. Then Ulric, seated on his mount near the pole, suddenly murmured, "What in the name of all the gods . . . Archers!"

A volley of arrows followed. A baaing sound filled the night. Shadows jumped, and shadows fell.

"Archers!" Ulric shouted again.

But Renfrew strode to his side. "Stop! We are firing at sheep," he said contemptuously. "Nothing but sheep."

Mellyora tried to stare through the shadows.

"Ah, my beauty!" Renfrew walked to her and touched her cheek, saying softly, "Sorry, my lady, you are not saved. They are nothing but sheep. Poor lady. Are you weary, in pain? Perhaps even my bed will look good to you this night!"

"Sheep!" Ulric swore from his mount. "More of them, hundreds of them!"

Indeed, there were. Frightened, maddened, and by the hundreds, they came. They'd been shot down, but now, there were more. Sheep were running, leaping, and baaing everywhere.

And more came over the hilltop, terrified, jumping on the men, causing chaos. The warriors swore; they dropped their weapons to fend off the sheep. Some were laughing, making fun of Scottish shepherds, men who couldn't even keep track of their animals. They began to chase after the creatures, trying to catch them with their hands. Some men shouted that there were enough dead ones, others shouted that they were a diversion from the endless waiting.

Diversion, Mellyora thought.

And then, in the midst of the chaos, the horsemen came.

She heard a cry, a hoarse, terrible battle cry, and exhilarated, she lifted her head.

Waryk.

He was in the lead, riding Mercury over the natural stone barrier as if he were a winged horse. Behind him, Angus came, and Daro, and the others. Rider after rider, taking the enemy by surprise.

Renfrew swore. He turned to her, gripping the pole and staring at her with eyes of pure hatred and fury. He moved away from her, toward one of the fires lit in the dark, and he started kicking the kindling around her log. The heat rose instantly. She could feel the blaze. It would catch her clothing and the pole, and then consume her, in a matter of minutes.

"Burn in hell, lady. Burn in hell," he told her, drawing his sword.

Mercury was flying across what was now becoming a battlefield littered with dead men, horses, and sheep. Renfrew stood before her. Mercury bore down on him.

Waryk was in full armor, his head helmeted, his surcoat covering his mail. He wielded his sword deftly.

And he cut down Renfrew where he stood. A single, lethal slash of his weapon cut across Renfrew's side, where his mail was weakest. Waryk's sword rose again, slammed down on Renfrew's helmet. The man fell, blood spouting from his lips, his sightless eyes.

"Waryk!" Mellyora shrieked.

Ignoring the flames that were beginning to rise, Waryk urged Mercury up on the dais. With a slash of his sword, he broke the bonds tying her to the pole. She started to fall. Mercury's hoofbeats clattered nervously over the kindling. Waryk quickly bent low from his horse's back, slipped an arm around her, and swept her up.

Mercury leapt from the rising blaze. Clinging to Waryk with what strength she had, Mellyora was vaguely aware that her uncle fought to the one side, and Angus to the other. They covered Waryk's ride as he raced hard toward the stone dividing enemy camps. Yet there, a rider challenged Waryk, and she ducked, screaming, as a sword slashed her way. Waryk's blade rose to meet it. With her head down, she saw the Viking taking aim with his pike. She reached to her ankle for her knife and threw wildly.

She hit his arm. He screamed, his weapon fell. Waryk turned Mercury, ready to fight the man, but Daro had gone after him, and they were engaged in bloody combat. Spinning again, clinging to Waryk, Mellyora trembled, realizing that her husband's forces had taken these murderers completely by surprise.

He spurred Mercury, leading the horse into another flying leap over the stone, and they raced downhill.

He rode with her far from the battlefield, to where his camp had been. He moved through the tents and doused fires to a quiet copse by the stream. There, he dismounted with her in her arms. By the stream, he knelt, tearing off his helmet. His eyes touched hers, he searched her face anxiously.

"Waryk . . ."

"Lady . . ."

"M'laird!" she whispered.

She reached up, her arms no longer in such agony, now that she could touch him.

But he was anxious, so anxious. "Did they hurt you, Mellyora, you couldn't stand, you can barely move . . ."

"Too long standing tied," she said. She tried to smile. "You took your time!" she whispered.

"My apologies! I did my best, approaching without cover of artillery, and we might not have reached you."

"Oh, Waryk, you came for me!"

"Aye, lady. I will always come. Mellyora, you are the prize," he said very softly. "I have very definitely earned you."

She smiled, caught his hand, kissed it.

He cradled her against him, then swore, realized that he drew her against mail. "Ah, my love, this is a most difficult time and place to express quite all that I'm feeling."

She could hear the sound of the battle, and she closed her eyes, praying that her uncle would live, that the men who had come to her rescue would survive. Then she realized that she was hearing something closer. Movement, closer to them. She opened her eyes, and a cry of warning tore from her lips. "Waryk . . ."

He was up instantly, reaching for his sword. She had warned him in time.

He had killed Renfrew to rescue her from the fire. They had seen enough of the fighting to know who would prevail. But Ulric had not been killed, and he had followed them.

The two men circled one another. Ulric was the first to raise his weapon. Hammering blow after hammering blow fell upon Waryk. Mellyora tried to rise, afraid that Waryk couldn't bear the strain, that Ulric was besting him.

"You killed my father, you deserve to die!" Ulric screamed.

"I avenged my father, murdered by yours!"

"You should have been dead, a nit among lice."

"Ah, but I didn't die."

"No," Ulric said, "you didn't die. So know this. I had your wife; she was delicious. When you die now, she will welcome me as laird of her castle," Ulric taunted. "I didn't rape her, Waryk. She came to me, made love to me, asked me to kill you."

Mellyora gasped, stunned at such a lie, yet knowing that Ulric meant for Waryk to lose his temper, to doubt her . . .

To falter.

He did not.

"Do you think that I believe that?" Waryk queried in return, deftly avoiding a blow.

"I had your wife, fool. I, and Renfrew. And you'll never know whose brat she carries, eh, man? Your line dies with you. It should have died with your father, nit."

Waryk suddenly sent his blade flying against Ulric again and again with a deafening clamor. "My wife is alive, and with me, bastard, and that is what matters."

"Nay, fool, it is your father's line you fought to keep, but my son will have your isle!" Ulric told him, striding forward, his sword in both hands as he prepared for another series of blows.

But this time, Waryk made no effort to ward off the blows. He spun around, swinging upward with his father's claymore, catching Ulric below the mail, and piercing his abdomen. Stunned, Ulric dropped his sword, grabbed his stomach, and fell to his knees.

Waryk stood above him. "Nay, sir, whatever child has the isle will be mine." He turned back to Mellyora. She tried to rise to throw her arms around him. She must have come to her feet too quickly. The world began to spin.

"Waryk . . ."

She fell against him; night faded to black. She vaguely heard his words as he caught her in his arms.

"My love, my love . . ."

Phagin, who reached them at last, assured him that Mellyora would be well, and Phagin stayed with her while he directed his men, collecting their wounded, seeing to the burial of the dead.

The battle was an undisputed victory.

Many of Renfrew's Normans were slain, many begged mercy, and were sent to Stirling; their fate, Waryk had decided, the king must determine. Renfrew had made his private battle part of a war between kings, and so David must make final decisions.

Ulric's Vikings were slain, or fled to the North. They were so disbanded that Waryk couldn't see them making much trouble again.

Their victory celebration was wild. Vikings, Scotsmen, Normans, English.

They feasted on lamb roast.

Mellyora awoke, and came from the tent where she had rested, in the middle of the celebration. Her hair spilling down her back, she was dressed in a plain blue gown, and she seemed very young, innocent and pure as she walked to him. The men stopped in their drinking and cavorting, and a huge cry went out to her.

Waryk rose, she came into his arms, and together, they watched Phagin play sennachie, telling the story of the great battle of Blue Isle, the beautiful lady who had stopped the slaughter, and the brave warrior laird who had ridden to take his lady from the flames.

She fell asleep again in his arms. He held her tenderly, carried her to her tent, and lay at her side through the night.

He and Daro hadn't said much to one another. It wasn't necessary. They had formed a friendship based on trust both had learned the hard way. They had drunk too much with one another right after the battle, but even that had been good.

Life itself was good.

His wife had survived, and she lay in his arms. And that was all, he realized, that he had needed. She was, indeed, the prize he had fought for.

In the morning, Mellyora was stronger. And still, for the journey home, Waryk insisted she ride before him on Mercury. She didn't mind. She felt warm, secure, and cherished.

As they started out, others were near them. Phagin had created his magnificent poem, of course, but today, he told her about the battle in more graphic and dramatic terms. Daro told her his version of the battle. Peter tried to describe the meeting between Daro and Waryk. Angus, of course, had to tell a tale as well, and it was good to listen to them all, they were her world, and they had come together.

She was content to listen, smiling. Then Geoffrey, returned to his duties of carrying her husband's armor, rode by their side, and he, too, became a storyteller, telling Waryk about her courage in defying Ulric when he meant to murder Eleanora. And how she had nearly, and most cleverly, saved herself along with the castle, if it hadn't been for the treachery within. Waryk was grave then, looking down at her, and she closed her eyes, then opened them to his. "I wish I could swear that I will never leave you again," he said softly. "But I am the king's champion . . ."

"And we now know the truth about all the dangers within," she said, smiling. "I will be safe in the future," she promised.

It was only much later in the day that they managed to ride on ahead alone, and have a certain amount of privacy, and a chance to talk.

And Mellyora at last managed to twist in her husband's arms, and tell him, "You have to know this. And that I'm not lying, nor saying these words to ease your soul in any way. Ulric meant to torment you whether he lived or died. He never did touch me, Waryk. He didn't have the opportunity."

His arms tightened around her. "My lady, I would have wanted him dead for any hurt to you."

"But he wanted vengeance against you in any way. He wanted you to think that I might carry his child rather than yours. But—"

"My lady, it wouldn't have mattered."

The tremor and depth of his husky, masculine voice thrilled her. She curled her fingers over his where they rested on Mercury's reins.

"You wanted your own child. It was more important to you than anything in the world—" she protested.

He set his hand on her cheek, turning her head toward his. He looked down at her, blue eyes warmer than a summer day, dark hair handsomely rakish as it fell against his forehead. "Matters of importance change, Mellyora. Nothing mattered to me at all when he took you, except that I get you back alive."

She felt herself trembling as he held her. "But you wanted your own family so very much."

He shrugged. "I have discovered family to be the people who surround you, who love you, to whom you are responsible, and who give you their loyalty in return. You are my family, my love. Any child of yours will be a child of mine."

She touched his face, still shaking. "But I am having your child, Waryk."

"So Phagin told me."

"I wanted to tell you before this all came about. I wanted to surprise you with the news. That's why I danced at your camp, why I wanted to be with you alone so much. I was so pleased because . . ."

"Aye?"

"I thought that you'd be so happy."

"I am happy."

"But you—"

"Mellyora, I am happy, thrilled that we are to have a child. I suppose that I am glad it is my child, in truth, it wouldn't have mattered. I have you, and I'll be far more careful in the future with you, I promise."

She smiled, leaning against his broad chest.

"Waryk?"

"Aye?"

"I love you."

He was silent for a moment.

"Well?"

"It has taken you long enough to say it!"

Her smiled deepened. "I never thought it possible. I love you so very much. I've learned about love, hurt, jealousy, fear, worry . . ."

"Never fear again, my love, for you needn't be jealous, or in pain. No matter where I am, my lady, my heart and soul are in your keeping. You are all I need."

She had never known such sweet pleasure. Then, even as he spoke, they crested a hill, and out in a sparkling sea, she saw their fortress.

"Waryk, we're home."

"Aye, lady."

"Our baby will be born there. Dozens of babies, perhaps."

"Dozens?"

"Well, several, at the very least. A very large family, my love."

He leaned his cheek against her head. "As you wish, my lady. The king once told me that I must create my own kin. What he never told me was that . . ."

"Aye?"

"I would find all I needed in you," he said softly.

She touched his cheek. "Who would have ever known . . ."

"Aye?"

"That I could come to so love and adore such an old, decrepit Norman knight!" she said, and smiled.

"Watch your tongue, wife," he warned with a growl.

"Oh, aye, sire. But you are part Norman. And I've heard there's a wee bit of Viking blood, and Celtic, of course, some Anglo-Saxon, maybe—"

"Aye, my lady, and you are Pictish, Celtic, and Viking. And our babe will be all things—"

"Scottish!" she said softly.

"Aye, it is what we are made of, as we come to peace with one another."

"And, m'laird, we are at peace, are we not?"

He arched a brow, a half smile tugging at his lips. "Well, I imagine we'll still have a few rather fierce arguments."

"For all the years to come," she agreed pleasantly. "What would life be without them?"

"Indeed, you are charming when you try to atone for your sins," he said gravely.

"My sins!" she exclaimed, and then saw the laughter in his eyes.

"You're terribly disobedient, as a wife, you know."

"Well, I am a Viking's daughter. And you're a fierce warrior, the king's champion. There are bound to be disagreements, but ... oh, Waryk! Look at the isle from here, the stone of the fortress is silver in the sunlight ... it's so beautiful."

"That it is," he agreed; then he queried, "Up to a race?"

"Always, my love."

He nudged Mercury hard, and they raced across the wild, windswept crags and green valleys of Scotland.

Home. Their land.

And the land of their unborn babe ...

And all their sons and daughters yet to be.

# Author's Note

I believe I was a very lucky child. Of course, I didn't think so as I was growing up; few children realize what they had at the time. As an adult, however, I've learned what can happen in the world, and so I know just how lucky I was.

I had loving parents.

Not rich ones, but loving ones. I remember wishing once that my last name might have been Astor, Vanderbilt, or Carnegie, but in fact, I now know that I wouldn't trade my name for any other in the world, not for any other reason than that it was my father's. I adored him; he was my first hero. He was tall and very handsome, quite bald by the time I knew him, a look-alike for Mr. Clean—for those of you who remember that dashing, animated character. He had the most wonderful blue eyes, and a knack for telling a story, so much so that to this day, I'm not always sure just what was—and wasn't—true.

He was a Scotsman—an American, of course, but his heritage was Scottish, and he fit it well, a tall, powerful man with the remnants of dark, wavy hair and Celtic blue eyes. He gave me my grandfather's sporan, all kinds of tales, and a love for the sound of bagpipes.

We tend to turn people into saints once they've died, to forget anything bad, remember only what was good. I know that he wasn't a saint. I know that at one time he had led a very wild life. But I know as well that he was a man who encouraged me in every hope and dream I ever had, who could be stern, who taught me, and who loved me. He tried to show my sister and me both the evil and the goodness in the world, and to learn to judge between. Naturally, we fought. I was very angry at him at times. I'm sure I caused a great amount of what hair he'd had left at my birth to fall out of his head. All that is part of being a parent, and being a child. He's been gone a very long time now, but it's strange—sometimes I can still hear his voice, see the flash of his smile, hear the sound of his laughter. I wish I might have known him as an adult—he died right before my twenty-first birthday. Sometimes, I see him in his grandchildren, and I'm glad, and I wish that he might have known them. But I do believe in God, and an afterlife, so I believe that he does see them, and that he watches out for them. I wish that they might have known him, but again, perhaps they do, for he lives in my memory, and I like to believe I have acquired his gift for storytelling.

I am blessed to still have my mother. She has been helping me in all kinds of ways as long as I can remember. I owe her so much. She remarried years after my father's death, a Mr. Bill Sherman, and to him, equally, I am grateful, for he has unfailingly helped me in all kinds of situations, and he has been the world's best stepparent.

This book is partially for my mom and Bill—my mother was born in Dublin, but her father's name was Johnston, which is, of course, a Scottish clan name, too.

But mainly, this book, this series, is for my father.

It is about the Graham clan, the first use of the name, and the Grahams who went down in history heroically, and not so heroically. In several instances, where little is known except vague dates and supposition, I have taken an author's liberty to fill in the gaps. I've tried to be true to Scottish history, mainly in showing just how many intriguing peoples went into the creation of the nation. It is written with a great deal of love—I am as proud of my Scottish heritage as I am of my father. In future books, I'll be introducing a Graham who was historically one of William Wallace's best friends and staunchest supporters. (How Randall Wallace and Mel Gibson missed him, I'll never know!) He perished in his support of the Scottish cause. And down the road a few centuries, I'll be using a Graham known either as 'Bonnie Dundee', if you were on his side, or 'Bloody Claverhouse', if you were not! History, of course, is slanted towards the beliefs and opinions of those who write it!

Anyway, that's for the future. Here, we come across the first man to have been a Graham, according to clan histories. He lived in a turbulent time. Like de Brus (the future Bruces), he arrived with King David in a Norman contingent. He married a Scottish heiress. That much we know. The rest is supposition. I have given my hero the title of laird before the Graham were actually so honored. Author's liberty—to those Grahams and Scots who know that we were 'Sirs' before 'lairds'—please bear with me.

So once again, to my dad.

He died with little except the devoted love of those around him, and in that, he died a very rich man. Just as he left me with riches untold—his unwavering belief in me, in dreams that must be realized. He died before he could see that I did live a dream—to write, and to publish. He taught me as well to appreciate all gifts in life, and so, I have the good sense to be grateful every day of my life that I am able to do something I love so much for a living.

Here goes—this work is dedicated to his memory.

For my father, Ellsworth Derue "Dan" Graham.
With all my love.

# Chronology

c6000BC: Earliest peoples arrive from Europe (Stone Age): Some used stone axes to clear land.

c4500BC: Second wave of immigrants arrive (New Stone Age or Neolithic). "Grooved ware," simple forms of pottery, found. They left behind important remains, perhaps most notably, their tombs and cairns.

c3500BC: Approximate date of the remarkable chambered tombs at Maes Howe, Orkney.

c3000BC: Carbon dating of the village at Skara Brae, also Orkney, showing houses built of stone, built-in beds, straw mattresses, skin spreads, kitchen utensils of bone and wood, and other more sophisticated tools.

c2500BC: 'Beaker' people arrive; neolithic people who will eventually move into the Bronze Age. Bronze Age to last until approximately 700BC.

c700BC: Iron Age begins—iron believed to have been brought by Hallstadt peoples from central Europe. Term 'Celts' now applied to these people, from the Greek *Keltoi*; they were considered by the Greeks and Romans to be barbarians. Two types of Celtic language, P-Celtic, and Q-Celtic.

c600–100BC: The earliest Celtic fortifications, including the broch, or large stone tower. Some offered fireplaces and freshwater wells. Crannogs, or island forts, were also built; these were structures often surrounded by spikes or walls of stakes. Souterrains were homes built into the earth, utilizing stone, some up to eighty feet long. The Celts become known for their warlike qualities as well as for their beautiful jewelry and colorful clothing; 'trousers' are introduced by the Celts, perhaps learned from Middle-Eastern societies. A rich variety of colors are used (perhaps forerunner to tartan plaids) as well as long tunics, skirts, and cloaks to be held by the artistically wrought brooches.

55BC: Julius Caesar invades southern Britain.

56BC: Julius Caesar attacks again, but again, the assault does not reach Scotland.

43AD: The Roman Plautius attacks; by the late 70s (AD), the Romans have come to Scottish land.

78–84AD: The Roman Agricola, newly appointed governor, born a Gaul, plans to attack the Celts. Beginning in 80AD, he launches a two-pronged full-scale attack. There are no roads, and he doesn't have time to build them as the Romans have done elsewhere in Britain. 30,000 Romans marched; they will be met by a like number of Caledonians. (Later to be called Picts for their custom of painting or tattooing their faces and bodies.) After the battle of Mons Graupius, the Roman historian Tacitus (son-in-law of Agricola) related that 10,000 Caledonians were killed, that they were defeated. However, the Romans retreat southward after orders to withdraw.

122AD: Hadrian arrives in Britain and orders the construction of his famous wall.

142AD: Antoninus Pius arrives with fresh troops due to continual trouble in Scotland. The Antonine Wall is built, and garrisoned for the following twenty years.

150–200AD: The Romans suffer setbacks. An epidemic kills much of the population, and Marcus Aurelius dies, to be followed by a succession of poor rulers.

c208AD: Severus comes to Britain and attacks in Scotland, dealing some cruel blows, but his will be the last major Roman invasion. He dies in York in 211AD, and the Caledonians are then free from Roman intervention, though they will occasionally venture south to Roman holdings on raids.

350–400AD: Saxon pirates raid from northwest Europe, forcing Picts southward over the wall. Fierce invaders arrive from Ireland: the *Scotti*, a word meaning raiders. Eventually, the country will take its name from these people.

c400AD: St. Ninian, a British Celtic bishop, builds a monastery church at Whithorn. It is known as Candida Casa. His missionaries might have pushed north as far as the Orkney Islands; they were certainly responsible for bringing Christianity to much of the country.

c450AD: The Romans abandon Britain altogether. Powerful Picts invade lower Britain, and the Romanized people ask for help from Jutes, Angles, and Saxons. Scotland then basically divided between four peoples; Picts, Britons, Angles, and the Scotti of Dalriada. 'Clan' life begins—the word *clann* meaning "children" in Gaelic. Family groups are kin with the most important, possibly strongest, man becoming chief of his family and extended family. As generations go by, the clans grow larger, and more powerful.

500–700AD: The Angles settle and form two kingdoms, Deira and Bernicia. Aethelfrith, king from 593–617AD, wins a victory against the Scotia at Degsastan and severely crushes the Britons—who are left in a tight position between the Picts and Angles. He seizes the throne of King Edwin of Deira as well, causing bloodshed between the two kingdoms for the next fifty years, keeping the Angles busy and preventing warfare between them and their Pictish and Scottish neighbors. c500, Fergus MacErc and his brothers, Angus and Lorne, brought a fresh migration of Scotia from Ireland to Dalriada, and though the communities had been close (between Ireland and Scotland), they soon after began to pull away. By the late 500s, St. Columba came to Iona, creating a strong kingship there, and spreading Christianity even farther than St.

Ninian had gone. In 685AD at Nechtansmere, the Angles are severely defeated by the Picts; their king Ecgfrith is slain, and his army is half slaughtered. This prevents Scotland from becoming part of England at an early date.

787AD: The first Viking raid, according to the Anglo-Saxon chronicle. In 797, Lindisfarne is viciously attacked, and the monastery is destroyed. "From the Fury of the Northmen, deliver us, oh, Lord!" becomes a well-known cry.

843AD: Kenneth MacAlpian, son of a Scots king, who is also descended from Pictish kings through his maternal lineage, claims and wins the Pictish throne as well as his own. It is not an easy task as he sets forth to combine his two peoples into the country of Scotland. Soon after becoming king of the Picts and the Scotia, he moves his capital from Dunadd to Scone, and has the 'Stone of Destiny' brought there, now known as the Stone of Scone. (And recently returned to Scotland.)

The savage Viking raids become one focus that will help to unite the Picts and the Scots. Despite the raids and the battles, by the tenth century, many of the Vikings are settling in Scotland. The Norse kings rule the Orkneys through powerful jarls, and they maintain various other holdings in the country, many in the Hebrides. The Vikings will become a fifth main people to make up the Scottish whole. Kenneth is followed by a number of kings that are his descendants, but not necessarily immediate heirs, nor is the Pictish system of accepting the maternal line utilized. It appears that a powerful member of the family, supported by other powerful members, comes to the throne.

878AD: Alfred (the Great) of Wessex defeats the Danes. (They will take up residence in East Anglia and, at times, rule various parts of England.)

1018AD: Kenneth's descendant, Malcolm II, finally wins a victory over the Angles at Carham, bringing Lothian under Scottish rule. In this same year, the king of the Britons of Strathclyde dies without an heir. Duncan, Malcolm's heir, has a claim to the throne through his maternal ancestry.

1034AD: Malcolm dies, and Duncan, his grandson, succeeds him as king of a Scotland that now includes the Pictish, Scottish, Anglo, and Briton lands, and pushes into English lands.

1040AD: Duncan is killed by MacBeth, the Mormaer (or high official) of Moray, who claims the throne through his own ancestry, and that of his wife. Despite Shakespeare's version, he is suspected of having been a good king, and a good Christian—going on pilgrimage to Rome in 1050AD.

1057AD: MacBeth is killed by Malcolm III, Duncan's son. (Malcolm had been raised in England.) Malcolm is known as Malcolm Canmore, or Ceann Mor, or Big Head.

1059AD: Malcolm marries Ingibjorg, a Norse noblewoman, probably the daughter of Thorfinn the Mighty.

1066AD: Harold, king of England, rushes to the north of his country to battle an invading Norse army. Harold wins the battle, only to rush back south, to Hastings, to meet another invading force.

1066AD: William the Conqueror invades England and slays Harold, the Saxon King.

1069AD: Malcolm III marries (as his second wife) Princess Margaret, sister to the deposed Edgar Atheling, the Saxon heir to the English throne. Soon after, he launches a series of raids into England, feeling justified in that his brother-in-law has a very real claim to the English throne. England retaliates.

1071AD: Malcolm is forced to pay homage to William the Conqueror at Abernathy. Despite the battles between them, Malcolm remains popular among the English.

1093AD: While attacking Northumberland (some say to circumvent a Norman invasion), Malcolm is killed in ambush. Queen Margaret dies three days later. Scotland falls into turmoil. Malcolm's brother Donald Ban, raised in the Hebrides under Norse influence, seizes the throne and overthrows Norman policy for Viking.

1094AD: William Rufus, son of William the Conqueror, sends Malcolm's oldest son, Duncan, who has been a hostage in England, to overthrow his uncle, Donald. Duncan overthrows Donald, but is murdered himself, and Donald returns to the throne.

1097AD: Edgar, Duncan's half-brother, is sent to Scotland with an Anglo-Norman army, and Donald is chased out once again. He brings in many Norman knights and families, and makes peace with Magnus Barelegs, the King of Norway, formally ceding to him lands in the Hebrides which has been a holding already for a very long time.

1107AD: Edgar dies; his brother, Alexander succeeds him, but rules only the land between Forth and Spey; his younger brother, David, rules south of the Forth. Alexander's sister, Maud, had become the wife of Henry I of England, and Alexander has married Henry's daughter by a previous marriage, Sibylla. These matrimonial alliances make a terribly strong bond between the Scottish and English royal houses.

1124AD: Alexander dies. David (also raised in England) inherits the throne for all Scotland. He is destined to rule for nearly thirty years, to be a powerful king who will create burghs, a stronger church, a number of towns, and introduce a sound system of justice. He will be a patron of arts and learning. Having married an heiress, he is also an English noble, being Earl of Northampton and Huntington, and Prince of Cumbria. He brings feudalism to Scotland, and many friends, including de Brus, whose descendants will include Robert Bruce, fitzAllen, who will become High Steward—and, of course, a man named Sir William Graham.

Turn the page
for a sample of Shannon Drake's next
hardcover novel

# CONQUER THE NIGHT

*coming in February, 2000.*

# Conquer the Night

K yra stood before the fire in the main hall of the old stone
tower at Seacairn, watching as the flames rose and leapt,
crimson and gold, at the whim of the drafts that ceaselessly filled
the fortress.

No. No. Never.

The simple words filled her soul. She longed to shout, scream,
cry out so loudly that the rafters would tremble with her denial,
that the stone itself would shake and shudder with the force of
her denial.

She turned from the fire and raced up the curving stairs to
the chapel above the main hall. She stared at the main altar, but
turned from it. Far to the right of it was a shrine to the Virgin,
and it was there that she fled, falling to her knees, her skirts
billowing out around her. "No, no, no! Don't let it happen.
Blessed Mary, give me strength! I will enter any bargain with
God, or so help me, lady, forgive me, but I would deal with
Satan himself to escape what fate destines for me. Dear Lord,
but I'd rather die than—"

She broke off, startled by the thunderous sound of a ram slamming against the main gate of the castle. It was an ancient fortifica-
tion strengthened and enlarged by each power to lay claim to the
land, for hers was border country, where it seemed that every
race known to Scotland had once ruled. Now, under the ruthless
dominance of Edward I, the castle was in English hands. And
with Scotland in turmoil since the death of the Maiden of Norway,
vicious battle could come at any time. The man who held a castle
was he who ruled it, no matter what his nationality.

"My lady!"

Kyra rose and spun around as her maid, Ingrid, tore into the chapel.

"What is happening?"

"They've come, milady! Marauders, murderers, wildmen, savages! Horrible, heathen Scots out of the Highlands!"

Ingrid was young, a buxom girl who had been raised in a convent and was convinced that men were savages. This being true, then Scotsmen were little more than the lowest, most barbarous beasts.

Kyra rushed to the arrow slit and looked down. It was true. Mounted men, some in chain and plate armor, some in leather, some with little more than sharpened shovel poles or sickles as weapons, were shrieking fierce battle cries and bearing down upon the castle. They had already breached the outer gate and were into the bailey, fighting the meager forces left behind by Lord Kinsey Darrow, the Englishman granted rule here by Edward of England. She could see the hand-to-hand combat being waged.

She could hear the screams and cries of the dying, see the spatter of blood as battle-axes and swords met flesh and blood. Someone cried out that those who surrendered would be granted mercy—more than the Scots had received at the hands of the Englishmen.

"God help me!" she breathed, backing away from the window.

"They've come for you, my lady!" Ingrid said. "They've come for you, because of what Lord Darrow—"

"Ingrid, enough!" came a firm masculine voice. "Say nothing more to your lady!"

Again, Kyra spun around. His head hooded, face shrouded by the wool of his garment, Father Michael Corrigan had come quietly into the chapel. She had long thought that the spiritual leader of this fortress, though an Irishman, gave his sympathy—and his prayers—to the Scots.

"What does it matter what she says?" Kyra asked him, fighting to remain calm. "They have breached the walls. They are here, quite simply. Lord Darrow's men have fallen or surrendered. The enemy will be here any minute. The truth is that we're all about to be murdered by heathens—"

"I rather doubt they've come to do murder—"

"Oh, come, now, Father, do you see what happens below—"

"Indeed, my lady, they've come for vengeance. They've come

for the castle, for its origins are ancient and Gaelic, and—I dare say—they've come for you."

His face lay in shadow, yet she knew that he watched her. Was there vengeance in his heart as well as in the souls of the enemy below? Or was he simply detached, wondering if she would dissolve hopelessly into tears or attempt to throw herself from the battlements in despair.

"The soldiers out there will die for you."

She lifted her chin. "They must not do so. If the barbarians can be induced to offer mercy in any way—"

"Darrow herded fighters and farmers alike into a barn and set fire to it, Lady Kyra. Difficult to ask mercy in return—"

"Lady Kyra!"

She spun. Captain Tyler Miller of the castle guard had come. He fell on a knee before her. "Sweet Jesu, lady, we will gladly die in your defense, but I'm afraid there's no help in it. Perhaps there's a way for you to flee—"

"Captain Tyler, I beg you, get up. And I command that you surrender your men if you believe there's any hope of mercy."

"But, my lady, perhaps we can buy time with our lives—"

"I'll not have you imperil my soul with your lives, Captain Tyler, please. Leave me to my defenses. Hold the wildmen off if you can, but in Lord Darrow's name, I command you to surrender when all is lost."

Tyler bowed and spun around.

"They will be quickly bested," Father Corrigan commented.

"God help me then!" Kyra said fiercely. God help her, yes. How strange, that she had just come here, so desperately seeking intervention from the Virgin for the life she had been destined to lead.

How strangely prayers were answered!

What in God's name was she going to do?

"God help me!" she repeated to herself in a whisper. But Father Corrigan was listening. He smiled. "Remember, my child—God helps those who help themselves, my lady."

"Indeed, Father? Then by His grace, with your blessing, I will seek to help myself!"

"Lay down your arms!" Arryn cried, for though his first opponent inside the bailey once they had breached the outer walls had been a large, well-muscled, and experienced warrior, he now faced a slim man, probably no more than a lad, and the way he swung his sword showed training, but no experience.

"Nay, I cannot!"

The lad swung; a noble gesture. His sword fell short of its target, that target being Arryn's midsection. Arryn sat atop his great bay destrier—obtained several years ago from a fallen English cavalryman—and could have easily brought his own weapon down upon the fellow's neck and shoulders.

"Lad, give it up! You're beaten."

"Aye, and I'll meet the hangman, or find death at a stake, or—"

"Lay down your weapon, you fool! I don't punish children for the misfortune of their birth!" Arryn cried.

The lad hesitated, then laid down his sword. As he did so, Arryn heard his name called. He swung the handsome bay around. Jay MacDonald, head of the fighting members of his clan in this war, was rushing through the bailey to reach him.

"He's gone—Lord Darrow is gone. They say he heard that an army of wildmen was nearly upon him—and that he ran!"

"Aye, so 'tis true, the rat has sprung the trap!" Arryn said, spitting down into the dirt. God, it hurt! His anger and frustration were so great that they actually created a physical pain within him. His heart hurt, his soul hurt. What Kinsey Darrow had done was unforgivable, not to be forgotten. And all under the full blessing of the English king! There was nothing to do when such atrocities were law, except to defy the law. In a land where there was no justice, there was little left for a man except the pursuit of revenge. And by God, if not today, he would have his revenge. Kinsey Darrow would die, and die by his sword, or else his life would be readily, gladly given in forfeit. As it was, by God, Arryn could not live with his dreams, for they haunted him; he heard her screams into the night, and even into the dawn, and those screams would rip him apart as long as he lived. Perhaps, even, through all eternity.

"Arryn, did you hear me? Edward's wretched coward of a lackey is not here!" Jay said.

"You're certain?"

Jay indicated the corner where the castle guards stood, their weapons cast into a heap before them as they waited, eyes darting nervously as they surveyed their Scottish foe. "Ask the lad, Arryn. Lord Darrow rode out this morning."

"It's true?" He had yet to see the boy's face, for Kinsey Darrow was a rich, landed knight with the resources to arm his men well. The lad wore a helmet with a fitted faceplate and tightly knit mail with heavy plates as well. A tunic with Darrow's colors and crest lay over his armor, but didn't conceal its fine workmanship.

The lad lifted his helmet. As Arryn had suspected, he was very young. He stood tall still, and though obviously afraid, he meant to stand his ground, but speak honestly. He looked at Arryn and nodded. "Aye, sir, 'tis true. Lord Darrow came here to meet his lady, but received a message soon after from the Earl of Harringford, and departed with half his forces."

Arryn arched a brow, leaning down against the bay's neck to better study the boy's freckled face. "Came here to meet his lady?"

"Aye, sir."

"And he met with her?"

"Aye, sir."

"And he rode out with her?"

"Nay, sir, he did not."

"Then she remains?" Arryn queried, glancing over at Jay.

"Aye, sir, she remains."

"This is the Lady Kyra we're speaking about?"

"Aye, sir, the Lady Kyra." He appeared flushed and unhappy at that. "But, sir—"

"Lad, get to the wall with you, no harm will befall you," Arryn said.

"But, sir—"

"Now, lad," Arryn said, his voice low, a warning note within it.

The lad turned, still tall, proud, and headed toward the other prisoners grouped against the inner wall of the tower.

"Arryn," Jay said, "I assume you'll be going for Darrow's lady—"

"Aye, Jay."

"You're thinking revenge—"

"Aye, that I am."

"To take what is his."

Arryn lifted a hand with a gesture of impatience. "I intend to take the castle and the woman. What else would you have me do?"

Jay grinned suddenly. "Well, she could be ugly as sin, of course."

"Indeed."

"Wrinkled beyond all measure. She is rich, but wealth is certainly not always accompanied by youth or beauty."

Arryn studied his friend for a moment, wanting to feel the same sense of humor. He could not. Bile formed in his stomach.

"If she is as ugly as sin, as wrinkled as a prune, it will not matter. She is Darrow's, and that is all that counts. Was Darrow's. No more. She is at my mercy." He inhaled and exhaled, feeling as if he breathed in bitterness. "Nothing here is for pleasure. It is vengeance, Jay. She is simply to be used, ruined."

"Aye, but . . . is such vengeance humanly possible if a maid is preposterously ugly—"

"Have mercy, Jay."

Jay, his helmet in his hand, smoothed back his rich brown hair. "Ah, there's the word! You've granted mercy to these men—"

"But you would have me grant mercy as well to the woman who encouraged Darrow in his vicious and bloodthirsty behavior?"

"Arryn, perhaps—"

Arryn leaned downward, his gloved hand curling into a fist he slammed against his chest. "Sweet Jesus, I cannot forget or forgive what happened!"

"But she could be quite simply repulsive!" Jay stated.

"Then I will meet her in the dark, with a sack upon her head! Come, we've taken the bailey, now the towers must fall to us!"

He spurred his horse, leaving Jay to rush behind him to his own mount. Angered, restless, still feeling the pursuit of inner demons, Arryn rode hard to the great gate at the main tower. He called out orders, commanding his men to bombard the structure with a ram, which they did. Defenders overhead shouted, threatened; they would hurl down oil, flaming arrows to set them all ablaze. One fellow, in particular, shouted down that he would burn with them in hell.

"Seize the great oak shield and continue ramming the gate!" Arryn commanded, and his men quickly backed away for the shield they had fashioned of heavy oak, a piece of siege machinery that protected them like a wooden roof from the missiles cast down from the arrow slits in the main tower that stretched above them.

The door shuddered.

The flames cast down burned, smoked, and went out. The oil dripped off the curve of the shield.

The ram thundered against the door.

"Hold! For mercy's sake, we will surrender!"

Arryn lifted his visor and looked up. The same fellow who had sworn to burn with them all in hell was the one offering the surrender.

"You protect Lord Darrow's lady, sir. You would give up so easily?" he queried mockingly.

"You've granted mercy to the soldiers in the bailey. I am Tyler, captain of the guard, and I've heard, Sir Arryn, that you keep your word, and you're not like some of the other heathens who demand surrender, and then incinerate those who have begged mercy. Swear mercy to us, and I will open the gates. Thus you will have taken a castle you can still defend."

"Aye, I swear mercy. But I ask again, what of your lady?"

"She, too, must cast herself upon your mercy. We are too few; we have no more oil, no arrows, and we are poorly armed. And . . ."

He hesitated, looking down. "Sir Arryn, we've heard of the fate of so many of your people. We beg pardon. We're not all vicious dogs, sir."

"Open the gates then," Arryn commanded.

"Your word—"

"I've given my word."

The great gates to the main tower of the fortress creaked open. Arryn nudged his horse forward, only to realize that Jay had ridden behind him. "Take care—it could be a trap."

"I must lead the way in," Arryn murmured.

He spurred the bay lightly; the horse pranced prettily and swiftly, making its way across the threshold into the stone entry. He held his sword at the ready, and it still dripped the blood of Englishmen. But the threat was not necessary; the soldiers from the inner tower had laid down their weapons. There were only five of them. One stepped forward, helmet in his hand, offering his sword to Arryn. Arryn dismounted from the bay and accepted the sword. Jay came behind him, along with Nathan Fitzhugh and Patrick MacCullough. The other guards turned over their weapons in total surrender.

"Where is the Lady Kyra?" Arryn asked, careful to continue speaking his native Gaelic.

Tyler hesitated, wincing. "In the chapel."

Arryn started by him.

"Sir!" Tyler called.

Arryn paused, looking back.

"You swore mercy."

"To you, I swore mercy."

"But—"

"Get them outside, to the wall with the others," Arryn commanded.

"Aye, Arryn," Jay agreed, watching as Arryn strode toward the winding stairs. "Arryn, there might still be danger—"

"This danger, Jay, I'll face alone. Secure the fortress," Arryn said. He continued on up the stairs to the chapel, anxious, his blood racing and burning in a turmoil.

He reached the top of the stairs, and through a short hallway, came to the chapel.

And there, before the altar, a woman knelt.

Her head was bowed; she was deep in prayer. But she heard him. He saw her back stiffen. It was a broad back.

"Lady Kyra!"

Slowly, she rose. Even more slowly, she turned to him.

She wasn't *repulsive*. That would be far too strong a word.

She was simply . . .

Serviceable.

She reminded him of a good draft horse. She was, naturally, as broad at the shoulders as she was at the back. Her cheekbones were broad. Her jaw was broad. She was . . .

Broad. Aye, yes, broad.

The fever of fury that had brought him here seemed momentarily to still. His blood seemed to run like ice. No, she was not repulsive. She was as appealing as a solid cow.

Cruel, he told himself. She had her good points. Her eyes were powder blue, her hair was white blond. Her little lips were quivering away. She didn't look like the cunning woman who might have made demands upon a man like Lord Darrow, forcing him to heinous and cruel excesses in his bid to gain greater riches beneath King Edward.

No, she did not look the type . . .

He had come for revenge. She had been party to brutality and tragedy; nothing in life came without a price. She belonged to Darrow—she and her estates. He meant to see that she and her property did not become important additions to his quest for ever-greater power, a power that allowed him to torture and murder the Scots at will.

He had told Jay she would pay, indeed. Even if it meant a darkened room and a sack over her head.

Her broad head.

He removed his helmet and neck defenses, setting them down on a pew.

"So . . ." he stated, sword sheathed, hands behind his back as he walked toward her. "You are Lady Kyra."

She was silent, not understanding his Gaelic, he thought.

Approaching her, he felt all the more ill. Seize Darrow's woman, use her, hurt her, cut into Darrow's flesh and soul the way that she and Darrow had cut into his . . .

Could he ever have carried it through? He had killed often enough in battle. Yet, murder, and the murder of a woman, even if she were guilty of complicity in the most heinous of crimes against humanity, seemed beyond his capabilities. So why take this revenge at all?

"No one left to guard you," he mused, shaking his head. He stared at her flat, expressionless, bovine face again. "Oh, I am sorry, but . . . 'tis no great wonder! Nevertheless, you'll have to come with me—"

He started to reach for her. Just as he did so, he saw a flying shape—like a shadow of darkness—coming toward him. He spun around just in time to ward off a blow as a figure in a dark cloak came toward him, a knife raised high.

"Ah, a defender at last!" he cried out.

Swift movement had allowed him to ward off the first strike, but the cloaked defender was swiftly at him again, spinning around with supple grace and speed to try to stab a knife into his throat. Again, he deflected the blow, seizing the man by the back of the cloak, throwing him forward with impetus to allow himself time to draw his sword once again.

He tried to make out the fellow's face, but beneath the hood, the man wore a faceplate with a helm of mail.

"Surrender yourself!" Arryn commanded, lifting his blade.

The cloaked figure also carried a sword.

*Fine,* Arryn thought. *To the death let it be.*

He advanced, ready for the battle, fury and fire filling his veins once again. He dared not think often of what had happened, horrible things beyond the subjugation of a country, a people.

Crimes of man against man, crimes he could not believe that God could sit in Heaven and allow. With vicious, furious movements, he strode forward, his sword battering every thrust and swing of his opponent's weapon.

But the fellow was brave. He spun, flew atop a pew, fought from the rim of the altar itself. All the while, the Lady Kyra babbled and blubbered, crying out strange warnings, gasps, screams of panic.

He ignored her.

This was a fight he could fight.

His enemy flew from the altar to a pew, swinging his sword deftly. Arryn ducked the blow with a split second to spare, then spun. The fellow was giving rise to leap around again, and once again, Arryn spun to give his weapon impetus. Step after step, he battered his enemy with a rain of blows that sent the fellow falling backward again, again, until he was against the wall.

His sword fell to his side.

"So you do surrender!" Arryn whispered huskily, advancing.

The fellow swiftly lifted his blade, nearly slicing Arryn's chin. Arryn danced backward in the nick of time.

The fellow sped past him, tearing toward the entry.

Toward escape.

"Nay, my good fellow, nay, I think not!" Arryn cried, and leaping forward, he caught hold of the cloak, giving such a tug upon it that the fellow, a light man at that, was spun furiously in a circle. As he turned, Arryn stepped forward, tripping him so that his spin finished in a heavy sprawl upon the cold stone floor of the chapel. Oddly enough, they were directly beneath a beautifully carved statue of the Virgin Mary.

"Now, do you surrender?"

The cloaked figure shook its head.

The fellow had protected his face and head, but wore no body armor. Arryn raised his sword in a certain threat, lightly placing the tip just above the heart.

"Now, my good man, speak quickly, for though you've been an able combatant, my patience is at a low ebb, and you must know, dark deeds have brought me here, and vengeance will be found with the blood of some poor beings!"

"Bastard Scotsman, do it!" the fellow hissed.

Startled, he moved his weapon. "Ah . . . a sword through the heart would be preferable to a hangman's noose? Or disemboweling. Castration . . . a few of the tortures Darrow so enjoys inflicting upon his captured enemies."

"Do it!"

"No!"

The shriek came from the Lady Kyra. Arryn kept his sword against his victim's chest as he turned with surprise toward Darrow's lady.

"I should spare this fellow? Is he your lover, by chance, milady? A man far more concerned with your welfare than the lord who left you here?"

The lady went suddenly still, in grave discomfort, so it seemed.

Curious, Arryn raised his sword again, as if he would thrust it through the fallen man's heart.

"No!" the blond, broad Lady Kyra cried again.

"Who is he, let me see."

He knelt, wrenching the chain and plate head armor from his fallen enemy.

And there he froze.

For no man gazed up at him, but a woman. Eyes of emerald green fire challenged his in a blaze of hate and fury. A wealth of reddish gold hair tangled around her beautifully formed features. She made a man give pause, forced him to catch his breath.

"Ah!" he muttered, forcing himself to remember his place. "The only man among these English proves to be a woman." He leaned toward her. "So who are you?"

She didn't reply. She had lost her sword, but he realized that she carried a knife still, and was ready to spring for him, attack him. Cut his throat.

He caught her wrist and wrenched the weapon from her. "I am Sir Arryn Graham. Do you know me, madam?"

She didn't reply, but stared stonily at him. He smiled slowly, having no intention of speaking in anything other than Gaelic at the moment. "You will tell me who you are, or I will slice your ears from your head, then your nose from your face. A little trick learned from Lord Darrow."

The woman didn't reply. He started to twist the knife in his hands.

"*She* is the Lady Kyra!" the very broad blond woman suddenly cried out.

Ahh . . .

Was it true? Yes. He could see it in the flashing emerald eyes of the beauty sprawled before him.

Despite himself, despite hatred, anguish, and revenge, he felt his limbs burn, his blood find fire, his body quicken.

"Lady Kyra!" he breathed.

No man of flesh and blood could find the need to place a sack over this damsel's head.

"Aye, indeed!" she spat out, thrusting his knife aside, sitting up, and trying to slide back from him. She smoothed a strand of tangled gold hair from her face. "I am the Lady Kyra. But trust me, sir, I do not know you."

For a moment, her complete pride and reckless defiance amused him.

He rose, reaching for her hand, wrenching her to her feet. "But you will know me, my lady. You will come to know me very well. Indeed, from this moment onward, you will know no one *but* me." All humor and amusement left his eyes. "Indeed, lady, in payment for those so woefully misused and abused in your name, you will know me very, very well."